EVERYMAN'S POCKET CLASSICS

GHOST STORIES

EDITED BY PETER WASHINGTON

EVERYMAN'S POCKET CLASSICS
Alfred A. Knopf New York London Toronto

THIS IS A BORZOI BOOK

PUBLISHED BY ALFRED A. KNOPF

This selection by Peter Washington first published in
Everyman's Library, 2008

A list of acknowledgments to copyright owners appears at the back
of this volume.

 Published in the United States by Alfred A. Knopf,
a division of Random House, Inc., New York, and in Canada by
Random House of Canada Limited, Toronto. Distributed by
Random House, Inc., New York. Published in the United Kingdom
by Everyman's Library, Northburgh House, 10 Northburgh Street,
London EC1V 0AT, and distributed by Random House (UK) Ltd.

US website: www.randomhouse.com/everymans

ISBN: 978-0-307-26924-9 (US)
978-1-84159-601-3 (UK)

A CIP catalogue reference for this book is available from the
British Library

Library of Congress Cataloging-in-Publication Data
Ghost stories / edited by Peter Washington.
p. cm.—(Everyman's pocket classics)
ISBN 978-0-307-26924-9 (alk. paper)
1. Ghost stories, English. 2. Ghost stories, American.
I. Peter Washington.
PR1309.G5G47 2008 2008006499
823'.0873308—dc22

Typography by Peter B. Willberg

Typeset in the UK by AccComputing, North Barrow, Somerset

Printed a[illegible] by GGP Media GmbH, Pössneck

GHOST STORIES

Contents

ROBERT LOUIS STEVENSON

THE BODY-SNATCHER

EVERY NIGHT IN the year, four of us sat in the small parlour of the George at Debenham – the undertaker, and the landlord, and Fettes, and myself. Sometimes there would be more; but blow high, blow low, come rain or snow or frost, we four would be each planted in his own particular armchair. Fettes was an old drunken Scotchman, a man of education obviously, and a man of some property, since he lived in idleness. He had come to Debenham years ago, while still young, and by a mere continuance of living had grown to be an adopted townsman. His blue camlet cloak was a local antiquity, like the church-spire. His place in the parlour at the George, his absence from church, his old, crapulous, disreputable vices, were all things of course in Debenham. He had some vague Radical opinions and some fleeting infidelities, which he would now and again set forth and emphasize with tottering slaps upon the table. He drank rum – five glasses regularly every evening; and for the greater portion of his nightly visit to the George sat, with his glass in his right hand, in a state of melancholy alcoholic saturation. We called him the Doctor, for he was supposed to have some special knowledge of medicine, and had been known, upon a pinch, to set a fracture or reduce a dislocation; but beyond these slight particulars, we had no knowledge of his character and antecedents.

One dark winter night – it had struck nine some time before the landlord joined us – there was a sick man in the

George, a great neighbouring proprietor suddenly struck down with apoplexy on his way to Parliament; and the great man's still greater London doctor had been telegraphed to his bedside. It was the first time that such a thing had happened in Debenham, for the railway was but newly open, and we were all proportionately moved by the occurrence.

'He's come,' said the landlord, after he had filled and lighted his pipe.

'He?' said I. 'Who? – not the doctor?'

'Himself,' replied our host.

'What is his name?'

'Doctor Macfarlane,' said the landlord.

Fettes was far through his third tumbler, stupidly fuddled, now nodding over, now staring mazily around him; but at the last word he seemed to awaken, and repeated the name 'Macfarlane' twice, quietly enough the first time, but with sudden emotion at the second.

'Yes,' said the landlord, 'that's his name, Doctor Wolfe Macfarlane.'

Fettes became instantly sober; his eyes awoke, his voice became clear, loud, and steady, his language forcible and earnest. We were all startled by the transformation, as if a man had risen from the dead.

'I beg your pardon,' he said, 'I am afraid I have not been paying much attention to your talk. Who is this Wolfe Macfarlane?' And then, when he had heard the landlord out, 'It cannot be, it cannot be,' he added; 'and yet I would like well to see him face to face.'

'Do you know him, Doctor?' asked the undertaker, with a gasp.

'God forbid!' was the reply. 'And yet the name is a strange one; it were too much to fancy two. Tell me, landlord, is he old?'

'Well,' said the host, 'he's not a young man, to be sure, and his hair is white; but he looks younger than you.'

'He is older, though; years older. But,' with a slap upon the table, 'it's the rum you see in my face – rum and sin. This man, perhaps, may have an easy conscience and a good digestion. Conscience! Hear me speak. You would think I was some good, old, decent Christian, would you not? But no, not I; I never canted. Voltaire might have canted if he'd stood in my shoes; but the brains' – with a rattling fillip on his bald head – 'the brains were clear and active, and I saw and made no deductions.'

'If you know this doctor,' I ventured to remark, after a somewhat awful pause, 'I should gather that you do not share the landlord's good opinion.'

Fettes paid no regard to me.

'Yes,' he said, with sudden decision, 'I must see him face to face.'

There was another pause, and then a door was closed rather sharply on the first floor, and a step was heard upon the stair.

'That's the doctor,' cried the landlord. 'Look sharp, and you can catch him.'

It was but two steps from the small parlour to the door of the old George Inn; the wide oak staircase landed almost in the street; there was room for a Turkey rug and nothing more between the threshold and the last round of the descent; but this little space was every evening brilliantly lit up, not only by the light upon the stair and the great signal lamp below the sign, but by the warm radiance of the bar-room window. The George thus brightly advertised itself to passers-by in the cold street. Fettes walked steadily to the spot, and we, who were hanging behind, beheld the two men meet, as one of them had phrased it, face to face.

Dr Macfarlane was alert and vigorous. His white hair set off his pale and placid, although energetic, countenance. He was richly dressed in the finest of broadcloth and the whitest of linen, with a great gold watch-chain, and studs and spectacles of the same precious material. He wore a broad-folded tie, white and speckled with lilac, and he carried on his arm a comfortable driving-coat of fur. There was no doubt but he became his years, breathing, as he did, of wealth and consideration; and it was a surprising contrast to see our parlour sot – bald, dirty, pimpled, and robed in his old camlet cloak – confront him at the bottom of the stairs.

'Macfarlane!' he said somewhat loudly, more like a herald than a friend.

The great doctor pulled up short on the fourth step, as though the familiarity of the address surprised and somewhat shocked his dignity.

'Toddy Macfarlane!' repeated Fettes.

The London man almost staggered. He stared for the swiftest of seconds at the man before him, glanced behind him with a sort of scare, and then in a startled whisper, 'Fettes!' he said, 'you!'

'Ay,' said the other, 'me! Did you think I was dead too? We are not so easy shut of our acquaintance.'

'Hush, hush!' exclaimed the doctor. 'Hush, hush! this meeting is so unexpected – I can see you are unmanned. I hardly knew you, I confess, at first; but I am overjoyed – overjoyed to have this opportunity. For the present it must be how-d'ye-do and good-bye in one, for my fly is waiting, and I must not fail the train; but you shall – let me see – yes – you shall give me your address, and you can count on early news of me. We must do something for you, Fettes. I fear you are out at elbows; but we must see to that for auld lang syne, as once we sang at suppers.'

'Money!' cried Fettes; 'money from you! The money that I had from you is lying where I cast it in the rain.'

Dr Macfarlane had talked himself into some measure of superiority and confidence, but the uncommon energy of this refusal cast him back into his first confusion.

A horrible, ugly look came and went across his almost venerable countenance. 'My dear fellow,' he said, 'be it as you please; my last thought is to offend you. I would intrude on none. I will leave you my address, however—'

'I do not wish it – I do not wish to know the roof that shelters you,' interrupted the other. 'I heard your name; I feared it might be you; I wished to know if, after all, there were a God; I know now that there is none. Begone!'

He still stood in the middle of the rug, between the stair and doorway; and the great London physician, in order to escape, would be forced to step to one side. It was plain that he hesitated before the thought of this humiliation. White as he was, there was a dangerous glitter in his spectacles; but while he still paused uncertain, he became aware that the driver of his fly was peering in from the street at this unusual scene and caught a glimpse at the same time of our little body from the parlour, huddled by the corner of the bar. The presence of so many witnesses decided him at once to flee. He crouched together, brushing on the wainscot, and made a dart like a serpent, striking for the door. But his tribulation was not entirely at an end, for even as he was passing Fettes clutched him by the arm and these words came in a whisper, and yet painfully distinct, 'Have you seen it again?'

The great rich London doctor cried out aloud with a sharp, throttling cry; he dashed his questioner across the open space, and, with his hands over his head, fled out of the door like a detected thief. Before it had occurred to one of us to make a movement the fly was already rattling toward the station. The scene was over like a dream, but the dream had left proofs and traces of its passage. Next day the servant found the fine gold spectacles broken on the threshold, and that very night we were all standing breathless by the bar-room window, and Fettes at our side, sober, pale, and resolute in look.

'God protect us, Mr Fettes!' said the landlord, coming first into possession of his customary senses. 'What in the universe is all this? These are strange things you have been saying.'

Fettes turned toward us; he looked us each in succession in the face. 'See if you can hold your tongues,' said he. 'That man Macfarlane is not safe to cross; those that have done so already have repented it too late.'

And then, without so much as finishing his third glass, far less waiting for the other two, he bade us good-bye and went forth, under the lamp of the hotel, into the black night.

We three turned to our places in the parlour, with the big red fire and four clear candles; and as we recapitulated what had passed, the first chill of our surprise soon changed into a glow of curiosity. We sat late; it was the latest session I have known in the old George. Each man, before we parted, had his theory that he was bound to prove; and none of us had any nearer business in this world than to track out the past of our condemned companion, and surprise the secret that he shared with the great London doctor. It is no great boast, but I believe I was a better hand at worming out a story than either of my fellows at the George; and perhaps there is now no other man alive who could narrate to you the following foul and unnatural events.

In his young days Fettes studied medicine in the schools

of Edinburgh. He had talent of a kind, the talent that picks up swiftly what it hears and readily retails it for its own. He worked little at home; but he was civil, attentive, and intelligent in the presence of his masters. They soon picked him out as a lad who listened closely and remembered well; nay, strange as it seemed to me when I first heard it, he was in those days well favoured, and pleased by his exterior. There was, at that period, a certain extramural teacher of anatomy, whom I shall here designate by the letter K. His name was subsequently too well known. The man who bore it skulked through the streets of Edinburgh in disguise, while the mob that applauded at the execution of Burke called loudly for the blood of his employer. But Mr K— was then at the top of his vogue; he enjoyed a popularity due partly to his own talent and address, partly to the incapacity of his rival, the university professor. The students, at least, swore by his name, and Fettes believed himself, and was believed by others, to have laid the foundations of success when he acquired the favour of this meteorically famous man. Mr K— was a *bon vivant* as well as an accomplished teacher; he liked a sly illusion no less than a careful preparation. In both capacities Fettes enjoyed and deserved his notice, and by the second year of his attendance he held the half-regular position of second demonstrator, or sub-assistant in his class.

In this capacity the charge of the theatre and lecture-room devolved in particular upon his shoulders. He had to answer for the cleanliness of the premises and the conduct of the other students, and it was a part of his duty to supply, receive, and divide the various subjects. It was with a view to this last – at that time very delicate – affair that he was lodged by Mr K— in the same wynd, and at last in the same building, with the dissecting-rooms. Here, after a night of turbulent pleasures, his hand still tottering, his sight still misty and confused, he would be called out of bed in the black hours before the winter dawn by the unclean and desperate interlopers who supplied the table. He would open the door to these men, since infamous throughout the land. He would help them with their tragic burden, pay them their sordid price, and remain alone, when they were gone, with the unfriendly relics of humanity. From such a scene he would return to snatch another hour or two of slumber, to repair the abuses of the night, and refresh himself for the labours of the day.

Few lads could have been more insensible to the impressions of a life thus passed among the ensigns of mortality. His mind was closed against all general considerations. He was incapable of interest in the fate and fortunes of another, the slave of his own desires and low ambitions. Cold, light, and selfish in the last resort, he had that modicum of prudence, miscalled morality, which keeps a man from inconvenient drunkenness or punishable theft. He coveted, besides, a measure of consideration from his masters and his fellow-pupils, and he had no desire to fail conspicuously in the external parts of life. Thus he made it his pleasure to gain some distinction in his studies, and day after day rendered unimpeachable eye-service to his employer, Mr K—. For his day of work he indemnified himself by nights of roaring, blackguardly enjoyment; and when that balance had been struck, the organ that he called his conscience declared itself content.

The supply of subjects was a continual trouble to him as well as to his master. In that large and busy class, the raw material of the anatomist kept perpetually running out; and the business thus rendered necessary was not only unpleasant in itself, but threatened dangerous consequences to all who were concerned. It was the policy of Mr K— to ask no questions in his dealings with the trade. 'They bring the body, and we pay the price,' he used to say, dwelling on the alliteration – '*quid pro quo*'. And, again, and somewhat profanely, 'Ask no questions,' he would tell his assistants, 'for conscience' sake.' There was no understanding that the subjects were provided by the crime of murder. Had that idea been broached to him in words, he would have recoiled in horror; but the lightness of his speech upon so grave a matter was, in itself, an offence against good manners, and a temptation to the men with whom he dealt. Fettes, for instance, had often remarked to himself upon the singular freshness of the bodies. He had been struck again and again by the hangdog, abominable looks of the ruffians who came to him before the dawn; and putting things together clearly in his private thoughts, he perhaps attributed a meaning too immoral and too categorical to the unguarded counsels of his master. He understood his duty, in short, to have three branches: to take what was brought, to pay the price, and to avert the eye from any evidence of crime.

One November morning this policy of silence was put sharply to the test. He had been awake all night with a racking toothache – pacing his room like a caged beast or throwing himself in fury on his bed – and had fallen at last into that profound, uneasy slumber that so often follows on a night of pain, when he was awakened by the third or fourth angry repetition of the concerted signal. There was a thin, bright moonshine; it was bitter cold, windy, and frosty; the town had not yet awakened, but an indefinable stir already preluded the noise and business of the day. The ghouls had come later than usual, and they seemed more than usually eager to be gone. Fettes, sick with sleep, lighted them upstairs. He heard their grumbling Irish voices through a dream; and as they stripped the sack from their sad merchandise he leaned dozing, with his shoulder propped against the wall; he had to shake himself to find the men their money. As he did so his eyes lighted on the dead face. He started; he took two steps nearer, with the candle raised.

'God Almighty!' he cried. 'That is Jane Galbraith!'

The men answered nothing, but they shuffled nearer the door.

'I know her, I tell you,' he continued. 'She was alive and hearty yesterday. It's impossible she can be dead; it's impossible you should have got this body fairly.'

'Sure, sir, you're mistaken entirely,' said one of the men.

But the other looked Fettes darkly in the eyes, and demanded the money on the spot.

It was impossible to misconceive the threat or to exaggerate the danger. The lad's heart failed him. He stammered some excuses, counted out the sum, and saw his hateful visitors depart. No sooner were they gone than he hastened to confirm his doubts. By a dozen unquestionable marks he identified the girl he had jested with the day before. He saw, with horror, marks upon her body that might well betoken violence. A panic seized him, and he took refuge in his room. There he reflected at length over the discovery that he had made; considered soberly the bearing of Mr K—'s instructions and the danger to himself of interference in so serious a business, and at last, in sore perplexity, determined to wait for the advice of his immediate superior, the class assistant.

This was a young doctor, Wolfe Macfarlane, a high favourite among all the reckless students, clever, dissipated, and unscrupulous to the last degree. He had travelled and studied abroad. His manners were agreeable and a little forward. He was an authority on the stage, skilful on the ice or the links with skate or golf-club; he dressed with nice audacity, and, to put the finishing touch upon his glory, he kept a gig and a strong trotting-horse. With Fettes he was on terms of intimacy; indeed, their relative positions called for some community of life; and when subjects were scarce the pair would drive far into the country in Macfarlane's gig, visit and desecrate some lonely graveyard, and return before dawn with their booty to the door of the dissecting-room.

On that particular morning Macfarlane arrived somewhat earlier than his wont. Fettes heard him, and met him on the stairs, told him his story, and showed him the cause of his alarm. Macfarlane examined the marks on her body.

'Yes,' he said, with a nod, 'it looks fishy.'

'Well, what should I do?' asked Fettes.

'Do?' repeated the other. 'Do you want to do anything? Least said soonest mended, I should say.'

'Some one else might recognize her,' objected Fettes. 'She was as well known as the Castle Rock.'

'We'll hope not,' said Macfarlane, 'and if anybody does – well, you didn't, don't you see, and there's an end. The fact is, this has been going on too long. Stir up the mud, and you'll get K— into the most unholy trouble; you'll be in a shocking box yourself. So will I, if you come to that. I should like to know how any one of us would look, or what the devil we should have to say for ourselves, in any Christian witness-box. For me, you know there's one thing certain – that, practically speaking, all our subjects have been murdered.'

'Macfarlane!' cried Fettes.

'Come now!' sneered the other. 'As if you hadn't suspected it yourself!'

'Suspecting is one thing—'

'And proof another. Yes, I know; and I'm as sorry as you are this should have come here,' tapping the body with his cane. 'The next best thing for me is not to recognize it; and,' he added coolly, 'I don't. You may, if you please. I don't dictate, but I think a man of the world would do as I do; and I may add, I fancy that is what K— would look for at our hands. The question is, Why did he choose us two for his assistants? And I answer, Because he didn't want old wives.'

This was the tone of all others to affect the mind of a lad like Fettes. He agreed to imitate Macfarlane. The body of the unfortunate girl was duly dissected, and no one remarked or appeared to recognize her.

One afternoon, when his day's work was over, Fettes dropped into a popular tavern and found Macfarlane sitting with a stranger. This was a small man, very pale and dark, with coal-black eyes. The cut of his features gave a promise of intellect and refinement which was but feebly realized in his manners, for he proved, upon a nearer acquaintance, coarse, vulgar, and stupid. He exercised, however, a very remarkable control over Macfarlane; issued orders like the Great Bashaw; became inflamed at the least discussion or delay, and commented rudely on the servility with which he was obeyed. This most offensive person took a fancy to Fettes on the spot, plied him with drinks, and honoured him with unusual confidences on his past career. If a tenth part of what he confessed were true, he was a very loathsome rogue; and the lad's vanity was tickled by the attention of so experienced a man.

'I'm a pretty bad fellow myself,' the stranger remarked, 'but Macfarlane is the boy – Toddy Macfarlane I call him. Toddy, order your friend another glass.' Or it might be, 'Toddy, you jump up and shut the door.' 'Toddy hates me,' he said again. 'Oh, yes, Toddy, you do!'

'Don't you call me that confounded name,' growled Macfarlane.

'Hear him! Did you ever see the lads play knife? He would like to do that all over my body,' remarked the stranger.

'We medicals have a better way than that,' said Fettes. 'When we dislike a dead friend of ours, we dissect him.'

Macfarlane looked up sharply, as though this jest were scarcely to his mind.

The afternoon passed. Gray, for that was the stranger's name, invited Fettes to join them at dinner, ordered a feast so sumptuous that the tavern was thrown into commotion, and when all was done commanded Macfarlane to settle the bill. It was late before they separated; the man Gray was incapably drunk. Macfarlane, sobered by his fury, chewed the cud of the money he had been forced to squander and the slights he had been obliged to swallow. Fettes, with various liquors singing in his head, returned home with devious footsteps and a mind entirely in abeyance. Next day Macfarlane was absent from the class, and Fettes smiled to himself as he imagined him still squiring the intolerable Gray from tavern to tavern. As soon as the hour of liberty had struck he posted from place to place in quest of his last night's companions. He could find them, however, nowhere; so returned early to his rooms, went early to bed, and slept the sleep of the just.

At four in the morning he was awakened by the well-known signal. Descending to the door, he was filled with astonishment to find Macfarlane with his gig, and in the gig one of those long and ghastly packages with which he was so well acquainted.

'What?' he cried. 'Have you been out alone? How did you manage?'

But Macfarlane silenced him roughly, bidding him turn

to business. When they had got the body upstairs and laid it on the table, Macfarlane made at first as if he were going away. Then he paused and seemed to hesitate; and then, 'You had better look at the face,' said he, in tones of some constraint. 'You had better,' he repeated, as Fettes only stared at him in wonder.

'But where, and how, and when did you come by it?' cried the other.

'Look at the face,' was the only answer.

Fettes was staggered; strange doubts assailed him. He looked from the young doctor to the body, and then back again. At last, with a start, he did as he was bidden. He had almost expected the sight that met his eyes, and yet the shock was cruel. To see, fixed in the rigidity of death and naked on that coarse layer of sackcloth, the man whom he had left well clad and full of meat and sin upon the threshold of a tavern, awoke, even in the thoughtless Fettes, some of the terrors of the conscience. It was a *cras tibi* which re-echoed in his soul, that two whom he had known should have come to lie upon these icy tables. Yet these were only secondary thoughts. His first concern regarded Wolfe. Unprepared for a challenge so momentous, he knew not how to look his comrade in the face. He durst not meet his eye, and he had neither words nor voice at his command.

It was Macfarlane himself who made the first advance. He came up quietly behind and laid his hand gently but firmly on the other's shoulder.

'Richardson,' said he, 'may have the head.'

Now Richardson was a student who had long been anxious for that portion of the human subject to dissect. There was no answer, and the murderer resumed: 'Talking of business, you must pay me; your accounts, you see, must tally.'

Fettes found a voice, the ghost of his own: 'Pay you!' he cried. 'Pay you for that?'

'Why, yes, of course you must. By all means and on every possible account, you must,' returned the other. I dare not give it for nothing, you dare not take it for nothing; it would compromise us both. This is another case like Jane Galbraith's. The more things are wrong the more we must act as if all were right. Where does old K— keep his money?'

'There,' answered Fettes hoarsely, pointing to a cupboard in the corner.

'Give me the key, then,' said the other calmly, holding out his hand.

There was an instant's hesitation, and the die was cast. Macfarlane could not suppress a nervous twitch, the infinitesimal mark of an immense relief, as he felt the key between his fingers. He opened the cupboard, brought out pen and ink and a paper-book that stood in one compartment, and separated from the funds in a drawer a sum suitable to the occasion.

'Now, look here,' he said, 'there is the payment made – first proof of your good faith: first step to your security. You have now to clinch it by a second. Enter the payment in your book, and then you for your part may defy the devil.'

The next few seconds were for Fettes an agony of thought; but in balancing his terrors it was the most immediate that triumphed. Any future difficulty seemed almost welcome if he could avoid a present quarrel with Macfarlane. He set down the candle which he had been carrying all this time, and with a steady hand entered the date, the nature, and the amount of the transaction.

'And now,' said Macfarlane, 'it's only fair that you should pocket the lucre. I've had my share already. By-the-bye, when a man of the world falls into a bit of luck, has a few shillings extra in his pocket – I'm ashamed to speak of it, but there's a rule of conduct in the case. No treating, no purchase of expensive class-books, no squaring of old debts; borrow, don't lend.'

'Macfarlane,' began Fettes, still somewhat hoarsely, 'I have put my neck in a halter to oblige you.'

'To oblige me?' cried Wolfe. 'Oh, come! You did, as near as I can see the matter, what you downright had to do in self-defence. Suppose I got into trouble, where would you be? This second little matter flows clearly from the first. Mr Gray is the continuation of Miss Galbraith. You can't begin and then stop. If you begin, you must keep on beginning; that's the truth. No rest for the wicked.'

A horrible sense of blackness and the treachery of fate seized hold upon the soul of the unhappy student.

'My God!' he cried, 'but what have I done? and when did I begin? To be made a class assistant – in the name of reason, where's the harm in that? Service wanted the position; Service might have got it. Would *he* have been where *I* am now!'

'My dear fellow,' said Macfarlane, 'what a boy you are! What harm *has* come to you? What harm *can* come to you if you hold your tongue? Why, man, do you know what this life is? There are two squads of us – the lions and the lambs. If you're a lamb, you'll come to lie upon these tables like Gray or Jane Galbraith; if you're a lion, you'll live and drive a horse like me, like K—, like all the world with any wit or courage. You're staggered at the first. But look at K—! My dear fellow, you're clever, you have pluck. I like you, and K— likes you. You were born to lead the hunt; and I tell you, on my honour and my experience of life, three days from now you'll laugh at all these scarecrows like a High School boy at a farce.'

And with that Macfarlane took his departure and drove off up the wynd in his gig to get under cover before daylight. Fettes was thus left alone with his regrets. He saw the miserable peril in which he stood involved. He saw, with inexpressible dismay, that there was no limit to his weakness, and that, from concession to concession, he had fallen from the arbiter of Macfarlane's destiny to his paid and helpless accomplice. He would have given the world to have been a little braver at the time, but it did not occur to him that he might still be brave. The secret of Jane Galbraith and the cursed entry in the day-book closed his mouth.

Hours passed; the class began to arrive; the members of the unhappy Gray were dealt out to one and to another, and received without remark. Richardson was made happy with the head; and before the hour of freedom rang Fettes trembled with exultation to perceive how far they had already gone toward safety.

For two days he continued to watch, with increasing joy, the dreadful process of disguise.

On the third day Macfarlane made his appearance. He had been ill, he said; but he made up for lost time by the energy with which he directed the students. To Richardson in particular he extended the most valuable assistance and advice, and that student, encouraged by the praise of the demonstrator, burned high with ambitious hopes, and saw the medal already in his grasp.

Before the week was out Macfarlane's prophecy had been fulfilled. Fettes had outlived his terrors and had forgotten his baseness. He began to plume himself upon his courage, and had so arranged the story in his mind that he could look back on these events with an unhealthy pride. Of his accomplice he saw but little. They met, of course, in the business of the class; they received their orders together from

Mr K—. At times they had a word or two in private, and Macfarlane was from first to last particularly kind and jovial. But it was plain that he avoided any reference to their common secret; and even when Fettes whispered to him that he had cast in his lot with the lions and forsworn the lambs, he only signed to him smilingly to hold his peace.

At length an occasion arose which threw the pair once more into a closer union. Mr K— was again short of subjects; pupils were eager, and it was a part of this teacher's pretensions to be always well supplied. At the same time there came the news of a burial in the rustic graveyard of Glencorse. Time has little changed the place in question. It stood then, as now, upon a cross road, out of call of human habitations, and buried fathom deep in the foliage of six cedar trees. The cries of the sheep upon the neighbouring hills, the streamlets upon either hand, one loudly singing among pebbles, the other dripping furtively from pond to pond, the stir of the wind in mountainous old flowering chestnuts, and once in seven days the voice of the bell and the old tunes of the precentor, were the only sounds that disturbed the silence around the rural church. The Resurrection Man – to use a by-name of the period – was not to be deterred by any of the sanctities of customary piety. It was part of his trade to despise and desecrate the scrolls and trumpets of old tombs, the paths worn by the feet of worshippers and mourners, and the offerings and the inscriptions of bereaved affection. To rustic neighbourhoods, where love is more than commonly tenacious, and where some bonds of blood or fellowship unite the entire society of a parish, the body-snatcher, far from being repelled by natural respect, was attracted by the ease and safety of the task. To bodies that had been laid in earth, in joyful expectation of a far different awakening, there came that hasty, lamp-lit, terror-haunted resurrection of the spade and mattock. The coffin was forced, the cerements torn, and the melancholy relics, clad in sackcloth, after being rattled for hours on moonless byways, were at length exposed to uttermost indignities before a class of gaping boys.

Somewhat as two vultures may swoop upon a dying lamb, Fettes and Macfarlane were to be let loose upon a grave in that green and quiet resting-place. The wife of a farmer, a woman who had lived for sixty years, and been known for nothing but good butter and a godly conversation, was to be rooted from her grave at midnight and carried, dead and naked, to that far-away city that she had always honoured with her Sunday's best; the place beside her family was to be empty till the crack of doom; her innocent and almost venerable members to be exposed to that last curiosity of the anatomist.

Late one afternoon the pair set forth, well wrapped in cloaks and furnished with a formidable bottle. It rained without remission – a cold, dense, lashing rain. Now and again there blew a puff of wind, but these sheets of falling water kept it down. Bottle and all, it was a sad and silent drive as far as Penicuik, where they were to spend the evening. They stopped once, to hide their implements in a thick bush not far from the churchyard, and once again at the Fisher's Tryst, to have a toast before the kitchen fire and vary their nips of whisky with a glass of ale. When they reached their journey's end the gig was housed, the horse was fed and comforted, and the two young doctors in a private room sat down to the best dinner and the best wine the house afforded. The lights, the fire, the beating rain upon the window, the cold, incongruous work that lay before them, added zest to their enjoyment of the meal.

With every glass their cordiality increased. Soon Macfarlane handed a little pile of gold to his companion.

'A compliment,' he said. 'Between friends these little d—d accommodations ought to fly like pipe-lights.'

Fettes pocketed the money, and applauded the sentiment to the echo. 'You are a philosopher,' he cried. 'I was an ass till I knew you. You and K— between you, by the Lord Harry! but you'll make a man of me.'

'Of course we shall,' applauded Macfarlane. 'A man? I tell you, it required a man to back me up the other morning. There are some big, brawling, forty-year-old cowards who would have turned sick at the look of the d—d thing; but not you – you kept your head. I watched you.'

'Well, and why not?' Fettes thus vaunted himself. 'It was no affair of mine. There was nothing to gain on the one side but disturbance, and on the other I could count on your gratitude, don't you see?' And he slapped his pocket till the gold pieces rang.

Macfarlane somehow felt a certain touch of alarm at these unpleasant words. He may have regretted that he had taught his young companion so successfully, but he had no time to interfere, for the other noisily continued in this boastful strain: –

'The great thing is not to be afraid. Now, between you and me, I don't want to hang – that's practical; but for all cant, Macfarlane, I was born with a contempt. Hell, God, Devil, right, wrong, sin, crime, and all the old gallery of curiosities – they may frighten boys, but men of the world, like you and me, despise them. Here's to the memory of Gray!'

It was by this time growing somewhat late. The gig, according to order, was brought round to the door with both lamps brightly shining, and the young men had to pay their bill and take the road. They announced that they were bound for Peebles, and drove in that direction till they were clear of the last houses of the town; then, extinguishing the lamps, returned upon their course, and followed a by-road toward Glencorse. There was no sound but that of their own passage, and the incessant, strident pouring of the rain. It was pitch dark; here and there a white gate or a white stone in the wall guided them for a short space across the night; but for the most part it was at a foot pace, and almost groping, that they picked their way through that resonant blackness to their solemn and isolated destination. In the sunken woods that traverse the neighbourhood of the burying-ground the last glimmer failed them, and it became necessary to kindle a match and re-illumine one of the lanterns of the gig. Thus, under the dripping trees, and environed by huge and moving shadows, they reached the scene of their unhallowed labours.

They were both experienced in such affairs, and powerful with the spade; and they had scarce been twenty minutes at their task before they were rewarded by a dull rattle on the coffin lid. At the same moment, Macfarlane, having hurt his hand upon a stone, flung it carelessly above his head. The grave, in which they now stood almost to the shoulders, was close to the edge of the plateau of the graveyard; and the gig lamp had been propped, the better to illuminate their labours, against a tree, and on the immediate verge of the steep bank descending to the stream. Chance had taken a sure aim with the stone. Then came a clang of broken glass; night fell upon them; sounds alternately dull and ringing announced the bounding of the lantern down the bank, and its occasional collision with the trees. A stone or two, which it had dislodged in its descent, rattled behind it into the profundities of the glen; and then silence, like night, resumed its sway; and they might bend their hearing to its utmost pitch, but naught was to be heard except the rain, now marching to the wind, now steadily falling over miles of open country.

They were so nearly at an end of their abhorred task that they judged it wisest to complete it in the dark. The coffin was exhumed and broken open; the body inserted in the dripping sack and carried between them to the gig; one mounted to keep it in its place, and the other, taking the horse by the mouth, groped along by wall and bush until they reached the wider road by the Fisher's Tryst. Here was a faint, diffused radiancy, which they hailed like daylight; by that they pushed the horse to a good pace and began to rattle along merrily in the direction of the town.

They had both been wetted to the skin during their operations, and now, as the gig jumped among the deep ruts, the thing that stood propped between them fell now upon one and now upon the other. At every repetition of the horrid contact each instinctively repelled it with the greater haste; and the process, natural although it was, began to tell upon the nerves of the companions. Macfarlane made some ill-favoured jest about the farmer's wife, but it came hollowly from his lips, and was allowed to drop in silence. Still their unnatural burden bumped from side to side; and now the head would be laid, as if in confidence, upon their shoulders, and now the drenching sackcloth would flap icily about their faces. A creeping chill began to possess the soul of Fettes. He peered at the bundle, and it seemed somehow larger than at first. All over the countryside, and from every degree of distance, the farm dogs accompanied their passage with tragic ululations; and it grew and grew upon his mind that some unnatural miracle had been accomplished, that some nameless change had befallen the dead body, and that it was in fear of their unholy burden that the dogs were howling.

'For God's sake,' said he, making a great effort to arrive at speech, 'for God's sake, let's have a light!'

Seemingly Macfarlane was affected in the same direction; for, though he made no reply, he stopped the horse, passed the reins to his companion, got down, and proceeded to kindle the remaining lamp. They had by that time got no farther than the cross-road down to Auchenclinny. The rain still poured as though the deluge were returning, and it was no easy matter to make a light in such a world of wet and darkness. When at last the flickering blue flame had been transferred to the wick and began to expand and clarify, and shed a wide circle of misty brightness round the gig, it became possible for the two young men to see each other and the thing they had along with them. The rain had moulded the rough sacking to the outlines of the body underneath; the head was distinct from the trunk, the shoulders plainly modelled; something at once spectral and human riveted their eyes upon the ghastly comrade of their drive.

For some time Macfarlane stood motionless, holding up the lamp. A nameless dread was swathed, like a wet sheet, about the body, and tightened the white skin upon the face of Fettes; a fear that was meaningless, a horror of what could not be, kept mounting to his brain. Another beat of the watch, and he had spoken. But his comrade forestalled him.

'That is not a woman,' said Macfarlane, in a hushed voice.

'It was a woman when we put her in,' whispered Fettes.

'Hold that lamp,' said the other. 'I must see her face.'

And as Fettes took the lamp his companion untied the fastenings of the sack and drew down the cover from the head. The light fell very clear upon the dark, well-moulded features and smooth-shaven cheeks of a too familiar countenance, often beheld in dreams of both of these young men. A wild yell rang up into the night; each leaped from his own side into the roadway: the lamp fell, broke, and was extinguished; and the horse, terrified by this unusual commotion, bounded and went off toward Edinburgh at a gallop, bearing along with it, sole occupant of the gig, the body of the dead and long-dissected Gray.

GUY DE MAUPASSANT

THE HORLA

Translated by Ernest Boyd

MAY 8. What a glorious day! I have spent the whole morning lying on the grass in front of my house, under the enormous plane-tree that forms a complete covering, shelter and shade for it. I love this country, and I love living here because it is here I have my roots, those deep-down slender roots that hold a man to the place where his forefathers were born and died, hold him to ways of thought and habits of eating, to customs as to particular foods, to local fashions of speech, to the intonations of country voices, to the scent of the soil, the villages, and the very air itself.

I love this house of mine where I grew up. From my windows I see the Seine flowing alongside my garden, beyond the high road, almost at my door, the great wide Seine, running from Rouen to Havre, covered with passing boats.

Away to the left, Rouen, the widespread town, with its blue roofs lying under the bristling host of Gothic belfries. They are beyond number, frail or sturdy, dominated by the leaden steeples of the cathedral, and filled with bells that ring out in the limpid air of fine mornings, sending me the sweet and far-off murmur of their iron tongues, a brazen song borne to me on the breeze, now louder, now softer, as it swells or dies away.

How beautiful this morning has been!

Towards eleven o'clock a long convoy of boats followed each other past my gate, behind a squat tug looking like a fly, and wheezing painfully as it vomited thick clouds of smoke.

After two English yachts whose crimson awnings rose and fell against the sky, came a splendid three-masted Brazilian, all white, gloriously clean and glittering. The sight of this ship filled me with such joy that I saluted her, I don't know why.

May 11. I have had a slight fever for the last few days; I feel ill or rather unhappy.

Whence come these mysterious influences that change our happiness to dejection and our self-confidence to discouragement? It is as if the air, the unseen air, were full of unknowable powers whose mysterious nearness we endure. I wake full of joy, my throat swelling with a longing to sing. Why? I go down to the water-side; and suddenly, after a short walk, I come back home wretched, as if some misfortune were waiting me there. Why? Has a chill shudder, passing lightly over my skin, shaken my nerves and darkened my spirit? Have the shapes of the clouds, or the colour of the day, the ever-changing colour of the visible world, troubled my mind as they slipped past my eyes? Does anyone know? Everything that surrounds us, everything that we see unseeing, everything that we brush past unknowing, everything that we touch impalpably, everything that we meet unnoticing, has on us, on the organs of our bodies, and through them on our thoughts, on our very hearts, swift, surprising and inexplicable effects.

How deep it is, this mystery of the Invisible! We cannot fathom it with our miserable senses, with our eyes that perceive neither the too small, nor the too great, nor the too near, nor the too distant, nor the inhabitants of a star, nor the inhabitants of a drop of water... with our ears that deceive us, transmitting the vibrations of the air to us as sonorous sounds. They are fairies who by a miracle transmute movement into sound, from which metamorphosis music is born, and make audible in song the mute quivering of nature . . . with our smell, feebler than a dog's . . . with our taste, that can only just detect the age of a wine.

If only we had other organs to work other miracles on our behalf, what things we could discover round us!

May 16. I am certainly ill, I have been so well since last month. I have a fever, a rotten fever, or rather a feverish weakness that oppresses my mind as wearily as my body. All day and every day I suffer this frightful sense of threatened danger, this apprehension of coming ill or approaching death, this presentiment which is doubtless the warning signal of a lurking disease germinating in my blood and my flesh.

May 18. I have just consulted my doctor, for I was not getting any sleep. He found that my pulse is rapid, my eyes dilated, my nerves on edge, but no alarming symptom of any kind. I am to take douches and drink bromide of potassium.

May 25. No change. My case is truly strange. As night falls, an incomprehensible uneasiness fills me, as if the night concealed a frightful menace directed at me. I dine in haste, then I try to read; but I don't understand the words: I can hardly make out the letters. So I walk backwards and forwards in my drawing-room, oppressed by a vague fear that I cannot throw off, fear of sleeping and fear of my bed.

About ten o'clock I go up to my room. The instant I am inside the room I double-lock the door and shut the windows; I am afraid . . . of what? I never dreaded anything before. . . . I open my cupboards, I look under my bed;

I listen . . . listen . . . to what? It's a queer thing that a mere physical ailment, some disorder in the blood perhaps, the jangling of a nerve thread, a slight congestion, the least disturbance in the functioning of this living machine of ours, so imperfect and so frail, can make a melancholic of the happiest of men and a coward of the bravest. Then I lie down, and wait for sleep as if I were waiting to be executed. I wait for it, dreading its approach; my heart beats, my legs tremble; my whole body shivers in the warmth of the bed-clothes, until the moment I fall suddenly on sleep, like a man falling into deep and stagnant waters, there to drown. Nowadays I never feel the approach of this perfidious sleep, that lurks near me, spying on me, ready to take me by the hand, shut my eyes, steal my strength.

I sleep – for a long time – two or three hours – then a dream – no – a nightmare seizes me. I feel that I am lying down and that I am asleep . . . I feel it and I know it . . . and I feel too that someone approaches me, looks at me, touches me, climbs on my bed, kneels on my chest, takes my neck between his hands and squeezes . . . squeezes . . . with all his might, strangling me.

I struggle madly, in the grip of the frightful impotence that paralyses us in dreams; I try to cry out – I can't; I try to move – I can't; panting, with the most frightful efforts, I try to turn round, to fling off this creature who is crushing and choking me – I can't do it.

And suddenly I wake up, terrified, covered with sweat. I light a candle. I am alone.

The crisis over – a crisis that happens every night – I fall at last into a quiet sleep, until daybreak.

June 2. My case has grown worse. What can be the matter with me? Bromide is useless; douches are useless.

Lately, by way of wearying a body already quite exhausted, I went for a tramp in the forest of Roumare. At first I thought that the fresh air, the clear sweet air, full of the scents of grass and trees, was pouring a new blood into my veins and a new strength into my heart. I followed a broad glade, then I turned towards Boville, by a narrow walk between two ranks of immensely tall trees that flung a thick green roof, almost a black roof, between the sky and me.

A sudden shudder ran through me, not a shudder of cold but a strange shudder of anguish.

I quickened my pace, uneasy at being alone in this wood, unreasonably, stupidly, terrified by the profound solitude. Abruptly I felt that I was being followed, that someone was on my heels, as near as near, touching me.

I swung round. I was alone. I saw behind me only the straight open walk, empty, high, terrifyingly empty; it stretched out in front of me too, as far as the eye could see, as empty, and frightening.

I shut my eyes. Why? And I began to turn round on my heel at a great rate like a top. I almost fell; I opened my eyes again; the trees were dancing; the earth was swaying; I was forced to sit down. Then, ah! I didn't know now which way I had been walking. Strange thought! Strange! Strange thought! I didn't know anything at all now. I took the right-hand way, and found myself back in the avenue that had led me into the middle of the forest.

June 3. The night has been terrible. I am going to go away for several weeks. A short journey will surely put me right.

July 2. Home again. I am cured. I have had, moreover, a delightful holiday. I visited Mont-Saint-Michel, which I didn't know.

What a vision one gets, arriving at Avranches as I did, towards dusk! The town lies on a slope, and I was taken into the public garden, at the end of the city. A cry of astonishment broke from me. A shoreless bay stretched before me, as far as eye could see: it lay between opposing coasts that vanished in distant mist; and in the midst of this vast tawny bay, under a gleaming golden sky, a strange hill, sombre and peaked, thrust up from the sands at its feet. The sun had just sunk, and on a horizon still riotous with colour was etched the outline of this fantastic rock that bore on its summit a fantastic monument.

At daybreak I went out to it. The tide was low, as on the evening before, and as I drew near it, the miraculous abbey grew in height before my eyes. After several hours' walking I reached the monstrous pile of stones that supports the little city dominated by the great church. I clambered up the steep narrow street, I entered the most wonderful Gothic dwelling made for God on this earth, as vast as a town, with innumerable low rooms hollowed out under the vaults and high galleries slung over slender columns. I entered this gigantic granite jewel, as delicate as a piece of lace, pierced everywhere by towers and airy belfries where twisting stairways climb, towers and belfries that by day against a blue sky and by night against a dark sky lift strange heads, bristling with chimeras, devils, fantastic beasts and monstrous flowers, and are linked together by slender carved arches.

When I stood on the top I said to the monk who accompanied me: 'What a glorious place you have here, Father!'

'We get strong winds,' he answered, and we fell into talk as we watched the incoming sea run over the sand and cover it with a steel cuirass.

The monk told me stories, all the old stories of this place, legends, always legends.

One of them particularly impressed me. The people of the district, those who lived on the Mount, declared that at night they heard voices on the sands, followed by the bleating of two she-goats, one that called loudly and one calling softly. Unbelievers insisted that it was the crying of sea birds which at one and the same time resembled bleatings and the wailing of human voices: but benighted fishermen swore that they had met an old shepherd wandering on the dunes, between two tides, round the little town flung so far out of the world. No one ever saw the head hidden in his cloak: he led, walking in front of them, a goat with the face of a man and a she-goat with the face of a woman; both of them had long white hair and talked incessantly, disputing in an unknown tongue, then abruptly ceased crying to begin a loud bleating.

'Do you believe it?' I asked the monk.

He murmured: 'I don't know.'

'If,' I went on, 'there existed on the earth beings other than ourselves, why have we not long ago learned to know them; why have you yourself not seen them? Why have I not seen them myself?'

He answered: 'Do we see the hundred thousandth part of all that exists? Think, there's the wind, the greatest force in nature, which throws down men, shatters buildings, uproots trees, stirs up the sea into watery mountains, destroys cliffs and tosses the tall ships against the shore, the wind that kills, whistles, groans, roars – have you seen it, can you see it? Nevertheless, it exists.'

Before his simple reasoning I fell silent. This man was either a seer or a fool. I should not have cared to say which; but I held my peace. What he had just said, I had often thought.

July 3. I slept badly; I am sure there is a feverish influence at work here, for my coachman suffers from the same trouble as myself. When I came home yesterday, I noticed his strange pallor.

'What's the matter with you, Jean?' I demanded.

'I can't rest these days, sir; I'm burning the candle at both ends. Since you went away, sir, I haven't been able to throw it off.'

The other servants are all right, however, but I am terrified of getting caught by it again.

July 4. It has surely caught me again. My old nightmares have come back. Last night I felt crouching on me someone who presses his mouth on mine and drinks my life between my lips. Yes, he sucked it from my throat like a leech. Then he rose from me, replete, and I awoke, so mangled, bruised, enfeebled, that I could not move. If this goes on for many days more, I shall certainly go away again.

July 5. Have I lost my reason? What has just happened, what I saw last night, is so strange that my head reels when I think of it.

Following my invariable custom in the evenings, I had locked my door; then, feeling thirsty, I drank half a glass of water and I happened to notice that my carafe was filled up right to its crystal stopper.

I lay down after this and fell into one of my dreadful slumbers, from which I was jerked about two hours later by a shock more frightful than any of the others.

Imagine a sleeping man, who has been assassinated, and who wakes with a knife through his lung, with the death rattle in his throat, covered with blood, unable to breathe, and on the point of death, understanding nothing – and there you have it.

When I finally recovered my sanity, I was thirsty again; I lit a candle and went towards the table where I had placed my carafe. I lifted it and held it over my glass; not a drop ran out. It was empty! It was completely empty. At first, I simply didn't understand; then all at once a frightful rush of emotion so overwhelmed me that I was forced to sit down, or say rather that I fell into a chair! Then I leaped up again and looked round me! Then I sat down again, lost in surprise and fear, in front of the transparent crystal. I gazed at it with a fixed stare, seeking an answer to the riddle. My hands were trembling. Had someone drunk the water? Who? I? It must have been me. Who could it have been but me? So I was a somnambulist, all unaware I was living the mysterious double life that raises the doubt whether there be not two selves in us, or whether, in moments when the spirit lies unconscious, an alien self, unknowable and unseen, inhabits the captive body that obeys this other self as it obeys us, obeys it more readily than it obeys us.

Oh, can anyone understand my frightful agony? Can anyone understand the feelings of a sane-minded, educated, thoroughly rational man, staring in abject terror through the glass of his carafe, where the water has disappeared while he slept? I remained there until daylight, not daring to go back to bed.

July 6. I am going mad. My carafe was emptied again last night – or rather, I emptied it.

But is it I? Is it I? Who can it be? Who? Oh, my God! Am I going mad? Who will save me?

July 10. I have just made some astonishing experiments. Listen!

On the 6th of July, before lying down in bed, I placed on my table wine, milk, water, bread and strawberries.

Someone drank – I drank – all the water, and a little of the milk. Neither the wine, nor the bread, nor the strawberries were touched.

On the 7th of July, I made the same experiment and got the same result.

On the 8th of July, I left out the water and the milk. Nothing was touched.

Finally, on the 9th of July, I placed only the water and milk on my table, taking care to wrap the carafes in white muslin cloths and to tie down the stoppers. Then I rubbed my lips, my beard and my hands with a charcoal pencil and lay down.

The usual overpowering sleep seized me, followed shortly by the frightful wakening. I had not moved, my bed-clothes themselves bore no marks. I rushed towards my table. The cloths wrapped round the bottles remained spotless. I untied the cords, shaking with fear. All the water had been drunk! All the milk had been drunk! Oh, my God! . . .

I am leaving for Paris at once.

July 13. Paris. I suppose I lost my head during the last few days! I must have been the sport of my disordered imagination, unless I really am a somnambulist or have fallen under one of those indubitable but hitherto inexplicable influences that we call suggestions. However that may be, my disorder came very near to lunacy, and twenty-four hours in Paris have been enough to restore my balance.

Yesterday I went to the races and made various calls. I felt myself endowed with new vital strength, and I ended my evening at the Théâtre Français. They were presenting a play by the younger Dumas; and his alert forceful intelligence completed my cure. There can be no doubt that loneliness is dangerous to active minds. We need round us men who think and talk. When we live alone for long periods, we people the void with phantoms.

I returned to the hotel in high spirits, walking along the boulevards. Amid the jostling of the crowd, I thought ironically on my terrors, on my hallucinations of a week ago, when I had believed, yes, believed that an invisible being dwelt in my body. How weak and shaken and speedily unbalanced our brains are immediately they are confronted by a tiny incomprehensible fact!

Instead of coming to a conclusion in these simple words: 'I do not understand because the cause eludes me,' at once we imagine frightening mysteries and supernatural powers.

July 14. *Fête de la République.* I walked through the streets. The rockets and the flags filled me with a childish joy. At the same time, it is vastly silly to be joyous on a set day by order of the government. The mob is an imbecile herd, as stupid in its patience as it is savage when roused. You say to it: 'Enjoy yourself,' and it enjoys itself. You say to it: 'Go and fight your neighbour.' It goes to fight. You say to it: 'Vote for the Emperor.' It votes for the Emperor. Then you say to it: 'Vote for the Republic.' And it votes for the Republic.

Its rulers are as besotted; but instead of obeying men they obey principles, which can only be half-baked, sterile and false in so much as they are principles, that is to say, ideas reputed certain and immutable, in this world where nothing is sure, since light and sound are both illusions.

July 16. Yesterday I saw some things that have profoundly disturbed me.

I dined with my cousin, Mme Sablé, whose husband commands the 76th light horse at Limoges. At her house

I met two young women, one of whom has married a doctor, Dr Parent, who devotes himself largely to nervous illnesses and the extraordinary discoveries that are the outcome of the recent experiments in hypnotism and suggestion.

He told us at length about the amazing results obtained by English scientists and by the doctors of the Nancy school.

The facts that he put forward struck me as so fantastic that I confessed myself utterly incredulous.

'We are,' he declared, 'on the point of discovering one of the most important secrets of nature, I mean one of the most important secrets on this earth; for there are certainly others as important, away yonder, in the stars. Since man began to think, since he learned to express and record his thoughts, he has felt the almost impalpable touch of a mystery impenetrable by his clumsy and imperfect senses, and he has tried to supplement the impotence of his organic powers by the force of his intelligence. While this intelligence was still in a rudimentary stage, this haunting sense of invisible phenomena clothed itself in terrors such as occur to simple minds. Thus are born popular theories of the supernatural, the legends of wandering spirits, fairies, gnomes, ghosts. I'll add the God-myth itself, since our conceptions of the artificer-creator, to whatever religion they belong, are really the most uninspired, the most unintelligent, the most inacceptable products of the fear-clouded brain of human beings. Nothing is truer than that saying of Voltaire's: "God has made man in His image, but man has retorted upon Him in kind."

'But for a little over a century we have had glimpse of a new knowledge. Mesmer and others have set our feet on a fresh path, and, more specially during the last four or five years, we have actually reached surprising results.'

My cousin, as incredulous as I, smiled. Dr Parent said to her: 'Shall I try to put you to sleep, madame?'

'Yes, do.'

She seated herself in an armchair, and he looked fixedly into her eyes, as if he were trying to fascinate her. As for me, I felt suddenly uneasy: my heart thumped, my throat contracted. I saw Mme Sablé's eyes grow heavy, her mouth twitch, her bosom rise and fall with her quick breathing.

Within ten minutes she was asleep.

'Go behind her,' said the doctor.

I seated myself behind her. He put a visiting-card in her hands and said to her: 'Here is a looking-glass: what can you see in it?'

'I see my cousin,' she answered.

'What is he doing?'

'He is twisting his moustache.'

'And now?'

'He is drawing a photograph from his pocket.'

'Whose photograph is it?'

'His.'

She was right! And this photograph had been sent me at my hotel only that very evening.

'What is he doing in the photograph?'

'He is standing, with his hat in his hand.'

Evidently she saw, in this card, this piece of white pasteboard, as she would have seen in a glass.

The young women, terrified, cried: 'That's enough, that's quite enough.'

But the doctor said authoritatively: 'You will get up tomorrow at eight o'clock; then you will call on your cousin at his hotel and you will beg him to lend you five thousand francs that your husband has asked you to get and will exact on his next leave.'

Then he woke her up.

On my way back to the hotel, I thought about this curious séance, and I was assailed by doubts, not of the absolutely unimpeachable good faith of my cousin, whom since our childhood I had looked upon as my sister, but of the possibility of trickery on the doctor's part. Had he concealed a looking-glass in his hand and held it before the slumbering young woman when he was holding before her his visiting-card? Professional conjurers do things as strange.

I had reached the hotel by now and I went to bed. Then in the morning, towards half past eight, I was roused by my man, who said to me:

'Mme Sablé wishes to speak to you at once, sir.'

I got hurriedly into my clothes and had her shown in.

She seated herself, very agitated, her eyes downcast, and, without lifting her veil, said:

'I have a great favour to ask you, my dear cousin.'

'What is it, my dear?'

'I hate to ask it of you, and yet I must. I need, desperately, five thousand francs.'

'You? You need it?'

'Yes, I, or rather my husband, who has laid it on me to get it.'

I was so astounded that I stammered as I answered her. I wondered whether she and Dr Parent were not actually making fun of me, whether it weren't a little comedy they had prepared beforehand and were acting very well.

But as I watched her closely my doubts vanished entirely. The whole affair was so distasteful to her that she was shaking with anguish, and I saw that her throat was quivering with sobs.

I knew that she was very rich and I added:

'What! do you mean to say that your husband can't call

on five thousand francs! Come, think. Are you sure he told you to ask me for it?'

She hesitated for a few moments as if she were making a tremendous effort to search her memory, then she answered:

'Yes . . . yes. . . . I'm quite sure.'

'Has he written to you?'

She hesitated again, reflecting. I guessed at the tortured striving of her mind. She didn't know. She knew nothing except that she had to borrow five thousand francs from me for her husband. Then she plucked up courage to lie.

'Yes, he has written to me.'

'But when? You didn't speak to me about it yesterday.'

'I got his letter this morning.'

'Can you let me see it?'

'No . . . no . . . no . . . it is very intimate . . . too personal. . . . I've . . . I've burned it.'

'Your husband must be in debt, then.'

Again she hesitated, then answered:

'I don't know.'

I told her abruptly:

'The fact is I can't lay my hands on five thousand francs at the moment, my dear.'

A kind of agonized wail broke from her.

'Oh, I implore you, I implore you, get it for me.'

She grew dreadfully excited, clasping her hands as if she were praying to me. The tone of her voice changed as I listened: she wept, stammering, torn with grief, goaded by the irresistible command that had been laid on her.

'Oh, I implore you to get it. . . . If you knew how unhappy I am! . . . I must have it to-day.'

I took pity on her.

'You shall have it at once, I promise you.'

'Thank you, thank you,' she cried. 'How kind you are!'

'Do you remember,' I went on, 'what happened at your house yesterday evening?'

'Yes.'

'Do you remember that Dr Parent put you to sleep?'

'Yes.'

'Very well, he ordered you to come this morning and borrow five thousand francs from me, and you are now obeying the suggestion.'

She considered this for a moment and answered:

'Because my husband wants it.'

I spent an hour trying to convince her, but I did not succeed in doing so.

When she left, I ran to the doctor's house. He was just going out, and he listened to me with a smile. Then he said:

'Now do you believe?'

'I must.'

'Let's go and call on your cousin.'

She was already asleep on a day bed, overwhelmed with weariness. The doctor felt her pulse, and looked at her for some time, one hand lifted towards her eyes that slowly closed under the irresistible compulsion of his magnetic force.

When she was asleep:

'Your husband has no further need for five thousand francs. You will forget that you begged your cousin to lend it to you, and if he speaks to you about it, you will not understand.'

Then he woke her up. I drew a note-case from my pocket.

'Here is what you asked me for this morning, my dear.'

She was so dumbfounded that I dared not press the matter. I did, however, try to rouse her memory, but she denied it fiercely, thought I was making fun of her and at last was ready to be angry with me.

Back at the hotel. The experience has disturbed me so profoundly that I could not bring myself to take lunch.

July 19. I have told several people about this adventure and been laughed at for my pains. I don't know what to think now. The wise man says: Perhaps?

July 21. I dined at Bougival, then I spent the evening at the rowing-club dance. There's no doubt that everything is a question of places and persons. To believe in the supernatural in the island of Grenouillère would be the height of folly... but at the top of Mont-Saint-Michel?... in the Indies? We are terrified under the influence of our surroundings. I am going home next week.

July 30. I have been home since yesterday. All is well.

August 2. Nothing fresh. The weather has been glorious. I spend my days watching the Seine run past.

August 4. The servants are quarrelling among themselves. They declare that someone breaks the glasses in the cupboard at night. My man blames the cook, who blames the housemaid, who blames the other two. Who is the culprit? It would take a mighty clever man to find out.

August 6. This time, I am not mad. I've seen something... I've seen something.... I've seen something.... I have no more doubts.... I've seen it.... I'm still cold to my finger-tips.... My nerves are still racked with terror.... I've seen it.

At two o'clock, in broad daylight, I was walking in my rose-garden... between the autumn roses that are just coming out.

As I paused to look at a *Géant des Batailles*, which bore three superb flowers, I saw, I distinctly saw, right under my eye, the stem of one of these roses bend as if an invisible hand had twisted it, then break as if the hand had plucked it. Then the flower rose, describing in the air the curve that an arm would have made carrying it towards a mouth, and it hung suspended in the clear air, quite alone, motionless, a terrifying scarlet splash three paces from my eyes.

I lost my head and flung myself on it, grasping at it. My fingers closed on nothing: it had disappeared. Then I was filled with a savage rage against myself; a rational serious-minded man simply does not have such hallucinations.

But was it really an hallucination? I turned round to look for the flower and my eyes fell on it immediately: it had just been broken off and was lying between the two roses that still remained on the branch.

Then I went back to the house, my senses reeling: now I was sure as sure as I am that day follows night, that there lived at my side an invisible being who fed on milk and water, who could touch things, take them, move them from one place to another, endowed therefore with a material nature, imperceptible to our senses though it was, and living beside me, under my roof. . . .

August 7. I slept quietly. He has drunk the water from my carafe, but he did not disturb my sleep.

I wonder if I am mad. Sometimes as I walk in the blazing sunshine along the river-bank, I am filled with doubts of my sanity, not the vague doubts I have been feeling, but precise and uncompromising doubts. I have seen madmen; I have known men who were intelligent, lucid, even exceptionally clear-headed in everything in life but on one point. They talked quite clearly, easily, and profoundly about everything, until suddenly their mind ran on to the rocks of their madness and was there rent in pieces, strewn to the winds and foundered in the fearful raging sea, filled with surging waves, fogs, squalls, that we call 'insanity'.

I should certainly have thought myself mad, absolutely mad, if I were not conscious, if I were not perfectly aware of my state of mind, if I did not get to the bottom of it and analyse it with such complete clearness. I must be, in fact, no worse than a sane man troubled with hallucinations. There must be some unknown disturbance in my brain, one of those disturbances that modern physiologists are trying to observe and elucidate; and this disturbance has opened a deep gulf in my mind, in the orderly and logical working of my thoughts. Similar phenomena take place in a dream that drags us through the most unreal phantasmagoria without sowing the least surprise in our minds because the mechanism of judgment, the controlling censor, is asleep, while the imaginative faculty wakes and works. Can one of the invisible strings that control my mental keyboard have become muted?

Sometimes, after an accident, a man loses his power to remember proper names or verbs or figures or only dates. The localization of all the different faculties of the mind is now proved. Is there anything surprising, therefore, in the idea that my power of examining the unreality of certain hallucinations has ceased to function in my brain just now?

I thought of all this as I walked by the side of the water. The sunlight flung a mantle of light across the river, clothing the earth with beauty, filling my thoughts with love of life, of the swallows whose swift flight is a joy to my eyes, of the riverside grasses whose shuddering whisper contents my ears.

Little by little, however, I fell prey to an inexplicable uneasiness. I felt as though some force, an occult force, were paralysing my movements, halting me, hindering me from going on any further, calling me back. I was oppressed by just such an unhappy impulse to turn back as one feels when a beloved person has been left at home ill and one is possessed by a foreboding that the illness has taken a turn for the worse.

So, in spite of myself, I turned back, sure that I should find bad news waiting in my house, a letter or a telegram. There was nothing; and I was left more surprised and uneasy than if I had had yet another fantastic vision.

August 8. Yesterday I spent a frightful night. He did not manifest himself again, but I felt him near me, spying on me, watching me, taking possession of me, dominating me and more to be feared when he hid himself in this way than if he gave notice of his constant invisible presence by supernatural phenomena.

However, I slept.

August 9. Nothing, but I am afraid.

August 10. Nothing; what will happen to-morrow?

August 11. Still nothing: I can't remain in my home any longer, with this fear and these thoughts in my mind: I shall go away.

August 12. Ten o'clock in the evening. I have been wanting to go away all day. I can't. I have been wanting to carry out the easy simple act that will set me free – go out – get into my carriage to go to Rouen – I can't. Why?

August 13. Under the affliction of certain maladies, all the resources of one's physical being seem crushed, all one's energy exhausted, one's muscles relaxed, one's bones grown as soft as flesh and one's flesh turned to water. In a strange and wretched fashion I suffer all these pains in my spiritual being. I have no strength, no courage, no control over myself, no power even to summon up my will. I can will nothing; but someone wills for me – and I obey.

August 14. I am lost. Someone has taken possession of my soul and is master of it; someone orders all my acts, all my movements, all my thoughts. I am no longer anything, I am only a spectator, enslaved, and terrified by all the things I do. I wish to go out. I cannot. He does not wish it; and I remain, dazed, trembling, in the arm-chair where he keeps me seated. I desire no more than to get up, to raise myself, so that I can think I am master of myself again. I can't do it. I am riveted to my seat; and my seat is fast to the ground, in such fashion that no force could lift us.

Then, all at once, I must, must, must go to the bottom of my garden and pick strawberries and eat them. Oh, my God! my God! my God! Is there a God? If there is one, deliver me, save me, help me! Pardon me! Pity me! Have mercy on me! How I suffer! How I am tortured! How terrible this is!

August 15. Well, think how my poor cousin was possessed and overmastered when she came to borrow five thousand francs from me. She submitted to an alien will that had entered into her, as if it were another soul, a parasitic tyrannical soul. Is the world coming to an end?

But what is this being, this invisible being who is ruling me? This unknowable creature, this wanderer from a supernatural race.

So Unseen Ones exist? Then why is it that since the

world began they have never manifested themselves in so unmistakable a fashion as they are now manifesting themselves to me? I have never read of anything like the things that are happening under my roof. If I could only leave it, if I could go away, fly far away and return no more, I should be saved, but I can't.

August 16. To-day I was able to escape for two hours, like a prisoner who finds the door of his cell accidentally left open. I felt that I was suddenly set free, that he had withdrawn himself. I ordered the horses to be put in the carriage as quickly as possible and I reached Rouen. Oh, what a joy it was to find myself able to tell a man: 'Go to Rouen,' and be obeyed!

I stopped at the library and I asked them to lend me the long treatise of Dr Hermann Herestauss on the unseen inhabitants of the antique and modern worlds.

Then, just as I was getting back into my carriage, with the words, 'To the station,' on my lips, I shouted – I didn't speak, I shouted – in a voice so loud that the passers-by turned round: 'Home,' and I fell, overwhelmed with misery, on to the cushions of my carriage. He had found me again and taken possession once more.

August 17. What a night! what a night! Nevertheless it seems to me that I ought to congratulate myself. I read until one o'clock in the morning. Hermann Herestauss, a doctor of philosophy and theogony, has written an account of all the invisible beings who wander among men or have been imagined by men's minds. He describes their origins, their domains, their power. But none of them is the least like the being who haunts me. It is as if man, the thinker, has had a foreboding vision of some new being, mightier than himself, who shall succeed him in this world; and, in his terror, feeling him draw near, and unable to guess at the nature of this master, he has created all the fantastic crowd of occult beings, dim phantoms born of fear.

Well, I read until one o'clock and then I seated myself near my open window to cool my head and my thoughts in the gentle air of night.

It was fine and warm. In other days how I should have loved such a night!

No moon. The stars wavered and glittered in the black depths of the sky. Who dwells in these worlds? What forms of life, what living creatures, what animals or plants do they hold? What more than we do the thinkers in those far-off universes know? What more can they do than we? What do they see that we do not know of? Perhaps one of them, some day or other, will cross the gulf of space and appear on our earth as a conqueror, just as in olden days the Normans crossed the sea to subdue wealthy nations.

We others are so infirm, so defenceless, so ignorant, so small, on this grain of dust that revolves and crumbles in a drop of water.

So dreaming, I fell asleep, in the fresh evening air.

I slept for about forty minutes and opened my eyes again without moving, roused by I know not what vague and strange emotions. At first I saw nothing, then all at once I thought that the page of a book lying open on my table had turned over of itself. Not a breath of air came in at the window. I was surprised and I sat waiting. About four minutes later, I saw, I saw, yes, I saw with my own eyes another page come up and turn back on the preceding one, as if a finger had folded it back. My armchair was empty, seemed empty; but I realized that he was there, he, sitting in my place and reading. In one wild spring, like the spring of a maddened beast resolved to eviscerate his trainer, I crossed the room to seize him and crush him and kill him. But before I had reached it my seat turned right over as if he had fled before me . . . my table rocked, my lamp fell and was extinguished, and my window slammed shut as if I had surprised a malefactor who had flung himself out into the darkness, tugging at the sashes with all his force.

So he had run away; he had been afraid, afraid of me, me!

Then . . . then . . . to-morrow . . . or the day after . . . or some day . . . I should be able to get him between my fingers, and crush him against the ground. Don't dogs sometimes bite and fly at their masters' throats?

August 18. I've been thinking things over all day. Oh, yes, I'll obey him, satisfy his impulses, do his will, make myself humble, submissive, servile. He is the stronger. But an hour will come. . . .

August 19. I know now. . . . I know. . . . I know everything! I have just read the following in the *Revue du Monde Scientifique*: 'A strange piece of news reaches us from Rio de Janeiro. Madness, an epidemic of madness, comparable to the contagious outbursts of dementia that attacked the peoples of Europe in the Middle Ages, is raging at this day in the district of San-Paulo. The distracted inhabitants are quitting their houses, deserting their villages, abandoning their fields, declaring themselves to be pursued, possessed and ordered about like a human herd by certain invisible but tangible beings, vampires of some kind, who feed on their vitality while they sleep, in addition to drinking milk and water without, apparently, touching any other form of food.

'Professor Don Pedro Henriquez, accompanied by several learned doctors, has set out for the district of San-Paulo, to study on the spot the origins and the forms taken by this surprising madness, and to suggest to the Emperor such measures as appear to him most likely to restore the delirious inhabitants to sanity.'

Ah! I remember, I remember the lovely three-masted Brazilian that sailed past my windows on the 8th of last May, on her way up the Seine. I thought her such a bonny, white, gay boat. The Being was on board her, come from over the sea, where his race is born. He saw me. He saw my house, white like the ship, and he jumped from the vessel to the bank. Oh, my God!

Now I know, I understand. The reign of man is at an end.

He is here, whom the dawning fears of primitive peoples taught them to dread. He who was exorcized by troubled priests, evoked in the darkness of night by wizards who yet never saw him materialize, to whom the foreboding vision of the masters who have passed through this world lent all the monstrous or gracious forms of gnomes, spirits, jinns, fairies and hobgoblins. Primitive terror visualized him in the crudest forms; later wiser men have seen him more clearly. Mesmer foresaw him, and it is ten years since doctors made the most exact inquiries into the nature of his power, even before he exercised it himself. They have been making a plaything of this weapon of the new God, this imposition of a mysterious will on the enslaved soul of man. They called it magnetism, hypnotism, suggestion . . . anything you like. I have seen them amusing themselves with this horrible power like foolish children. Woe to us! Cursed is man! He is here . . . the . . . the . . . what is his name? . . . the . . . it seems as if he were shouting his name in my ear and I cannot hear it . . . the . . . yes . . . he is shouting it. . . . I am listening. . . . I can't hear . . . again, tell me again . . . the . . . Horla. . . . I heard . . . the Horla . . . it is he . . . the Horla . . . he is here!

Oh, the vulture has been used to eat the dove, the wolf to eat the sheep; the lion to devour the sharp-horned buffalo; man to kill the lion with arrow, spear and gun; but the Horla is going to make of man what we have made of the horse and the cow: his thing, his servant and his food, by the mere force of his will. Woe to us!

But sometimes the beast rebels and kills his tamer... I too want... I could... but I must know him, touch him, see him. Scientists say that the eye of the beast is not like ours and does not see as ours does.... And my eye fails to show me this newcomer who is oppressing me.

Why? Oh, the words of the monk of Mont-Saint-Michel come to my mind: 'Do we see the hundred thousandth part of all that exists? Think, there's the wind, the greatest force in nature, which throws down men, shatters buildings, uproots trees, stirs up the sea into watery mountains, destroys cliffs and tosses the tall ships against the shore, the wind that kills, whistles, groans, roars – have you seen it, can you see it? Nevertheless, it exists.'

And I considered further: my eye is so weak, so imperfect, that it does not distinguish even solid bodies that have the transparency of glass. If a looking-glass that has no foil backing bars my path, I hurl myself against it as a bird that has got into a room breaks its head on the window-pane. How many other things deceive and mislead my eye? Then what is there to be surprised at in its failure to see a new body that offers no resistance to the passage of light?

A new being! why not? He must assuredly come! why should we be the last? Why is he not seen of our eyes as are all the beings created before us? Because his form is nearer perfection, his body finer and completer than ours – ours, which is so weak, so clumsily conceived, encumbered by organs always tired, always breaking down like a too complex mechanism, which lives like a vegetable or a beast, drawing its substance with difficulty from the air, the herbs of the field and meat, a living machine subject to sickness, deformity and corruption, drawing its breath in pain, ill-regulated, simple and fantastic, ingeniously ill-made, clumsily and delicately erected, the mere rough sketch of a being who could become intelligent and noble.

There have been so few kinds created in the world, from the bivalve to man. Why not one more, when we reach the end of the period of time that separates each successive appearance of a species from that which appeared before it?

Why not one more? Why not also new kinds of trees bearing monstrous flowers, blazing with colour and filling all the country-side with their perfume? Why not other elements than fire, air, earth and water? There are four, only four sources of our being! What a pity! Why not forty, four hundred, four thousand? How poor, niggardly and brutish is life! grudgingly given, meanly conceived, stupidly executed. Consider the grace of the elephant, the hippopotamus! The elegance of the camel!

You bid me consider the butterfly! a winged flower! I can imagine one vast as a hundred worlds, with wings for whose shape, beauty, colour, and sweep I cannot find any words. But I see it . . . it goes from star to star, refreshing and perfuming them with the soft, gracious wind of its passing. And the people of the upper air watch it pass, in an ecstasy of joy!

What is the matter with me? It is he, he, the Horla, who is haunting me, filling my head with these absurdities! He is in me, he has become my soul; I will kill him.

August 19. I will kill him. I have seen him! I was sitting at my table yesterday evening, making a great show of being very absorbed in writing. I knew quite well that he would come and prowl round me, very close to me, so close that I might be able to touch him, seize him, perhaps? And then! . . . then, I should be filled with the strength of desperation; I should have hands, knees, chest, face, teeth to strangle him, crush him, tear him, rend him.

With every sense quiveringly alert, I watched for him.

I had lit both my lamps and the eight candles on my chimney-piece, as if I thought I should be more likely to discover him by this bright light.

In front of me was my bed, an old oak four-poster; on my right, the fire-place; on my left, my door carefully shut, after I had left it open for a long time to attract him; behind me, a very tall cupboard with a mirror front, which I used every day to shave and dress by, and in which I always regarded myself from head to foot whenever I passed in front of it.

Well, I pretended to write to deceive him, because he was spying on me too; and, all at once, I felt, I was certain, that he was reading over my shoulder, that he was there, his breath on my ear.

I stood up, my hand outstretched, and turned round, so quickly that I almost fell. What do you think? . . . the room was as light as day, and I could not see myself in my looking-glass! It was empty, transparent, deep, filled with light! I was not reflected in it . . . and I was standing in front of it. I could see the wide limpid expanse of glass from top to bottom. And I stared at it with a distraught gaze: I daren't move another step, I daren't make another movement; nevertheless I felt that he was there, whose immaterial body had swallowed up my reflection, but that he would elude me still.

How frightened I was! A moment later my reflection began to appear in the depths of the looking-glass, in a sort of mist, as if I were looking at it through water; this water seemed to flow from left to right, slowly, so that moment by moment my reflection emerged more distinctly. It was like the passing of an eclipse. The thing that was concealing me appeared to possess no sharply defined outlines, but a kind of transparent opacity that gradually cleared.

At last I could see myself from head to foot, just as I saw myself every day when I looked in the glass.

I had seen him! The horror of it is still on me, making me shudder.

August 20. How can I kill him? Since I can't touch him? Poison? But he would see me put it in the water; and besides, would our poisons affect an immaterial body? No . . . no, they certainly would not. . . . Then how? . . . how?

August 21. I have sent for a locksmith from Rouen, and ordered him to fit my room with iron shutters, such as they have in certain hotels in Paris, to keep out robbers. He is to make me, also, a similar sort of door. Everyone thinks me a coward, but much I care for that!

* * *

September 10. Rouen, Hôtel Continental. It is done . . . it is done . . . but is he dead? My brain reels with what I have seen.

Yesterday the locksmith put up my iron shutters and my iron door, and I left everything open until midnight, although it began to get cold.

All at once I felt his presence, and I was filled with joy, a mad joy. I rose slowly to my feet, and walked about the room for a long time, so that he should suspect nothing; then I took off my boots and carelessly drew on my slippers;

then I closed my iron shutters, and, sauntering back towards the door, I double-locked it too. Then I walked back to the window and secured it with a padlock, putting the key in my pocket.

Suddenly I realized that he was prowling anxiously round me, he was afraid now, and commanding me to open them for him. I almost yielded: I did not yield, but, leaning on the door, I set it ajar, just wide enough for me to slip out backwards; and as I am very tall my head touched the lintel. I was sure that he could not have got out and I shut him in, alone, all alone. Thank God! I had him! Then I ran downstairs; in the drawing-room which is under my room, I took both my lamps and emptied the oil all over the carpet and the furniture, everything; then I set it on fire and I fled after having double-locked the main door.

And I went and hid myself at the bottom of my garden, in a grove of laurels. How long it took, how long! Everything was dark, silent, still, not a breath of air, not a star, mountains of unseen clouds that lay so heavily, so heavily, on my spirit.

I kept my gaze fixed on my house, and waited. How long it took! I was beginning to think that the fire had died out of itself, or that he, He, had put it out, when one of the lower windows fell in under the fierce breath of the fire and a flame, a great red and yellow flame, a long, curling, caressing flame, leaped up the white wall and pressed its kiss on the roof itself. A flood of light poured over trees, branches, leaves, and with that a shudder, a shudder of fear, ran through them. The birds woke; a dog howled: I thought the dawn was at hand. In a moment two more windows burst into flame and I saw that the lower half of my house was now one frightful furnace. But a cry, a frightful piercing agonized cry, a woman's cry, stabbed the night, and two skylights opened. I had forgotten my servants. I saw their distraught faces and their wildly waving arms. . . .

Then, frantic with horror, I began to run towards the village, shouting: 'Help! help! fire! fire!' I met people already on their way to the house and I turned back with them to look at it.

By now the house was no more than a horrible and magnificent funeral pyre, a monstrous pyre lighting up the whole earth, a pyre that was consuming men, and consuming Him, Him, my prisoner, the new Being, the new Master, the Horla!

The whole roof fell in with a sudden crash, and a volcano of flames leaped to the sky. Through all the windows open on the furnace, I saw the fiery vat, and I reflected that he was there, in this oven, dead. . . .

Dead? Perhaps? . . . His body? Perhaps that body through which light fell could not be destroyed by the methods that kill our bodies?

Suppose he is not dead? . . . Perhaps only time has power over the Invisible and Dreadful One. Why should this transparent, unknowable body, this body of the spirit, fear sickness, wounds, infirmity, premature destruction?

Premature destruction? The source of all human dread! After man, the Horla. After him who can die any day, any hour, any moment, by accidents of all kinds, comes he who can only die in his appointed day, hour and moment, when he has attained the limit of his existence.

No . . . no . . . I know, I know . . . he is not dead . . . so . . . so . . . I must kill myself, now.

HENRY JAMES

THE FRIENDS OF THE FRIENDS

I FIND, as you prophesied, much that's interesting, but little that helps the delicate question – the possibility of publication. Her diaries are less systematic than I hoped; she only had a blessed habit of noting and narrating. She summarized, she saved; she appears seldom indeed to have let a good story pass without catching it on the wing. I allude of course not so much to things she heard as to things she saw and felt. She writes sometimes of herself, sometimes of others, sometimes of the combination. It's under this last rubric that she's usually most vivid. But it's not, you will understand, when she's most vivid that she's always most publishable. To tell the truth she's fearfully indiscreet, or has at least all the material for making *me* so. Take as an instance the fragment I send you, after dividing it for your convenience into several small chapters. It is the contents of a thin blank-book which I have had copied out and which has the merit of being nearly enough a rounded thing, an intelligible whole. These pages evidently date from years ago. I've read with the liveliest wonder the statement they so circumstantially make and done my best to swallow the prodigy they leave to be inferred. These things would be striking, wouldn't they? to any reader; but can you imagine for a moment my placing such a document before the world, even though, as if she herself had desired the world should have the benefit of it, she has given her friends neither name nor initials? Have you any sort of clue to their identity? I leave her the floor.

I

I know perfectly of course that I brought it upon myself; but that doesn't make it any better. I was the first to speak of her to him – he had never even heard her mentioned. Even if I had happened not to speak some one else would have made up for it: I tried afterwards to find comfort in that reflection. But the comfort of reflections is thin: the only comfort that counts in life is not to have been a fool. That's a beatitude I shall doubtless never enjoy. 'Why, you ought to meet her and talk it over,' is what I immediately said. 'Birds of a feather flock together.' I told him who she was and that they were birds of a feather because if he had had in youth a strange adventure she had had about the same time just such another. It was well known to her friends – an incident she was constantly called on to describe. She was charming, clever, pretty, unhappy; but it was none the less the thing to which she had originally owed her reputation.

Being at the age of eighteen somewhere abroad with an aunt she had had a vision of one of her parents at the moment of death. The parent was in England, hundreds of miles away and so far as she knew neither dying nor dead. It was by day, in the museum of some great foreign town. She had passed alone, in advance of her companions, into a small room containing some famous work of art and occupied at that moment by two other persons. One of these was an old custodian; the second, before observing him, she took for a stranger, a tourist. She was merely conscious that he was bare-headed and seated on a bench. The instant her eyes rested on him however she beheld to her amazement her father, who, as if he had long waited for her, looked at her in singular distress, with an impatience that was akin to reproach. She rushed to him with a bewildered cry, 'Papa, what *is* it?' but this was followed by an exhibition of still livelier feeling when on her movement he simply vanished, leaving the custodian and her relations, who were at her heels, to gather round her in dismay. These persons, the official, the aunt, the cousins were therefore in a manner witnesses of the fact – the fact at least of the impression made on her; and there was the further testimony of a doctor who was attending one of the party and to whom it was immediately afterwards communicated. He gave her a remedy for hysterics but said to the aunt privately: 'Wait and see if something doesn't happen at home.' Something *had* happened – the poor father, suddenly and violently seized, had died that morning. The aunt, the mother's sister, received before the day was out a telegram announcing the event and requesting her to prepare her niece for it. Her niece was already prepared, and the girl's sense of this visitation remained of course indelible. We had all as her friends had it conveyed to us and had conveyed it creepily to each other. Twelve years had elapsed and as a woman who had made an unhappy marriage and lived apart from her husband she had become interesting from other sources; but since the name she now bore was a name frequently borne, and since moreover her judicial separation, as things were going, could hardly count as a distinction, it was usual to qualify her as 'the one, you know, who saw her father's ghost'.

As for him, dear man, he had seen his mother's. I had never heard of that till this occasion on which our closer, our pleasanter acquaintance led him, through some turn of the subject of our talk, to mention it and to inspire me in so doing with the impulse to let him know that he had a rival in the field – a person with whom he could compare notes. Later on his story became for him, perhaps because of my unduly repeating it, likewise a convenient worldly label; but it had not a year before been the ground on which he was introduced to me. He had other merits, just as she, poor thing! had others. I can honestly say that I was quite aware of them from the first – I discovered them sooner than he discovered mine. I remember how it struck me even at the time that his sense of mine was quickened by my having been able to match, though not indeed straight from my own experience, his curious anecdote. It dated, this anecdote, as hers did, from some dozen years before – a year in which, at Oxford, he had for some reason of his own been staying on into the 'Long'. He had been in the August afternoon on the river. Coming back into his room while it was still distinct daylight he found his mother standing there as if her eyes had been fixed on the door. He had had a letter from her that morning out of Wales, where she was staying with her father. At the sight of him she smiled with extraordinary radiance and extended her arms to him, and then as he sprang forward and joyfully opened his own she vanished from the place. He wrote to her that night, telling her what had happened; the letter had been carefully preserved. The next morning he heard of her death. He was through this chance of our talk extremely struck with the little prodigy I was able to produce for him. He had never encountered another case. Certainly they ought to meet, my friend and he; certainly they would have something in common. I would arrange this, wouldn't I? – if *she* didn't mind; for himself he didn't mind in the least. I had promised to speak to her of the matter as soon as possible, and within the week I was able to do so. She 'minded' as little as he; she was perfectly willing to see him. And yet no meeting was to occur – as meetings are commonly understood.

II

That's just half my tale – the extraordinary way it was hindered. This was the fault of a series of accidents; but the accidents continued for years and became, for me and for others, a subject of hilarity with either party. They were droll enough at first; then they grew rather a bore. The odd thing was that both parties were amenable: it wasn't a case of their being indifferent, much less of their being indisposed. It was one of the caprices of chance, aided I suppose by some opposition of their interests and habits. His were centred in his office, his eternal inspectorship, which left him small leisure, constantly calling him away and making him break engagements. He liked society, but he found it everywhere and took it at a run. I never knew at a given moment where he was, and there were times when for months together I never saw him. She was on her side practically suburban: she lived at Richmond and never went 'out'. She was a woman of distinction, but not of fashion, and felt, as people said, her situation. Decidedly proud and rather whimsical, she lived her life as she had planned it. There were things one could do with her, but one couldn't make her come to one's parties. One went indeed a little more than seemed quite convenient to hers, which consisted of her cousin, a cup of tea and the view. The tea was good; but the view was familiar, though perhaps not, like the cousin – a disagreeable old maid who had been of the group at the museum and with whom she now lived – offensively so. This connection with an inferior relative, which had partly an economical motive – she proclaimed her companion a marvellous manager – was one of the little perversities we had to forgive her. Another was her estimate of the proprieties created by her rupture with her husband. That was extreme – many persons called it even morbid. She made no advances; she cultivated scruples; she suspected, or I should perhaps rather say she remembered slights: she was one of the few women I have known whom that particular predicament had rendered modest rather than bold. Dear thing! she had some delicacy. Especially marked were the limits she had set to possible attentions from men: it was always her thought that her husband was waiting to pounce on her. She discouraged if she didn't forbid the visits of male persons not senile: she said she could never be too careful.

When I first mentioned to her that I had a friend whom fate had distinguished in the same weird way as herself I put her quite at liberty to say 'Oh, bring him out to see me!' I should probably have been able to bring him, and a situation perfectly innocent or at any rate comparatively simple would have been created. But she uttered no such word; she only said: 'I must meet him certainly; yes, I shall look out for him!' That caused the first delay, and meanwhile various things happened. One of them was that as time went on she made, charming as she was, more and more friends, and that it regularly befell that these friends were sufficiently also friends of his to bring him up in conversation. It was odd that without belonging, as it were, to the same world or, according to the horrid term, the same set, my baffled pair should have happened in so many cases to fall in with the same people and make them join in the funny chorus. She had friends who didn't know each other but who inevitably and punctually recommended *him*. She had also the sort of originality, the intrinsic interest that led her to be kept by each of us as a kind of private resource, cultivated jealously, more or less in secret, as a person whom one didn't meet in society, whom it was not for every one – whom it was not for the vulgar – to approach, and with whom therefore acquaintance was particularly difficult and particularly precious. We saw her separately, with appointments and conditions, and found it made on the whole for harmony not to tell each other. Somebody had always had a note from her still later than somebody else. There was some silly woman who for a long time, among the unprivileged, owed to three simple visits to Richmond a reputation for being intimate with 'lots of awfully clever out-of-the-way people'.

Every one has had friends it has seemed a happy thought to bring together, and every one remembers that his happiest thoughts have not been his greatest successes; but I doubt if there was ever a case in which the failure was in such direct proportion to the quantity of influence set in motion. It is really perhaps here the quantity of influence that was most remarkable. My lady and gentleman each declared to me and others that it was like the subject of a roaring farce. The reason first given had with time dropped out of sight and fifty better ones flourished on top of it. They were so awfully alike: they had the same ideas and tricks and tastes, the same prejudices and superstitions and heresies; they said the same things and sometimes did them; they liked and disliked the same persons and places, the same books, authors and styles; any one could see a certain identity even in their looks and their features. It established much of a propriety that they were in common parlance equally 'nice' and almost equally handsome. But the great sameness, for wonder and chatter, was their rare perversity in regard to being photographed. They were the only persons ever heard of who had never been 'taken' and who had a passionate objection to it. They just *wouldn't* be, for anything any one could say. I had loudly complained of this; him in particular I had so vainly desired to be able to show on my drawing-room chimney-piece in a Bond Street frame. It was at any rate the very liveliest of all the reasons why they ought to know each other – all the lively reasons reduced to naught by the strange law that had made them bang so many doors in each other's face, made them the buckets in the well, the two ends of the see-saw, the two parties in the state, so that when one was up the other was down, when one was out the other was in; neither by any possibility entering a house till the other had left it, or leaving it, all unawares, till the other was at hand. They only arrived when they had been given up, which was precisely also when they departed. They were in a word alternate and incompatible; they missed each other with an inveteracy that could be explained only by its being preconcerted. It was however so far from preconcerted that it had ended – literally after several years – by disappointing and annoying them. I don't think their curiosity was lively till it had been proved utterly vain. A great deal was of course done to help them, but it merely laid wires for them to trip. To give examples I should have to have taken notes; but I happen to remember that neither had ever been able to dine on the right occasion. The right occasion for each was the occasion that would be wrong for the other. On the wrong one they were most punctual, and there were never any but wrong ones. The very elements conspired and the constitution of man reinforced them. A cold, a headache, a bereavement, a storm, a fog, an earthquake, a cataclysm infallibly intervened. The whole business was beyond a joke.

Yet as a joke it had still to be taken, though one couldn't help feeling that the joke had made the situation serious, had produced on the part of each a consciousness, an awkwardness, a positive dread of the last accident of all, the only one with any freshness left, the accident that would bring them face to face. The final effect of its predecessors had been to kindle this instinct. They were quite ashamed – perhaps even a little of each other. So much preparation, so much frustration: what indeed could be good enough for it all to lead up to? A mere meeting would be mere flatness. Did I see them at the end of years, they often asked, just stupidly confronted? If they were bored by the joke they might be worse bored by something else. They made exactly the same reflections, and each in some manner was sure to hear of the other's. I really think it was this peculiar diffidence that finally controlled the situation. I mean that if they had failed for the first year or two because they couldn't help it they kept up the habit because they had – what shall I call it? – grown nervous. It really took some lurking volition to account for anything so absurd.

III

When to crown our long acquaintance I accepted his renewed offer of marriage it was humorously said, I know, that I had made the gift of his photograph a condition. This was so far true that I had refused to give him mine without it. At any rate I had him at last, in his high distinction, on the chimney-piece, where the day she called to congratulate me she came nearer than she had ever done to seeing him. He had set her in being taken an example which I invited her to follow; he had sacrificed his perversity – wouldn't she sacrifice hers? She too must give me something on my engagement – wouldn't she give me the companion-piece? She laughed and shook her head; she had headshakes whose impulse seemed to come from as far away as the breeze that stirs a flower. The companion-piece to the portrait of my future husband was the portrait of his future wife. She had taken her stand – she could depart from it as little as she could explain it. It was a prejudice, an *entêtement*, a vow – she would live and die unphotographed. Now too she was alone in that state: this was what she liked; it made her so much more original. She rejoiced in the fall of her late associate and looked a long time at his picture, about which she made no memorable remark, though she even turned it over to see the back. About our engagement she was charming – full of cordiality and sympathy. 'You've known him even longer than I've *not*,' she said, 'and that seems a very long time.' She understood how we had jogged together over hill and dale and how inevitable it was that we should now rest together. I'm definite about all this because what followed is so strange that it's a kind of relief to me to mark the point up to which our relations were as natural as ever. It was I myself who in a sudden madness altered and destroyed them. I see now that she gave me no pretext and that I only found one in the way she looked at the fine face in the Bond Street frame. How then would I have had her look at it? What I had wanted from the first was to make her care for him. Well, that was what I still wanted – up to the moment of her having promised me that he would on this occasion really aid me to break the silly spell that had kept them asunder. I had arranged with him to do his part if she would as triumphantly do hers. I was on a different footing now – I was on a footing to answer for him. I would positively engage that at five on the following Saturday he would be on that spot. He was out of town on pressing business; but pledged to keep his promise to the letter he would return on purpose and in abundant time. 'Are you perfectly sure?' I remember she asked, looking grave and considering: I thought she had turned a little pale. She was tired, she was indisposed: it was a pity he was to see her after all at so poor a moment. If he only *could* have seen her five years before!

However, I replied that this time I was sure and that success therefore depended simply on herself. At five o'clock on the Saturday she would find him in a particular chair I pointed out, the one in which he usually sat and in which – though this I didn't mention – he had been sitting when, the week before, he put the question of our future to me in the way that had brought me round. She looked at it in silence, just as she had looked at the photograph, while I repeated for the twentieth time that it was too preposterous it shouldn't somehow be feasible to introduce to one's dearest friend one's second self. '*Am* I your dearest friend?' she asked with a smile that for a moment brought back her beauty. I replied by pressing her to my bosom; after which she said: 'Well, I'll come. I'm extraordinarily afraid, but you may count on me.'

When she had left me I began to wonder what she was afraid of, for she had spoken as if she fully meant it. The next day, late in the afternoon, I had three lines from her: she had found on getting home the announcement of her husband's death. She had not seen him for seven years, but she wished me to know it in this way before I should hear of it in another. It made however in her life, strange and sad to say, so little difference that she would scrupulously keep her appointment. I rejoiced for her – I supposed it would make at least the difference of her having more money; but even in this diversion, far from forgetting that she had said she was afraid, I seemed to catch sight of a reason for her being so. Her fear as the evening went on became contagious, and the contagion took in my breast the form of a sudden panic. It wasn't jealousy – it was the dread of jealousy. I called myself a fool for not having been quiet till we were man and wife. After that I should somehow feel secure. It was only a question of waiting another month – a trifle surely for people who had waited so long. It had been plain enough she was nervous, and now that she was free she naturally wouldn't be less so. What was her nervousness therefore but a presentiment? She had been hitherto the victim of interference, but it was quite possible she would henceforth be the source of it. The victim in that case would be my simple self. What had the interference been but the finger of providence pointing out a danger? The danger was of course for poor *me*. It had been kept at bay by a series of accidents unexampled in their frequency; but the reign of accident was now visibly at an end. I had an intimate conviction that both parties would keep the tryst. It was more and more impressed upon me that they were approaching, converging. We had talked about breaking the spell; well, it would be effectually broken – unless indeed it should merely take another form and overdo their encounters as it had overdone their escapes. This was something I couldn't sit still for thinking of; it kept me awake – at midnight I was full of unrest. At last I felt there was only one way of laying the ghost. If the reign of accident was over I must just take up the succession. I sat down and wrote a hurried note which would meet him on his return and which as the servants had gone to bed I sallied forth bare-headed into the empty, gusty street to drop into the nearest pillar-box. It was to tell him that I shouldn't be able to be at home in the afternoon as I had hoped and that he must postpone his visit till dinner-time. This was an implication that he would find me alone.

IV

When accordingly at five she presented herself I naturally felt false and base. My act had been a momentary madness, but I had at least to be consistent. She remained an hour; he of course never came; and I could only persist in my perfidy.

I had thought it best to let her come; singular as this now seems to me I thought it diminished my guilt. Yet as she sat there so visibly white and weary, stricken with a sense of everything her husband's death had opened up, I felt an almost intolerable pang of pity and remorse. If I didn't tell her on the spot what I had done it was because I was too ashamed. I feigned astonishment – I feigned it to the end; I protested that if ever I had had confidence I had had it that day. I blush as I tell my story – I take it as my penance. There was nothing indignant I didn't say about him; I invented suppositions, attenuations; I admitted in stupefaction, as the hands of the clock travelled, that their luck hadn't turned. She smiled at this vision of their 'luck', but she looked anxious – she looked unusual: the only thing that kept me up was the fact that, oddly enough, she wore mourning – no great depths of crape, but simple and scrupulous black. She had in her bonnet three small black feathers. She carried a little muff of astrachan. This put me by the aid of some acute reflection a little in the right. She had written to me that the sudden event made no difference for her, but apparently it made as much difference as that. If she was inclined to the usual forms why didn't she observe that of not going the first day or two out to tea? There was some one she wanted so much to see that she couldn't wait till her husband was buried. Such a betrayal of eagerness made me hard and cruel enough to practise my odious deceit, though at the same time, as the hour waxed and waned, I suspected in her something deeper still than disappointment and somewhat less successfully concealed. I mean a strange underlying relief; the soft, low emission of the breath that comes when a danger is past. What happened as she spent her barren hour with me was that at last she gave him up. She let him go for ever. She made the most graceful joke of it that I've ever seen made of anything; but it was for all that a great date in her life. She spoke with her mild gaiety of all the other vain times, the long game of hide-and-seek, the unprecedented queerness of such a relation. For it *was*, or had been, a relation, wasn't it, hadn't it? That was just the absurd part of it. When she got up to go I said to her that it was more a relation than ever, but that I hadn't the face after what had occurred to propose to her for the present another opportunity. It was plain that the only valid opportunity would be my accomplished marriage. Of course she would be at my wedding? It was even to be hoped that *he* would.

'If *I* am, he won't be!' she declared with a laugh. I admitted there might be something in that. The thing was therefore to get us safely married first. 'That won't help us. Nothing will help us!' she said as she kissed me farewell. 'I shall never, never see him!' It was with those words she left me.

I could bear her disappointment as I've called it; but when a couple of hours later I received him at dinner I found that I couldn't bear his. The way my manœuvre might have affected him had not been particularly present to me; but the result of it was the first word of reproach that had ever yet dropped from him. I say 'reproach' because that expression is scarcely too strong for the terms in which he conveyed to me his surprise that under the extraordinary circumstances I should not have found some means not to deprive him of such an occasion. I might really have managed either not to be obliged to go out or to let their meeting take place all the same. They would probably have got on in my drawing-room without me. At this I quite broke down – I confessed my iniquity and the miserable reason of it. I had not put her off and I had not gone out; she had been there and after waiting for him an hour had departed in the belief that he had been absent by his own fault.

'She must think me a precious brute!' he exclaimed. 'Did she say of me – what she had a right to say?'

'I assure you she said nothing that showed the least feeling. She looked at your photograph, she even turned round the back of it, on which your address happens to be inscribed. Yet it provoked her to no demonstration. She doesn't care so much as all that.'

'Then why are you afraid of her?'

'It was not of her I was afraid. It was of you.'

'Did you think I would fall in love with her? You never alluded to such a possibility before,' he went on as I remained silent. 'Admirable person as you pronounced her, that wasn't the light in which you showed her to me.'

'Do you mean that if it *had* been you would have managed by this time to catch a glimpse of her? I didn't fear things then,' I added. 'I hadn't the same reason.'

He kissed me at this, and when I remembered that she had done so an hour or two before I felt for an instant as if he were taking from my lips the very pressure of hers. In spite of kisses the incident had shed a certain chill, and I suffered horribly from the sense that he had seen me guilty of a fraud. He had seen it only through my frank avowal, but I was as unhappy as if I had a stain to efface. I couldn't get over the manner of his looking at me when I spoke of her apparent indifference to his not having come. For the first time since I had known him he seemed to have expressed a doubt of my word. Before we parted I told him that I would undeceive her, start the first thing in the morning for Richmond and there let her know that he had been blameless. At this he kissed me again. I would expiate my sin, I said; I would humble myself in the dust; I would confess and ask to be forgiven. At this he kissed me once more.

V

In the train the next day this struck me as a good deal for him to have consented to; but my purpose was firm enough to carry me on. I mounted the long hill to where the view begins, and then I knocked at her door. I was a trifle mystified by the fact that her blinds were still drawn, reflecting that if in the stress of my compunction I had come early I had certainly yet allowed people time to get up.

'At home, mum? She has left home for ever.'

I was extraordinarily startled by this announcement of the elderly parlour-maid. 'She has gone away?'

'She's dead, mum, please.' Then as I gasped at the horrible word: 'She died last night.'

The loud cry that escaped me sounded even in my own ears like some harsh violation of the hour. I felt for the moment as if I had killed her; I turned faint and saw through a vagueness the woman hold out her arms to me. Of what next happened I have no recollection, nor of anything but my friend's poor stupid cousin, in a darkened room, after an interval that I suppose very brief, sobbing at me in a smothered accusatory way. I can't say how long it took me to understand, to believe and then to press back with an immense effort that pang of responsibility which, superstitiously, insanely, had been at first almost all I was conscious of. The doctor, after the fact, had been superlatively wise and clear: he was satisfied of a long-latent weakness of the heart, determined probably years before by the agitations and terrors to which her marriage had introduced her. She had had in those days cruel scenes with her husband, she had been in fear of her life. All emotion, everything in the nature of anxiety and suspense had been after that to be strongly deprecated, as in her marked cultivation of a quiet life she was evidently well aware; but who could say that any one, especially a 'real lady', could be successfully protected from every little rub? She had had one a day or two before in the news of her husband's death; for there were shocks of all kinds, not only those of grief and surprise. For that matter she had never dreamed of so near a release: it had looked uncommonly as if he would live as long as herself. Then in the evening, in town, she had manifestly had another: something must have happened there which it would be indispensable to clear up. She had come back very late – it was past eleven o'clock, and on being met in the hall by her cousin, who was extremely anxious, had said that she was tired and must rest a moment before mounting the stairs. They had passed together into the dining-room, her companion proposing a glass of wine and bustling to the sideboard to pour it out. This took but a moment, and when my informant turned round our poor friend had not had time to seat herself. Suddenly, with a little moan that was barely audible, she dropped upon the sofa. She was dead. What unknown 'little rub' had dealt her the blow? What shock, in the name of wonder, *had* she had in town? I mentioned immediately the only one I could imagine – her having failed to meet at my house, to which by invitation for the purpose she had come at five o'clock, the gentleman I was to be married to, who had been accidentally kept away and with whom she had no acquaintance whatever. This obviously counted for little; but something else might easily have occurred: nothing in the London streets was more possible than an accident, especially an accident in those desperate cabs. What had she done, where had she gone on leaving my house? I had taken for granted she had gone straight home. We both presently remembered that in her excursions to town she sometimes, for convenience, for refreshment, spent an hour or two at the 'Gentlewomen', the quiet little ladies' club, and I promised that it should be my first care to make at that establishment thorough inquiry. Then we entered the dim and dreadful chamber where she lay locked up in death and where, asking after a little to be left alone with her, I remained for half an hour. Death had made her, had kept her beautiful; but I felt above all, as I kneeled at her bed, that it had made her, had kept her silent. It had turned the key on something I was concerned to know.

On my return from Richmond and after another duty had been performed I drove to his chambers. It was the first time, but I had often wanted to see them. On the staircase, which, as the house contained twenty sets of rooms, was unrestrictedly public, I met his servant, who went back with me and ushered me in. At the sound of my entrance he appeared in the doorway of a further room, and the instant we were alone I produced my news: 'She's dead!'

'Dead?'

He was tremendously struck, and I observed that he had no need to ask whom, in this abruptness, I meant.

'She died last evening – just after leaving me.'

He stared with the strangest expression, his eyes searching mine as if they were looking for a trap. 'Last evening – after leaving you?' He repeated my words in stupefaction. Then he brought out so that it was in stupefaction I heard: 'Impossible! I saw her.'

'You "saw" her?'

'On that spot – where you stand.'

This called back to me after an instant, as if to help me to take it in, the great wonder of the warning of his youth. 'In the hour of death – I understand: as you so beautifully saw your mother.'

'Ah! *not* as I saw my mother – not that way, not that

way!' He was deeply moved by my news – far more moved, I perceived, than he would have been the day before: it gave me a vivid sense that, as I had then said to myself, there was indeed a relation between them and that he had actually been face to face with her. Such an idea, by its reassertion of his extraordinary privilege, would have suddenly presented him as painfully abnormal had he not so vehemently insisted on the difference. 'I saw her living – I saw her to speak to her – I saw her as I see you now!'

It is remarkable that for a moment, though only for a moment, I found relief in the more personal, as it were, but also the more natural of the two odd facts. The next, as I embraced this image of her having come to him on leaving me and of just what it accounted for in the disposal of her time, I demanded with a shade of harshness of which I was aware –

'What on earth did she come for?'

He had now had a minute to think – to recover himself and judge of effects, so that if it was still with excited eyes he spoke he showed a conscious redness and made an inconsequent attempt to smile away the gravity of his words.

'She came just to see me. She came – after what had passed at your house – so that we *should*, after all, at last meet. The impulse seemed to me exquisite, and that was the way I took it.'

I looked round the room where she had been – where she had been and I never had been.

'And was the way you took it the way she expressed it?'

'She only expressed it by being here and by letting me look at her. That was enough!' he exclaimed with a singular laugh.

I wondered more and more. 'You mean she didn't speak to you?'

'She said nothing. She only looked at me as I looked at her.'

'And you didn't speak either?'

He gave me again his painful smile. 'I thought of *you*. The situation was every way delicate. I used the finest tact. But she saw she had pleased me.' He even repeated his dissonant laugh.

'She evidently pleased you!' Then I thought a moment. 'How long did she stay?'

'How can I say? It seemed twenty minutes, but it was probably a good deal less.'

'Twenty minutes of silence!' I began to have my definite view and now in fact quite to clutch at it. 'Do you know you're telling me a story positively monstrous?'

He had been standing with his back to the fire; at this, with a pleading look, he came to me. 'I beseech you, dearest, to take it kindly.'

I could take it kindly, and I signified as much; but I couldn't somehow, as he rather awkwardly opened his arms, let him draw me to him. So there fell between us for an appreciable time the discomfort of a great silence.

VI

He broke it presently by saying: 'There's absolutely no doubt of her death?'

'Unfortunately none. I've just risen from my knees by the bed where they've laid her out.'

He fixed his eyes hard on the floor; then he raised them to mine. 'How does she look?'

'She looks – at peace.'

He turned away again, while I watched him; but after a moment he began: 'At what hour, then –?'

'It must have been near midnight. She dropped as she reached her house – from an affection of the heart which she knew herself and her physician knew her to have, but of which, patiently, bravely she had never spoken to me.'

He listened intently and for a minute he was unable to speak. At last he broke out with an accent of which the almost boyish confidence, the really sublime simplicity rings in my ears as I write: 'Wasn't she *wonderful*!' Even at the time I was able to do it justice enough to remark in reply that I had always told him so; but the next minute, as if after speaking he had caught a glimpse of what he might have made me feel, he went on quickly: 'You see that if she didn't get home till midnight—'

I instantly took him up. 'There was plenty of time for you to have seen her? How so,' I inquired, 'when you didn't leave my house till late? I don't remember the very moment – I was preoccupied. But you know that though you said you had lots to do you sat for some time after dinner. She, on her side, was all the evening at the "Gentlewomen". I've just come from there – I've ascertained. She had tea there; she remained a long, long time.'

'What was she doing all the long, long time?'

I saw that he was eager to challenge at every step my account of the matter; and the more he showed this the more I found myself disposed to insist on that account, to prefer with apparent perversity an explanation which only deepened the marvel and the mystery, but which, of the two prodigies it had to choose from, my reviving jealousy found easiest to accept. He stood there pleading with a candour that now seems to me beautiful for the privilege of having in spite of supreme defeat known the living woman; while I, with a passion I wonder at to-day, though it still smoulders in a manner in its ashes, could only reply that, through a strange gift shared by her with his mother and on her own side likewise hereditary, the miracle of his youth had been renewed for him, the miracle of hers for her. She had been to him – yes, and by an impulse as charming as he liked; but oh! she had not been in the body. It was a simple question of evidence. I had had, I assured him, a definite statement of what she had done – most of the time – at the little club. The place was almost empty, but the servants had noticed her. She had sat motionless in a deep chair by the drawing-room fire; she had leaned back her head, she had closed her eyes, she had seemed softly to sleep.

'I see. But till what o'clock?'

'There,' I was obliged to answer, 'the servants fail me a little. The portress in particular is unfortunately a fool, though even she too is supposed to be a Gentlewoman. She was evidently at that period of the evening, without a substitute and against regulations, absent for some little time from the cage in which it's her business to watch the comings and goings. She's muddled, she palpably prevaricates; so I can't positively, from her observation, give you an hour. But it was remarked toward half-past ten that our poor friend was no longer in the club.'

'She came straight here; and from here she went straight to the train.'

'She couldn't have run it so close,' I declared. 'That was a thing she particularly never did.'

'There was no need of running it close, my dear – she had plenty of time. Your memory is at fault about my having left you late: I left you, as it happens, unusually early. I'm sorry my stay with you seemed long; for I was back here by ten.'

'To put yourself into your slippers,' I rejoined, 'and fall asleep in your chair. You slept till morning – you saw her in a dream!' He looked at me in silence and with sombre eyes

– eyes that showed me he had some irritation to repress. Presently I went on: 'You had a visit, at an extraordinary hour, from a lady – *soit*: nothing in the world is more probable. But there are ladies and ladies. How in the name of goodness, if she was unannounced and dumb and you had into the bargain never seen the least portrait of her – how could you identify the person we're talking of?'

'Haven't I to absolute satiety heard her described? I'll describe her for you in every particular.'

'Don't!' I exclaimed with a promptness that made him laugh once more. I coloured at this, but I continued: 'Did your servant introduce her?'

'He wasn't here – he's always away when he's wanted. One of the features of this big house is that from the street-door the different floors are accessible practically without challenge. My servant makes love to a young person employed in the rooms above these, and he had a long bout of it last evening. When he's out on that job he leaves my outer door, on the staircase, so much ajar as to enable him to slip back without a sound. The door then only requires a push. She pushed it – that simply took a little courage.'

'A little? It took tons! And it took all sorts of impossible calculations.'

'Well, she had them – she made them. Mind you, I don't deny for a moment,' he added, 'that it was very, very wonderful!'

Something in his tone prevented me for a while from trusting myself to speak. At last I said: 'How did she come to know where you live?'

'By remembering the address on the little label the shop-people happily left sticking to the frame I had had made for my photograph.'

'And how was she dressed?'

'In mourning, my own dear. No great depths of crape, but simple and scrupulous black. She had in her bonnet three small black feathers. She carried a little muff of astrachan. She has near the left eye,' he continued, 'a tiny vertical scar—'

I stopped him short. 'The mark of a caress from her husband.' Then I added: 'How close you must have been to her!' He made no answer to this, and I thought he blushed, observing which I broke straight off. 'Well, good-bye.'

'You won't stay a little?' He came to me again tenderly, and this time I suffered him. 'Her visit had its beauty,' he murmured as he held me, 'but yours has a greater one.'

I let him kiss me, but I remembered, as I had remembered the day before, that the last kiss she had given, as I supposed, in this world had been for the lips he touched.

'I'm life, you see,' I answered. 'What you saw last night was death.'

'It was life – it was life!'

He spoke with a kind of soft stubbornness, and I disengaged myself. We stood looking at each other hard.

'You describe the scene – so far as you describe it at all – in terms that are incomprehensible. She was in the room before you knew it?'

'I looked up from my letter-writing – at that table under the lamp I had been wholly absorbed in it – and she stood before me.'

'Then what did you do?'

'I sprang up with an ejaculation, and she, with a smile, laid her finger, ever so warningly, yet with a sort of delicate dignity, to her lips. I knew it meant silence, but the strange thing was that it seemed immediately to explain and to justify her. We at any rate stood for a time that, as I've told you, I can't calculate, face to face. It was just as you and I stand now.'

'Simply staring?'

He impatiently protested. 'Ah! *we're* not staring!'

'Yes, but we're talking.'

'Well, *we* were – after a fashion.' He lost himself in the memory of it. 'It was as friendly as this.' I had on my tongue's point to ask if that were saying much for it, but I remarked instead that what they had evidently done was to gaze in mutual admiration. Then I inquired whether his recognition of her had been immediate. 'Not quite,' he replied, 'for of course I didn't expect her; but it came to me long before she went who she was – who she could only be.'

I thought a little. 'And how did she at last go?'

'Just as she arrived. The door was open behind her, and she passed out.'

'Was she rapid – slow?'

'Rather quick. But looking behind her,' he added, with a smile. 'I let her go, for I perfectly understood that I was to take it as she wished.'

I was conscious of exhaling a long, vague sigh. 'Well, you must take it now as *I* wish – you must let *me* go.'

At this he drew near me again, detaining and persuading me, declaring with all due gallantry that I was a very different matter. I would have given anything to have been able to ask him if he had touched her, but the words refused to form themselves: I knew well enough how horrid and vulgar they would sound. I said something else – I forget exactly what; it was feebly tortuous and intended to make him tell me without my putting the question. But he didn't tell me; he only repeated, as if from a glimpse of the propriety of soothing and consoling me, the sense of his declaration of some minutes before – the assurance that she was indeed exquisite, as I had always insisted, but that I was his 'real' friend and his very own for ever. This led me to reassert, in the spirit of my previous rejoinder, that I had at least the merit of being alive; which in turn drew from him again the flash of contradiction I dreaded. 'Oh, *she* was alive! she was, she was!'

'She was dead! she was dead!' I asseverated with an energy, a determination that it should *be* so, which comes back to me now almost as grotesque. But the sound of the word as it rang out filled me suddenly with horror, and all the natural emotion the meaning of it might have evoked in other conditions gathered and broke in a flood. It rolled over me that here was a great affection quenched and how much I had loved and trusted her. I had a vision at the same time of the lonely beauty of her end. 'She's gone – she's lost to us for ever!' I burst into sobs.

'That's exactly what I feel,' he exclaimed, speaking with extreme kindness and pressing me to him for comfort. 'She's gone; she's lost to us for ever: so what does it matter now?' He bent over me, and when his face had touched mine I scarcely knew if it were wet with my tears or with his own.

VII

It was my theory, my conviction, it became, as I may say, my attitude, that they had still never 'met'; and it was just on this ground that I said to myself it would be generous to ask him to stand with me beside her grave. He did so, very modestly and tenderly, and I assumed, though he himself clearly cared nothing for the danger, that the solemnity of the occasion, largely made up of persons who had known them both and had a sense of the long joke, would sufficiently deprive his presence of all light association. On the question of what had happened the evening of her death little more passed between us; I had been overtaken by a horror of the element of evidence. It seemed gross and prying on either hypothesis. He on his side had none to produce, none at least but a statement of his house-porter – on his own admission a most casual and intermittent personage – that between the hours of ten o'clock and midnight no less than three ladies in deep black had flitted in and out of the place. This proved far too much; we had neither of us any use for three. He knew that I considered I had accounted for every fragment of her time, and we dropped the matter as settled; we abstained from further discussion. What *I* knew however was that he abstained to please me rather than because he yielded to my reasons. He didn't yield – he was only indulgent; he clung to his interpretation because he liked it better. He liked it better, I held, because it had more to say to his vanity. That, in a similar position, would not have been its effect on me, though I had doubtless quite as much; but these are things of individual humour, as to which no person can judge for another. I should have supposed it more gratifying to be the subject of one of those inexplicable occurrences that are chronicled in thrilling books and disputed about at learned meetings; I could conceive, on the part of a being just engulfed in the infinite and still vibrating with human emotion, of nothing more fine and pure, more high and august than such an impulse of reparation, of admonition or even of curiosity. *That* was beautiful, if one would, and I should in his place have thought more of myself for being so distinguished. It was public that he had already, that he had long been distinguished, and what was this in itself but almost a proof? Each of the strange visitations contributed to establish the other. He had a different feeling; but he had also, I hasten to add, an unmistakable desire not to make a stand or, as they say, a fuss about it. I might believe what I liked – the more so that the whole thing was in a manner a mystery of my producing. It was an event of my history, a puzzle of my consciousness, not of his; therefore he would take about it any tone that struck me as convenient. We had both at all events other business on hand; we were pressed with preparations for our marriage.

Mine were assuredly urgent, but I found as the days went on that to believe what I 'liked' was to believe what I was more and more intimately convinced of. I found also that I didn't like it so much as that came to, or that the pleasure at all events was far from being the cause of my conviction. My obsession, as I may really call it and as I began to perceive, refused to be elbowed away, as I had hoped, by my sense of paramount duties. If I had a great deal to do I had still more to think about, and the moment came when my occupations were gravely menaced by my thoughts. I see it all now, I feel it, I live it over. It's terribly void of joy, it's full indeed to overflowing of bitterness; and yet I must do myself justice – I couldn't possibly be other than I was. The same strange impressions, had I to meet them again, would produce the same deep anguish, the same sharp doubts, the same still sharper certainties. Oh, it's all easier to remember than to write, but even if I could retrace the business hour by hour, could find terms for the inexpressible, the ugliness and the pain would quickly stay my hand. Let me then note very simply and briefly that a week before our wedding-day, three weeks after her death, I became fully aware that I had something very serious to look in the face and that if I was to make this effort I must make it on the spot and before another hour should elapse. My unextinguished jealousy – that was the Medusa-mask. It hadn't died with her death, it had lividly survived, and it was fed by suspicions unspeakable. They *would* be unspeakable to-day, that is, if I hadn't felt the sharp need of uttering them at the time. This need took possession of me – to save me, as it appeared, from my fate. When once it had done so I saw – in the urgency of the case, the diminishing hours and shrinking interval – only one issue, that of absolute promptness and frankness. I could at least not do him the wrong of delaying another day; I could at least treat my difficulty as too fine for a subterfuge. Therefore very quietly, but none the less abruptly and hideously, I put it before him on a certain evening that we must reconsider our situation and recognize that it had completely altered.

He stared bravely. 'How has it altered?'

'Another person has come between us.'

He hesitated a moment. 'I won't pretend not to know whom you mean.' He smiled in pity for my aberration, but he meant to be kind. 'A woman dead and buried!'

'She's buried, but she's not dead. She's dead for the world – she's dead for me. But she's not dead for *you*.'

'You hark back to the different construction we put on her appearance that evening?'

'No,' I answered, 'I hark back to nothing. I've no need of it. I've more than enough with what's before me.'

'And pray, darling, what is that?'

'You're completely changed.'

'By that absurdity?' he laughed.

'Not so much by that one as by other absurdities that have followed it.'

'And what may they have been?'

We had faced each other fairly, with eyes that didn't flinch; but his had a dim, strange light, and my certitude triumphed in his perceptible paleness. 'Do you really pretend,' I asked, 'not to know what they are?'

'My dear child,' he replied, 'you describe them too sketchily!'

I considered a moment. 'One may well be embarrassed to finish the picture! But from that point of view – and from the beginning – what was ever more embarrassing than your idiosyncrasy?'

He was extremely vague. 'My idiosyncrasy?'

'Your notorious, your peculiar power.'

He gave a great shrug of impatience, a groan of overdone disdain. 'Oh, my peculiar power!'

'Your accessibility to forms of life,' I coldly went on, 'your command of impressions, appearances, contacts closed – for our gain or our loss – to the rest of us. That was originally a part of the deep interest with which you inspired me – one of the reasons I was amused, I was indeed positively proud to know you. It was a magnificent distinction; it's a magnificent distinction still. But of course I had no prevision then of the way it would operate now; and even had that been the case I should have had none of the extraordinary way in which its action would affect me.'

'To what in the name of goodness,' he pleadingly inquired, 'are you fantastically alluding?' Then as I remained silent, gathering a tone for my charge, 'How in the world *does* it operate?' he went on; 'and how in the world are you affected?'

'She missed you for five years,' I said, 'but she never misses you now. You're making it up!'

'Making it up?' He had begun to turn from white to red.

'You see her – you see her: you see her every night!' He gave a loud sound of derision, but it was not a genuine one. 'She comes to you as she came that evening,' I declared; 'having tried it she found she liked it!' I was able, with God's help, to speak without blind passion or vulgar violence; but those were the exact words – and far from 'sketchy' they then appeared to me – that I uttered. He had turned away in his laughter, clapping his hands at my folly, but in an instant he faced me again with a change of expression that struck me. 'Do you dare to deny,' I asked, 'that you habitually see her?'

He had taken the line of indulgence, of meeting me half-way and kindly humouring me. At all events to my astonishment he suddenly said: 'Well, my dear, what if I do?'

'It's your natural right; it belongs to your constitution and to your wonderful if not perhaps quite enviable fortune. But you will easily understand that it separates us. I unconditionally release you.'

'Release me?'

'You must choose between me and her.'

He looked at me hard. 'I see.' Then he walked away a little, as if grasping what I had said and thinking how he had best treat it. At last he turned upon me afresh. 'How on earth do you know such an awfully private thing?'

'You mean because you've tried so hard to hide it? It *is* awfully private, and you may believe I shall never betray you. You've done your best, you've acted your part, you've behaved, poor dear! loyally and admirably. Therefore I've watched you in silence, playing my part too; I've noted every drop in your voice, every absence in your eyes, every effort in your indifferent hand: I've waited till I was utterly sure and miserably unhappy. How *can* you hide it when you're abjectly in love with her, when you're sick almost to death with the joy of what she gives you?' I checked his quick protest with a quicker gesture. 'You love her as you've *never* loved, and, passion for passion, she gives it straight back! She rules you, she holds you, she has you all! A woman, in such a case as mine, divines and feels and sees; she's not an idiot who has to be credibly informed. You come to me mechanically, compunctiously, with the dregs of your tenderness and the remnant of your life. I can renounce you, but I can't share you; the best of you is hers; I know what it is and I freely give you up to her for ever!'

He made a gallant fight, but it couldn't be patched up; he repeated his denial, he retracted his admission, he ridiculed my charge, of which I freely granted him moreover the indefensible extravagance. I didn't pretend for a moment that we were talking of common things; I didn't pretend for a moment that he and she were common people. Pray, if they *had* been, how should I ever have cared for them? They had enjoyed a rare extension of being and they had caught me up in their flight; only I couldn't breathe in such an air and I promptly asked to be set down. Everything in the facts was monstrous, and most of all my lucid perception of them; the only thing allied to nature and truth was my having to act on that perception. I felt after I had spoken in this sense that my assurance was complete; nothing had been wanting to it but the sight of my effect on him. He disguised indeed the effect in a cloud of chaff, a diversion that gained him time and covered his retreat. He challenged my sincerity, my sanity, almost my humanity, and that of course widened our breach and confirmed our rupture. He did everything in short but convince me either that I was wrong or that he was unhappy: we separated and I left him to his inconceivable communion.

He never married, any more than I've done. When six years later, in solitude and silence, I heard of his death I hailed it as a direct contribution to my theory. It was sudden, it was never properly accounted for, it was surrounded by circumstances in which – for oh, I took them to pieces! – I distinctly read an intention, the mark of his own hidden hand. It was the result of a long necessity, of an unquenchable desire. To say exactly what I mean, it was a response to an irresistible call.

W. W. JACOBS

THE MONKEY'S PAW

I

WITHOUT, THE NIGHT was cold and wet; but in the small parlour of Laburnum Villa the blinds were drawn and the fire burned brightly. Father and son were at chess; the former, who possessed ideas about the game involving radical changes, putting his king into such sharp and unnecessary perils that it even provoked comment from the white-haired old lady knitting placidly by the fire.

'Hark at the wind,' said Mr White, who, having seen a fatal mistake after it was too late, was amiably desirous of preventing his son from seeing it.

'I'm listening,' said the latter, grimly surveying the board as he stretched out his hand. 'Check.'

'I should hardly think that he'd come to-night,' said his father, with his hand poised over the board.

'Mate,' replied the son.

'That's the worst of living so far out,' bawled Mr White, with sudden and unlooked-for violence; 'of all the beastly, slushy, out-of-the-way places to live in, this is the worst. Path's a bog, and the road's a torrent. I don't know what people are thinking about. I suppose because only two houses in the road are let, they think it doesn't matter.'

'Never mind, dear,' said his wife soothingly; 'perhaps you'll win the next one.'

Mr White looked up sharply, just in time to intercept a knowing glance between mother and son. The words died away on his lips, and he hid a guilty grin in his thin grey beard.

'There he is,' said Herbert White, as the gate banged to loudly and heavy footsteps came toward the door.

The old man rose with hospitable haste and, opening the door, was heard condoling with the new arrival. The new arrival also condoled with himself, so that Mrs White said, 'Tut, tut!' and coughed gently as her husband entered the room, followed by a tall, burly man, beady of eye and rubicund of visage.

'Sergeant-Major Morris,' he said, introducing him.

The sergeant-major shook hands, and taking the proffered seat by the fire, watched contentedly while his host got out whisky and tumblers and stood a small copper kettle on the fire.

At the third glass his eyes got brighter, and he began to talk, the little family circle regarding with eager interest this visitor from distant parts, as he squared his broad shoulders in the chair and spoke of wild scenes and doughty deeds; of wars and plagues and strange peoples.

'Twenty-one years of it,' said Mr White, nodding at his wife and son. 'When he went away he was a slip of a youth in the warehouse. Now look at him.'

'He don't look to have taken much harm,' said Mrs White politely.

'I'd like to go to India myself,' said the old man, 'just to look round a bit, you know.'

'Better where you are,' said the sergeant-major, shaking his head. He put down the empty glass, and sighing softly, shook it again.

'I should like to see those old temples and fakirs and jugglers,' said the old man. 'What was that you started telling me the other day about a monkey's paw or something, Morris?'

'Nothing,' said the soldier hastily. 'Leastways nothing worth hearing.'

'Monkey's paw?' said Mrs White curiously.

'Well, it's just a bit of what you might call magic, perhaps,' said the sergeant-major offhandedly.

His three listeners leaned forward eagerly. The visitor absentmindedly put his empty glass to his lips and then set it down again. His host filled it for him.

'To look at,' said the sergeant-major, fumbling in his pocket, 'it's just an ordinary little paw, dried to a mummy.'

He took something out of his pocket and proffered it. Mrs White drew back with a grimace, but her son, taking it, examined it curiously.

'And what is there special about it?' inquired Mr White as he took it from his son, and having examined it, placed it upon the table.

'It had a spell put on it by an old fakir,' said the sergeant-major, 'a very holy man. He wanted to show that fate ruled people's lives, and that those who interfered with it did so to their sorrow. He put a spell on it so that three separate men could each have three wishes from it.'

His manner was so impressive that his hearers were conscious that their light laughter jarred somewhat.

'Well, why don't you have three, sir?' said Herbert White cleverly.

The soldier regarded him in the way that middle age is wont to regard presumptuous youth. 'I have,' he said quietly and his blotchy face whitened.

'And did you really have the three wishes granted?' asked Mrs White.

'I did,' said the sergeant-major, and his glass tapped against his strong teeth.

'And has anybody else wished?' persisted the old lady.

'The first man had his three wishes. Yes,' was the reply; 'I don't know what the first two were, but the third was for death. That's how I got the paw.'

His tones were so grave that a hush fell upon the group.

'If you've had your three wishes, it's no good to you now, then, Morris,' said the old man at last. 'What do you keep it for?'

The soldier shook his head. 'Fancy I suppose,' he said slowly. 'I did have some idea of selling it, but I don't think I will. It has caused enough mischief already. Besides, people won't buy. They think it's a fairy tale, some of them; and those who do think anything of it want to try it first and pay me afterward.'

'If you could have another three wishes,' said the old man, eyeing him keenly, 'would you have them?'

'I don't know,' said the other. 'I don't know.'

He took the paw, and dangling it between his forefinger and thumb, suddenly threw it upon the fire. White, with a slight cry, stooped down and snatched it off.

'Better let it burn,' said the soldier solemnly.

'If you don't want it, Morris,' said the other, 'give it to me.'

'I won't,' said his friend doggedly. 'I threw it on the fire. If you keep it, don't blame me for what happens. Pitch it on the fire again like a sensible man.'

The other shook his head and examined his new possession closely. 'How do you do it?' he inquired.

'Hold it up in your right hand and wish aloud,' said the sergeant-major, 'but I warn you of the consequences.'

'Sounds like the *Arabian Nights*,' said Mrs White, as she rose and began to set the supper. 'Don't you think you might wish for four pairs of hands for me?'

Her husband drew the talisman from his pocket, and

then all three burst into laughter as the sergeant-major, with a look of alarm on his face, caught him by the arm.

'If you must wish,' he said gruffly, 'wish for something sensible.'

Mr White dropped it back in his pocket, and placing chairs, motioned his friend to the table. In the business of supper the talisman was partly forgotten, and afterward the three sat listening in an enthralled fashion to a second instalment of the soldier's adventures in India.

'If the tale about the monkey's paw is not more truthful than those he has been telling us,' said Herbert, as the door closed behind their guest, just in time to catch the last train, 'we shan't make much out of it.'

'Did you give him anything for it, father?' inquired Mrs White, regarding her husband closely.

'A trifle,' said he, colouring slightly. 'He didn't want it, but I made him take it. And he pressed me again to throw it away.'

'Likely,' said Herbert, with pretended horror. 'Why, we're going to be rich, and famous, and happy. Wish to be an emperor, father, to begin with; then you can't be henpecked.'

He darted round the table, pursued by the maligned Mrs White armed with an antimacassar.

Mr White took the paw from his pocket and eyed it dubiously. 'I don't know what to wish for, and that's a fact,' he said slowly. 'It seems to me I've got all I want.'

'If you only cleared the house, you'd be quite happy, wouldn't you!' said Herbert, with his hand on his shoulder. 'Well, wish for two hundred pounds, then; that'll just do it.'

His father, smiling shamefacedly at his own credulity, held up the talisman, as his son, with a solemn face, somewhat marred by a wink at his mother, sat down at the piano and struck a few impressive chords.

'I wish for two hundred pounds,' said the old man distinctly.

A fine crash from the piano greeted the words, interrupted by a shuddering cry from the old man. His wife and son ran toward him.

'It moved,' he cried, with a glance of disgust at the object as it lay on the floor. 'As I wished, it twisted in my hand like a snake.'

'Well, I don't see the money,' said his son, as he picked it up and placed it on the table, 'and I bet I never shall.'

'It must have been your fancy, father,' said his wife, regarding him anxiously.

He shook his head. 'Never mind, though; there's no harm done, but it gave me a shock all the same.'

They sat down by the fire again while the two men finished their pipes. Outside, the wind was higher than ever, and the old man started nervously at the sound of a door banging upstairs. A silence unusual and depressing settled upon all three, which lasted until the old couple rose to retire for the night.

'I expect you'll find the cash tied up in a big bag in the middle of your bed,' said Herbert, as he bade them good night, 'and something horrible squatting up on top of the wardrobe watching you as you pocket your ill-gotten gains.'

He sat alone in the darkness, gazing at the dying fire, and seeing faces in it. The last face was so horrible and so simian that he gazed at it in amazement. It got so vivid that, with a little uneasy laugh, he felt on the table for a glass containing a little water to throw over it. His hand grasped the monkey's paw, and with a little shiver he wiped his hand on his coat and went up to bed.

II

In the brightness of the wintry sun next morning as it streamed over the breakfast table he laughed at his fears. There was an air of prosaic wholesomeness about the room which it had lacked on the previous night, and the dirty, shrivelled little paw was pitched on the side-board with a carelessness which betokened no great belief in its virtues.

'I suppose all old soldiers are the same,' said Mrs White. 'The idea of our listening to such nonsense! How could wishes be granted in these days? And if they could, how could two hundred pounds hurt you, father?'

'Might drop on his head from the sky,' said the frivolous Herbert.

'Morris said the things happened so naturally,' said his father, 'that you might if you so wished attribute it to coincidence.'

'Well, don't break into the money before I come back,' said Herbert as he rose from the table. 'I'm afraid it'll turn you into a mean, avaricious man, and we shall have to disown you.'

His mother laughed, and following him to the door, watched him down the road; and returning to the breakfast table, was very happy at the expense of her husband's credulity. All of which did not prevent her from scurrying to the door at the postman's knock, nor prevent her from referring somewhat shortly to retired sergeant-majors of bibulous habits when she found that the post brought a tailor's bill.

'Herbert will have some more of his funny remarks, I expect, when he comes home,' she said, as they sat at dinner.

'I dare say,' said Mr White, pouring himself out some beer, 'but for all that, the thing moved in my hand; that I'll swear to.'

'You thought it did,' said the old lady, soothingly.

'I say it did,' replied the other. 'There was no thought about it; I had just – What's the matter?'

His wife made no reply She was watching the mysterious movements of a man outside, who, peering in an undecided fashion at the house, appeared to be trying to make up his mind to enter. In mental connexion with the two hundred pounds, she noticed that the stranger was well dressed, and wore a silk hat of glossy newness. Three times he paused at the gate, and then walked on again. The fourth time he stood with his hand upon it, and then with sudden resolution flung it open and walked up the path. Mrs White at the same moment placed her hands behind her, and hurriedly unfastening the strings of her apron, put that useful article of apparel beneath the cushion of her chair.

She brought the stranger, who seemed ill at ease, into the room. He gazed at her furtively and listened in a preoccupied fashion as the old lady apologized for the appearance of the room, and her husband's coat, a garment which he usually reserved for the garden. She then waited as patiently as her sex would permit, for him to broach his business, but he was at first strangely silent.

'I – was asked to call,' he said at last, and stooped and picked a piece of cotton from his trousers. 'I come from "Maw and Meggins".'

The old lady started. 'Is anything the matter?' she asked breathlessly. 'Has anything happened to Herbert? What is it? What is it?'

Her husband interposed. 'There, there, mother,' he said hastily. 'Sit down, and don't jump to conclusions. You've not brought bad news, I'm sure, sir'; and he eyed the other wistfully.

'I'm sorry—' began the visitor.

'Is he hurt?' demanded the mother wildly.

The visitor bowed in assent. 'Badly hurt,' he said quietly, 'but he is not in any pain.'

'Oh, thank God!' said the old woman, clasping her hands. 'Thank God for that! Thank—'

She broke off suddenly as the sinister meaning of the assurance dawned upon her and she saw the awful confirmation of her fears in the other's averted face. She caught her breath, and turning to her slower-witted husband, laid her trembling old hand upon his. There was a long silence.

'He was caught in the machinery,' said the visitor at length in a low voice.

'Caught in the machinery,' repeated Mr White, in a dazed fashion, 'yes.'

He sat staring blankly out at the window, and taking his wife's hand between his own, pressed it as he had been wont to do in their old courting days nearly forty years before.

'He was the only one left to us,' he said, turning gently to the visitor. 'It is hard.'

The other coughed, and rising, walked slowly to the window. 'The firm wished me to convey their sincere sympathy with you in your great loss,' he said, without looking round. 'I beg that you will understand I am only their servant and merely obeying orders.'

There was no reply; the old woman's face was white, her eyes staring, and her breath inaudible; on the husband's face was a look such as his friend the sergeant might have carried into his first action.

'I was to say that Maw and Meggins disclaim all responsibility,' continued the other. 'They admit to no liability at all, but in consideration of your son's services, they wish to present you with a certain sum as compensation.'

Mr White dropped his wife's hand, and rising to his feet, gazed with a look of horror at his visitor. His dry lips shaped the words, 'How much?'

'Two hundred pounds,' was the answer.

Unconscious of his wife's shriek, the old man smiled faintly put out his hands like a sightless man, and dropped, a senseless heap, to the floor.

III

In the huge new cemetery, some two miles distant, the old people buried their dead, and came back to the house steeped in shadow and silence. It was all over so quickly that at first they could hardly realize it, and remained in a state of expectation as though of something else to happen – something else which was to lighten this load, too heavy for old hearts to bear.

But the days passed, and expectation gave place to resignation – the hopeless resignation of the old, sometimes miscalled apathy. Sometimes they hardly exchanged a word, for now they had nothing to talk about, and their days were long to weariness.

It was about a week after that the old man, waking suddenly in the night, stretched out his hand and found himself alone. The room was in darkness, and the sound of subdued weeping came from the window. He raised himself in bed and listened.

'Come back,' he said tenderly. 'You will be cold.'

'It is colder for my son,' said the old woman, and wept afresh.

The sound of her sobs died away on his ears. The bed was warm, and his eyes heavy with sleep. He dozed fitfully, and then slept until a sudden wild cry from his wife awoke him with a start.

'*The paw!*' she cried wildly. 'The monkey's paw!'

He started up in alarm. 'Where? Where is it? What's the matter?'

She came stumbling across the room toward him. 'I want it,' she said quietly. 'You've not destroyed it?'

'It's in the parlour, on the bracket,' he replied, marvelling. 'Why?'

She cried and laughed together, and bending over, kissed his cheek.

'I only just thought of it,' she said hysterically. 'Why didn't I think of it before? Why didn't *you* think of it?'

'Think of what?' he questioned.

'The other two wishes,' she replied rapidly. 'We've only had one.'

'Was not that enough?' he demanded fiercely.

'No,' she cried triumphantly; 'we'll have one more. Go down and get it quickly, and wish our boy alive again.'

The man sat up in bed and flung the bedclothes from his quaking limbs. 'Good God, you are mad!' he cried, aghast.

'Get it,' she panted; 'get it quickly and wish— Oh, my boy, my boy!'

Her husband struck a match and lit the candle. 'Get back to bed,' he said unsteadily. 'You don't know what you are saying.'

'We had the first wish granted,' said the old woman feverishly; 'why not the second?'

'A coincidence,' stammered the old man.

'Go and get it and wish,' cried his wife, quivering with excitement.

The old man turned and regarded her, and his voice shook. 'He has been dead ten days, and besides he – I would not tell you else, but – I could only recognize him by his clothing. If he was too terrible for you to see then, how now?'

'Bring him back,' cried the old woman, and dragged him toward the door. 'Do you think I fear the child I have nursed?'

He went down in the darkness, and felt his way to the parlour, and then to the mantelpiece. The talisman was in its place, and a horrible fear that the unspoken wish might bring his mutilated son before him ere he could escape from the room seized upon him, and he caught his breath as he found that he had lost the direction of the door. His brow cold with sweat, he felt his way round the table, and groped along the wall until he found himself in the small passage with the unwholesome thing in his hand.

Even his wife's face seemed changed as he entered the room. It was white and expectant, and to his fears seemed to have an unnatural look upon it. He was afraid of her.

'*Wish!*' she cried, in a strong voice.

'It is foolish and wicked,' he faltered.

'*Wish!*' repeated his wife.

He raised his hand. 'I wish my son alive again.'

The talisman fell to the floor, and he regarded it fearfully. Then he sank trembling into a chair as the old woman, with burning eyes, walked to the window and raised the blind.

He sat until he was chilled with the cold, glancing occasionally at the figure of the old woman peering through the window. The candle-end, which had burned below the rim of the china candlestick, was throwing pulsating shadows on the ceiling and walls, until, with a flicker larger than the rest, it expired. The old man, with an unspeakable sense of relief at the failure of the talisman, crept back to his bed, and a minute or two afterward the old woman came silently and apathetically beside him.

Neither spoke, but lay silently listening to the ticking of

the clock. A stair creaked, and a squeaky mouse scurried noisily through the wall. The darkness was oppressive, and after lying for some time screwing up his courage, he took the box of matches, and striking one, went downstairs for a candle.

At the foot of the stairs the match went out, and he paused to strike another; and at the same moment a knock, so quiet and stealthy as to be scarcely audible, sounded on the front door.

The matches fell from his hand and spilled in the passage. He stood motionless, his breath suspended until the knock was repeated. Then he turned and fled swiftly back to his room, and closed the door behind him. A third knock sounded through the house.

'*What's that?*' cried the old woman, starting up.

'A rat,' said the old man in shaking tones – 'a rat. It passed me on the stairs.'

His wife sat up in bed listening. A loud knock resounded through the house.

'It's Herbert!' she screamed. 'It's Herbert!'

She ran to the door, but her husband was before her, and catching her by the arm, held her tightly.

'What are you going to do?' he whispered hoarsely.

'It's my boy; it's Herbert!' she cried, struggling mechanically. 'I forgot it was two miles away. What are you holding me for? Let go. I must open the door.'

'For God's sake don't let it in,' cried the old man, trembling.

'You're afraid of your own son,' she cried, struggling. 'Let me go. I'm coming, Herbert; I'm coming.'

There was another knock, and another. The old woman with a sudden wrench broke free and ran from the room. Her husband followed to the landing, and called after her appealingly as she hurried downstairs. He heard the chain rattle back and the bottom bolt drawn slowly and stiffly from the socket. Then the old woman's voice, strained and panting.

'The bolt,' she cried loudly. 'Come down. I can't reach it.'

But her husband was on his hands and knees groping wildly on the floor in search of the paw. If he could only find it before the thing outside got in. A perfect fusillade of knocks reverberated through the house, and he heard the scraping of a chair as his wife put it down in the passage against the door. He heard the creaking of the bolt as it came slowly back, and at the same moment he found the monkey's paw, and frantically breathed his third and last wish.

The knocking ceased suddenly, although the echoes of it were still in the house. He heard the chair drawn back, and the door opened. A cold wind rushed up the staircase, and a long loud wail of disappointment and misery from his wife gave him courage to run down to her side, and then to the gate beyond. The street lamp flickering opposite shone on a quiet and deserted road.

M. R. JAMES

'OH, WHISTLE, AND I'LL COME TO YOU, MY LAD'

'I SUPPOSE YOU will be getting away pretty soon, now Full term is over, Professor,' said a person not in the story to the Professor of Ontography, soon after they had sat down next to each other at a feast in the hospitable hall of St James's College.

The Professor was young, neat, and precise in speech.

'Yes,' he said; 'my friends have been making me take up golf this term, and I mean to go to the East Coast – in point of fact to Burnstow – (I dare say you know it) for a week or ten days, to improve my game. I hope to get off to-morrow.'

'Oh, Parkins,' said his neighbour on the other side, 'if you are going to Burnstow, I wish you would look at the site of the Templars' preceptory, and let me know if you think it would be any good to have a dig there in the summer.'

It was, as you might suppose, a person of antiquarian pursuits who said this, but, since he merely appears in this prologue, there is no need to give his entitlements.

'Certainly,' said Parkins, the Professor: 'if you will describe to me whereabouts the site is, I will do my best to give you an idea of the lie of the land when I get back; or I could write to you about it, if you would tell me where you are likely to be.'

'Don't trouble to do that, thanks. It's only that I'm thinking of taking my family in that direction in the Long, and it occurred to me that, as very few of the English preceptories have ever been properly planned, I might have an opportunity of doing something useful on off-days.'

The Professor rather sniffed at the idea that planning out a preceptory could be described as useful. His neighbour continued:

'The site – I doubt if there is anything showing above ground – must be down quite close to the beach now. The sea has encroached tremendously, as you know, all along that bit of coast. I should think, from the map, that it must be about three-quarters of a mile from the Globe Inn, at the north end of the town. Where are you going to stay?'

'Well, *at* the Globe Inn as a matter of fact,' said Parkins; 'I have engaged a room there. I couldn't get in anywhere else; most of the lodging-houses are shut up in winter, it seems; and, as it is, they tell me that the only room of any size I can have is really a double-bedded one, and that they haven't a corner in which to store the other bed, and so on. But I must have a fairly large room, for I am taking some books down, and mean to do a bit of work; and though I don't quite fancy having an empty bed – not to speak of two – in what I may call for the time being my study, I suppose I can manage to rough it for the short time I shall be there.'

'Do you call having an extra bed in your room roughing it, Parkins?' said a bluff person opposite. 'Look here, I shall come down and occupy it for a bit; it'll be company for you.'

The Professor quivered, but managed to laugh in a courteous manner.

'By all means, Rogers; there's nothing I should like better. But I'm afraid you would find it rather dull; you don't play golf, do you?'

'No, thank Heaven!' said rude Mr Rogers.

'Well, you see, when I'm not writing I shall most likely be out on the links, and that, as I say, would be rather dull for you, I'm afraid.'

'Oh, I don't know! There's certain to be somebody I know

in the place; but, of course, if you don't want me, speak the word, Parkins; I shan't be offended. Truth, as you always tell us, is never offensive.'

Parkins was, indeed, scrupulously polite and strictly truthful. It is to be feared that Mr Rogers sometimes practised upon his knowledge of these characteristics. In Parkins's breast there was a conflict now raging, which for a moment or two did not allow him to answer. That interval being over, he said:

'Well, if you want the exact truth, Rogers, I was considering whether the room I speak of would really be large enough to accommodate us both comfortably; and also whether (mind, I shouldn't have said this if you hadn't pressed me) you would not constitute something in the nature of a hindrance to my work.'

Rogers laughed loudly.

'Well done, Parkins!' he said. 'It's all right. I promise not to interrupt your work; don't you disturb yourself about that. No, I won't come if you don't want me; but I thought I should do so nicely to keep the ghosts off.' Here he might have been seen to wink and to nudge his next neighbour. Parkins might also have been seen to become pink. 'I beg pardon, Parkins,' Rogers continued; 'I oughtn't to have said that. I forgot you didn't like levity on these topics.'

'Well,' Parkins said, 'as you have mentioned the matter, I freely own that I do *not* like careless talk about what you call ghosts. A man in my position,' he went on, raising his voice a little, 'cannot, I find, be too careful about appearing to sanction the current beliefs on such subjects. As you know, Rogers, or as you ought to know; for I think I have never concealed my views—'

'No, you certainly have not, old man,' put in Rogers *sotto voce*.

'—I hold that any semblance, any appearance of concession to the view that such things might exist is equivalent to a renunciation of all that I hold most sacred. But I'm afraid I have not succeeded in securing your attention.'

'Your *undivided* attention, was what Dr Blimber actually *said*,'* Rogers interrupted, with every appearance of an earnest desire for accuracy. 'But I beg your pardon, Parkins: I'm stopping you.'

'No, not at all,' said Parkins. 'I don't remember Blimber; perhaps he was before my time. But I needn't go on. I'm sure you know what I mean.'

'Yes, yes,' said Rogers, rather hastily – 'just so. We'll go into it fully at Burnstow, or somewhere.'

In repeating the above dialogue I have tried to give the impression which it made on me, that Parkins was something of an old woman – rather hen-like, perhaps, in his little ways; totally destitute, alas! of the sense of humour, but at the same time dauntless and sincere in his convictions, and a man deserving of the greatest respect. Whether or not the reader has gathered so much, that was the character which Parkins had.

On the following day Parkins did, as he had hoped, succeed in getting away from his college, and in arriving at Burnstow. He was made welcome at the Globe Inn, was safely installed in the large double-bedded room of which we have heard, and was able before retiring to rest to arrange his materials for work in apple-pie order upon a commodious table which occupied the outer end of the room, and was surrounded on three sides by windows looking out seaward; that is to say, the central window looked straight out to sea, and those on the left and right commanded prospects along the shore

* Mr Rogers was wrong, *vide Dombey and Son*, chapter xii.

to the north and south respectively. On the south you saw the village of Burnstow. On the north no houses were to be seen, but only the beach and the low cliff backing it. Immediately in front was a strip – not considerable – of rough grass, dotted with old anchors, capstans, and so forth; then a broad path; then the beach. Whatever may have been the original distance between the Globe Inn and the sea, not more than sixty yards now separated them.

The rest of the population of the inn was, of course, a golfing one, and included few elements that call for a special description. The most conspicuous figure was, perhaps, that of an *ancien militaire*, secretary of a London club, and possessed of a voice of incredible strength, and of views of a pronouncedly Protestant type. These were apt to find utterance after his attendance upon the ministrations of the Vicar, an estimable man with inclinations towards a picturesque ritual, which he gallantly kept down as far as he could out of deference to East Anglian tradition.

Professor Parkins, one of whose principal characteristics was pluck, spent the greater part of the day following his arrival at Burnstow in what he had called improving his game, in company with this Colonel Wilson: and during the afternoon – whether the process of improvement were to blame or not, I am not sure – the Colonel's demeanour assumed a colouring so lurid that even Parkins jibbed at the thought of walking home with him from the links. He determined, after a short and furtive look at that bristling moustache and those incarnadined features, that it would be wiser to allow the influences of tea and tobacco to do what they could with the Colonel before the dinner-hour should render a meeting inevitable.

'I might walk home to-night along the beach,' he reflected – 'yes, and take a look – there will be light enough for that –

at the ruins of which Disney was talking. I don't exactly know where they are, by the way; but I expect I can hardly help stumbling on them.'

This he accomplished, I may say, in the most literal sense, for in picking his way from the links to the shingle beach his foot caught, partly in a gorse-root and partly in a biggish stone, and over he went. When he got up and surveyed his surroundings, he found himself in a patch of somewhat broken ground covered with small depressions and mounds. These latter, when he came to examine them, proved to be simply masses of flints embedded in mortar and grown over with turf. He must, he quite rightly concluded, be on the site of the preceptory he had promised to look at. It seemed not unlikely to reward the spade of the explorer; enough of the foundations was probably left at no great depth to throw a good deal of light on the general plan. He remembered vaguely that the Templars, to whom this site had belonged, were in the habit of building round churches, and he thought a particular series of the humps or mounds near him did appear to be arranged in something of a circular form. Few people can resist the temptation to try a little amateur research in a department quite outside their own, if only for the satisfaction of showing how successful they would have been had they only taken it up seriously. Our Professor, however, if he felt something of this mean desire, was also truly anxious to oblige Mr Disney. So he paced with care the circular area he had noticed, and wrote down its rough dimensions in his pocket-book. Then he proceeded to examine an oblong eminence which lay east of the centre of the circle, and seemed to his thinking likely to be the base of a platform or altar. At one end of it, the northern, a patch of the turf was gone – removed by some boy or other creature *feræ naturæ*. It might, he thought, be as well to probe the soil here for evidences of masonry, and he took out his knife and began scraping away the earth. And now followed another little discovery: a portion of soil fell inward as he scraped, and disclosed a small cavity. He lighted one match after another to help him to see of what nature the hole was; but the wind was too strong for them all. By tapping and scratching the sides with his knife, however, he was able to make out that it must be an artificial hole in masonry. It was rectangular, and the sides, top, and bottom, if not actually plastered, were smooth and regular. Of course it was empty. No! As he withdrew the knife he heard a metallic clink, and when he introduced his hand it met with a cylindrical object lying on the floor of the hole. Naturally enough, he picked it up, and when he brought it into the light, now fast fading, he could see that it, too, was of man's making – a metal tube about four inches long, and evidently of some considerable age.

By the time Parkins had made sure that there was nothing else in this odd receptacle, it was too late and too dark for him to think of undertaking any further search. What he had done had proved so unexpectedly interesting that he determined to sacrifice a little more of the daylight on the morrow to archaeology. The object which he now had safe in his pocket was bound to be of some slight value at least, he felt sure.

Bleak and solemn was the view on which he took a last look before starting homeward. A faint yellow light in the west showed the links, on which a few figures moving towards the club-house were still visible, the squat martello tower, the lights of Aldsey village, the pale ribbon of sands intersected at intervals by black wooden groynes, the dim and murmuring sea. The wind was bitter from the north, but was at his back when he set out for the Globe. He quickly rattled and clashed through the shingle and gained the sand, upon which, but for the groynes which had to be got over every few yards, the going was both good and quiet. One last look behind, to measure the distance he had made since leaving the ruined Templars' church, showed him a prospect of company on his walk, in the shape of a rather indistinct personage, who seemed to be making great efforts to catch up with him, but made little, if any, progress. I mean that there was an appearance of running about his movements, but that the distance between him and Parkins did not seem materially to lessen. So, at least, Parkins thought, and decided that he almost certainly did not know him, and that it would be absurd to wait until he came up. For all that, company, he began to think, would really be very welcome on that lonely shore, if only you could choose your companion. In his unenlightened days he had read of meetings in such places which even now would hardly bear thinking of. He went on thinking of them, however, until he reached home, and particularly of one which catches most people's fancy at some time of their childhood. 'Now I saw in my dream that Christian had gone but a very little way when he saw a foul fiend coming over the field to meet him.' 'What should I do now,' he thought, 'if I looked back and caught sight of a black figure sharply defined against the yellow sky, and saw that it had horns and wings? I wonder whether I should stand or run for it. Luckily, the gentleman behind is not of that kind, and he seems to be about as far off now as when I saw him first. Well, at this rate he won't get his dinner as soon as I shall; and, dear me! it's within a quarter of an hour of the time now. I must run!'

Parkins had, in fact, very little time for dressing. When he met the Colonel at dinner, Peace – or as much of her as that gentleman could manage – reigned once more in the military bosom; nor was she put to flight in the hours of bridge that followed dinner, for Parkins was a more than respectable player. When, therefore, he retired towards twelve o'clock, he felt that he had spent his evening in quite a satisfactory way, and that, even for so long as a fortnight or three weeks, life at the Globe would be supportable under similar conditions – 'especially,' thought he, 'if I go on improving my game.'

As he went along the passages he met the boots of the Globe, who stopped and said:

'Beg your pardon, sir, but as I was a-brushing your coat just now there was somethink fell out of the pocket. I put it on your chest of drawers, sir, in your room, sir – a piece of a pipe or somethink of that, sir. Thank you, sir. You'll find it on your chest of drawers, sir – yes, sir. Good night, sir.'

The speech served to remind Parkins of his little discovery of that afternoon. It was with some considerable curiosity that he turned it over by the light of his candles. It was of bronze, he now saw, and was shaped very much after the manner of the modern dog-whistle; in fact it was – yes, certainly it was – actually no more nor less than a whistle. He put it to his lips, but it was quite full of a fine, caked-up sand or earth, which would not yield to knocking, but must be loosened with a knife. Tidy as ever in his habits, Parkins cleared out the earth on to a piece of paper, and took the latter to the window to empty it out. The night was clear and bright, as he saw when he had opened the casement, and he stopped for an instant to look at the sea and note a belated wanderer stationed on the shore in front of the inn. Then he shut the window, a little surprised at the late hours people kept at Burnstow, and took his whistle to the light again. Why, surely there were marks on it, and not merely marks, but letters! A very little rubbing rendered the deeply-cut inscription quite legible, but the professor had to confess, after some earnest thought, that the meaning of it was as obscure to him as the writing on the wall to Belshazzar. There were legends both on the front and on the back of the whistle. The one read thus:

FLA
FUR BIS
FLE

The other:

卐 QUIS EST ISTE QUI UENIT 卐

'I ought to be able to make it out,' he thought; 'but I suppose I am a little rusty in my Latin. When I come to think of it, I don't believe I even know the word for a whistle. The long one does seem simple enough. It ought to mean, "Who is this who is coming?" Well, the best way to find out is evidently to whistle for him.'

He blew tentatively and stopped suddenly, startled and yet pleased at the note he had elicited. It had a quality of infinite distance in it, and, soft as it was, he somehow felt it must be audible for miles round. It was a sound, too, that seemed to have the power (which many scents possess) of forming pictures in the brain. He saw quite clearly for a moment a vision of a wide, dark expanse at night, with a fresh wind blowing, and in the midst a lonely figure – how employed, he could not tell. Perhaps he would have seen more had not the picture been broken by the sudden surge of a gust of wind against his casement, so sudden that it made him look up, just in time to see the white glint of a sea-bird's wing somewhere outside the dark panes.

The sound of the whistle had so fascinated him that he

could not help trying it once more, this time more boldly. The note was little, if at all, louder than before, and repetition broke the illusion – no picture followed, as he had half hoped it might. 'But what is this? Goodness! what force the wind can get up in a few minutes! What a tremendous gust! There! I knew that window-fastening was no use! Ah! I thought so – both candles out. It's enough to tear the room to pieces.'

The first thing was to get the window shut. While you might count twenty Parkins was struggling with the small casement, and felt almost as if he were pushing back a sturdy burglar, so strong was the pressure. It slackened all at once, and the window banged to and latched itself. Now to relight the candles and see what damage, if any, had been done. No, nothing seemed amiss; no glass even was broken in the casement. But the noise had evidently roused at least one member of the household: the Colonel was to be heard stumping in his stockinged feet on the floor above, and growling.

Quickly as it had risen, the wind did not fall at once. On it went, moaning and rushing past the house, at times rising to a cry so desolate that, as Parkins disinterestedly said, it might have made fanciful people feel quite uncomfortable; even the unimaginative, he thought after a quarter of an hour, might be happier without it.

Whether it was the wind, or the excitement of golf, or of the researches in the preceptory that kept Parkins awake, he was not sure. Awake he remained, in any case, long enough to fancy (as I am afraid I often do myself under such conditions) that he was the victim of all manner of fatal disorders: he would lie counting the beats of his heart, convinced that it was going to stop work every moment, and would entertain grave suspicions of his lungs, brain, liver, etc. – suspicions which he was sure would be dispelled by the return of daylight, but which until then refused to be put aside. He found a little vicarious comfort in the idea that someone else was in the same boat. A near neighbour (in the darkness it was not easy to tell his direction) was tossing and rustling in his bed, too.

The next stage was that Parkins shut his eyes and determined to give sleep every chance. Here again over-excitement asserted itself in another form – that of making pictures. *Experto crede*, pictures do come to the closed eyes of one trying to sleep, and are often so little to his taste that he must open his eyes and disperse them.

Parkins's experience on this occasion was a very distressing one. He found that the picture which presented itself to him was continuous. When he opened his eyes, of course, it went; but when he shut them once more it framed itself afresh, and acted itself out again, neither quicker nor slower than before. What he saw was this:

A long stretch of shore – shingle edged by sand, and intersected at short intervals with black groynes running down to the water – a scene, in fact, so like that of his afternoon's walk that, in the absence of any landmark, it could not be distinguished therefrom. The light was obscure, conveying an impression of gathering storm, late winter evening, and slight cold rain. On this bleak stage at first no actor was visible. Then, in the distance, a bobbing black object appeared; a moment more, and it was a man running, jumping, clambering over the groynes, and every few seconds looking eagerly back. The nearer he came the more obvious it was that he was not only anxious, but even terribly frightened, though his face was not to be distinguished. He was, moreover, almost at the end of his strength. On he came; each successive obstacle seemed to cause him more difficulty than the last. 'Will he get over this next one?' thought Parkins; 'it seems a little higher than the others.' Yes; half climbing, half throwing himself, he did get over, and fell all in a heap on the other side (the side nearest to the spectator). There, as if really unable to get up again, he remained crouching under the groyne, looking up in an attitude of painful anxiety.

So far no cause whatever for the fear of the runner had been shown; but now there began to be seen, far up the shore, a little flicker of something light-coloured moving to and fro with great swiftness and irregularity. Rapidly growing larger, it, too, declared itself as a figure in pale, fluttering draperies, ill-defined. There was something about its motion which made Parkins very unwilling to see it at close quarters. It would stop, raise arms, bow itself toward the sand, then run stooping across the beach to the water-edge and back again; and then, rising upright, once more continue its course forward at a speed that was startling and terrifying. The moment came when the pursuer was hovering about from left to right only a few yards beyond the groyne where the runner lay in hiding. After two or three ineffectual castings hither and thither it came to a stop, stood upright, with arms raised high, and then darted straight forward towards the groyne.

It was at this point that Parkins always failed in his resolution to keep his eyes shut. With many misgivings as to incipient failure of eyesight, over-worked brain, excessive smoking, and so on, he finally resigned himself to light his candle, get out a book, and pass the night waking, rather than be tormented by this persistent panorama, which he saw clearly enough could only be a morbid reflection of his walk and his thoughts on that very day.

The scraping of match on box and the glare of light must have startled some creatures of the night – rats or what not

– which he heard scurry across the floor from the side of his bed with much rustling. Dear, dear! the match is out! Fool that it is! But the second one burnt better, and a candle and book were duly procured, over which Parkins pored till sleep of a wholesome kind came upon him, and that in no long space. For about the first time in his orderly and prudent life he forgot to blow out the candle, and when he was called next morning at eight there was still a flicker in the socket and a sad mess of guttered grease on the top of the little table.

After breakfast he was in his room, putting the finishing touches to his golfing costume – fortune had again allotted the Colonel to him for a partner – when one of the maids came in.

'Oh, if you please,' she said, 'would you like any extra blankets on your bed, sir?'

'Ah! thank you,' said Parkins. 'Yes, I think I should like one. It seems likely to turn rather colder.'

In a very short time the maid was back with the blanket.

'Which bed should I put it on, sir?' she asked.

'What? Why, that one – the one I slept in last night,' he said, pointing to it.

'Oh yes! I beg your pardon, sir, but you seemed to have tried both of 'em; leastways, we had to make 'em both up this morning.'

'Really? How very absurd!' said Parkins. 'I certainly never touched the other, except to lay some things on it. Did it actually seem to have been slept in?'

'Oh yes, sir!' said the maid. 'Why, all the things was crumpled and throwed about all ways, if you'll excuse me, sir – quite as if anyone 'adn't passed but a very poor night, sir.'

'Dear me,' said Parkins. 'Well, I may have disordered it more than I thought when I unpacked my things. I'm very sorry to have given you the extra trouble, I'm sure. I expect a friend of mine soon, by the way – a gentleman from Cambridge – to come and occupy it for a night or two. That will be all right, I suppose, won't it?'

'Oh yes, to be sure, sir. Thank you, sir. It's no trouble, I'm sure,' said the maid, and departed to giggle with her colleagues.

Parkins set forth, with a stern determination to improve his game.

I am glad to be able to report that he succeeded so far in this enterprise that the Colonel, who had been rather repining at the prospect of a second day's play in his company, became quite chatty as the morning advanced; and his voice boomed out over the flats, as certain also of our own minor poets have said, 'like some great bourdon in a minster tower'.

'Extraordinary wind, that, we had last night,' he said. 'In my old home we should have said someone had been whistling for it.'

'Should you, indeed!' said Parkins. 'Is there a superstition of that kind still current in your part of the country?'

'I don't know about superstition,' said the Colonel. 'They believe in it all over Denmark and Norway, as well as on the Yorkshire coast; and my experience is, mind you, that there's generally something at the bottom of what these country-folk hold to, and have held to for generations. But it's your drive' (or whatever it might have been: the golfing reader will have to imagine appropriate digressions at the proper intervals).

When conversation was resumed, Parkins said, with a slight hesitancy:

'Apropos of what you were saying just now, Colonel, I think I ought to tell you that my own views on such subjects are very strong. I am, in fact, a convinced disbeliever in what is called the "supernatural".'

'What!' said the Colonel, 'do you mean to tell me you don't believe in second-sight, or ghosts, or anything of that kind?'

'In nothing whatever of that kind,' returned Parkins firmly.

'Well,' said the Colonel, 'but it appears to me at that rate, sir, that you must be little better than a Sadducee.'

Parkins was on the point of answering that, in his opinion, the Sadducees were the most sensible persons he had ever read of in the Old Testament; but, feeling some doubt as to whether much mention of them was to be found in that work, he preferred to laugh the accusation off.

'Perhaps I am,' he said; 'but— Here, give me my cleek, boy! – Excuse me one moment, Colonel.' A short interval. 'Now, as to whistling for the wind, let me give you my theory about it. The laws which govern winds are really not at all perfectly known – to fisher-folk and such, of course, not known at all. A man or woman of eccentric habits, perhaps, or a stranger, is seen repeatedly on the beach at some unusual hour, and is heard whistling. Soon afterwards a violent wind rises; a man who could read the sky perfectly or who possessed a barometer could have foretold that it would. The simple people of a fishing-village have no barometers, and only a few rough rules for prophesying weather. What more natural than that the eccentric personage I postulated should be regarded as having raised the wind, or that he or she should clutch eagerly at the reputation of being able to do so? Now, take last night's wind: as it happens, I myself was whistling. I blew a whistle twice, and the wind seemed to come absolutely in answer to my call. If anyone had seen me—'

The audience had been a little restive under this harangue, and Parkins had, I fear, fallen somewhat into the tone of a lecturer; but at the last sentence the Colonel stopped.

'Whistling, were you?' he said. 'And what sort of whistle did you use? Play this stroke first.' Interval.

'About that whistle you were asking, Colonel. It's rather a curious one. I have it in my— No; I see I've left it in my room. As a matter of fact; I found it yesterday.'

And then Parkins narrated the manner of his discovery of the whistle, upon hearing which the Colonel grunted, and opined that, in Parkins's place, he should himself be careful about using a thing that had belonged to a set of Papists, of whom, speaking generally, it might be affirmed that you never knew what they might not have been up to. From this topic he diverged to the enormities of the Vicar, who had given notice on the previous Sunday that Friday would be the Feast of St Thomas the Apostle, and that there would be service at eleven o'clock in the church. This and other similar proceedings constituted in the Colonel's view a strong presumption that the Vicar was a concealed Papist, if not a Jesuit; and Parkins, who could not very readily follow the Colonel in this region, did not disagree with him. In fact, they got on so well together in the morning that there was no talk on either side of their separating after lunch.

Both continued to play well during the afternoon, or, at least, well enough to make them forget everything else until the light began to fail them. Not until then did Parkins remember that he had meant to do some more investigating at the preceptory; but it was of no great importance, he reflected. One day was as good as another; he might as well go home with the Colonel.

As they turned the corner of the house, the Colonel was almost knocked down by a boy who rushed into him at the very top of his speed, and then, instead of running away, remained hanging on to him and panting. The first words of the warrior were naturally those of reproof and objurgation, but he very quickly discerned that the boy was almost speechless with fright. Inquiries were useless at first. When the boy got his breath he began to howl, and still clung to the Colonel's legs. He was at last detached, but continued to howl.

'What in the world *is* the matter with you? What have you been up to? What have you seen?' said the two men.

'Ow, I seen it wive at me out of the winder,' wailed the boy, 'and I don't like it.'

'What window?' said the irritated Colonel. 'Come, pull yourself together, my boy.'

'The front winder it was, at the 'otel,' said the boy. At this point Parkins was in favour of sending the boy home, but the Colonel refused; he wanted to get to the bottom of it, he said; it was most dangerous to give a boy such a fright as this one had had, and if it turned out that people had been playing jokes, they should suffer for it in some way. And by a series of questions he made out this story: The boy had been playing about on the grass in front of the Globe with some others; then they had gone home to their teas, and he was just going, when he happened to look up at the front winder and see it a-wiving at him. *It* seemed to be a figure of some sort, in white as far as he knew – couldn't see its face; but it wived at him, and it warn't a right thing – not to say not a right person. Was there a light in the room? No, he didn't think to look if there was a light. Which was the window? Was it the top one or the second one? The seckind one it was – the big winder what got two little uns at the sides.

'Very well, my boy,' said the Colonel, after a few more questions. 'You run away home now. I expect it was some person trying to give you a start. Another time, like a brave English boy, you just throw a stone – well, no, not that exactly, but you go and speak to the waiter, or to Mr Simpson, the landlord, and – yes – and say that I advised you to do so.'

The boy's face expressed some of the doubt he felt as to the likelihood of Mr Simpson's lending a favourable ear to his complaint, but the Colonel did not appear to perceive this, and went on:

'And here's a sixpence – no, I see it's a shilling – and you be off home, and don't think any more about it.'

The youth hurried off with agitated thanks, and the Colonel and Parkins went round to the front of the Globe and reconnoitred. There was only one window answering to the description they had been hearing.

'Well, that's curious,' said Parkins; 'it's evidently my window the lad was talking about. Will you come up for a moment, Colonel Wilson? We ought to be able to see if anyone has been taking liberties in my room.'

They were soon in the passage, and Parkins made as if to open the door. Then he stopped and felt in his pockets.

'This is more serious than I thought,' was his next remark. 'I remember now that before I started this morning I locked the door. It is locked now, and, what is more, here is the key.' And he held it up. 'Now,' he went on, 'if the servants are in the habit of going into one's room during the day when one is away, I can only say that – well, that I don't approve of it at all.' Conscious of a somewhat weak climax, he busied himself in opening the door (which was indeed locked) and in lighting candles. 'No,' he said, 'nothing seems disturbed.'

'Except your bed,' put in the Colonel.

'Excuse me, that isn't my bed,' said Parkins. 'I don't use

that one. But it does look as if someone had been playing tricks with it.'

It certainly did: the clothes were bundled up and twisted together in a most tortuous confusion. Parkins pondered.

'That must be it,' he said at last: 'I disordered the clothes last night in unpacking, and they haven't made it since. Perhaps they came in to make it, and that boy saw them through the window; and then they were called away and locked the door after them. Yes, I think that must be it.'

'Well, ring and ask,' said the Colonel, and this appealed to Parkins as practical.

The maid appeared, and, to make a long story short, deposed that she had made the bed in the morning when the gentleman was in the room, and hadn't been there since. No, she hadn't no other key. Mr Simpson he kep' the keys; he'd be able to tell the gentleman if anyone had been up.

This was a puzzle. Investigation showed that nothing of value had been taken, and Parkins remembered the disposition of the small objects on tables and so forth well enough to be pretty sure that no pranks had been played with them. Mr and Mrs Simpson furthermore agreed that neither of them had given the duplicate key of the room to any person whatever during the day. Nor could Parkins, fair-minded man as he was, detect anything in the demeanour of master, mistress, or maid that indicated guilt. He was much more inclined to think that the boy had been imposing on the Colonel.

The latter was unwontedly silent and pensive at dinner and throughout the evening. When he bade good night to Parkins, he murmured in a gruff undertone:

'You know where I am if you want me during the night.'

'Why, yes, thank you, Colonel Wilson, I think I do; but there isn't much prospect of my disturbing you, I hope. By the way,' he added, 'did I show you that old whistle I spoke of? I think not. Well, here it is.'

The Colonel turned it over gingerly in the light of the candle.

'Can you make anything of the inscription?' asked Parkins, as he took it back.

'No, not in this light. What do you mean to do with it?'

'Oh, well, when I get back to Cambridge I shall submit it to some of the archaeologists there, and see what they think of it; and very likely, if they consider it worth having, I may present it to one of the museums.'

''M!' said the Colonel. 'Well, you may be right. All I know is that, if it were mine, I should chuck it straight into the sea. It's no use talking, I'm well aware, but I expect that with you it's a case of live and learn. I hope so, I'm sure, and I wish you a good night.'

He turned away, leaving Parkins in act to speak at the bottom of the stair, and soon each was in his own bedroom.

By some unfortunate accident, there were neither blinds nor curtains to the windows of the Professor's room. The previous night he had thought little of this, but to-night there seemed every prospect of a bright moon rising to shine directly on his bed, and probably wake him later on. When he noticed this he was a good deal annoyed, but, with an ingenuity which I can only envy, he succeeded in rigging up, with the help of a railway-rug, some safety-pins, and a stick and umbrella, a screen which, if it only held together, would completely keep the moonlight off his bed. And shortly afterwards he was comfortably in that bed. When he had read a somewhat solid work long enough to produce a decided wish for sleep, he cast a drowsy glance round the room, blew out the candle, and fell back upon the pillow.

He must have slept soundly for an hour or more, when

a sudden clatter shook him up in a most unwelcome manner. In a moment he realized what had happened: his carefully-constructed screen had given way, and a very bright frosty moon was shining directly on his face. This was highly annoying. Could he possibly get up and reconstruct the screen? or could he manage to sleep if he did not?

For some minutes he lay and pondered over the possibilities; then he turned over sharply, and with all his eyes open lay breathlessly listening. There had been a movement, he was sure, in the empty bed on the opposite side of the room. To-morrow he would have it moved, for there must be rats or something playing about in it. It was quiet now. No! the commotion began again. There was a rustling and shaking: surely more than any rat could cause.

I can figure to myself something of the Professor's bewilderment and horror, for I have in a dream thirty years back seen the same thing happen; but the reader will hardly, perhaps, imagine how dreadful it was to him to see a figure suddenly sit up in what he had known was an empty bed. He was out of his own bed in one bound, and made a dash towards the window, where lay his only weapon, the stick with which he had propped his screen. This was, as it turned out, the worst thing he could have done, because the personage in the empty bed, with a sudden smooth motion, slipped from the bed and took up a position, with outspread arms, between the two beds, and in front of the door. Parkins watched it in a horrid perplexity. Somehow, the idea of getting past it and escaping through the door was intolerable to him; he could not have borne – he didn't know why – to touch it; and as for its touching him, he would sooner dash himself through the window than have that happen. It stood for the moment in a band of dark shadow, and he had not seen what its face was like. Now it began to move, in a stooping posture, and all at once the spectator realized, with some horror and some relief, that it must be blind, for it seemed to feel about it with its muffled arms in a groping and random fashion. Turning half away from him, it became suddenly conscious of the bed he had just left, and darted towards it, and bent over and felt the pillows in a way which made Parkins shudder as he had never in his life thought it possible. In a very few moments it seemed to know that the bed was empty, and then, moving forward into the area of light and facing the window, it showed for the first time what manner of thing it was.

Parkins, who very much dislikes being questioned about it, did once describe something of it in my hearing, and I gathered that what he chiefly remembers about it is a horrible, an intensely horrible, face *of crumpled linen*. What expression he read upon it he could not or would not tell, but that the fear of it went nigh to maddening him is certain.

But he was not at leisure to watch it for long. With formidable quickness it moved into the middle of the room, and, as it groped and waved, one corner of its draperies swept across Parkins's face. He could not – though he knew how perilous a sound was – he could not keep back a cry of disgust, and this gave the searcher an instant clue. It leapt towards him upon the instant, and the next moment he was half-way through the window backwards, uttering cry upon cry at the utmost pitch of his voice, and the linen face was thrust close into his own. At this, almost the last possible second, deliverance came, as you will have guessed: the Colonel burst the door open, and was just in time to see the dreadful group at the window. When he reached the figures only one was left. Parkins sank forward into the room in a faint, and before him on the floor lay a tumbled heap of bed-clothes.

Colonel Wilson asked no questions, but busied himself in keeping everyone else out of the room and in getting Parkins back to his bed; and himself, wrapped in a rug, occupied the other bed for the rest of the night. Early on the next day Rogers arrived, more welcome than he would have been a day before, and the three of them held a very long consultation in the Professor's room. At the end of it the Colonel left the hotel door carrying a small object between his finger and thumb, which he cast as far into the sea as a very brawny arm could send it. Later on the smoke of a burning ascended from the back premises of the Globe.

Exactly what explanation was patched up for the staff and visitors at the hotel I must confess I do not recollect. The Professor was somehow cleared of the ready suspicion of delirium tremens, and the hotel of the reputation of a troubled house.

There is not much question as to what would have happened to Parkins if the Colonel had not intervened when he did. He would either have fallen out of the window or else lost his wits. But it is not so evident what more the creature that came in answer to the whistle could have done than frighten. There seemed to be absolutely nothing material about it save the bed-clothes of which it had made itself a body. The Colonel, who remembered a not very dissimilar occurrence in India, was of opinion that if Parkins had closed with it it could really have done very little, and that its one power was that of frightening. The whole thing, he said, served to confirm his opinion of the Church of Rome.

There is really nothing more to tell, but, as you may imagine, the Professor's views on certain points are less clear cut than they used to be. His nerves, too, have suffered: he cannot even now see a surplice hanging on a door quite unmoved, and the spectacle of a scarecrow in a field late on a winter afternoon has cost him more than one sleepless night.

SAKI

THE OPEN WINDOW

'MY AUNT WILL be down presently, Mr Nuttel,' said a very self-possessed young lady of fifteen; 'in the meantime you must try and put up with me.'

Framton Nuttel endeavoured to say the correct something which should duly flatter the niece of the moment without unduly discounting the aunt that was to come. Privately he doubted more than ever whether these formal visits on a succession of total strangers would do much towards helping the nerve cure which he was supposed to be undergoing.

'I know how it will be,' his sister had said when he was preparing to migrate to this rural retreat; 'you will bury yourself down there and not speak to a living soul, and your nerves will be worse than ever from moping. I shall just give you letters of introduction to all the people I know there. Some of them, as far as I can remember, were quite nice.'

Framton wondered whether Mrs Sappleton, the lady to whom he was presenting one of the letters of introduction, came into the nice division.

'Do you know many of the people round here?' asked the niece, when she judged that they had had sufficient silent communion.

'Hardly a soul,' said Framton. 'My sister was staying here, at the rectory, you know, some four years ago, and she gave me letters of introduction to some of the people here.'

He made the last statement in a tone of distinct regret.

'Then you know practically nothing about my aunt?' pursued the self-possessed young lady.

'Only her name and address,' admitted the caller. He was wondering whether Mrs Sappleton was in the married or widowed state. An undefinable something about the room seemed to suggest masculine habitation.

'Her great tragedy happened just three years ago,' said the child; 'that would be since your sister's time.'

'Her tragedy?' asked Framton; somehow in this restful country spot tragedies seemed out of place.

'You may wonder why we keep that window wide open on an October afternoon,' said the niece, indicating a large French window that opened on to a lawn.

'It is quite warm for the time of the year,' said Framton; 'but has that window got anything to do with the tragedy?'

'Out through that window, three years ago to a day, her husband and her two young brothers went off for their day's shooting. They never came back. In crossing the moor to their favourite snipe-shooting ground they were all three engulfed in a treacherous piece of bog. It had been that dreadful wet summer, you know, and places that were safe in other years gave way suddenly without warning. Their bodies were never recovered. That was the dreadful part of it.' Here the child's voice lost its self-possessed note and became falteringly human. 'Poor aunt always thinks that they will come back some day, they and the little brown spaniel that was lost with them, and walk in at that window just as they used to do. That is why the window is kept open every evening till it is quite dusk. Poor dear aunt, she has often told me how they went out, her husband with his white waterproof coat over his arm, and Ronnie, her youngest brother, singing, "Bertie, why do you bound?" as he always did to tease her, because she said it got on her nerves. Do you know, sometimes on still, quiet evenings like this, I almost get a creepy feeling that they will all walk in through that window—'

She broke off with a little shudder. It was a relief to Framton when the aunt bustled into the room with a whirl of apologies for being late in making her appearance.

'I hope Vera has been amusing you?' she said.

'She has been very interesting,' said Framton.

'I hope you don't mind the open window,' said Mrs Sappleton briskly; 'my husband and brothers will be home directly from shooting, and they always come in this way. They've been out for snipe in the marshes to-day, so they'll make a fine mess over my poor carpets. So like you men-folk, isn't it?'

She rattled on cheerfully about the shooting and the scarcity of birds, and the prospects for duck in the winter. To Framton it was all purely horrible. He made a desperate but only partially successful effort to turn the talk on to a less ghastly topic; he was conscious that his hostess was giving him only a fragment of her attention, and her eyes were constantly straying past him to the open window and the lawn beyond. It was certainly an unfortunate coincidence that he should have paid his visit on this tragic anniversary.

'The doctors agree in ordering me complete rest, an absence of mental excitement, and avoidance of anything in the nature of violent physical exercise,' announced Framton, who laboured under the tolerably widespread delusion that total strangers and chance acquaintances are hungry for the least detail of one's ailments and infirmities, their cause and cure. 'On the matter of diet they are not so much in agreement,' he continued.

'No?' said Mrs Sappleton, in a voice which only replaced a yawn at the last moment. Then she suddenly brightened into alert attention – but not to what Framton was saying.

'Here they are at last!' she cried. 'Just in time for tea, and don't they look as if they were muddy up to the eyes!'

Framton shivered slightly and turned towards the niece with a look intended to convey sympathetic comprehension. The child was staring out through the open window with dazed horror in her eyes. In a chill shock of nameless fear Framton swung round in his seat and looked in the same direction.

In the deepening twilight three figures were walking across the lawn towards the window; they all carried guns under their arms, and one of them was additionally burdened with a white coat hung over his shoulders. A tired brown spaniel kept close at their heels. Noiselessly they neared the house, and then a hoarse young voice chanted out of the dusk: 'I said, Bertie, why do you bound?'

Framton grabbed wildly at his stick and hat; the hall-door, the gravel-drive, and the front gate were dimly noted stages in his headlong retreat. A cyclist coming along the road had to run into the hedge to avoid imminent collision.

'Here we are, my dear,' said the bearer of the white mackintosh, coming in through the window; 'fairly muddy, but most of it's dry. Who was that who bolted out as we came up?'

'A most extraordinary man, a Mr Nuttel,' said Mrs Sappleton; 'could only talk about his illnesses, and dashed off without a word of good-bye or apology when you arrived. One would think he had seen a ghost.'

'I expect it was the spaniel,' said the niece calmly; 'he told me he had a horror of dogs. He was once hunted into a cemetery somewhere on the banks of the Ganges by a pack of pariah dogs, and had to spend the night in a newly dug grave with the creatures snarling and grinning and foaming just above him. Enough to make any one lose their nerve.'

Romance at short notice was her speciality.

KATHERINE MANSFIELD

THE DAUGHTERS OF THE LATE COLONEL

I

THE WEEK AFTER was one of the busiest weeks of their lives. Even when they went to bed it was only their bodies that lay down and rested; their minds went on, thinking things out, talking things over, wondering, deciding, trying to remember where . . .

Constantia lay like a statue, her hands by her sides, her feet just overlapping each other, the sheet up to her chin. She stared at the ceiling.

'Do you think father would mind if we gave his top-hat to the porter?'

'The porter?' snapped Josephine. 'Why ever the porter? What a very extraordinary idea!'

'Because,' said Constantia slowly, 'he must often have to go to funerals. And I noticed at – at the cemetery that he only had a bowler.' She paused. 'I thought then how very much he'd appreciate a top-hat. We ought to give him a present, too. He was always very nice to father.'

'But,' cried Josephine, flouncing on her pillow and staring across the dark at Constantia, 'father's head!' And suddenly, for one awful moment, she nearly giggled. Not, of course, that she felt in the least like giggling. It must have been habit. Years ago, when they had stayed awake at night talking, their beds had simply heaved. And now the porter's head, disappearing, popped out, like a candle, under father's hat. . . . The giggle mounted, mounted; she clenched her hands; she fought it down; she frowned fiercely at the dark and said 'Remember' terribly sternly.

'We can decide to-morrow,' she said.

Constantia had noticed nothing; she sighed.

'Do you think we ought to have our dressing-gowns dyed as well?'

'Black?' almost shrieked Josephine.

'Well, what else?' said Constantia. 'I was thinking – it doesn't seem quite sincere, in a way, to wear black out of doors and when we're fully dressed, and then when we're at home—'

'But nobody sees us,' said Josephine. She gave the bed-clothes such a twitch that both her feet became uncovered and she had to creep up the pillows to get them well under again.

'Kate does,' said Constantia. 'And the postman very well might.'

Josephine thought of her dark-red slippers, which matched her dressing-gown, and of Constantia's favourite indefinite green ones which went with hers. Black! Two black dressing-gowns and two pairs of black woolly slippers, creeping off to the bathroom like black cats.

'I don't think it's absolutely necessary,' said she.

Silence. Then Constantia said, 'We shall have to post the papers with the notice in them to-morrow to catch the Ceylon mail.... How many letters have we had up till now?'

'Twenty-three.'

Josephine had replied to them all, and twenty-three times when she came to 'We miss our dear father so much' she had broken down and had to use her handkerchief, and on some of them even to soak up a very light-blue tear with an edge of blotting-paper. Strange! She couldn't have put it on – but twenty-three times. Even now, though, when she said over to herself sadly 'We miss our dear father *so* much,' she could have cried if she'd wanted to.

'Have you got enough stamps?' came from Constantia.

'Oh, how can I tell?' said Josephine crossly. 'What's the good of asking me that now?'

'I was just wondering,' said Constantia mildly.

Silence again. There came a little rustle, a scurry, a hop.

'A mouse,' said Constantia.

'It can't be a mouse because there aren't any crumbs,' said Josephine.

'But it doesn't know there aren't,' said Constantia.

A spasm of pity squeezed her heart. Poor little thing! She wished she'd left a tiny piece of biscuit on the dressing-table. It was awful to think of it not finding anything. What would it do?

'I can't think how they manage to live at all,' she said slowly.

'Who?' demanded Josephine.

And Constantia said more loudly than she meant to, 'Mice.'

Josephine was furious. 'Oh, what nonsense, Con!' she said. 'What have mice got to do with it? You're asleep.'

'I don't think I am,' said Constantia. She shut her eyes to make sure. She was.

Josephine arched her spine, pulled up her knees, folded her arms so that her fists came under her ears, and pressed her cheek hard against the pillow.

II

Another thing which complicated matters was they had Nurse Andrews staying on with them that week. It was their own fault; they had asked her. It was Josephine's idea. On the morning – well, on the last morning, when the doctor had gone, Josephine had said to Constantia, 'Don't you think it would be rather nice if we asked Nurse Andrews to stay on for a week as our guest?'

'Very nice,' said Constantia.

'I thought,' went on Josephine quickly, 'I should just say this afternoon, after I've paid her, "My sister and I would be very pleased, after all you've done for us, Nurse Andrews, if you would stay on for a week as our guest." I'd have to put that in about being our guest in case—'

'Oh, but she could hardly expect to be paid!' cried Constantia.

'One never knows,' said Josephine sagely.

Nurse Andrews had, of course, jumped at the idea. But it was a bother. It meant they had to have regular sit-down meals at the proper times, whereas if they'd been alone they could just have asked Kate if she wouldn't have minded bringing them a tray wherever they were. And meal-times now that the strain was over were rather a trial.

Nurse Andrews was simply fearful about butter. Really they couldn't help feeling that about butter, at least, she took advantage of their kindness. And she had that maddening habit of asking for just an inch more bread to finish what she had on her plate, and then, at the last mouthful, absent-mindedly – of course it wasn't absent-mindedly – taking another helping. Josephine got very red when this happened, and she fastened her small, bead-like eyes on the tablecloth as if she saw a minute strange insect creeping through the web of it. But Constantia's long, pale face lengthened and set, and she gazed away – away – far over the desert, to where that line of camels unwound like a thread of wool....

'When I was with Lady Tukes,' said Nurse Andrews, 'she had such a dainty little contrayvance for the buttah. It was a silvah Cupid balanced on the – on the bordah of a glass dish, holding a tayny fork. And when you wanted some buttah you simply pressed his foot and he bent down and speared you a piece. It was quite a gayme.'

Josephine could hardly bear that. But 'I think those things are very extravagant' was all she said.

'But whey?' asked Nurse Andrews, beaming through her eyeglasses. 'No one, surely, would take more buttah than one wanted – would one?'

'Ring, Con,' cried Josephine. She couldn't trust herself to reply.

And proud young Kate, the enchanted princess, came in to see what the old tabbies wanted now. She snatched away their plates of mock something or other and slapped down a white, terrified blancmange.

'Jam, please, Kate,' said Josephine kindly.

Kate knelt and burst open the sideboard, lifted the lid of the jam-pot, saw it was empty, put it on the table, and stalked off.

'I'm afraid,' said Nurse Andrews a moment later, 'there isn't any.'

'Oh, what a bother!' said Josephine. She bit her lip. 'What had we better do?'

Constantia looked dubious. 'We can't disturb Kate again,' she said softly.

Nurse Andrews waited, smiling at them both. Her eyes wandered, spying at everything behind her eyeglasses. Constantia in despair went back to her camels. Josephine frowned heavily – concentrated. If it hadn't been for this idiotic woman she and Con would, of course, have eaten their blancmange without. Suddenly the idea came.

'I know,' she said. 'Marmalade. There's some marmalade in the sideboard. Get it, Con.'

'I hope,' laughed Nurse Andrews – and her laugh was like a spoon tinkling against a medicine-glass – 'I hope it's not very bittah marmalayde.'

III

But, after all, it was not long now, and then she'd be gone for good. And there was no getting over the fact that she had been very kind to father. She had nursed him day and night at the end. Indeed, both Constantia and Josephine felt privately she had rather overdone the not leaving him at the very last. For when they had gone in to say good-bye Nurse Andrews had sat beside his bed the whole time, holding his wrist and pretending to look at her watch. It couldn't have been necessary. It was so tactless, too. Supposing father had wanted to say something – something private to them. Not that he had. Oh, far from it! He lay there, purple, a dark, angry purple in the face, and never even looked at them when they came in. Then, as they were standing there, wondering what to do, he had suddenly opened one eye. Oh, what a difference it would have made, what a difference to their memory of him, how much easier to tell people about it, if he had only opened both! But no – one eye only. It glared at them a moment and then . . . went out.

IV

It had made it very awkward for them when Mr Farolles, of St John's, called the same afternoon.

'The end was quite peaceful, I trust?' were the first words he said as he glided towards them through the dark drawing-room.

'Quite,' said Josephine faintly. They both hung their

heads. Both of them felt certain that eye wasn't at all a peaceful eye.

'Won't you sit down?' said Josephine.

'Thank you, Miss Pinner,' said Mr Farolles gratefully. He folded his coat-tails and began to lower himself into father's armchair, but just as he touched it he almost sprang up and slid into the next chair instead.

He coughed. Josephine clasped her hands; Constantia looked vague.

'I want you to feel, Miss Pinner,' said Mr Farolles, 'and you, Miss Constantia, that I'm trying to be helpful. I want to be helpful to you both, if you will let me. These are the times,' said Mr Farolles, very simply and earnestly, 'when God means us to be helpful to one another.'

'Thank you very much, Mr Farolles,' said Josephine and Constantia.

'Not at all,' said Mr Farolles gently. He drew his kid gloves through his fingers and leaned forward. 'And if either of you would like a little Communion, either or both of you, here *and* now, you have only to tell me. A little Communion is often very help – a great comfort,' he added tenderly.

But the idea of a little Communion terrified them. What! In the drawing-room by themselves – with no – no altar or anything! The piano would be much too high, thought Constantia, and Mr Farolles could not possibly lean over it with the chalice. And Kate would be sure to come bursting in and interrupt them, thought Josephine. And supposing the bell rang in the middle? It might be somebody important – about their mourning. Would they get up reverently and go out, or would they have to wait . . . in torture?

'Perhaps you will send round a note by your good Kate if you would care for it later,' said Mr Farolles.

'Oh yes, thank you very much!' they both said.

Mr Farolles got up and took his black straw hat from the round table.

'And about the funeral,' he said softly. 'I may arrange that – as your dear father's old friend and yours, Miss Pinner – and Miss Constantia?'

Josephine and Constantia got up too.

'I should like it to be quite simple,' said Josephine firmly, 'and not too expensive. At the same time, I should like—'

'A good one that will last,' thought dreamy Constantia, as if Josephine were buying a night-gown. But, of course, Josephine didn't say that. 'One suitable to our father's position.' She was very nervous.

'I'll run round to our good friend Mr Knight,' said Mr Farolles soothingly. 'I will ask him to come and see you. I am sure you will find him very helpful indeed.'

V

Well, at any rate, all that part of it was over, though neither of them could possibly believe that father was never coming back. Josephine had had a moment of absolute terror at the cemetery, while the coffin was lowered, to think that she and Constantia had done this thing without asking his permission. What would father say when he found out? For he was bound to find out sooner or later. He always did. 'Buried. You two girls had me *buried*!' She heard his stick thumping. Oh, what would they say? What possible excuse could they make? It sounded such an appallingly heartless thing to do. Such a wicked advantage to take of a person because he happened to be helpless at the moment. The other people seemed to treat it all as a matter of course. They were strangers; they couldn't be expected to understand that father was the very last person for such a thing to happen to. No, the entire blame for it all would fall on her and Constantia. And the expense, she thought, stepping into the tight-buttoned cab. When she had to show him the bills. What would he say then?

She heard him absolutely roaring. 'And do you expect me to pay for this gimcrack excursion of yours?'

'Oh,' groaned poor Josephine aloud, 'we shouldn't have done it, Con!'

And Constantia, pale as a lemon in all that blackness, said in a frightened whisper, 'Done what, Jug?'

'Let them bu-bury father like that,' said Josephine, breaking down and crying into her new, queer-smelling mourning handkerchief.

'But what else could we have done?' asked Constantia wonderingly. 'We couldn't have kept him, Jug – we couldn't have kept him unburied. At any rate, not in a flat that size.'

Josephine blew her nose; the cab was dreadfully stuffy.

'I don't know,' she said forlornly. 'It is all so dreadful. I feel we ought to have tried to, just for a time at least. To make perfectly sure. One thing's certain' – and her tears sprang out again – 'father will never forgive us for this – never!'

VI

Father would never forgive them. That was what they felt more than ever when, two mornings later, they went into his room to go through his things. They had discussed it quite calmly. It was even down on Josephine's list of things to be done. *Go through father's things and settle about them.* But that was a very different matter from saying after breakfast:

'Well, are you ready, Con?'

'Yes, Jug – when you are.'

'Then I think we'd better get it over.'

It was dark in the hall. It had been a rule for years never to disturb father in the morning, whatever happened. And now they were going to open the door without knocking even. . . . Constantia's eyes were enormous at the idea; Josephine felt weak in the knees.

'You – you go first,' she gasped, pushing Constantia.

But Constantia said, as she always had said on those occasions, 'No, Jug, that's not fair. You're eldest.'

Josephine was just going to say – what at other times she wouldn't have owned to for the world – what she kept for her very last weapon, 'But you're tallest,' when they noticed that the kitchen door was open, and there stood Kate. . . .

'Very stiff,' said Josephine, grasping the door-handle and doing her best to turn it. As if anything ever deceived Kate!

It couldn't be helped. That girl was . . . Then the door was shut behind them, but – but they weren't in father's room at all. They might have suddenly walked through the wall by mistake into a different flat altogether. Was the door just behind them? They were too frightened to look. Josephine knew that if it was it was holding itself tight shut; Constantia felt that, like the doors in dreams, it hadn't any handle at all. It was the coldness which made it so awful. Or the whiteness – which? Everything was covered. The blinds were down, a cloth hung over the mirror, a sheet hid the bed; a huge fan of white paper filled the fire-place. Constantia timidly put out her hand; she almost expected a snowflake to fall. Josephine felt a queer tingling in her nose, as if her nose was freezing. Then a cab klop-klopped over the cobbles below, and the quiet seemed to shake into little pieces.

'I had better pull up a blind,' said Josephine bravely.

'Yes, it might be a good idea,' whispered Constantia.

They only gave the blind a touch, but it flew up and the cord flew after, rolling round the blind-stick, and the little tassel tapped as if trying to get free. That was too much for Constantia.

'Don't you think – don't you think we might put it off for another day?' she whispered.

'Why?' snapped Josephine, feeling, as usual, much better now that she knew for certain that Constantia was terrified. 'It's got to be done. But I do wish you wouldn't whisper, Con.'

'I didn't know I was whispering,' whispered Constantia.

'And why do you keep on staring at the bed?' said Josephine, raising her voice almost defiantly. 'There's nothing *on* the bed.'

'Oh, Jug, don't say so!' said poor Connie. 'At any rate, not so loudly.'

Josephine felt herself that she had gone too far. She took a wide swerve over to the chest of drawers, put out her hand, but quickly drew it back again.

'Connie!' she gasped, and she wheeled round and leaned with her back against the chest of drawers.

'Oh, Jug – what?'

Josephine could only glare. She had the most extraordinary feeling that she had just escaped something simply awful. But how could she explain to Constantia that father was in the chest of drawers? He was in the top drawer with his handkerchiefs and neckties, or in the next with his shirts and pyjamas, or in the lowest of all with his suits. He was watching there, hidden away – just behind the door-handle – ready to spring.

She pulled a funny old-fashioned face at Constantia, just as she used to in the old days when she was going to cry.

'I can't open,' she nearly wailed.

'No, don't, Jug,' whispered Constantia earnestly. 'It's

much better not to. Don't let's open anything. At any rate, not for a long time.'

'But – but it seems so weak,' said Josephine, breaking down.

'But why not be weak for once, Jug?' argued Constantia, whispering quite fiercely. 'If it is weak.' And her pale stare flew from the locked writing-table – so safe – to the huge glittering wardrobe, and she began to breathe in a queer, panting way. 'Why shouldn't we be weak for once in our lives, Jug? It's quite excusable. Let's be weak – be weak, Jug. It's much nicer to be weak than to be strong.'

And then she did one of those amazingly bold things that she'd done about twice before in their lives: she marched over to the wardrobe, turned the key, and took it out of the lock. Took it out of the lock and held it up to Josephine, showing Josephine by her extraordinary smile that she knew what she'd done – she'd risked deliberately father being in there among his overcoats.

If the huge wardrobe had lurched forward, had crashed down on Constantia, Josephine wouldn't have been surprised. On the contrary, she would have thought it the only suitable thing to happen. But nothing happened. Only the room seemed quieter than ever, and bigger flakes of cold air fell on Josephine's shoulders and knees. She began to shiver.

'Come, Jug,' said Constantia, still with that awful callous smile; and Josephine followed just as she had that last time, when Constantia had pushed Benny into the round pond.

VII

But the strain told on them when they were back in the dining-room. They sat down, very shaky, and looked at each other.

'I don't feel I can settle to anything,' said Josephine, 'until I've had something. Do you think we could ask Kate for two cups of hot water?'

'I really don't see why we shouldn't,' said Constantia carefully. She was quite normal again. 'I won't ring. I'll go to the kitchen door and ask her.'

'Yes, do,' said Josephine, sinking down into a chair. 'Tell her, just two cups, Con, nothing else – on a tray.'

'She needn't even put the jug on, need she?' said Constantia, as though Kate might very well complain if the jug had been there.

'Oh no, certainly not! The jug's not at all necessary. She can pour it direct out of the kettle,' cried Josephine, feeling that would be a labour-saving indeed.

Their cold lips quivered at the greenish brims. Josephine curved her small red hands round the cup; Constantia sat up and blew on the wavy steam, making it flutter from one side to the other.

'Speaking of Benny,' said Josephine.

And though Benny hadn't been mentioned Constantia immediately looked as though he had.

'He'll expect us to send him something of father's, of course. But it's so difficult to know what to send to Ceylon.'

'You mean things get unstuck so on the voyage,' murmured Constantia.

'No, lost,' said Josephine sharply. 'You know there's no post. Only runners.'

Both paused to watch a black man in white linen drawers running through the pale fields for dear life, with a large brown-paper parcel in his hands. Josephine's black man was tiny; he scurried along glistening like an ant. But there was something blind and tireless about Constantia's tall, thin fellow, which made him, she decided, a very unpleasant person indeed. . . . On the veranda, dressed all in white and wearing a cork helmet, stood Benny. His right hand shook up and down, as father's did when he was impatient. And behind him, not in the least interested, sat Hilda, the unknown sister-in-law. She swung in a cane rocker and flicked over the leaves of the *Tatler*.

'I think his watch would be the most suitable present,' said Josephine.

Constantia looked up; she seemed surprised.

'Oh, would you trust a gold watch to a native?'

'But, of course, I'd disguise it,' said Josephine. 'No one would know it was a watch.' She liked the idea of having to make a parcel such a curious shape that no one could possibly guess what it was. She even thought for a moment of hiding the watch in a narrow cardboard corset-box that she'd kept by her for a long time, waiting for it to come in for something. It was such beautiful, firm cardboard. But, no, it wouldn't be appropriate for this occasion. It had lettering on it: *Medium Women's 28. Extra Firm Busks.* It would be almost too much of a surprise for Benny to open that and find father's watch inside.

'And, of course, it isn't as though it would be going – ticking, I mean,' said Constantia, who was still thinking of the native love of jewellery. 'At least,' she added, 'it would be very strange if after all that time it was.'

VIII

Josephine made no reply. She had flown off on one of her tangents. She had suddenly thought of Cyril. Wasn't it more usual for the only grandson to have the watch? And then dear Cyril was so appreciative and a gold watch meant so much to a young man. Benny, in all probability, had quite got out of the habit of watches; men so seldom wore waistcoats in those hot climates. Whereas Cyril in London wore them from year's end to year's end. And it would be so nice for her and Constantia, when he came to tea, to know it was there. 'I see you've got on grandfather's watch, Cyril.' It would be somehow so satisfactory.

Dear boy! What a blow his sweet, sympathetic little note had been! Of course they quite understood; but it was most unfortunate.

'It would have been such a point, having him,' said Josephine.

'And he would have enjoyed it so,' said Constantia, not thinking what she was saying.

However, as soon as he got back he was coming to tea with his aunties. Cyril to tea was one of their rare treats.

'Now, Cyril, you mustn't be frightened of our cakes. Your Auntie Con and I bought them at Buszard's this morning. We know what a man's appetite is. So don't be ashamed of making a good tea.'

Josephine cut recklessly into the rich dark cake that stood for her winter gloves or the soling and heeling of Constantia's only respectable shoes. But Cyril was most unmanlike in appetite.

'I say, Aunt Josephine, I simply can't. I've only just had lunch, you know.'

'Oh, Cyril, that can't be true! It's after four,' cried Josephine. Constantia sat with her knife poised over the chocolate-roll.

'It is, all the same,' said Cyril. 'I had to meet a man at Victoria, and he kept me hanging about till . . . there was only time to get lunch and to come on here. And he gave me – phew' – Cyril put his hand to his forehead – 'a terrific blow-out,' he said.

It was disappointing – to-day of all days. But still he couldn't be expected to know.

'But you'll have a meringue, won't you, Cyril?' said Aunt Josephine. 'These meringues were bought specially for you. Your dear father was so fond of them. We were sure you are, too.'

'I *am*, Aunt Josephine,' cried Cyril ardently. 'Do you mind if I take half to begin with?'

'Not at all, dear boy; but we mustn't let you off with that.'

'Is your dear father still so fond of meringues?' asked Auntie Con gently. She winced faintly as she broke through the shell of hers.

'Well, I don't quite know, Auntie Con,' said Cyril breezily.

At that they both looked up.

'Don't know?' almost snapped Josephine. 'Don't know a thing like that about your own father, Cyril?'

'Surely,' said Auntie Con softly.

Cyril tried to laugh it off. 'Oh, well,' he said, 'it's such a long time since—' He faltered. He stopped. Their faces were too much for him.

'Even *so*,' said Josephine.

And Auntie Con looked.

Cyril put down his teacup. 'Wait a bit,' he cried. 'Wait a bit, Aunt Josephine. What am I thinking of?'

He looked up. They were beginning to brighten. Cyril slapped his knee.

'Of course,' he said, 'it was meringues. How could I have forgotten? Yes, Aunt Josephine, you're perfectly right. Father's most frightfully keen on meringues.'

They didn't only beam. Aunt Josephine went scarlet with pleasure; Auntie Con gave a deep, deep sigh.

'And now, Cyril, you must come and see father,' said Josephine. 'He knows you were coming to-day.'

'Right,' said Cyril, very firmly and heartily. He got up from his chair; suddenly he glanced at the clock.

'I say, Auntie Con, isn't your clock a bit slow? I've got to meet a man at – at Paddington just after five. I'm afraid I shan't be able to stay very long with grandfather.'

'Oh, he won't expect you to stay *very* long!' said Aunt Josephine.

Constantia was still gazing at the clock. She couldn't make up her mind if it was fast or slow. It was one or the other, she felt almost certain of that. At any rate, it had been.

Cyril still lingered. 'Aren't you coming along, Auntie Con?'

'Of course,' said Josephine, 'we shall all go. Come on, Con.'

IX

They knocked at the door, and Cyril followed his aunts into grandfather's hot, sweetish room.

'Come on,' said Grandfather Pinner. 'Don't hang about. What is it? What've you been up to?'

He was sitting in front of a roaring fire, clasping his stick. He had a thick rug over his knees. On his lap there lay a beautiful pale yellow silk handkerchief.

'It's Cyril, father,' said Josephine shyly. And she took Cyril's hand and led him forward.

'Good afternoon, grandfather,' said Cyril, trying to take his hand out of Aunt Josephine's. Grandfather Pinner shot his eyes at Cyril in the way he was famous for. Where was Auntie Con? She stood on the other side of Aunt Josephine; her long arms hung down in front of her; her hands were clasped. She never took her eyes off grandfather.

'Well,' said Grandfather Pinner, beginning to thump, 'what have you got to tell me?'

What had he, what had he got to tell him? Cyril felt himself smiling like a perfect imbecile. The room was stifling, too.

But Aunt Josephine came to his rescue. She cried brightly, 'Cyril says his father is still very fond of meringues, father dear.'

'Eh?' said Grandfather Pinner, curving his hand like a purple meringue-shell over one ear.

Josephine repeated, 'Cyril says his father is still very fond of meringues.'

'Can't hear,' said old Colonel Pinner. And he waved Josephine away with his stick, then pointed with his stick to Cyril. 'Tell me what she's trying to say,' he said.

(My God!) 'Must I?' said Cyril, blushing and staring at Aunt Josephine.

'Do, dear,' she smiled. 'It will please him so much.'

'Come on, out with it!' cried Colonel Pinner testily, beginning to thump again.

And Cyril leaned forward and yelled, 'Father's still very fond of meringues.'

At that Grandfather Pinner jumped as though he had been shot.

'Don't shout!' he cried. 'What's the matter with the boy? *Meringues!* What about 'em?'

'Oh, Aunt Josephine, must we go on?' groaned Cyril desperately.

'It's quite all right, dear boy,' said Aunt Josephine, as though he and she were at the dentist's together. 'He'll understand in a minute.' And she whispered to Cyril, 'He's getting a bit deaf; you know.' Then she leaned forward and really bawled at Grandfather Pinner, 'Cyril only wanted to tell you, father dear, that *his* father is still very fond of meringues.'

Colonel Pinner heard that time, heard and brooded, looking Cyril up and down.

'What an esstrordinary thing!' said old Grandfather Pinner. 'What an esstrordinary thing to come all this way here to tell me!'

And Cyril felt it *was*.

'Yes, I shall send Cyril the watch,' said Josephine.

'That would be very nice,' said Constantia. 'I seem to remember last time he came there was some little trouble about the time.'

X

They were interrupted by Kate bursting through the door in her usual fashion, as though she had discovered some secret panel in the wall.

'Fried or boiled?' asked the bold voice.

Fried or boiled? Josephine and Constantia were quite bewildered for the moment. They could hardly take it in.

'Fried or boiled what, Kate?' asked Josephine, trying to begin to concentrate.

Kate gave a loud sniff. 'Fish.'

'Well, why didn't you say so immediately?' Josephine reproached her gently. 'How could you expect us to understand, Kate? There are a great many things in this world, you know, which are fried or boiled.' And after such a display of courage she said quite brightly to Constantia, 'Which do you prefer, Con?'

'I think it might be nice to have it fried,' said Constantia. 'On the other hand, of course, boiled fish is very nice. I think I prefer both equally well . . . Unless you . . . In that case –'

'I shall fry it,' said Kate, and she bounced back, leaving their door open and slamming the door of her kitchen.

Josephine gazed at Constantia; she raised her pale eyebrows until they rippled away into her pale hair. She got up.

She said in a very lofty, imposing way, 'Do you mind following me into the drawing-room, Constantia? I've something of great importance to discuss with you.'

For it was always to the drawing-room they retired when they wanted to talk over Kate.

Josephine closed the door meaningly. 'Sit down, Constantia,' she said, still very grand. She might have been receiving Constantia for the first time. And Con looked round vaguely for a chair, as though she felt indeed quite a stranger.

'Now the question is,' said Josephine, bending forward, 'whether we shall keep her or not.'

'That is the question,' agreed Constantia.

'And this time,' said Josephine firmly, 'we must come to a definite decision.'

Constantia looked for a moment as though she might begin going over all the other times, but she pulled herself together and said, 'Yes, Jug.'

'You see, Con,' explained Josephine, 'everything is so changed now.' Constantia looked up quickly. 'I mean,' went on Josephine, 'we're not dependent on Kate as we were.' And she blushed faintly. 'There's not father to cook for.'

'That is perfectly true,' agreed Constantia. 'Father certainly doesn't want any cooking now whatever else—'

Josephine broke in sharply, 'You're not sleepy, are you, Con?'

'Sleepy, Jug?' Constantia was wide-eyed.

'Well, concentrate more,' said Josephine sharply, and she returned to the subject. 'What it comes to is, if we did' – and this she barely breathed, glancing at the door – 'give Kate notice' – she raised her voice again – 'we could manage our own food.'

'Why not?' cried Constantia. She couldn't help smiling.

The idea was so exciting. She clasped her hands. 'What should we live on, Jug?'

'Oh, eggs in various forms!' said Jug, lofty again. 'And, besides, there are all the cooked foods.'

'But I've always heard,' said Constantia, 'they are considered so very expensive.'

'Not if one buys them in moderation,' said Josephine. But she tore herself away from this fascinating bypath and dragged Constantia after her.

'What we've got to decide now, however, is whether we really do trust Kate or not.'

Constantia leaned back. Her flat little laugh flew from her lips.

'Isn't it curious, Jug,' said she, 'that just on this one subject I've never been able to quite make up my mind?'

XI

She never had. The whole difficulty was to prove anything. How did one prove things, how could one? Suppose Kate had stood in front of her and deliberately made a face. Mightn't she very well have been in pain? Wasn't it impossible, at any rate, to ask Kate if she was making a face at her? If Kate answered 'No' – and, of course, she would say 'No' – what a position! How undignified! Then, again, Constantia suspected, she was almost certain that Kate went to her chest of drawers when she and Josephine were out, not to take things but to spy. Many times she had come back to find her amethyst cross in the most unlikely places, under her lace ties or on top of her evening Bertha. More than once she had laid a trap for Kate. She had arranged things in a special order and then called Josephine to witness.

'You see, Jug?'

'Quite, Con.'

'Now we shall be able to tell.'

But, oh dear, when she did go to look, she was as far off from a proof as ever! If anything was displaced, it might so very well have happened as she closed the drawer; a jolt might have done it so easily.

'You come, Jug, and decide. I really can't. It's too difficult.'

But after a pause and a long glare Josephine would sigh, 'Now you've put the doubt into my mind, Con, I'm sure I can't tell myself.'

'Well, we can't postpone it again,' said Josephine. 'If we postpone it this time—'

XII

But at that moment in the street below a barrel-organ struck up. Josephine and Constantia sprang to their feet together.

'Run, Con,' said Josephine. 'Run quickly. There's sixpence on the—'

Then they remembered. It didn't matter. They would never have to stop the organ-grinder again. Never again would she and Constantia be told to make that monkey take his noise somewhere else. Never would sound that loud, strange bellow when father thought they were not hurrying enough. The organ-grinder might play there all day and the stick would not thump.

It never will thump again,
It never will thump again,

played the barrel-organ.

What was Constantia thinking? She had such a strange smile; she looked different. She couldn't be going to cry.

'Jug, Jug,' said Constantia softly, pressing her hands together. 'Do you know what day it is? It's Saturday. It's a week to-day, a whole week.'

A week since father died,
A week since father died,

cried the barrel-organ. And Josephine, too, forgot to be practical and sensible; she smiled faintly, strangely. On the Indian carpet there fell a square of sunlight, pale red; it came and went and came – and stayed, deepened – until it shone almost golden.

'The sun's out,' said Josephine, as though it really mattered.

A perfect fountain of bubbling notes shook from the barrel-organ, round, bright notes, carelessly scattered.

Constantia lifted her big, cold hands as if to catch them, and then her hands fell again. She walked over to the mantelpiece to her favourite Buddha. And the stone and gilt image, whose smile always gave her such a queer feeling, almost a pain and yet a pleasant pain, seemed to-day to be more than smiling. He knew something; he had a secret. 'I know something that you don't know,' said her Buddha. Oh, what was it, what could it be? And yet she had always felt there was . . . something.

The sunlight pressed through the windows, thieved its way in, flashed its light over the furniture and the photographs. Josephine watched it. When it came to mother's photograph, the enlargement over the piano, it lingered as though puzzled to find so little remained of mother, except the ear-rings shaped like tiny pagodas and a black feather boa. Why did the photographs of dead people always fade so? wondered Josephine. As soon as a person was dead their photograph died too. But, of course, this one of mother was very old. It was thirty-five years old. Josephine remembered standing on a chair and pointing out that feather boa to Constantia and telling her that it was a snake that had killed their mother in Ceylon.... Would everything have been different if mother hadn't died? She didn't see why. Aunt Florence had lived with them until they had left school, and they had moved three times and had their yearly holiday and ... and there'd been changes of servants, of course.

Some little sparrows, young sparrows they sounded, chirped on the window-ledge. *Yeep – eyeep – yeep*. But Josephine felt they were not sparrows, not on the window-ledge. It was inside her, that queer little crying noise. *Yeep – eyeep – yeep*. Ah, what was it crying, so weak and forlorn?

If mother had lived, might they have married? But there had been nobody for them to marry. There had been father's Anglo-Indian friends before he quarrelled with them. But after that she and Constantia never met a single man except clergymen. How did one meet men? Or even if they'd met them, how could they have got to know men well enough to be more than strangers? One read of people having adventures, being followed, and so on. But nobody had ever followed Constantia and her. Oh yes, there had been one year at Eastbourne a mysterious man at their boarding-house who had put a note on the jug of hot water outside their bedroom door! But by the time Connie had found it the steam had made the writing too faint to read; they couldn't even make out to which of them it was addressed. And he had left next day. And that was all. The rest had been looking after father and at the same time keeping out of father's way. But now? But now? The thieving sun touched Josephine gently. She lifted her face. She was drawn over to the window by gentle beams....

Until the barrel-organ stopped playing Constantia stayed before the Buddha, wondering, but not as usual, not vaguely. This time her wonder was like longing. She remembered the times she had come in here, crept out of bed in her night-gown when the moon was full, and lain on the floor with her arms outstretched, as though she was crucified. Why? The big, pale moon had made her do it. The horrible dancing figures on the carved screen had leered at her and she hadn't minded. She remembered too how, whenever they were at the seaside, she had gone off by herself and got as close to the sea as she could, and sung something, something she had made up, while she gazed all over that restless water. There had been this other life, running out, bringing things home in bags, getting things on approval, discussing them with Jug, and taking them back to get more things on approval, and arranging father's trays and trying not to annoy father. But it all seemed to have happened in a kind of tunnel. It wasn't real. It was only when she came out of the tunnel into the moonlight or by the sea or into a thunderstorm that she really felt herself. What did it mean? What was it she was always wanting? What did it all lead to? Now? Now?

She turned away from the Buddha with one of her vague gestures. She went over to where Josephine was standing. She wanted to say something to Josephine, something frightfully important, about – about the future and what . . .

'Don't you think perhaps—' she began.

But Josephine interrupted her. 'I was wondering if now—' she murmured. They stopped; they waited for each other.

'Go on, Con,' said Josephine.

'No, no, Jug; after you,' said Constantia.

'No, say what you were going to say. You began,' said Josephine.

'I . . . I'd rather hear what you were going to say first,' said Constantia.

'Don't be absurd, Con.'

'Really, Jug.'

'Connie!'

'Oh, *Jug*!'

A pause. Then Constantia said faintly, 'I can't say what I was going to say, Jug, because I've forgotten what it was . . . that I was going to say.'

Josephine was silent for a moment. She stared at a big cloud where the sun had been. Then she replied shortly, 'I've forgotten too.'

P. G. WODEHOUSE

HONEYSUCKLE COTTAGE

'DO YOU BELIEVE in ghosts?' asked Mr Mulliner abruptly.

I weighed the question thoughtfully. I was a little surprised, for nothing in our previous conversation had suggested the topic.

'Well,' I replied, 'I don't like them, if that's what you mean. I was once butted by one as a child.'

'Ghosts. Not goats.'

'Oh, ghosts? Do I believe in ghosts?'

'Exactly.'

'Well, yes – and no.'

'Let me put it another way,' said Mr Mulliner, patiently. 'Do you believe in haunted houses? Do you believe that it is possible for a malign influence to envelop a place and work a spell on all who come within its radius?'

I hesitated.

'Well, no – and yes.'

Mr Mulliner sighed a little. He seemed to be wondering if I was always as bright as this.

'Of course,' I went on, 'one has read stories. Henry James's *Turn of the Screw* . . .'

'I am not talking about fiction.'

'Well, in real life – Well, look here, I once, as a matter of fact, did meet a man who knew a fellow—'

'My distant cousin James Rodman spent some weeks in a haunted house,' said Mr Mulliner, who, if he has a fault, is not a very good listener. 'It cost him five thousand pounds. That is to say, he sacrificed five thousand pounds by not remaining there. Did you ever,' he asked, wandering, it seemed to me, from the subject, 'hear of Leila J. Pinckney?'

Naturally I had heard of Leila J. Pinckney. Her death some years ago has diminished her vogue, but at one time it was impossible to pass a book-shop or a railway bookstall without seeing a long row of her novels. I had never myself actually read any of them, but I knew that in her particular line of literature, the Squashily Sentimental, she had always been regarded by those entitled to judge as pre-eminent. The critics usually headed their reviews of her stories with the words: –

ANOTHER PINCKNEY

or sometimes, more offensively:–

ANOTHER PINCKNEY!!!

And once, dealing with, I think, *The Love Which Prevails*, the literary expert of the *Scrutinizer* had compressed his entire critique into the single phrase 'Oh, God!'

'Of course,' I said. 'But what about her?'

'She was James Rodman's aunt.'

'Yes?'

'And when she died James found that she had left him five thousand pounds and the house in the country where she had lived for the last twenty years of her life.'

'A very nice little legacy.'

'Twenty years,' repeated Mr Mulliner. 'Grasp that, for it has a vital bearing on what follows. Twenty years, mind you, and Miss Pinckney turned out two novels and twelve short stories regularly every year, besides a monthly page of Advice to Young Girls in one of the magazines. That is to say, forty of her novels and no fewer than two hundred and forty of her short stories were written under the roof of Honeysuckle Cottage.'

'A pretty name.'

'A nasty, sloppy name,' said Mr Mulliner severely, 'which should have warned my distant cousin James from the start. Have you a pencil and a piece of paper?' He scribbled for a while, poring frowningly over columns of figures. 'Yes,' he said, looking up, 'if my calculations are correct, Leila J. Pinckney wrote in all a matter of nine million one hundred and forty thousand words of glutinous sentimentality at Honeysuckle Cottage, and it was a condition of her will that James should reside there for six months in every year. Failing to do this, he was to forfeit the five thousand pounds.'

'It must be great fun making a freak will,' I mused. 'I often wish I was rich enough to do it.'

'This was not a freak will. The conditions are perfectly understandable. James Rodman was a writer of sensational mystery stories, and his aunt Leila had always disapproved of his work. She was a great believer in the influence of environment, and the reason why she inserted that clause in her will was that she wished to compel James to move from London to the country. She considered that living in London hardened him and made his outlook on life sordid. She often asked him if he thought it quite nice to harp so much on sudden death and blackmailers with squints. Surely, she said, there were enough squinting blackmailers in the world without writing about them.

'The fact that Literature meant such different things to these two had, I believe, caused something of a coolness between them, and James had never dreamed that he would be remembered in his aunt's will. For he had never concealed his opinion that Leila J. Pinckney's style of writing revolted him, however dear it might be to her enormous public. He held rigid views on the art of the novel, and always maintained that an artist with a true reverence for his craft should not descend to goo-ey love stories, but should stick austerely to revolvers, cries in the night, missing papers, mysterious Chinamen and dead bodies – with or without gash in throat. And not even the thought that his aunt had dandled him on her knee as a baby could induce him to stifle his literary conscience to the extent of pretending to enjoy her work. First, last and all the time, James Rodman had held the opinion – and voiced it fearlessly – that Leila J. Pinckney wrote bilge.

'It was a surprise to him, therefore, to find that he had been left this legacy. A pleasant surprise, of course. James was making quite a decent income out of the three novels and eighteen short stories which he produced annually, but an author can always find a use for five thousand pounds. And, as for the cottage, he had actually been looking about for a little place in the country at the very moment when he received the lawyer's letter. In less than a week he was installed at his new residence.'

James's first impressions of Honeysuckle Cottage were, he tells me, wholly favourable. He was delighted with the place. It was a low, rambling, picturesque old house with funny little chimneys and a red roof, placed in the middle of the most charming country. With its oak beams, its trim garden, its trilling birds and its rose-hung porch, it was the ideal spot for a writer. It was just the sort of place, he reflected whimsically, which his aunt had loved to write about in her books. Even the apple-cheeked old housekeeper who attended to his needs might have stepped straight our of one of them.

It seemed to James that his lot had been cast in pleasant

places. He had brought down his books, his pipes and his golfclubs, and was hard at work finishing the best thing he had ever done. *The Secret Nine* was the title of it; and on the beautiful summer afternoon on which this story opens he was in the study, hammering away at his typewriter, at peace with the world. The machine was running sweetly, the new tobacco he had bought the day before was proving admirable, and he was moving on all six cylinders to the end of a chapter.

He shoved in a fresh sheet of paper, chewed his pipe thoughtfully for a moment, then wrote rapidly:

'For an instant Lester Gage thought that he must have been mistaken. Then the noise came again, faint but unmistakable – a soft scratching on the outer panel.

'His mouth set in a grim line. Silently, like a panther, he made one quick step to the desk, noiselessly opened a drawer, drew out his automatic. After that affair of the poisoned needle, he was taking no chances. Still in dead silence, he tiptoed to the door; then, flinging it suddenly open, he stood there, his weapon poised.

'On the mat stood the most beautiful girl he had ever beheld. A veritable child of Faërie. She eyed him for a moment with a saucy smile; then with a pretty, roguish look of reproof shook a dainty fore-finger at him.

' "I believe you've forgotten me, Mr Gage!" she fluted with a mock severity which her eyes belied.'

James stared at the paper dumbly. He was utterly perplexed. He had not had the slightest intention of writing anything like this. To begin with, it was a rule with him, and one which he never broke, to allow no girls to appear in his stories. Sinister landladies, yes, and naturally any amount of adventuresses with foreign accents, but never under any pretext what may be broadly described as girls.

A detective story, he maintained, should have no heroine. Heroines only held up the action and tried to flirt with the hero when he should have been busy looking for clues, and then went and let the villain kidnap them by some childishly simple trick. In his writing, James was positively monastic.

And yet here was this creature with her saucy smile and her dainty fore-finger horning in at the most important point in the story. It was uncanny.

He looked once more at his scenario. No, the scenario was all right.

In perfectly plain words it stated that what happened when the door opened was that a dying man fell in and after gasping, 'The beetle! Tell Scotland Yard that the blue beetle is—' expired on the hearth-rug, leaving Lester Gage not unnaturally somewhat mystified. Nothing whatever about any beautiful girls.

In a curious mood of irritation, James scratched out the offending passage, wrote in the necessary corrections and put the cover on the machine. It was at this point that he heard William whining.

The only blot on this paradise which James had so far been able to discover was the infernal dog, William. Belonging nominally to the gardener, on the very first morning he had adopted James by acclamation, and he maddened and infuriated James. He had a habit of coming and whining under the window when James was at work. The latter would ignore this as long as he could; then, when the thing became insupportable, would bound out of his chair, to see the animal standing on the gravel, gazing expectantly up at him with a stone in his mouth. William had a weak-minded passion for chasing stones; and on the first day James, in a rash spirit of camaraderie, had flung one for him. Since then James had thrown no more stones; but he had thrown any number of other solids, and the garden was littered with objects ranging from match boxes to a plaster statuette of the young Joseph prophesying before Pharaoh. And still William came and whined, an optimist to the last.

The whining, coming now at a moment when he felt irritable and unsettled, acted on James much as the scratching on the door had acted on Lester Gage. Silently, like a panther, he made one quick step to the mantelpiece, removed from it a china mug beating the legend A Present from Clacton-on-Sea, and crept to the window.

And as he did so a voice outside said, 'Go away, sir, go away!' and there followed a short, high-pitched bark which was certainly not William's. William was a mixture of Airedale, setter, bull terrier, and mastiff; and when in vocal mood, favoured the mastiff side of his family.

James peered out. There on the porch stood a girl in blue. She held in her arms a small fluffy white dog, and she was endeavouring to foil the upward movement toward this of the blackguard William. William's mentality had been arrested some years before at the point where he imagined that everything in the world had been created for him to eat. A bone, a boot, a steak, the back wheel of a bicycle – it was all one to William. If it was there he tried to eat it. He had even made a plucky attempt to devour the remains of the young Joseph prophesying before Pharaoh. And it was perfectly plain now that he regarded the curious wriggling object in the girl's arms purely in the light of a snack to keep body and soul together till dinner-time.

'William!' bellowed James.

William looked courteously over his shoulder with eyes that beamed with the pure light of a life's devotion, wagged the whiplike tail which he had inherited from his bull-terrier ancestor and resumed his intent scrutiny of the fluffy dog.

'Oh, please!' cried the girl. 'This great rough dog is frightening poor Toto.'

The man of letters and the man of action do not always go hand in hand, but practice had made James perfect in handling with a swift efficiency any situation that involved William. A moment later that canine moron, having received the present from Clacton in the short ribs, was scuttling round the corner of the house, and James had jumped through the window and was facing the girl.

She was an extraordinarily pretty girl. Very sweet and fragile she looked as she stood there under the honeysuckle with the breeze ruffling a tendril of golden hair that strayed from beneath her coquettish little hat. Her eyes were very big and very blue, her rose-tinted face becomingly flushed. All wasted on James, though. He disliked all girls, and particularly the sweet, droopy type.

'Did you want to see somebody?' he asked stiffly.

'Just the house,' said the girl, 'if it wouldn't be giving any trouble. I do so want to see the room where Miss Pinckney wrote her books. This is where Leila J. Pinckney used to live, isn't it?'

'Yes; I am her nephew. My name is James Rodman.'

'Mine is Rose Maynard.'

James led the way into the house, and she stopped with a cry of delight on the threshold of the morning-room.

'Oh, how too perfect!' she cried. 'So this was her study?'

'Yes.'

'What a wonderful place it would be for you to think in if you were a writer too.'

James held no high opinion of women's literary taste, but nevertheless he was conscious of an unpleasant shock.

'I am a writer,' he said coldly. 'I write detective stories.'

'I – I'm afraid' – she blushed – 'I'm afraid I don't often read detective stories.'

'You no doubt prefer,' said James, still more coldly, 'the sort of thing my aunt used to write.'

'Oh, I love her stories!' cried the girl, clasping her hands ecstatically. 'Don't you?'

'I cannot say that I do.'

'What?'

'They are pure apple sauce,' said James sternly, 'just nasty blobs of sentimentality, thoroughly untrue to life.'

The girl stared.

'Why, that's just what's so wonderful about them, their trueness to life! You feel they might all have happened. I don't understand what you mean.'

They were walking down the garden now. James held the gate open for her and she passed through into the road.

'Well, for one thing,' he said, 'I decline to believe that a marriage between two young people is invariably preceded by some violent and sensational experience in which they both share.'

'Are you thinking of *Scent o' the Blossom*, where Edgar saves Maud from drowning?'

'I am thinking of every single one of my aunt's books.' He looked at her curiously. He had just got the solution of a mystery which had been puzzling him for some time. Almost from the moment he had set eyes on her she had seemed somehow strangely familiar. It now suddenly came to him why it was that he disliked her so much. 'Do you know,' he said, 'you might be one of my aunt's heroines yourself? You're just the sort of girl she used to love to write about.'

Her face lit up.

'Oh, do you really think so?' She hesitated. 'Do you know

what I have been feeling ever since I came here? I've been feeling that you are exactly like one of Miss Pinckney's heroes.'

'No, I say, really!' said James, revolted.

'Oh, but you are! When you jumped through that window it gave me quite a start. You were so exactly like Claude Masterson in *Heather o' the Hills*.'

'I have not read *Heather o' the Hills*,' said James, with a shudder.

'He was very strong and quiet, with deep, dark, sad eyes.'

James did not explain that his eyes were sad because her society gave him a pain in the neck. He merely laughed scornfully.

'So now, I suppose,' he said, 'a car will come and knock you down and I shall carry you gently into the house and lay you – Look out!' he cried.

It was too late. She was lying in a little huddled heap at his feet. Round the corner a large automobile had come bowling, keeping with an almost affected precision to the wrong side of the road. It was now receding into the distance, the occupant of the tonneau, a stout red-faced gentleman in a fur coat, leaning out over the back. He had bared his head – not, one fears, as a pretty gesture of respect and regret, but because he was using his hat to hide the number plate.

The dog Toto was unfortunately uninjured.

James carried the girl gently into the house and laid her on the sofa in the morning-room. He rang the bell and the apple-cheeked housekeeper appeared.

'Send for the doctor,' said James. 'There has been an accident.'

The housekeeper bent over the girl.

'Eh, dearie, dearie!' she said. 'Bless her sweet pretty face!'

The gardener, he who technically owned William, was routed out from among the young lettuces and told to fetch Doctor Brady. He separated his bicycle from William, who was making a light meal off the left pedal, and departed on his mission. Doctor Brady arrived and in due course he made his report.

'No bones broken, but a number of nasty bruises. And, of course, the shock. She will have to stay here for some time Rodman. Can't be moved.'

'Stay here! But she can't! It isn't proper.'

'Your housekeeper will act as a chaperone.'

The doctor sighed. He was a stolid-looking man of middle age with side-whiskers.

'A beautiful girl, that, Rodman,' he said.

'I suppose so,' said James.

'A sweet, beautiful girl. An elfin child.'

'A what?' cried James, starting.

This imagery was very foreign to Doctor Brady as he knew him. On the only previous occasion on which they had had any extended conversation, the doctor had talked exclusively about the effect of too much protein on the gastric juices.

'An elfin child; a tender, fairy creature. When I was looking at her just now, Rodman, I nearly broke down. Her little hand lay on the coverlet like some white lily floating on the surface of a still pool, and her dear, trusting eyes gazed up at me.'

He pottered off down the garden, still babbling, and James stood staring after him blankly. And slowly, like some cloud athwart a summer sky, there crept over James's heart the chill shadow of a nameless fear.

* * *

It was about a week later that Mr Andrew McKinnon, the senior partner in the well-known firm of literary agents, McKinnon & Gooch, sat in his office in Chancery Lane, frowning thoughtfully over a telegram. He rang the bell.

'Ask Mr Gooch to step in here.' He resumed his study of the telegram. 'Oh, Gooch,' he said when his partner appeared, 'I've just had a curious wire from young Rodman. He seems to want to see me very urgently.'

Mr Gooch read the telegram.

'Written under the influence of some strong mental excitement,' he agreed. 'I wonder why he doesn't come to the office if he wants to see you so badly.'

'He's working very hard, finishing that novel for Prodder & Wiggs. Can't leave it, I suppose. Well, it's a nice day. If you will look after things here I think I'll motor down and let him give me lunch.'

As Mr McKinnon's car reached the crossroads a mile from Honeysuckle Cottage, he was aware of a gesticulating figure by the hedge. He stopped the car.

'Morning, Rodman.'

'Thank God, you've come!' said James. It seemed to Mr McKinnon that the young man looked paler and thinner. 'Would you mind walking the rest of the way? There's something I want to speak to you about.'

Mr McKinnon alighted; and James, as he glanced at him, felt cheered and encouraged by the very sight of the man. The literary agent was a grim, hard-bitten person, to whom, when he called at their offices to arrange terms, editors kept their faces turned so that they might at least retain their back collar studs. There was no sentiment in Andrew McKinnon. Editresses of society papers practised their blandishments on him in vain, and many a publisher had waked screaming in the night, dreaming that he was signing a McKinnon contract.

'Well, Rodman,' he said, 'Prodder & Wiggs have agreed to our terms. I was writing to tell you so when your wire arrived. I had a lot of trouble with them, but it's fixed at 20 per cent., rising to 25, and two hundred pounds advance royalties on day of publication.'

'Good!' said James absently. 'Good! McKinnon, do you remember my aunt, Leila J. Pinckney?'

'Remember her? Why, I was her agent all her life.'

'Of course. Then you know the sort of tripe she wrote.'

'No author,' said Mr McKinnon reprovingly, 'who pulls down a steady twenty thousand pounds a year writes tripe.'

'Well anyway, you know her stuff.'

'Who better?'

'When she died she left me five thousand pounds and her house, Honeysuckle Cottage. I'm living there now. McKinnon, do you believe in haunted houses?'

'No.'

'Yet I tell you solemnly that Honeysuckle Cottage is haunted!'

'By your aunt?' said Mr McKinnon, surprised.

'By her influence. There's a malignant spell over the place; a sort of miasma of sentimentalism. Everybody who enters it succumbs.'

'Tut-tut! You mustn't have these fancies.'

'They aren't fancies.'

'You aren't seriously meaning to tell me—'

'Well, how do you account for this? That book you were speaking about, which Prodder & Wiggs are to publish – *The Secret Nine*. Every time I sit down to write it a girl keeps trying to sneak in.'

'Into the room?'

'Into the story.'

'You don't want a love interest in your sort of book,' said Mr McKinnon, shaking his head. 'It delays the action.'

'I know it does. And every day I have to keep shooing this infernal female out. An awful girl, McKinnon. A soppy, soupy, treacly, drooping girl with a roguish smile. This morning she tried to butt in on the scene where Lester Gage is trapped in the den of the mysterious leper.'

'No!'

'She did, I assure you. I had to rewrite three pages before I could get her out of it. And that's not the worst. Do you know, McKinnon, that at this moment I am actually living the plot of a typical Leila May Pinckney novel in just the setting she always used! And I can see the happy ending coming nearer every day! A week ago a girl was knocked down by a car at my door and I've had to put her up, and every day I realize more clearly that sooner or later I shall ask her to marry me.'

'Don't do it,' said Mr McKinnon, a stout bachelor. 'You're too young to marry.'

'So was Methuselah,' said James, a stouter. 'But all the same I know I'm going to do it. It's the influence of this awful house weighing upon me. I feel like an eggshell in a maelstrom. I am being sucked on by a force too strong for me to resist. This morning I found myself kissing her dog!'

'No!'

'I did! And I loathe the little beast. Yesterday I got up at dawn and plucked a nosegay of flowers for her, wet with the dew.'

'Rodman!'

'It's a fact. I laid them at her door and went downstairs kicking myself all the way. And there in the hall was the apple-checked housekeeper regarding me archly. If she didn't murmur "Bless their sweet young hearts!" my ears deceived me.'

'Why don't you pack up and leave?'

'If I do I lose the five thousand pounds.'

'Ah!' said Mr McKinnon.

'I can understand what has happened. It's the same with all haunted houses. My aunt's subliminal ether vibrations have woven themselves into the texture of the place, creating an atmosphere which forces the ego of all who come in contact with it to attune themselves to it. It's either that or something to do with the fourth dimension.'

Mr McKinnon laughed scornfully.

'Tut-tut!' he said again. 'This is pure imagination. What has happened is that you've been working too hard. You'll see this precious atmosphere of yours will have no effect on me.'

'That's exactly why I asked you to come down. I hoped you might break the spell.'

'I will that,' said Mr McKinnon jovially.

The fact that the literary agent spoke little at lunch caused James no apprehension. Mr McKinnon was ever a silent trencherman. From time to time James caught him stealing a glance at the girl, who was well enough to come down to meals now, limping pathetically, but he could read nothing in his face. And yet the mere look of his face was a consolation. It was so solid, so matter of fact, so exactly like an unemotional coconut.

'You've done me good,' said James with a sigh of relief, as he escorted the agent down the garden to his car after lunch. 'I felt all along that I could rely on your rugged common sense. The whole atmosphere of the place seems different now.'

Mr McKinnon did nor speak for a moment. He seemed to be plunged in thought.

'Rodman,' he said, as he got into his car, 'I've been thinking over that suggestion of yours of putting a love interest into *The Secret Nine*. I think you're wise. The story needs it. After all, what is there greater in the world than love? Love – love – aye, it's the sweetest word in the language. Put in a heroine and let her marry Lester Gage.'

'If,' said James grimly, 'she does succeed in worming her way in she'll jolly well marry the mysterious leper. But look here, I don't understand—'

'It was seeing that girl that changed me,' proceeded Mr McKinnon. And as James stared at him aghast, tears suddenly filled his hard-boiled eyes. He openly snuffled. 'Aye, seeing her sitting there under the roses, with all that smell of honeysuckle and all. And the birdies singing so sweet in the garden and the sun lighting up her bonny face. The puir wee lass!' he muttered, dabbing at his eyes. 'The puir bonny wee lass! Rodman,' he said, his voice quivering, 'I've decided that we're being hard on Prodder & Wiggs. Wiggs has had sickness in his home lately. We mustn't be hard on a man who's had sickness in his home, hey, laddie? No, no! I'm going to take back that contract and alter it to a flat 12 per cent. and no advance royalties.'

'What!'

'But you shan't lose by it, Rodman. No, no, you shan't lose by it, my manny. I am going to waive my commission. The puir bonny wee lass!'

The car rolled off down the road. Mr McKinnon, seated in the back, was blowing his nose violently.

'This is the end!' said James.

It is necessary at this point to pause and examine James Rodman's position with an unbiased eye. The average man, unless he puts himself in James's place, will be unable to appreciate it. James, he will feel, was making a lot of fuss about nothing. Here he was, drawing daily closer and closer to a charming girl with big blue eyes, and surely rather to be envied than pitied.

But we must remember that James was one of Nature's bachelors. And no ordinary man, looking forward dreamily to a little home of his own with a loving wife putting out his slippers and changing the gramophone records, can realize the intensity of the instinct for self-preservation which animates Nature's bachelors in times of peril.

James Rodman had a congenital horror of matrimony. Though a young man, he had allowed himself to develop a great many habits which were as the breath of life to him; and these habits, he knew instinctively, a wife would shoot to pieces within a week of the end of the honeymoon.

James liked to breakfast in bed; and, having breakfasted, to smoke in bed and knock the ashes out on the carpet. What wife would tolerate this practice?

James liked to pass his days in a tennis shirt, grey flannel trousers and slippers. What wife ever rests until she has inclosed her husband in a stiff collar, tight boots and a morning suit and taken him with her to *thés musicales*?

These and a thousand other thoughts of the same kind flashed through the unfortunate young man's mind as the days went by, and every day that passed seemed to draw him nearer to the brink of the chasm. Fate appeared to be taking a malicious pleasure in making things as difficult for him as possible. Now that the girl was well enough to leave her bed, she spent her time sitting in a chair on the sun-sprinkled porch, and James had to read to her – and poetry, at that; and not the jolly, wholesome sort of poetry the boys are turning out nowadays, either – good, honest stuff about sin and gas works and decaying corpses – but the old-fashioned kind with rhymes in it, dealing almost exclusively with love. The weather, moreover, continued superb. The honeysuckle cast its sweet scent on the gentle breeze; the roses over the porch stirred and nodded; the flowers in the garden were lovelier than ever; the birds sang their little throats sore. And every evening there was a magnificent sunset. It was almost as if Nature were doing it on purpose.

At last James intercepted Doctor Brady as he was leaving after one of his visits and put the thing to him squarely:

'When is that girl going?'

The doctor patted him on the arm.

'Not yet, Rodman,' he said in a low, understanding voice. 'No need to worry yourself about that. Mustn't be moved for days and days and days – I might almost say weeks and weeks and weeks.'

'Weeks and weeks!' cried James.

'And weeks,' said Doctor Brady. He prodded James roguishly in the abdomen. 'Good luck to you, my boy, good luck to you,' he said.

It was some small consolation to James that the mushy physician immediately afterward tripped over William on his way down the path and broke his stethoscope. When a man is up against it like James every little helps.

He was walking dismally back to the house after this conversation when he was met by the apple-cheeked housekeeper.

'The little lady would like to speak to you, sir,' said the apple-cheeked exhibit, rubbing her hands.

'Would she?' said James hollowly.

'So sweet and pretty she looks, sir – oh, sir, you wouldn't believe! Like a blessed angel sitting there with her dear eyes all a-shining.'

'Don't do it!' cried James with extraordinary vehemence. 'Don't do it!'

He found the girl propped up on the cushions and thought once again how singularly he disliked her. And yet, even as he thought this, some force against which he had to fight madly was whispering to him, 'Go to her and take that little hand! Breathe into that little ear the burning words that will make that little face turn away crimsoned with blushes!' He wiped a bead of perspiration from his forehead and sat down.

'Mrs Stick-in-the-Mud – what's her name? – says you want to see me.'

The girl nodded.

'I've had a letter from Uncle Henry. I wrote to him as soon as I was better and told him what had happened, and he is coming here to-morrow morning.'

'Uncle Henry?'

'That's what I call him, but he's really no relation. He is my guardian. He and daddy were officers in the same regiment, and when daddy was killed, fighting on the Afghan frontier, he died in Uncle Henry's arms and with his last breath begged him to take care of me.'

James started. A sudden wild hope had waked in his heart. Years ago, he remembered, he had read a book of his aunt's entitled *Rupert's Legacy*, and in that book –

'I'm engaged to marry him,' said the girl quietly.

'Wow!' shouted James.

'What?' asked the girl, startled.

'Touch of cramp,' said James. He was thrilling all over. That wild hope had been realized.

'It was daddy's dying wish that we should marry,' said the girl.

'And dashed sensible of him, too; dashed sensible,' said James warmly.

'And yet,' she went on, a little wistfully, 'I sometimes wonder—'

'Don't!' said James. 'Don't! You must respect daddy's dying wish. There's nothing like daddy's dying wish; you can't beat it. So he's coming here to-morrow, is he? Capital, capital! To lunch, I suppose? Excellent! I'll run down and tell Mrs Who-Is-It to lay in another chop.'

It was with a gay and uplifted heart that James strolled the garden and smoked his pipe next morning. A great cloud seemed to have rolled itself away from him. Everything was for the best in the best of all possible worlds. He had finished *The Secret Nine* and shipped it off to Mr McKinnon, and now as he strolled there was shaping itself in his mind a corking plot about a man with only half a face who lived in a secret den and terrorized London with a series of shocking murders. And what made them so shocking was the fact that each of the victims, when discovered, was found to have only half a face too. The rest had been chipped off, presumably by some blunt instrument.

The thing was coming out magnificently, when suddenly his attention was diverted by a piercing scream. Out of the bushes fringing the river that ran beside the garden burst the apple-cheeked housekeeper.

'Oh, sir! Oh, sir! Oh, sir!'

'What is it?' demanded James irritably.

'Oh, sir! Oh, sir! Oh, sir!'

'Yes, and then what?'

'The little dog, sir! He's in the river!'

'Well, whistle him to come out.'

'Oh, sir, do come quick! He'll be drowned!'

James followed her through the bushes, taking off his

coat as he went. He was saying to himself, 'I will not rescue this dog. I do not like the dog. It is high time he had a bath, and in any case it would be much simpler to stand on the bank and fish for him with a rake. Only an ass out of a Leila J. Pinckney book would dive into a beastly river to save—'

At this point he dived. Toto, alarmed by the splash, swam rapidly for the bank, but James was too quick for him. Grasping him firmly by the neck, he scrambled ashore and ran for the house, followed by the housekeeper.

The girl was seated on the porch. Over her there bent the tall soldierly figure of a man with keen eyes and greying hair. The housekeeper raced up.

'Oh, miss! Toto! In the river! He saved him! He plunged in and saved him!'

The girl drew a quick breath.

'Gallant, damme! By Jove! By gad! Yes, gallant, by George!' exclaimed the soldierly man.

The girl seemed to wake from a reverie.

'Uncle Henry, this is Mr Rodman. Mr Rodman, my guardian, Colonel Carteret.'

'Proud to meet you, sir,' said the colonel, his honest blue eyes glowing as he fingered his short crisp moustache. 'As fine a thing as I ever heard of, damme!'

'Yes, you are brave – brave,' the girl whispered.

'I am wet – wet,' said James, and went upstairs to change his clothes.

When he came down for lunch, he found to his relief that the girl had decided not to join them, and Colonel Carteret was silent and preoccupied. James, exerting himself in his capacity of host, tried him with the weather, golf, India, the Government, the high cost of living, first-class cricket, the modern dancing craze, and murderers he had met, but the other still preserved that strange, absent-minded silence. It was only when the meal was concluded and James had produced cigarettes that he came abruptly out of his trance.

'Rodman,' he said, 'I should like to speak to you.'

'Yes?' said James, thinking it was about time.

'Rodman,' said Colonel Carteret, 'or rather, George – I may call you George?' he added, with a sort of wistful diffidence that had a singular charm.

'Certainly,' replied James, 'if you wish it. Though my name is James.'

'James, eh? Well, well, it amounts to the same thing, eh, what, damme, by gad?' said the colonel with a momentary return of his bluff soldierly manner. 'Well, then, James, I have something that I wish to say to you. Did Miss Maynard – did Rose happen to tell you anything about myself in – er – in connection with herself?'

'She mentioned that you and she were engaged to be married.'

The colonel's tightly drawn lips quivered.

'No longer,' he said.

'What?'

'No, John, my boy.'

'James.'

'No, James, my boy, no longer. While you were upstairs changing your clothes she told me – breaking down, poor child, as she spoke – that she wished our engagement to be at an end.'

James half rose from the table, his cheeks blanched.

'You don't mean that!' he gasped.

Colonel Carteret nodded. He was staring out of the window, his fine eyes set in a look of pain.

'But this is nonsense!' cried James. 'This is absurd! She – she mustn't be allowed to chop and change like this. I mean to say, it – it isn't fair—'

'Don't think of me, my boy.'

'I'm not – I mean, did she give any reason?'

'Her eyes did.'

'Her eyes did?'

'Her eyes, when she looked at you on the porch, as you stood there – young, heroic – having just saved the life of the dog she loves. It is you who won that tender heart, my boy.'

'Now listen,' protested James, 'you aren't going to sit there and tell me that a girl falls in love with a man just because he saves her dog from drowning?'

'Why, surely,' said Colonel Carteret, surprised. 'What better reason could she have?' He sighed. 'It is the old, old story, my boy. Youth to youth. I am an old man. I should have known – I should have foreseen – yes, youth to youth.'

'You aren't a bit old.'

'Yes, yes.'

'No, no.'

'Yes, yes.'

'Don't keep on saying yes, yes!' cried James, clutching at his hair. 'Besides, she wants a steady old buffer – a steady, sensible man of medium age – to look after her.'

Colonel Carteret shook his head with a gentle smile.

'This is mere quixotry, my boy. It is splendid of you to take this attitude; but no, no.'

'Yes, yes.'

'No, no.' He gripped James's hand for an instant, then rose and walked to the door. 'That is all I wished to say, Tom.'

'James.'

'James. I just thought that you ought to know how matters stood. Go to her, my boy, go to her, and don't let any thought of an old man's broken dream keep you from pouring out what is in your heart. I am an old soldier, lad, an old soldier. I have learned to take the rough with the smooth. But I think – I think I will leave you now. I – I should – should like to be alone for a while. If you need me you will find me in the raspberry bushes.'

He had scarcely gone when James also left the room. He took his hat and stick and walked blindly out of the garden, he knew not whither. His brain was numbed. Then, as his powers of reasoning returned, he told himself that he should have foreseen this ghastly thing. If there was one type of character over which Leila J. Pinckney had been wont to spread herself, it was the pathetic guardian who loves his ward but relinquishes her to the younger man. No wonder the girl had broken off the engagement. Any elderly guardian who allowed himself to come within a mile of Honeysuckle Cottage was simply asking for it. And then, as he turned to walk back, a sort of dull defiance gripped James. Why, he asked, should he be put upon in this manner? If the girl liked to throw over this man, why should he be the goat?

He saw his way clearly now. He just wouldn't do it, that was all. And if they didn't like it they could lump it.

Full of a new fortitude, he strode in at the gate. A tall, soldierly figure emerged from the raspberry bushes and came to meet him.

'Well?' said Colonel Carteret.

'Well?' said James defiantly.

'Am I to congratulate you?'

James caught his keen blue eye and hesitated. It was not going to be so simple as he had supposed.

'Well – er—' he said.

Into the keen blue eyes there came a look that James had not seen there before. It was the stern, hard look which – probably – had caused men to bestow upon this old soldier the name of Cold-Steel Carteret.

'You have not asked Rose to marry you?'

'Er – no; not yet.'

The keen blue eyes grew keener and bluer.

'Rodman,' said Colonel Carteret in a strange, quiet voice, 'I have known that little girl since she was a tiny child. For years she has been all in all to me. Her father died in my arms and with his last breath bade me see that no harm came to his darling. I have nursed her through mumps, measles – aye, and chicken pox – and I live but for her happiness.' He paused, with a significance that made James's toes curl. 'Rodman,' he said, 'do you know what I would do to any man who trifled with that little girl's affections?' He reached in his hip pocket and an ugly-looking revolver glittered in the sunlight. 'I would shoot him like a dog.'

'Like a dog?' faltered James.

'Like a dog,' said Colonel Carteret. He took James's arm and turned him toward the house. 'She is on the porch. Go to her. And if—' He broke off. 'But tut!' he said in a kindlier tone. 'I am doing you an injustice, my boy. I know it.'

'Oh, you are,' said James fervently.

'Your heart is in the right place.'

'Oh, absolutely,' said James.

'Then go to her, my boy. Later on you may have something to tell me. You will find me in the strawberry beds.'

It was very cool and fragrant on the porch. Overhead, little breezes played and laughed among the roses. Somewhere in the distance sheep bells tinkled, and in the shrubbery a thrush was singing its even-song.

Seated in her chair behind a wicker table laden with tea

things, Rose Maynard watched James as he shambled up the path.

'Tea's ready,' she called gaily. 'Where is Uncle Henry?' A look of pity and distress flitted for a moment over her flower-like face. 'Oh, I – I forgot,' she whispered.

'He is in the strawberry beds,' said James in a low voice.

She nodded unhappily.

'Of course, of course. Oh, why is life like this?' James heard her whisper.

He sat down. He looked at the girl. She was leaning back with closed eyes, and he thought he had never seen such a little squirt in his life. The idea of passing his remaining days in her society revolted him. He was stoutly opposed to the idea of marrying anyone; but if, as happens to the best of us, he ever were compelled to perform the wedding glide, he had always hoped it would be with some lady golf champion who would help him with his putting, and thus, by bringing his handicap down a notch or two, enable him to save something from the wreck, so to speak. But to link his lot with a girl who read his aunt's books and liked them; a girl who could tolerate the presence of the dog Toto; a girl who clasped her hands in pretty, childish joy when she saw a nasturtium in bloom – it was too much. Nevertheless, he took her hand and began to speak.

'Miss Maynard – Rose—'

She opened her eyes and cast them down. A flush had come into her cheeks. The dog Toto at her side sat up and begged for cake, disregarded.

'Let me tell you a story. Once upon a time there was a lonely man who lived in a cottage all by himself—'

He stopped. Was it James Rodman who was talking this bilge?

'Yes?' whispered the girl.

'—but one day there came to him out of nowhere a little fairy princess. She—'

He stopped again, but this time not because of the sheer shame of listening to his own voice. What caused him to interrupt his tale was the fact that at this moment the tea table suddenly began to rise slowly in the air, tilting as it did so a considerable quantity of hot tea on to the knees of his trousers.

'Ouch!' cried James, leaping.

The table continued to rise, and then fell sideways, revealing the homely countenance of William, who, concealed by the cloth, had been taking a nap beneath it. He moved slowly forward, his eyes on Toto. For many a long day William had been desirous of putting to the test, once and for all, the problem of whether Toto was edible or not. Sometimes he thought yes, at other times no. Now seemed an admirable opportunity for a definite decision. He advanced on the object of his experiment, making a low whistling noise through his nostrils, nor unlike a boiling kettle. And Toto, after one long look of incredulous horror, tucked his shapely tail between his legs and, turning, raced for safety. He had laid a course in a bee line for the open garden gate, and William, shaking a dish of marmalade off his head a little petulantly, galloped ponderously after him. Rose Maynard staggered to her feet.

'Oh, save him!' she cried.

Without a word James added himself to the procession. His interest in Toto was but tepid. What he wanted was to get near enough to William to discuss with him that matter of the tea on his trousers. He reached the road and found that the order of the runners had not changed. For so small a dog, Toto was moving magnificently. A cloud of dust rose as he skidded round the corner. William followed. James followed William.

And so they passed Farmer Birkett's barn, Farmer Giles' cow shed, the place where Farmer Willetts' pigsty used to be before the big fire, and the Bunch of Grapes public house, Jno Biggs propr., licensed to sell tobacco, wines and spirits. And it was as they were turning down the lane that leads past Farmer Robinson's chicken run that Toto, thinking swiftly, bolted abruptly into a small drain pipe.

'William!' roared James, coming up at a canter. He stopped to pluck a branch from the hedge and swooped darkly on.

William had been crouching before the pipe, making a noise like a bassoon into its interior; but now he rose and came beamingly to James. His eyes were aglow with chumminess and affection; and placing his forefeet on James's chest, he licked him three times on the face in rapid succession. And as he did so, something seemed to snap in James. The scales seemed to fall from James's eyes. For the first time he saw William as he really was, the authentic type of dog that saves his master from a frightful peril. A wave of emotion swept over him.

'William!' he muttered. 'William!'

William was making an early supper off a half brick he had found in the road. James stooped and patted him fondly.

'William,' he whispered, 'you knew when the time had come to change the conversation, didn't you, old boy!' He straightened himself. 'Come, William,' he said. Another four miles and we reach Meadowsweet Junction. Make it snappy and we shall just catch the up express, first stop London.'

William looked up into his face and it seemed to James that he gave a brief nod of comprehension and approval. James turned. Through the trees to the east he could see the red roof of Honeysuckle Cottage, lurking like some evil dragon in ambush.

Then, together, man and dog passed silently into the sunset.

That (concluded Mr Mulliner) is the story of my distant cousin James Rodman. As to whether it is true, that, of course, is an open question. I, personally, am of opinion that it is. There is no doubt that James did go to live at Honeysuckle Cottage and, while there, underwent some experience which has left an ineradicable mark upon him. His eyes to-day have that unmistakable look which is to be seen only in the eyes of confirmed bachelors whose feet have been dragged to the very brink of the pit and who have gazed at close range into the naked face of matrimony.

And, if further proof be needed, there is William. He is now James's inseparable companion. Would any man be habitually seen in public with a dog like William unless he had some solid cause to be grateful to him, – unless they were linked together by some deep and imperishable memory? I think not. Myself when I observe William coming along the street, I cross the road and look into a shop window till he has passed. I am not a snob, but I dare not risk my position in Society by being seen talking to that curious compound.

Nor is the precaution an unnecessary one. There is about William a shameless absence of appreciation of class distinctions which recalls the worst excesses of the French Revolution. I have seen him with these eyes chivvy a pomeranian belonging to a Baroness in her own right from near the Achilles Statue to within a few yards of the Marble Arch.

And yet James walks daily with him in Piccadilly. It is surely significant.

L. P. HARTLEY

W.S.

THE FIRST POSTCARD came from Forfar.

> I thought you might like a picture of Forfar,

it began.

> You have always been so interested in Scotland, and that is one reason why I am interested in you. I have enjoyed all your books, but do you really get to grips with people? I doubt it. Try to think of this as a handshake from your devoted admirer, *W.S.*

Like other novelists, Walter Streeter was used to getting communications from strangers. Generally they were friendly but sometimes they were critical. In either case he always answered them, for he was conscientious. But answering them took up the time and energy he needed for his writing, so that he was rather relieved that W.S. had given no address. The photograph of Forfar was uninteresting and he tore it up. His anonymous correspondent's criticism, however, lingered in his mind. Did he really fail to come to grips with his characters? Perhaps he did. He was aware that in most cases they were either projections of his own personality, or, in different forms, the antitheses of it. The Me and the Not Me. Perhaps W.S. had spotted this. Not for the first time Walter made a vow to be more objective.

About ten days later arrived another postcard, this time from Berwick-on-Tweed.

What do you think of Berwick-on-Tweed?

it said.

> Like you, it's on the Border. I hope this doesn't sound rude. I don't mean that you are a border-line case! You know how much I admire your stories. Some people call them other-worldly. I think you should plump for one world or the other. Another warm handshake from *W.S.*

Walter Streeter pondered over this and began to wonder about the sender. Was his correspondent a man or a woman? It looked like a man's handwriting – commercial, unself-conscious, and the criticism was like a man's. On the other hand, it was like a woman to probe – to want to make him feel at the same time flattered and unsure of himself. He felt the faint stirrings of curiosity but soon dismissed them; he was not a man to experiment with acquaintances. Still, it was odd to think of this unknown person speculating about him, sizing him up. Other-worldly, indeed! He re-read the last two chapters he had written. Perhaps they didn't have their feet firm on the ground. Perhaps he was too ready to escape, as other novelists were nowadays, into an ambiguous world, a world where the conscious mind did not have things too much its own way. But did that matter? He threw the picture of Berwick-on-Tweed into his November fire and tried to write; but the words came haltingly, as though contending with an extra-strong barrier of self-criticism. And as the days passed, he became uncomfortably aware of self-division, as though someone had taken hold of his personality and was pulling it apart. His work was no longer homogeneous; there were two strains in it, unreconciled and opposing, and it went much slower as he tried to resolve the discord. Never mind, he thought: perhaps I was getting into a groove. These difficulties may be growing pains; I may have tapped a new source of supply. If only I could correlate the two and make their conflict fruitful, as many artists have!

The third postcard showed a picture of York Minster.

> I know you are interested in cathedrals,

it said.

> I'm sure this isn't a sign of megalomania in your case, but smaller churches are sometimes more rewarding. I'm seeing a good many churches on my way south. Are you busy writing or are you looking around for ideas? Another hearty handshake from your friend, *W.S.*

It was true that Walter Streeter was interested in cathedrals. Lincoln Cathedral had been the subject of one of his youthful fantasies and he had written about it in a travel book. And it was also true that he admired mere size and was inclined to under-value parish churches. But how could W.S. have known that? And was it really a sign of megalomania? And who was W.S. anyhow?

For the first time it struck him that the initials were his own. No, not for the first time. He had noticed it before, but they were such commonplace initials; they were Gilbert's, they were Maugham's, they were Shakespeare's – a common possession. Anyone might have them. Yet now it seemed to him an odd coincidence; and the idea came into his mind – suppose I have been writing postcards to myself? People did such things, especially people with split personalities. Not that he was one of them, of course. And yet there was this unexplained development – the dichotomy in his writing, which had now extended from his thought to his style, making one paragraph languorous with semicolons and subordinate clauses, and another sharp and incisive with main verbs and full-stops.

He looked at the handwriting again. It had seemed the perfection of ordinariness – anybody's hand – so ordinary as perhaps to be disguised. Now he fancied he saw in it resemblances to his own. He was just going to pitch the postcard in the fire when suddenly he decided not to. I'll show it to somebody, he thought.

His friend said, 'My dear fellow, it's all quite plain. The woman's a lunatic. I'm sure it's a woman. She has probably fallen in love with you and wants to make you interested in her. I should pay no attention whatsoever. People in the public eye are always getting letters from lunatics. If they worry you, destroy them without reading them. That sort of person is often a little psychic, and if she senses that she's getting a rise out of you, she'll go on.'

For a moment Walter Streeter felt reassured. A woman, a little mouse-like creature, who had somehow taken a fancy to him! What was there to feel uneasy about in that? Then his subconscious mind, searching for something to torment him with, and assuming the authority of logic, said: Supposing those postcards are a lunatic's, and you are writing them to yourself; doesn't it follow that you must be a lunatic too? He tried to put the thought away from him; he tried to destroy the postcard as he had the others. But something in him wanted to preserve it. It had become a piece of him, he felt. Yielding to an irresistible compulsion, which he dreaded, he found himself putting it behind the clock on the chimney-piece. He couldn't see it, but he knew that it was there.

He now had to admit to himself that the postcard business had become a leading factor in his life. It had created a new area of thoughts and feelings and they were most unhelpful. His being was strung up in expectation of the next postcard.

Yet when it came it took him as the others had, completely by surprise. He could not bring himself to look at the picture.

I am coming nearer,

the postcard said;

> I have got as near as Coventry. Have you ever been sent to Coventry? I have, in fact you sent me. It isn't a pleasant experience, I can tell you. Perhaps we shall come to grips after all. I advised you to come to grips with your characters, didn't I? Have I given you any new ideas? If I have, you ought to thank me, for they are what novelists want, I understand. I have been re-reading your novels, living in them, I might say. Je vous serre la main. As always. *W.S.*

A wave of panic surged up in Walter Streeter. How was it that he had never noticed, all this time, the most significant fact about the postcards – that each one came from a place geographically closer to him than the last? *I am coming nearer.* Had his mind, unconsciously self-protective, worn blinkers? If it had, he wished he could put them back. He took an atlas and idly traced W.S.'s itinerary. An interval of eighty miles or so seemed to separate the stopping-places. Walter lived in a large West Country town about that distance from Coventry.

Should he show the postcards to an alienist? But what could an alienist tell him? He would not know, what Walter wanted to know, whether he had anything to fear from W.S.

Better go to the police. The police were used to dealing with poison-pens. If they laughed at him, so much the better.

They did not laugh, however. They said they thought the postcards were a hoax and that W.S. would never show up in the flesh. Then they asked if there was anyone who had a grudge against him. 'No one that I know of,' Walter said.

They, too, took the view that the writer was probably a woman. They told him not to worry but to let them know if further postcards came.

A little comforted. Walter went home. The talk with the police had done him good. He thought it over. It was quite true what he had told them – that he had no enemies. He was not a man of strong personal feelings; such feelings as he had went into his books. In his books he had drawn some pretty nasty characters. Not of recent years, however. Of recent years he had felt a reluctance to draw a very bad man or woman: he thought it morally irresponsible and artistically unconvincing, too. There was good in everyone: Iagos were a myth. Latterly – but he had to admit that it was several weeks since he laid pen to paper, so much had this ridiculous business of the postcards weighed upon his mind – if he had to draw a really wicked person he represented him as a Communist or a Nazi – someone who had deliberately put off his human characteristics. But in the past, when he was younger and more inclined to see things as black or white, he had let himself go once or twice. He did not remember his old books very well but there was a character in one, *The Outcast*, into whom he had really got his knife. He had written about him with extreme vindictiveness, just as if he was a real person whom he was trying to show up. He had experienced a curious pleasure in attributing every kind of wickedness to this man. He never gave him the benefit of the doubt. He never felt a twinge of pity for him, even when he paid the penalty for his misdeeds on the gallows. He had so worked himself up that the idea of this dark creature, creeping about brimful of malevolence, had almost frightened him.

Odd that he couldn't remember the man's name. He took the book down from the shelf and turned the pages – even now they affected him uncomfortably. Yes, here it was, William . . . William . . . he would have to look back to find the surname, William Stainsforth.

His own initials.

He did not think the coincidence meant anything, but it coloured his mind and weakened its resistance to his obsession. So uneasy was he that when the next postcard came, it came as a relief.

Does this remind you of anything?

he read, and involuntarily turned the postcard over. He saw a picture of a gaol – Gloucester gaol. He stared at it as if it could tell him something, then with an effort went on reading.

> I am quite close now. My movements, as you may have guessed, are not quite under my control, but all being well, I look forward to seeing you some time this weekend. Then we can really come to grips. I wonder if you'll recognize me! It won't be the first time you have given me hospitality. Ti stringo la mano. As always. *W.S.*

Walter took the postcard straight to the police station, and asked if he could have police protection over the weekend. The officer in charge smiled at him and said he was quite sure it was a hoax: but he would tell someone to keep an eye on the place.

'You still have no idea who it could be?' he asked.

Walter shook his head.

It was Tuesday. Walter Streeter had plenty of time to think about the weekend. At first he felt he would not be able to live through the interval but, strange to say, his confidence increased instead of waning. He set himself to work as though he could work, and presently he found he could –

differently from before, and, he thought, better. It was as though the nervous strain he had been living under had, like an acid, dissolved a layer of non-conductive thought that came between him and his subject: he was nearer to it now, and instead of responding only too readily to his stage directions, his characters gave themselves wholeheartedly to all the tests he put them to. So passed the days, and the dawn of Friday seemed like any other day until something jerked him out of his self-induced trance, and suddenly he asked himself. 'When does a weekend begin?'

A long weekend begins on Friday. At that his panic returned. He went to the street door and looked out. It was a suburban, unfrequented street of detached Regency houses like his own. They had tall square gateposts, some crowned with semi-circular iron brackets holding lanterns. Most of these were out of repair, only two or three were ever lit. A car went slowly down the street; some people crossed it; everything was normal.

Several times that day he went to look and saw nothing unusual, and when Saturday came, bringing no postcard. his panic had almost subsided. He nearly rang up the police to tell them not to bother to send anyone after all.

But they were as good as their word: they did send someone. Between tea and dinner, the time when weekend guests most commonly arrive, Walter went to the door and there, between two unlit gateposts, he saw a policeman standing – the first policeman he had ever seen in Charlotte Street. At the sight, and the relief it brought him, he realized how anxious he had been. Now he felt safer than he had ever felt in his life, and also a little ashamed at having given extra trouble to a hard-worked body of men. Should he go and speak to his unknown guardian, offer him a cup of tea or a drink? It would be nice to hear him laugh at Walter's fancies.

But no – somehow he felt his security the greater when its source was impersonal and anonymous. 'PC Smith' was somehow less impressive than 'police protection'.

Several times from an upper window (he didn't like to open the door and stare) he made sure that his guardian was still there: and once, for added proof, he asked his housekeeper to verify the strange phenomenon. Disappointingly, she came back saying she had seen no policeman; but she was not very good at seeing things, and when Walter went a few minutes later, he saw him plain enough. The man must walk about, of course; perhaps he had been taking a stroll when Mrs Kendal looked.

It was contrary to his routine to work after dinner but to-night he did – he felt so much in the vein. Indeed, a sort of exaltation possessed him; the words ran off his pen; it would be foolish to check the creative impulse for the sake of a little extra sleep. On, on. They were right who said the small hours were the time to work. When his housekeeper came in to say good night, he scarcely raised his eyes.

In the warm, snug little room the silence purred around him like a kettle. He did not even hear the door-bell till it had been ringing for some time.

A visitor at this hour?

His knees trembling, he went to the door, scarcely knowing what he expected to find; so what was his relief, on opening it, to see the doorway filled by the tall figure of a policeman. Without waiting for the man to speak, 'Come in, come in, my dear fellow,' he exclaimed. He held his hand out, but the policeman did not take it. 'You must have been very cold standing out there. I didn't know that it was snowing, though,' he added, seeing the snowflakes on the policeman's cape and helmet. 'Come in and warm yourself.'

'Thanks,' said the policeman. 'I don't mind if I do.'

Walter knew enough of the phrases used by men of the policeman's stamp not to mistake this for a grudging acceptance. 'This way,' he prattled on. 'I was writing in my study. By Jove, it *is* cold, I'll turn the gas on more. Now won't you take your traps off, and make yourself at home?'

'I can't stay long,' the policeman said, 'I've got a job to do, as *you* know.'

'Oh, yes,' said Walter, 'such a silly job, a sinecure.' He stopped, wondering if the policeman would know what a sinecure was. 'I suppose you know what it's about – the postcards?'

The policeman nodded.

'But nothing can happen to me as long as you are here,' said Walter. 'I shall be as safe . . . as safe as houses. Stay as long as you can, and have a drink.'

'I never drink on duty,' said the policeman. Still in his cape and helmet, he looked round. 'So this is where you work?' he said.

'Yes, I was writing when you rang.'

'Some poor devil's for it, I expect,' the policeman said.

'Oh, why?' Walter was hurt by his unfriendly tone, and noticed how hard his gooseberry eyes were.

'I'll tell you in a minute,' said the policeman, and then the telephone bell rang. Walter excused himself and hurried from the room.

'This is the police station,' said a voice. 'Is that Mr Streeter?'

Walter said it was.

'Well, Mr Streeter, how is everything at your place? All right, I hope? I'll tell you why I ask. I'm sorry to say we quite forgot about that little job we were going to do for you. Bad co-ordination, I'm afraid.'

'But,' said Walter, 'you did send someone.'

'No, Mr Streeter, I'm afraid we didn't.'

'But there's a policeman here, here in this very house. There was a pause, then his interlocutor said, in a less casual voice:

'He can't be one of our chaps. Did you see his number by any chance?'

'No.'

After another pause the voice said:

'Would you like us to send somebody now?'

'Yes, p – please.'

'All right then, we'll be with you in a jiffy.'

Walter put back the receiver. What now? he asked himself. Should he barricade the door? Should he run out into the street? Should he try to rouse his housekeeper? A policeman of any sort was something to be reckoned with: but a *rogue* policeman! A law-keeper turned law-breaker, roaming about loose, savaging people! How long would it take the real police to come? What was a jiffy in terms of minutes? While he was debating, the door opened and his guest came in.

'No room's private when the street door's once passed,' he said. 'Had you forgotten I was a policeman?'

'Was?' said Walter, edging away from him. 'You *are* a policeman.'

'I have been other things as well,' the policeman said. 'Thief, pimp, blackmailer, not to mention murderer. *You* should know.'

The policeman, if such he was, seemed to be moving towards him and Walter suddenly became alive to the importance of small distances – the space between the sideboard and the table, and between one chair and another.

'I don't know what you mean,' he said. 'Why do you

speak like that? I've never done you any harm. I've never set eyes on you before.'

'Oh, haven't you?' the man said. 'But you've thought about me, and' – his voice rose – 'you've written about me. You got some fun out of me, didn't you? Now I'm going to get some fun out of you. You made me just as nasty as you could. Wasn't that doing me harm? You didn't think what it would feel like to be me, did you? You didn't put yourself in my place, did you? You hadn't any pity for me, had you? Well, I'm not going to have any pity for you.'

'But I tell you,' cried Walter, clutching the table's edge, 'I don't know you!'

'And now you say you don't know me! You did all that to me and then forgot me.' His voice became a whine, charged with self-pity. 'You forgot William Stainsforth.'

'William Stainsforth!'

'Yes. I was your scapegoat, wasn't I? You unloaded all your self-dislike on me. You felt pretty good while you were writing about me. Now, as one W.S. to another, what shall I do, if I behave in character?'

'I – I don't know,' muttered Walter.

'You don't know?' Stainsforth sneered. 'You ought to know, you fathered me. What would William Stainsforth do if he met his old dad in a quiet place, his kind old dad who made him swing?'

Walter could only stare at him.

'You know what he'd do as well as I,' said Stainsforth. Then his face changed and he said abruptly, 'No you don't, because you never really understood me. I'm not so black as you painted me.' He paused and a flame of hope flickered in Walter's breast. 'You never gave me a chance, did you? Well, I'm going to give you one. That shows you never understood me, doesn't it?'

Walter nodded.

'And there's another thing you have forgotten.

'What is that?'

'I was a kid once,' the ex-policeman said.

Walter said nothing.

'You admit that?' said William Stainsforth grimly. 'Well, if you can tell me of one virtue you ever credited me with – just one kind thought – just one redeeming feature—'

'Yes?' said Walter, trembling.

'Well, then I'll let you off.'

'And if I can't?' whispered Walter.

'Well, then, that's just too bad. We'll have to come to grips and you know what that means. You took off one of my arms but I've still got the other. "Stainsforth of the iron arm" you called me.'

Walter began to pant.

'I'll give you two minutes to remember,' Stainsforth said.

They both looked at the clock. At first the stealthy movement of the hand paralysed Walter's thought. He stared at William Stainsforth's face, his cruel, crafty face, which seemed to be always in shadow, as if it was something the light could not touch. Desperately he searched his memory for the one fact that would save him; but his memory, clenched like a fist, would give up nothing. 'I must invent something,' he thought, and suddenly his mind relaxed and he saw, printed on it like a photograph, the last page of the book. Then, with the speed and magic of a dream, each page appeared before him in perfect clarity until the first was reached, and he realized with overwhelming force that what he looked for was not there. In all that evil there was not one hint of good. And he felt, compulsively and with a kind of exultation that unless he testified to this, the cause of goodness everywhere would be betrayed.

'There's nothing to be said for you!' he shouted. 'Of all your dirty tricks this is the dirtiest! You want me to whitewash you, do you. Why, the very snowflakes on you are turning black! How dare you ask me for a character? I've given you one already! God forbid that I should ever say a good word for you! I'd rather die!'

Stainsforth's one arm shot out. 'Then die!' he said.

The police found Walter Streeter slumped across the dining table. His body was still warm, but he was dead. It was easy to tell how he died, for not only had his mauled, limp hand been shaken, but his throat too. He had been strangled. Of his assailant there was no trace. And how he came to have snowflakes on him remained a mystery, for no snow was reported from any district on the day he died.

EDITH WHARTON

THE LOOKING GLASS

I

MRS ATTLEE HAD never been able to understand why there was any harm in giving people a little encouragement when they needed it.

Sitting back in her comfortable armchair by the fire, her working days over, and her muscular masseuse's hands lying swollen and powerless on her knee, she was at leisure to turn the problem over, and ponder it as there had never been time to do before.

Mrs Attlee was so infirm now that, when her widowed daughter-in-law was away for the day, her granddaughter Moyra Attlee had to stay with her until the kitchen girl had prepared the cold supper, and could come in and sit in the parlour.

'You'd be surprised, you know, my dear, to find how discouraged the grand people get, in those big houses with all the help, and the silver dinner plates, and a bell always handy if the fire wants poking, or the pet dog asks for a drink. . . . And what'd a masseuse be good for, if she didn't jolly up their minds a little along with their muscles? – as Dr Welbridge used to say to me many a time, when he'd given me a difficult patient. And he always gave me the most difficult,' she added proudly.

She paused, aware (for even now little escaped her) that Moyra had ceased to listen, but accepting the fact resignedly, as she did most things in the slow decline of her days.

'It's a fine afternoon,' she reflected, 'and likely she's fidgety because there's a new movie on; or that young fellow's fixed it up to get back earlier from New York. . . .'

She relapsed into silence, following her thoughts; but presently, as happens with old people, they came to the surface again.

'And I hope I'm a good Catholic, as I said to Father Divott the other day, and at peace with heaven, if ever I was took suddenly – but no matter what happens I've got to risk my punishment for the wrong I did to Mrs Clingsland, because as long as I've never repented it there's no use telling Father Divott about it. Is there?'

Mrs Attlee heaved an introspective sigh. Like many humble persons of her kind and creed, she had a vague idea that a sin unrevealed was, as far as the consequences went, a sin uncommitted; and this conviction had often helped her in the difficult task of reconciling doctrine and practice.

II

Moyra Attlee interrupted her listless stare down the empty Sunday street of the New Jersey suburb, and turned an astonished glance on her grandmother.

'Mrs Clingsland? A wrong you did to Mrs Clingsland?'

Hitherto she had lent an inattentive ear to her grandmother's ramblings; the talk of old people seemed to be a language hardly worth learning. But it was not always so with Mrs Attlee's. Her activities among the rich had ceased before the first symptoms of the financial depression; but her tenacious memory was stored with pictures of the luxurious days of which her granddaughter's generation, even in a wider world, knew only by hearsay. Mrs Attlee had a gift for evoking in a few words scenes of half-understood opulence and leisure, like a guide leading a stranger through the gallery of a palace in the twilight, and now and then lifting a lamp to a shimmering Rembrandt or a jeweled Rubens; and it was particularly when she mentioned Mrs Clingsland that Moyra caught these dazzling glimpses. Mrs Clingsland had always been something more than a name to the Attlee family. They knew (though they did not know why) that it was through her help that Grandmother Attlee had been able, years ago, to buy the little house at Montclair, with a patch of garden behind it, where, all through the depression, she had held out, thanks to fortunate investments made on the advice of Mrs Clingsland's great friend, the banker.

'She had so many friends, and they were all high-up people, you understand. Many's the time she'd say to me: "Cora" (think of the loveliness of her calling me Cora), "Cora, I'm going to buy some Golden Flyer shares on Mr Stoner's advice; Mr Stoner of the National Union Bank, you know. He's getting me in on the ground floor, as they say, and if you want to step in with me, why come along. There's nothing too good for you, in my opinion," she used to say. And, as it turned out, those shares have kept their head above water all through the bad years, and now I think they'll see me through, and be there when I'm gone, to help out you children.'

To-day Moyra Attlee heard the revered name with a new interest. The phrase: 'The wrong I did to Mrs Clingsland', had struck through her listlessness, rousing her to sudden curiosity. What could her grandmother mean by saying she had done a wrong to the benefactress whose bounties she was never tired of recording? Moyra believed her grandmother to be a very good woman – certainly she had been wonderfully generous in all her dealings with her children and grandchildren; and it seemed incredible that, if there had been one grave lapse in her life, it should have taken the form of an injury to Mrs Clingsland. True, whatever the lapse was, she seemed to have made peace with herself about it; yet it was clear that its being unconfessed lurked disquietingly in the back of her mind.

'How can you say you ever did harm to a friend like Mrs Clingsland, Gran?'

Mrs Attlee's eyes grew sharp behind her spectacles, and she fixed them half distrustfully on the girl's face. But in a moment she seemed to recover herself. 'Not harm, I don't say; I'll never think I harmed her. Bless you, it wasn't to harm her I'd ever have lifted a finger. All I wanted was to help. But when you try to help too many people at once, the devil sometimes takes note of it. You see, there's quotas nowadays for everything, doing good included, my darling.'

Moyra made an impatient movement. She did not care to hear her grandmother philosophize. 'Well – but you said you did a wrong to Mrs Clingsland.'

Mrs Attlee's sharp eyes seemed to draw back behind a mist of age. She sat silent, her hands lying heavily over one another in their tragic uselessness.

'What would *you* have done, I wonder,' she began suddenly, 'if you'd ha' come in on her that morning, and seen her laying in her lovely great bed, with the lace a yard deep on the sheets, and her face buried in the pillows, so I knew she was crying? Would you have opened your bag same as usual, and got out your cocoanut cream and talcum powder, and the nail polishers, and all the rest of it, and waited there like a statue till she turned over to you; or'd you have gone up to her, and turned her softly round, like you would a baby, and said to her: "Now, my dear, I guess you can tell Cora Attlee what's the trouble"? Well, that's what I did, anyhow; and there she was, with her face streaming with tears, and looking like a martyred saint on an altar, and when I said to her: "Come, now, you tell me, and it'll help you," she just sobbed out: "Nothing can ever help me, now I've lost it." '

' "Lost what?" I said, thinking first of her boy, the Lord help me, though I'd heard him whistling on the stairs as I went up; but she said: "My beauty, Cora – I saw it suddenly slipping out of the door from me this morning". . . . Well, at that I had to laugh, and half angrily too. "Your beauty," I said to her, "and is that all? And me that thought it was your husband, or your son – or your fortune even. If it's only your beauty, can't I give it back to you with these hands of mine? But what are you saying to me about beauty, with that seraph's face looking up at me this minute?" I said to her, for she angered me as if she'd been blaspheming.'

'Well, was it true?' Moyra broke in, impatient and yet curious.

'True that she'd lost her beauty?' Mrs Attlee paused to consider. 'Do you know how it is, sometimes when you're doing a bit of fine darning, sitting by the window in the afternoon; and one minute it's full daylight, and your needle seems to find the way of itself; and the next minute you say: "Is it my eyes?" because the work seems blurred; and presently you see it's the daylight going, stealing away, soft-like, from your corner, though there's plenty left overhead. Well – it was that way with her. . . .'

But Moyra had never done fine darning, or strained her eyes in fading light, and she intervened again, more impatiently: 'Well, what did she do?'

Mrs Attlee once more reflected. 'Why, she made me tell her every morning that it wasn't true; and every morning she believed me a little less. And she asked everybody in the house, beginning with her husband, poor man – him so bewildered when you asked him anything outside of his business, or his club or his horses, and never noticing any difference in her looks since the day he'd led her home as his bride, twenty years before, maybe. . . .

'But there – nothing he could have said, if he'd had the wit to say it, would have made any difference. From the day she saw the first little line around her eyes she thought of herself as an old woman, and the thought never left her for more than a few minutes at a time. Oh, when she was dressed up, and laughing, and receiving company, then I don't say the faith in her beauty wouldn't come back to her, and go to her head like champagne; but it wore off quicker than champagne, and I've seen her run upstairs with the foot of a girl, and then, before she'd tossed off her finery, sit down in a heap in front of one of her big looking glasses – it was looking glasses everywhere in her room – and stare and stare till the tears ran down over her powder.'

'Oh, well, I suppose it's always hateful growing old,' said Moyra, her indifference returning.

Mrs Attlee smiled retrospectively. 'How can I say that, when my own old age has been made so peaceful by all her goodness to me?'

Moyra stood up with a shrug. 'And yet you tell me you acted wrong to her. How am I to know what you mean?'

Her grandmother made no answer. She closed her eyes, and leaned her head against the little cushion behind her neck. Her lips seemed to murmur, but no words came. Moyra reflected that she was probably falling asleep, and that when she woke she would not remember what she had been about to reveal.

'It's not much fun sitting here all this time, if you can't even keep awake long enough to tell me what you mean about Mrs Clingsland,' she grumbled.

Mrs Attlee roused herself with a start.

III

Well (she began) you know what happened in the war – I mean, the way all the fine ladies, and the poor shabby ones too, took to running to the mediums and the clairvoyants, or whatever the stylish folk call 'em. The women had to have news of their men; and they were made to pay high enough for it.... Oh, the stories I used to hear – and the price paid wasn't only money, either! There was a fair lot of swindlers and blackmailers in the business, there was. I'd sooner have trusted a gypsy at a fair... but the women just *had* to go to them.

Well, my dear, I'd always had a way of seeing things; from the cradle, even. I don't mean reading the tea leaves, or dealing the cards; that's for the kitchen. No, no; I mean, feeling there's things about you, behind you, whispering over your shoulder.... Once my mother, on the Connemara hills, saw the leprechauns at dusk; and she said they smelt fine and high, too.... Well, when I used to go from one grand house to another, to give my massage and face treatment, I got more and more sorry for those poor wretches that the soothsaying swindlers were dragging the money out of for a pack of lies; and one day I couldn't stand it any longer, and though I knew the Church was against it, when I saw one lady nearly crazy, because for months she'd had no news of her boy at the front, I said to her: 'If you'll come over to my place to-morrow, I might have a word for you.' And the wonder of it was that I *had*! For that night I dreamt a message came saying there was good news for her, and the next day, sure enough, she had a cable, telling her her son had escaped from a German camp....

After that the ladies came in flocks – in flocks fairly... you're too young to remember, child; but your mother could tell you. Only she wouldn't, because after a bit the priest got wind of it, and then it had to stop . . . so she won't even talk of it any more. But I always said: how could I help it? For I *did* see things, and hear things, at that time. . . . And of course the ladies were supposed to come just for the face treatment . . . and was I to blame if I kept hearing those messages for them, poor souls, or seeing things they wanted me to see?

It's no matter now, for I made it all straight with Father Divott years ago; and now nobody comes after me any more, as you can see for yourself. And all I ask is to be left alone in my chair. . . .

But with Mrs Clingsland – well, that was different. To begin with, she was the patient I liked best. There was nothing she wouldn't do for you, if ever for a minute you could get her to stop thinking of herself . . . and that's saying a good deal, for a rich lady. Money's an armour, you see; and there's few cracks in it. But Mrs Clingsland was a loving nature, if only anybody'd shown her how to love. . . . Oh, dear, and wouldn't she have been surprised if you'd told her that! Her that thought she was living up to her chin in love and love-making. But as soon as the lines began to come about her eyes, she didn't believe in it any more. And she had to be always hunting for new people to tell her she was as beautiful as ever; because she wore the others out, forever asking them: 'Don't you think I'm beginning to go off a little?' – till finally fewer and fewer came to the house, and as far as a poor masseuse like me can judge, I didn't much fancy the looks of those that did; and I saw Mr Clingsland didn't either.

But there was the children, you'll say. I know, I know! And she did love her children in a way; only it wasn't their way. The girl, who was a good bit the eldest, took after her father: a plain face and plain words. Dogs and horses and athletics. With her mother she was cold and scared; so her mother was cold and scared with her. The boy was delicate when he was little, so she could curl him up, and put him into black velvet pants, like that boy in the book – little Lord Something. But when his long legs grew out of the pants, and they sent him to school, she said he wasn't her own little cuddly baby any more; and it riles a growing boy to hear himself talked about like that.

She had good friends left, of course; mostly elderly ladies they were, of her own age (for she *was* elderly now; the change had come), who used to drop in often for a gossip; but, bless your heart, they weren't much help, for what she wanted, and couldn't do without, was the gaze of men struck dumb by her beauty. And that was what she couldn't get any longer, except she paid for it. And even so –!

For, you see, she was too quick and clever to be humbugged long by the kind that tried to get things out of her. How she used to laugh at the old double-chinners trotting round to the nightclubs with their boy friends! She laughed at old ladies in love; and yet she couldn't bear to be out of love, though she knew she was getting to be an old lady herself.

Well, I remember one day another patient of mine, who'd never had much looks beyond what you can buy in Fifth Avenue, laughing at me about Mrs Clingsland, about her dread of old age, and her craze for admiration – and as I listened, I suddenly thought: 'Why, we don't either of us know anything about what a beautiful woman suffers when she loses her beauty. For you and me, and thousands like us, beginning to grow old is like going from a bright warm room to one a little less warm and bright; but to a beauty like Mrs Clingsland it's like being pushed out of an illuminated ballroom, all flowers and chandeliers, into the winter night and the snow.' And I had to bite the words back, not to say them to my patient. . . .

IV

Mrs Clingsland brightened up a little when her own son grew up and went to college. She used to go over and see him now and again; or he'd come home for the holidays. And he used to take her out for lunch, or to dance at those cabaret places; and when the headwaiters took her for his sweetheart she'd talk about it for a week. But one day a hall porter said: 'Better hurry up, mister. There's your mother waiting for you over there, looking clean fagged out'; and after that she didn't go round with him so much.

For a time she used to get some comfort out of telling me about her early triumphs; and I used to listen patiently, because I knew it was safer for her to talk to me than to the flatterers who were beginning to get round her.

You mustn't think of her, though, as an unkind woman. She was friendly to her husband, and friendly to her children; but they meant less and less to her. What she wanted was a looking glass to stare into; and when her own people took enough notice of her to serve as looking glasses, which wasn't often, she didn't much fancy what she saw there. I think this was about the worst time of her life. She lost a tooth; she began to dye her hair; she went into retirement to have her face lifted, and then got frightened, and came out again looking like a ghost, with a pouch under one eye, where they'd begun the treatment. . . .

I began to be really worried about her then. She got sour and bitter toward everybody, and I seemed to be the only person she could talk out to. She used to keep me by for hours, always paying for the appointments she made me miss, and going over the same thing again and again; how when she was young and came into a ballroom, or a restaurant or a theatre, everybody stopped what they were doing to turn and look at her – even the actors on the stage did, she said; and it was the truth, I dare say. But that was over. . . .

Well, what could I say to her? She'd heard it all often enough. But there were people prowling about in the background that I didn't like the look of; people, you understand, who live on weak women that can't grow old. One day she showed me a love letter. She said she didn't know the man who'd sent it; but she knew about him. He was a Count Somebody; a foreigner. He'd had adventures. Trouble in his own country, I guess. . . . She laughed and tore the letter up. Another came from him, and I saw that too – but I didn't see her tear it up.

'Oh, I know what he's after,' she said. 'Those kind of men are always looking out for silly old women with money. . . . Ah,' says she, 'it was different in old times. I remember one day I'd gone into a florist's to buy some violets, and I saw a young fellow there; well, maybe he was a little younger than me – but I looked like a girl still. And when he saw me he just stopped short with what he was saying to the florist, and his face turned so white I thought he was going to faint. I bought my violets; and as I went out a violet dropped from the bunch, and I saw him stoop and pick it up, and hide it away as if it had been money he'd stolen. . . . Well,' she says, 'a few days after that I met him at a dinner, and it turned out he was the son of a friend of mine, a woman older than myself, who'd married abroad. He'd been brought up in England, and had just come to New York to take up a job there. . . .'

She lay back with her eyes closed, and a quiet smile on her poor tormented face. 'I didn't know it then, but I suppose that was the only time I've ever been in love. . . .' For a while she didn't say anything more, and I noticed the tears beginning to roll down her cheeks. 'Tell me about it, now do, you poor soul,' I says; for I thought, this is better for her than fandangoing with that oily count whose letter she hasn't torn up.

'There's so little to tell,' she said. 'We met only four or five times – and then Harry went down on the "Titanic".'

'Mercy,' says I, 'and was it all those years ago?'

'The years don't make any difference, Cora,' she says. 'The way he looked at me I know no one ever worshiped me as he did.'

'And did he tell you so?' I went on, humouring her; though I felt kind of guilty towards her husband.

'Some things don't have to be told,' says she, with the smile of a bride. 'If only he hadn't died, Cora.... It's the sorrowing for him that's made me old before my time.' (Before her time! And her well over fifty.)

Well, a day or two after that I got a shock. Coming out of Mrs Clingsland's front door as I was going into it I met a woman I'd know among a million if I was to meet her again in hell – where I will, I know, if I don't mind my steps.... You see, Moyra, though I broke years ago with all that crystal-reading, and table-rapping, and what the Church forbids, I was mixed up in it for a time (till Father Divott ordered me to stop), and I knew, by sight at any rate, most of the big mediums and their touts. And this woman on the doorstep was a tout, one of the worst and most notorious in New York; I knew cases where she'd sucked people dry selling them the news they wanted, like she was selling them a forbidden drug. And all of a sudden it came to me that I'd heard it said that she kept a foreign count, who was sucking *her* dry – and I gave one jump home to my own place, and sat down there to think it over.

I saw well enough what was going to happen. Either she'd persuade my poor lady that the count was mad over her beauty, and get a hold over her that way; or else – and this was worse – she'd make Mrs Clingsland talk, and get at the story of the poor young man called Harry, who was drowned, and bring her messages from him; and that might go on forever, and bring in more money than the count. . . .

Well, Moyra, could I help it? I was so sorry for her, you see. I could see she was sick and fading away, and her will weaker than it used to be; and if I was to save her from those gangsters I had to do it right away, and make it straight with my conscience afterward – if I could. . . .

V

I don't believe I ever did such hard thinking as I did that night. For what was I after doing? Something that was against my Church and against my own principles; and if ever I got found out, it was all up with me – me, with my thirty years' name of being the best masseuse in New York, and none honester, nor more respectable!

Well, then, I says to myself, what'll happen if that woman gets hold of Mrs Clingsland? Why, one way or another, she'll bleed her white, and then leave her without help or comfort. I'd seen households where that had happened, and I wasn't going to let it happen to my poor lady. What I was after was to make her believe in herself again, so that she'd be in a kindlier mind toward others . . . and by the next day I'd thought my plan out, and set it going.

It wasn't so easy, neither; and I sometimes wonder at my nerve. I'd figured it out that the other woman would have to work the stunt of the young man who was drowned, because I was pretty sure Mrs Clingsland, at the last minute, would shy away from the count. Well, then, thinks I, I'll work the same stunt myself – but how?

You see, dearie, those big people, when they talk and write to each other, they use lovely words we ain't used to; and I was afraid if I began to bring messages to her, I'd word them wrong, and she'd suspect something. I knew I could work it the first day or the second; but after that I wasn't so sure. But there was no time to lose, and when I went back to her next morning I said: 'A queer thing happened to me last night. I guess it was the way you spoke to me about that gentleman – the one on the "Titanic". Making me see him as clear as if he was in the room with us—' and at that I had her sitting up in bed with her great eyes burning into me like gimlets. 'Oh, Cora, perhaps he *is*! Oh, tell me quickly what happened!'

'Well, when I was laying in my bed last night something came to me from him. I knew at once it was from him; it was a word he was telling me to bring you. . . .'

I had to wait then, she was crying so hard, before she could listen to me again; and when I went on she hung on to me, saving the word, as if I'd been her Saviour. The poor woman!

The message I'd hit on for that first day was easy enough. I said he'd told me to tell her he'd always loved her. It went down her throat like honey, and she just lay there and tasted it. But after a while she lifted up her head. 'Then why didn't he tell me so?' says she.

'Ah,' says I, 'I'll have to try to reach him again, and ask him that.' And that day she fairly drove me off on my other jobs, for fear I'd be late getting home, and too tired to hear him if he came again. 'And he *will* come, Cora; I know he will! And you must be ready for him, and write down everything. I want every word written down the minute he says it, for fear you'll forget a single one.'

Well, that was a new difficulty. Writing wasn't ever my

strong point; and when it came to finding the words for a young gentleman in love who'd gone down on the 'Titanic', you might as well have asked me to write a Chinese dictionary. Not that I couldn't imagine how he'd have felt; but I didn't for Mary's grace know how to say it for him.

But it's wonderful, as Father Divott says, how Providence sometimes seems to be listening behind the door. That night when I got home I found a message from a patient, asking me to go to see a poor young fellow she'd befriended when she was better off – he'd been her children's tutor, I believe – who was down and out, and dying in a miserable rooming house down here at Montclair. Well, I went; and I saw at once why he hadn't kept this job, or any other job. Poor fellow, it was the drink; and now he was dying of it. It was a pretty bad story, but there's only a bit of it belongs to what I'm telling you.

He was a highly educated gentleman, and as quick as a flash, and before I'd half explained, he told me what to say, and wrote out the message for me. I remember it now. 'He was so blinded by your beauty that he couldn't speak – and when he saw you the next time, at that dinner, in your bare shoulders and your pearls, he felt farther away from you than ever. And he walked the streets till morning, and then went home, and wrote you a letter; but he didn't dare to send it after all.'

This time Mrs Clingsland swallowed it down like champagne. Blinded by her beauty; struck dumb by love of her! Oh, but that's what she'd been thirsting and hungering for all these years. Only, once it had begun, she had to have more of it, and always more . . . and my job didn't get any easier.

Luckily, though, I had that young fellow to help me; and after a while, when I'd given him a hint of what it was all about, he got as much interested as I was, and began to fret for me the days I didn't come.

But, my, what questions she asked. 'Tell him, if it's true that I took his breath away that first evening at dinner, to describe to you how I was dressed. They must remember things like that even in the other world, don't you think so? And you say he noticed my pearls?'

Luckily she'd described that dress to me so often that I had no difficulty about telling the young man what to say – and so it went on, and it went on, and one way or another I managed each time to have an answer that satisfied her. But one day, after Harry'd sent her a particularly lovely message from the Over There (as those people call it) she burst into tears and cried out: 'Oh, why did he never say things like that to me when we were together?'

That was a poser, as they say; I couldn't imagine why he hadn't. Of course I knew it was all wrong and immoral, anyway; but, poor thing, I don't see who it can hurt to help the love-making between a sick woman and a ghost. And I'd taken care to say a Novena against Father Divott finding me out.

Well, I told the poor young man what she wanted to know, and he said: 'Oh, you can tell her an evil influence came between them. Someone who was jealous, and worked against him – here, give me a pencil, and I'll write it out. . . .' and he pushed out his hot twitching hand for the paper.

That message fairly made her face burn with joy. 'I knew it – I always knew it!' She flung her thin arms about me, and kissed me. 'Tell me again, Cora, how he said I looked the first day he saw me. . . .'

'Why, you must have looked as you look now,' says I to her, 'for there's twenty years fallen from your face.' And so there was.

What helped me to keep on was that she'd grown so much gentler and quieter. Less impatient with the people who waited on her, more understanding with the daughter and Mr Clingsland. There was a different atmosphere in the house. And sometimes she'd say: 'Cora, there must be poor souls in trouble, with nobody to hold out a hand to them; and I want you to come to me when you run across anybody like that.' So I used to keep that poor young fellow well looked after, and cheered up with little dainties. And you'll never make me believe there was anything wrong in that – or in letting Mrs Clingsland help me out with the new roof on this house, either.

But there was a day when I found her sitting up in bed when I came in, with two red spots on her thin cheeks. And all the peace had gone out of her poor face. 'Why, Mrs Clingsland, my dear, what's the matter?' But I could see well enough what it was. Somebody'd been undermining her belief in spirit communications, or whatever they call them, and she'd been crying herself into a fever, thinking I'd made up all I'd told her. 'How do I know you're a medium, anyhow,' she flung out at me with pitiful furious eyes, 'and not taking advantage of me with all this stuff every morning?'

Well, the queer thing was that I took offence at that, not because I was afraid of being found out, but because – heaven help us! – I'd somehow come to believe in that young man Harry and his love-making, and it made me angry to be treated as a fraud. But I kept my temper and my tongue, and went on with the message as if I hadn't heard her; and she was ashamed to say any more to me. The quarrel between us lasted a week; and then one day, poor soul, she said, whimpering like a drug taker: 'Cora, I can't get on without the messages you bring me. The ones I get through other people don't sound like Harry – and yours do.'

I was so sorry for her then that I had hard work not to cry with her; but I kept my head, and answered quietly: 'Mrs Clingsland, I've been going against my Church, and risking my immortal soul, to get those messages through to you; and if you've found others that can help you, so much the better for me, and I'll go and make my peace with Heaven this very evening,' I said.

'But the other messages don't help me, and I don't want to disbelieve in you,' she sobbed out. 'Only lying awake all night and turning things over, I get so miserable. I shall die if you can't prove to me that it's really Harry speaking to you.'

I began to pack up my things. 'I can't prove that, I'm afraid,' I says in a cold voice, turning away my head so she wouldn't see the tears running down my cheeks.

'Oh, but you must, Cora, or I shall die!' she entreated me; and she looked as if she would, the poor soul.

'How can I prove it to you?' I answered. For all my pity for her, I still resented the way she'd spoken; and I thought how glad I'd be to get the whole business off my soul that very night in the confessional.

She opened her great eyes and looked up at me; and I seemed to see the wraith of her young beauty looking out of them. 'There's only one way,' she whispered.

'Well,' I said, still offended, 'what's the way?'

'You must ask him to repeat to you that letter he wrote, and didn't dare send to me. I'll know instantly then if you're in communication with him, and if you are I'll never doubt you any more.'

Well, I sat down and gave a laugh. 'You think it's as easy as that to talk with the dead, do you?'

'I think he'll know I'm dying too, and have pity on me, and do as I ask.' I said nothing more, but packed up my things and went away.

VI

That letter seemed to me a mountain in my path; and the poor young man, when I told him, thought so too. 'Ah, that's too difficult,' he said. But he told me he'd think it over, and do his best – and I was to come back the next day if I could. 'If only I knew more about her – or about *him*. It's damn difficult, making love for a dead man to a woman you've never seen,' says he with his little cracked laugh. I couldn't deny that it was; but I knew he'd do what he could, and I could see that the difficulty of it somehow spurred him on, while me it only cast down.

So I went back to his room the next evening; and as I climbed the stairs I felt one of those sudden warnings that sometimes used to take me by the throat.

'It's as cold as ice on these stairs,' I thought, 'and I'll wager there's no one made up the fire in his room since morning.' But it wasn't really the cold I was afraid of; I could tell there was worse than that waiting for me.

I pushed open the door and went in. 'Well,' says I, as cheerful as I could, 'I've got a pint of champagne and a thermos of hot soup for you; but before you get them you've got to tell me—'

He laid there in his bed as if he didn't see me, though his eyes were open; and when I spoke to him he didn't answer. I tried to laugh. 'Mercy!' I says, 'are you so sleepy you can't even look round to see the champagne? Hasn't that slut of a woman been in to 'tend to the stove for you? The room's as cold as death—' I says, and at the word I stopped short. He neither moved nor spoke; and I felt that the cold came from him, and not from the empty stove. I took hold of his hand, and held the cracked looking glass to his lips; and I knew he was gone to his Maker. I drew his lids down, and fell on my knees beside the bed. 'You shan't go without a prayer, you poor fellow,' I whispered to him, pulling out my beads.

But though my heart was full of mourning I dursn't pray for long, for I knew I ought to call the people of the house. So I just muttered a prayer for the dead, and then got to my feet again. But before calling in anybody I took a quick look around; for I said to myself it would be better not to leave about any of those bits he'd written down for me. In the shock of finding the poor young man gone I'd clean forgotten all about the letter; but I looked among his few books and papers for anything about the spirit messages, and found nothing. After that I turned back for a last look at him, and a last blessing; and then it was, fallen on the floor and half under the bed, I saw a sheet of paper scribbled over in pencil in his weak writing. I picked it up, and, holy Mother, it was the letter! I hid it away quick in my bag, and I stooped down and kissed him. And then I called the people in.

Well, I mourned the poor young man like a son, and I had a busy day arranging things, and settling about the funeral with the lady that used to befriend him. And with all there was to do I never went near Mrs Clingsland nor so much as thought of her, that day or the next; and the day after that there was a frantic message, asking what had happened, and saying she was very ill, and I was to come quick, no matter how much else I had to do.

I didn't more than half believe in the illness; I've been about too long among the rich not to be pretty well used to their scares and fusses. But I knew Mrs Clingsland was just pining to find out if I'd got the letter, and that my only chance of keeping my hold over her was to have it ready in my bag when I went back. And if I didn't keep my hold over her, I knew what slimy hands were waiting in the dark to pull her down.

Well, the labour I had copying out that letter was so great that I didn't hardly notice what was in it; and if I thought about it at all, it was only to wonder if it wasn't worded too plainlike, and if there oughtn't to have been more long words in it, coming from a gentleman to his lady. So with one thing and another I wasn't any too easy in my mind when I appeared again at Mrs Clingsland's; and if ever I wished myself out of a dangerous job, my dear, I can tell you that was the day. . . .

I went up to her room, the poor lady, and found her in bed, and tossing about, her eyes blazing, and her face full of all the wrinkles I'd worked so hard to rub out of it; and the sight of her softened my heart. After all, I thought, these people don't know what real trouble is; but they've manufactured something so like it that it's about as bad as the genuine thing.

'Well,' she said in a fever, 'well, Cora – the letter? Have you brought me the letter?'

I pulled it out of my bag, and handed it to her; and then I sat down and waited, my heart in my boots. I waited a long time, looking away from her; you couldn't stare at a lady who was reading a message from her sweetheart, could you?

I waited a long time; she must have read the letter very slowly, and then reread it. Once she sighed, ever so softly; and once she said: 'Oh, Harry, no, no – how foolish' . . . and laughed a little under her breath. Then she was still again for so long that at last I turned my head and took a stealthy look at her. And there she lay on her pillows, the hair waving over them, the letter clasped tight in her hands, and her face smoothed out the way it was years before, when I first knew her. Yes – those few words had done more for her than all my labour.

'Well – ?' said I, smiling a little at her.

'Oh, Cora – now at last he's spoken to me, really spoken.' And the tears were running down her young cheeks.

I couldn't hardly keep back my own, the heart was so light in me. 'And now you'll believe in me, I hope, ma'am, won't you?'

'I was mad ever to doubt you, Cora. . . .' She lifted the letter to her breast, and slipped it in among her laces. 'How did you manage to get it, you darling, you?'

Dear me, thinks I, and what if she asks me to get her another one like it, and then another? I waited a moment, and then I spoke very gravely. 'It's not an easy thing, ma'am, coaxing a letter like that from the dead.' And suddenly, with a start, I saw that I'd spoken the truth. It *was* from the dead that I'd got it.

'No, Cora; I can well believe it. But this is a treasure I can live on for years. Only you must tell me how I can repay you. . . . In a hundred years I could never do enough for you,' she says.

Well, that word went to my heart; but for a minute I didn't know how to answer. For it was true. I'd risked my soul, and that was something she couldn't pay me for; but then maybe I'd saved hers in getting her away from those foul people, so the whole business was more of a puzzle to me than ever. But then I had a thought that made me easier.

'Well, ma'am, the day before yesterday I was with a young man about the age of – of your Harry; a poor young man, without health or hope, lying sick in a mean rooming house. I used to go there and see him sometimes—'

Mrs Clingsland sat up in bed in a flutter of pity. 'Oh, Cora, how dreadful! Why did you never tell me? You must hire a better room for him at once. Has he a doctor? Has he a nurse? Quick – give me my checkbook!'

'Thank you, ma'am. But he don't need no nurse nor no doctor; and he's in a room underground by now. All I wanted to ask you for,' said I at length, though I knew I might have got a king's ransom from her, 'is money enough to have a few masses said for his soul – because maybe there's no one else to do it.'

I had hard work making her believe there was no end to the masses you could say for a hundred dollars; but somehow it's comforted me ever since that I took no more from her that day. I saw to it that Father Divott said the masses and got a good bit of the money; so he was a sort of accomplice too, though he never knew it.

ELIZABETH BOWEN

THE HAPPY AUTUMN FIELDS

THE FAMILY WALKING party, though it comprised so many, did not deploy or straggle over the stubble but kept in a procession of threes and twos. Papa, who carried his Alpine stick, led, flanked by Constance and little Arthur. Robert and Cousin Theodore, locked in studious talk, had Emily attached but not quite abreast. Next came Digby and Lucius, taking, to left and right, imaginary aim at rooks. Henrietta and Sarah brought up the rear.

It was Sarah who saw the others ahead on the blond stubble, who knew them, knew what they were to each other, knew their names and knew her own. It was she who felt the stubble under her feet, and who heard it give beneath the tread of the others a continuous different more distant soft stiff scrunch. The field and all these outlying fields in view knew as Sarah knew that they were Papa's. The harvest had been good and was now in: he was satisfied – for this afternoon he had made the instinctive choice of his most womanly daughter, most nearly infant son. Arthur, whose hand Papa was holding, took an anxious hop, a skip and a jump to every stride of the great man's. As for Constance – Sarah could often see the flash of her hat-feather as she turned her head, the curve of her close bodice as she turned her torso. Constance gave Papa her attention but not her thoughts, for she had already been sought in marriage.

The landowner's daughters, from Constance down, walked with their beetle-green, mole or maroon skirts gathered up and carried clear of the ground, but for Henrietta, who was still ankle-free. They walked inside a continuous stuffy sound, but left silence behind them. Behind them, rooks that had risen and circled, sun striking blue from their blue-black wings, planed one by one to the earth and settled to peck again. Papa and the boys were dark-clad as the rooks but with no sheen, but for their white collars.

It was Sarah who located the thoughts of Constance, knew what a twisting prisoner was Arthur's hand, felt to the depths of Emily's pique at Cousin Theodore's inattention, rejoiced with Digby and Lucius at the imaginary fall of so many rooks. She fell back, however, as from a rocky range, from the converse of Robert and Cousin Theodore. Most she knew that she swam with love at the nearness of Henrietta's young and alert face and eyes which shone with the sky and queried the afternoon.

She recognized the colour of valediction, tasted sweet sadness, while from the cottage inside the screen of trees wood-smoke rose melting pungent and blue. This was the eve of the brothers' return to school. It was like a Sunday; Papa had kept the late aftemoon free; all (all but one) encircling Robert, Digby and Lucius, they walked the estate the brothers would not see again for so long. Robert, it could be felt, was not unwilling to return to his books; next year he would go to college like Theodore; besides, to all this they saw he was not the heir. But in Digby and Lucius aiming and popping hid a bodily grief, the repugnance of victims, though these two were further from being heirs than Robert.

Sarah said to Henrietta: 'To think they will not be here to-morrow!'

'*Is* that what you are thinking about?' Henrietta asked, with her subtle taste for the truth.

'More, I was thinking that you and I will be back again by one another at table . . .'

'You know we are always sad when the boys are going, but we are never sad when the boys have gone.' The sweet reciprocal guilty smile that started on Henrietta's lips finished on those of Sarah. 'Also,' the young sister said, 'we know this is only something happening again. It happened last year, and it will happen next. But oh how should I feel, and how should you feel, if it were something that had not happened before?'

'For instance, when Constance goes to be married?'

'Oh, I don't mean *Constance*!' said Henrietta.

'So long,' said Sarah, considering, 'as, whatever it is, it happens to both of us?' She must never have to wake in the early morning except to the bird-like stirrings of Henrietta, or have her cheek brushed in the dark by the frill of another pillow in whose hollow did not repose Henrietta's cheek. Rather than they should cease to lie in the same bed she prayed they might lie in the same grave. 'You and I will stay as we are,' she said, 'then nothing can touch one without touching the other.'

'So you say; so I hear you say!' exclaimed Henrietta, who then, lips apart, sent Sarah her most tormenting look. 'But I cannot forget that you chose to be born without me; that you would not wait—' But here she broke off, laughed outright and said: 'Oh, *see*!'

Ahead of them there had been a dislocation. Emily took advantage of having gained the ridge to kneel down to tie her bootlace so abruptly that Digby all but fell over her, with an exclamation. Cousin Theodore had been civil enough to pause beside Emily, but Robert, lost to all but what he was saying, strode on, head down, only just not colliding into Papa and Constance, who had turned to look back. Papa, astounded, let go of Arthur's hand, whereupon Arthur fell flat on the stubble.

'Dear me,' said the affronted Constance to Robert.

Papa said, 'What is the matter there? May I ask, Robert, where you are going, sir? Digby, remember that is your sister Emily.'

'Cousin Emily is in trouble,' said Cousin Theodore.

Poor Emily, telescoped in her skirts and by now scarlet under her hatbrim, said in a muffled voice: 'It is just my bootlace, Papa.'

'Your bootlace, Emily?'

'I was just tying it.'

'Then you had better tie it. – Am I to think,' said Papa, looking round them all, 'that you must all go down like a pack of ninepins because Emily has occasion to stoop?'

At this Henrietta uttered a little whoop, flung her arms round Sarah, buried her face in her sister and fairly suffered with laughter. She could contain this no longer; she shook all over. Papa, who found Henrietta so hopelessly out of order that he took no notice of her except at table, took no notice, simply giving the signal for the others to collect themselves and move on. Cousin Theodore, helping Emily to her feet, could be seen to see how her heightened colour became her, but she dispensed with his hand chillily, looked elsewhere, touched the brooch at her throat and said: 'Thank you, I have not sustained an accident.' Digby apologized to Emily, Robert to Papa and Constance. Constance righted Arthur, flicking his breeches over with her handkerchief. All fell into their different steps and resumed their way.

Sarah, with no idea how to console laughter, coaxed, 'Come, come, come,' into Henrietta's ear. Between the girls and the others the distance widened; it began to seem that they would be left alone.

'And why not?' said Henrietta, lifting her head in answer to Sarah's thought.

They looked around them with the same eyes. The shorn uplands seemed to float on the distance, which extended dazzling to tiny blue glassy hills. There was no end to the afternoon, whose light went on ripening now they had scythed the corn. Light filled the silence which, now Papa and the others were out of hearing, was complete. Only screens of trees intersected and knolls made islands in the vast fields. The mansion and the home farm had sunk for ever below them in the expanse of woods, so that hardly a ripple showed where the girls dwelled.

The shadow of the same rook circling passed over Sarah then over Henrietta, who in their turn cast one shadow across the stubble. 'But, Henrietta, we cannot stay here for ever.'

Henrietta immediately turned her eyes to the only lonely plume of smoke, from the cottage. 'Then let us go and visit the poor old man. He is dying and the others are happy. One day we shall pass and see no more smoke; then soon his roof will fall in, and we shall always be sorry we did not go to-day.'

'But he no longer remembers us any longer.'

'All the same, he will feel us there in the door.'

'But can we forget this is Robert's and Digby's and Lucius's goodbye walk? It would be heartless of both of us to neglect them.'

'Then how heartless Fitzgeorge is!' smiled Henrietta.

'Fitzgeorge is himself the eldest and in the Army. Fitzgeorge I'm afraid is not an excuse for us.'

A resigned sigh, or perhaps the pretence of one, heaved up Henrietta's still narrow bosom. To delay matters for just a moment more she shaded her eyes with one hand, to search the distance like a sailor looking for a sail. She gazed with hope and zeal in every direction but that in which she and Sarah were bound to go. Then – 'Oh, but Sarah, here *they* are, coming – they are!' she cried. She brought out her handkerchief and began to fly it, drawing it to and fro through the windless air.

In the glass of the distance, two horsemen came into view, cantering on a grass track between the fields. When the track dropped into a hollow they dropped with it, but by now the drumming of hoofs was heard. The reverberation filled the land, the silence and Sarah's being; not watching for the riders to reappear she instead fixed her eyes on her sister's handkerchief which, let hang limp while its owner intently waited, showed a bitten corner as well as a damson stain. Again it became a flag, in furious motion. – 'Wave too, Sarah, wave too! Make your bracelet flash!'

'They must have seen us if they will ever see us,' said Sarah, standing still as a stone.

Henrietta's waving at once ceased. Facing her sister she crunched up her handkerchief, as though to stop it acting a lie. 'I can see you are shy,' she said in a dead voice. 'So shy you won't even wave to *Fitzgeorge*?'

Her way of not speaking the *other* name had a hundred meanings; she drove them all in by the way she did not look at Sarah's face. The impulsive breath she had caught stole silently out again, while her eyes – till now at their brightest, their most speaking – dulled with uncomprehending solitary alarm. The ordeal of awaiting Eugene's approach thus became for Sarah, from moment to moment, torture.

Fitzgeorge, Papa's heir, and his friend Eugene, the young neighbouring squire, struck off the track and rode up at a trot with their hats doffed. Sun striking low turned Fitzgeorge's flesh to coral and made Eugene blink his dark eyes. The young men reined in; the girls looked up at the horses. 'And my father, Constance, the others?' Fitzgeorge demanded, as though the stubble had swallowed them.

'Ahead, on the way to the quarry, the other side of the hill.'

'We heard you were all walking together,' Fitzgeorge said, seeming dissatisfied.

'We are following.'

'What, alone?' said Eugene, speaking for the first time.

'Forlorn!' glittered Henrietta, raising two mocking hands.

Fitzgeorge considered, said 'Good' severely, and signified to Eugene that they would ride on. But too late: Eugene had dismounted. Fitzgeorge saw, shrugged and flicked his horse to a trot; but Eugene led his slowly between the sisters. Or rather, Sarah walked on his left hand, the horse on his right and Henrietta the other side of the horse. Henrietta, acting like somebody quite alone, looked up at the sky, idly holding one of the empty stirrups. Sarah, however, looked at the ground, with Eugene inclined as though to speak but not speaking. Enfolded, dizzied, blinded as though inside a wave, she could feel his features carved in brightness above her. Alongside the slender stepping of his horse, Eugene matched his naturally long free step to hers. His elbow was through the reins; with his fingers he brushed back the lock that his bending to her had sent falling over his forehead. She recorded the sublime act and knew what smile shaped his lips. So each without looking trembled before an image, while slow colour burned up the curves of her cheeks. The consummation would be when their eyes met.

At the other side of the horse, Henrietta began to sing. At once her pain, like a scientific ray, passed through the horse and Eugene to penetrate Sarah's heart.

We surmount the skyline: the family come into our view, we into theirs. They are halted, waiting, on the decline to the quarry. The handsome statufied group in strong yellow sunshine, aligned by Papa and crowned by Fitzgeorge, turn their judging eyes on the laggards, waiting to close their ranks round Henrietta and Sarah and Eugene. One more moment and it will be too late; no further communication will be possible. Stop oh stop Henrietta's heartbreaking singing! Embrace her close again! Speak the only possible word! Say – oh, say what? Oh, the word is lost!

'Henrietta . . .'

A shock of striking pain in the knuckles of the outflung hand – Sarah's? The eyes, opening, saw that the hand had struck, not been struck: there was a corner of a table. Dust, whitish and gritty, lay on the top of the table and on the telephone. Dull but piercing white light filled the room and what was left of the ceiling; her first thought was that it must have snowed. If so, it was winter now.

Through the calico stretched and tacked over the window came the sound of a piano: someone was playing Tchaikowsky badly in a room without windows or doors. From somewhere else in the hollowness came a cascade of hammering. Close up, a voice: 'Oh, *awake*, Mary?' It came from the other side of the open door, which jutted out between herself and the speaker – he on the threshold, she lying on the uncovered mattress of a bed. The speaker added: 'I had been going away.'

Summoning words from somewhere she said: 'Why? I didn't know you were here.'

'Evidently – Say, who is "Henrietta"?'

Despairing tears filled her eyes. She drew back her hurt hand, began to suck at the knuckle and whimpered, 'I've hurt myself.'

A man she knew to be 'Travis', but failed to focus, came

round the door saying: 'Really I don't wonder.' Sitting down on the edge of the mattress he drew her hand away from her lips and held it: the act, in itself gentle, was accompanied by an almost hostile stare of concern. 'Do listen, Mary,' he said. 'While you've slept I've been all over the house again, and I'm less than ever satisfied that it's safe. In your normal senses you'd never attempt to stay here. There've been alerts, and more than alerts, all day; one more bang anywhere near, which may happen at any moment, could bring the rest of this down. You keep telling me that you have things to see to – but do you know what chaos the rooms are in? Till they've gone ahead with more clearing, where can you hope to start? And if there *were* anything you could do, you couldn't do it. Your own nerves know that, if you don't: it was almost frightening, when I looked in just now, to see the way you were sleeping – you've shut up shop.'

She lay staring over his shoulder at the calico window. He went on: 'You don't like it here. Your self doesn't like it. Your will keeps driving your self, but it can't be driven the whole way – it makes its own get-out: sleep. Well, I want you to sleep as much as you (really) do. But *not* here. So I've taken a room for you in a hotel; I'm going now for a taxi; you can practically make the move without waking up.'

'No, I can't get into a taxi without waking.'

'Do you realize you're the last soul left in the terrace?'

'Then who is that playing the piano?'

'Oh, one of the furniture-movers in Number Six. I didn't count the jaquerie; of course *they're* in possession – unsupervised, teeming, having a high old time. While I looked in on you in here ten minutes ago they were smashing out that conservatory at the other end. Glass being done in in cold blood – it was brutalizing. You never batted an eyelid; in fact, I thought you smiled.' He listened. 'Yes, the piano –

they are highbrow all right. You know there's a workman downstairs lying on your blue sofa looking for pictures in one of your French books?'

'No,' she said, 'I've no idea who is there.'

'Obviously. With the lock blown off your front door anyone who likes can get in and out.'

'Including you.'

'Yes. I've had a word with a chap about getting that lock back before to-night. As for you, you don't know what is happening.'

'I did,' she said, locking her fingers before her eyes.

The unreality of this room and of Travis's presence preyed on her as figments of dreams that one knows to be dreams can do. This environment's being in semi-ruin struck her less than its being some sort of device or trap; and she rejoiced, if anything, in its decrepitude. As for Travis, he had his own part in the conspiracy to keep her from the beloved two. She felt he began to feel he was now unmeaning. She was struggling not to contemn him, scorn him for his ignorance of Henrietta, Eugene, her loss. His possessive angry fondness was part, of course, of the story of him and Mary, which like a book once read she remembered clearly but with indifference. Frantic at being delayed here, while the moment awaited her in the cornfield, she all but afforded a smile at the grotesquerie of being saddled with Mary's body and lover. Rearing up her head from the bare pillow, she looked, as far as the crossed feet, along the form inside which she found herself trapped: the irrelevant body of Mary, weighted down to the bed, wore a short black modern dress, flaked with plaster. The toes of the black suède shoes by their sickly whiteness showed Mary must have climbed over fallen ceilings; dirt engraved the fate-lines in Mary's palms.

This inspired her to say: 'But I've made a start; I've been pulling out things of value or things I want.'

For answer Travis turned to look down, expressively, at some object out of her sight, on the floor close by the bed. '*I* see,' he said, 'a musty old leather box gaping open with God knows what – junk, illegible letters, diaries, yellow photographs, chiefly plaster and dust. Of all things, Mary! – after a missing will?'

'Everything one unburies seems the same age.'

'Then what are these, where do they come from – family stuff?'

'No idea,' she yawned into Mary's hand. 'They may not even be mine. Having a house like this that had empty rooms must have made me store more than I knew, for years. I came on these, so I wondered. Look if you like.'

He bent and began to go through the box – it seemed to her, not unsuspiciously. While he blew grit off packets and fumbled with tapes she lay staring at the exposed laths of the ceiling, calculating. She then said: 'Sorry if I've been cranky, about the hotel and all. Go away just for two hours, then come back with a taxi, and I'll go quiet. Will that do?'

'Fine – except why not now?'

'*Travis...*'

'Sorry. It shall be as you say... You've got some good morbid stuff in this box, Mary – so far as I can see at a glance. The photographs seem more your sort of thing. Comic but lyrical. All of one set of people – a beard, a gun and a pot hat, a schoolboy with a moustache, a phaeton drawn up in front of mansion, a group on steps, a *carte de visite* of two young ladies hand-in-hand in front of a painted field—'

'*Give that to me!*'

She instinctively tried and failed, to unbutton the bosom of Mary's dress: it offered no hospitality to the photograph.

So she could only fling herself over on the mattress, away from Travis, covering the two faces with her body. Racked by that oblique look of Henrietta's she recorded, too, a sort of personal shock at having seen Sarah for the first time.

Travis's hand came over her, and she shuddered. Wounded, he said: 'Mary...'

'Can't you leave *me* alone?'

She did not move or look till he had gone out saying: 'Then, in two hours.' She did not therefore see him pick up the dangerous box, which he took away under his arm, out of her reach.

They were back. Now the sun was setting behind the trees, but its rays passed dazzling between the branches into the beautiful warm red room. The tips of the ferns in the jardinière curled gold, and Sarah, standing by the jardinière, pinched at a leaf of scented geranium. The carpet had a great centre wreath of pomegranates, on which no tables or chairs stood, and its whole circle was between herself and the others.

No fire was lit yet, but where they were grouped was a hearth. Henrietta sat on a low stool, resting her elbow above her head on the arm of Mamma's chair, looking away intently as though into a fire, idle. Mamma embroidered, her needle slowed down by her thoughts; the length of tatting with roses she had already done overflowed stiffly over her supple skirts. Stretched on the rug at Mamma's feet, Arthur looked through an album of Swiss views, not liking them but vowed to be very quiet. Sarah, from where she stood, saw fuming cataracts and null eternal snows as poor Arthur kept turning over the pages, which had tissue paper between.

Against the white marble mantelpiece stood Eugene. The

dark red shadows gathering in the drawing-room as the trees drowned more and more of the sun would reach him last, perhaps never: it seemed to Sarah that a lamp was lighted behind his face. He was the only gentleman with the ladies: Fitzgeorge had gone to the stables, Papa to give an order; Cousin Theodore was consulting a dictionary; in the gun-room Robert, Lucius and Digby went through the sad rites, putting away their guns. All this was known to go on but none of it could be heard.

This particular hour of subtle light – not to be fixed by the clock, for it was early in winter and late in summer and in spring and autumn now, about Arthur's bed-time – had always, for Sarah, been Henrietta's. To be with her indoors or out, upstairs or down, was to share the same crepitation. Her spirit ran on past yours with a laughing shiver into an element of its own. Leaves and branches and mirrors in empty rooms became animate. The sisters rustled and scampered and concealed themselves where nobody else was in play that was full of fear, fear that was full of play. Till, by dint of making each other's hearts beat violently, Henrietta so wholly and Sarah so nearly lost all human reason that Mamma had been known to look at them searchingly as she sat instated for evening among the calm amber lamps.

But now Henrietta had locked the hour inside her breast. By spending it seated beside Mamma, in young imitation of Constance the Society daughter, she disclaimed for ever anything else. It had always been she who with one fierce act destroyed any toy that might be outgrown. She sat with straight back, poising her cheek remotely against her finger. Only by never looking at Sarah did she admit their eternal loss.

Eugene, not long returned from a foreign tour, spoke of travel, addressing himself to Mamma, who thought but did not speak of her wedding journey. But every now and then she had to ask Henrietta to pass the scissors or tray of carded wools, and Eugene seized every such moment to look at Sarah. Into eyes always brilliant with melancholy he dared begin to allow no other expression. But this in itself declared the conspiracy of still undeclared love. For her part she looked at him as though he, transfigured by the strange light, were indeed a picture, a picture who could not see her. The wallpaper now flamed scarlet behind his shoulder. Mamma, Henrietta, even unknowing Arthur were in no hurry to raise their heads.

Henrietta said: 'If I were a man I should take my bride to Italy.'

'There are mules in Switzerland,' said Arthur.

'Sarah,' said Mamma, who turned in her chair mildly, 'where are you, my love; do you never mean to sit down?'

'To Naples,' said Henrietta.

'Are you not thinking of Venice?' said Eugene.

'No,' returned Henrietta, 'why should I be? I should like to climb the volcano. But then I am not a man, and am still less likely ever to be a bride.'

'Arthur . . .' Mamma said.

'Mamma?'

'Look at the clock.'

Arthur sighed politely, got up and replaced the album on the circular table, balanced upon the rest. He offered his hand to Eugene, his cheek to Henrietta and to Mamma; then he started towards Sarah, who came to meet him. 'Tell me, Arthur,' she said, embracing him, 'what did you do to-day?'

Arthur only stared with his button blue eyes. 'You were there too; we went for a walk in the cornfield, with Fitzgeorge on his horse, and I fell down.' He pulled out of her arms and said: 'I must go back to my beetle.' He had difficulty, as always, in turning the handle of the mahogany door. Mamma waited till he had left the room, then said: 'Arthur is quite a man now; he no longer comes running to me when he has hurt himself. Why, I did not even know he had fallen down. Before we know, he will be going away to school too.' She sighed and lifted her eyes to Eugene. 'To-morrow is to be a sad day.'

Eugene with a gesture signified his own sorrow. The sentiments of Mamma could have been uttered only here in the drawing-room, which for all its size and formality was lyrical and almost exotic. There was a look like velvet in darker parts of the air; sombre window draperies let out gushes of lace; the music on the piano-forte bore tender titles, and the harp though unplayed gleamed in a corner, beyond sofas, whatnots, armchairs, occasional tables that all stood on tottering little feet. At any moment a tinkle might have been struck from the lustres' drops of the brighter day, a vibration from the musical instruments, or a quiver from the fringes and ferns. But the towering vases upon the consoles, the albums piled on the tables, the shells and figurines on the flights of brackets, all had, like the alabaster Leaning Tower of Pisa, an equilibrium of their own. Nothing would fall or change. And everything in the drawing-room was muted, weighted, pivoted by Mamma. When she added: 'We shall not feel quite the same,' it was to be understood that she would not have spoken thus from her place at the opposite end of Papa's table.

'Sarah,' said Henrietta curiously, 'what made you ask Arthur what he had been doing? Surely you have not forgotten to-day?'

The sisters were seldom known to address or question one another in public; it was taken that they knew each other's minds. Mamma, though untroubled, looked from one to the other. Henrietta continued: 'No day, least of all to-day, is like any other – Surely that must be true?' she said to Eugene. 'You will never forget my waving my handkerchief?'

Before Eugene had composed an answer, she turned to Sarah: 'Or *you*, them riding across the fields?'

Eugene also slowly turned his eyes on Sarah, as though awaiting with something like dread her answer to the question he had not asked. She drew a light little gold chair into the middle of the wreath of the carpet, where no one ever sat, and sat down. She said: 'But since then I think I have been asleep.'

'Charles the First walked and talked half an hour after his head was cut off,' said Henrietta mockingly. Sarah in anguish pressed the palms of her hands together upon a shred of geranium leaf.

'How else,' she said, 'could I have had such a bad dream?'

'That must be the explanation!' said Henrietta.

'A trifle fanciful,' said Mamma.

However rash it might be to speak at all, Sarah wished she knew how to speak more clearly. The obscurity and loneliness of her trouble was not to be borne. How could she put into words the feeling of dislocation, the formless dread that had been with her since she found herself in the drawing-room? The source of both had been what she must call her dream. How could she tell the others with what vehemence she tried to attach her being to each second, not because each was singular in itself, each a drop condensed from the mist of love in the room, but because she apprehended that the seconds were numbered? Her hope was that the others at least half knew. Were Henrietta and Eugene able to understand how completely, how nearly for ever, she had been swept from them, would they not without fail each grasp one of her hands? – She went so far as to throw her hands out, as though alarmed by a wasp. The shred of geranium fell to the carpet.

Mamma, tracing this behaviour of Sarah's to only one cause, could not but think reproachfully of Eugene. Delightful as his conversation had been, he would have done better had he paid this call with the object of interviewing Papa. Turning to Henrietta she asked her to ring for the lamps, as the sun had set.

Eugene, no longer where he had stood, was able to make no gesture towards the bell-rope. His dark head was under the tide of dusk; for, down on one knee on the edge of the wreath, he was feeling over the carpet for what had fallen from Sarah's hand. In the inevitable silence rooks on the return from the fields could be heard streaming over the house; their sound filled the sky and even the room, and it appeared so useless to ring the bell that Henrietta stayed quivering by Mamma's chair. Eugene rose, brought out his fine white handkerchief and, while they watched, enfolded carefully in it what he had just found, then returning the handkerchief to his breast pocket. This was done so deep in the reverie that accompanies any final act that Mamma instinctively murmured to Henrietta: 'But you will be my child when Arthur has gone.'

The door opened for Constance to appear on the threshold. Behind her queenly figure globes approached, swimming in their own light: these were the lamps for which Henrietta had not rung, but these first were put on the hall tables. 'Why, Mamma,' exclaimed Constance, 'I cannot see who is with you!'

'Eugene is with us,' said Henrietta, 'but on the point of asking if he may send for his horse.'

'Indeed?' said Constance to Eugene. 'Fitzgeorge has been asking for you, but I cannot tell where he is now.'

The figures of Emily, Lucius and Cousin Theodore criss-crossed the lamplight there in the hall, to mass behind Constance's in the drawing-room door. Emily, over her sister's shoulder, said: 'Mamma, Lucius wishes to ask you whether for once he may take his guitar to school.' – 'One objection, however,' said Cousin Theodore, 'is that Lucius's trunk is already locked and strapped.' 'Since Robert is taking his box of inks,' said Lucius, 'I do not see why I should not take my guitar.' – 'But Robert,' said Constance, 'will soon be going to college.'

Lucius squeezed past the others into the drawing-room in order to look anxiously at Mamma, who said: 'You have thought of this late; we must go and see.' The others parted to let Mamma, followed by Lucius, out. Then Constance, Emily and Cousin Theodore deployed and sat down in different parts of the drawing-room, to await the lamps.

'I am glad the rooks have done passing over,' said Emily, 'they make me nervous.' – 'Why?' yawned Constance haughtily, 'what do you think could happen?' Robert and Digby silently came in.

Eugene said to Sarah: 'I shall be back to-morrow.'

'But, oh—' she began. She turned to cry: 'Henrietta!'

'Why, what is the matter?' said Henrietta, unseen at the back of the gold chair. 'What could be sooner than to-morrow?'

'But something terrible may be going to happen.'

'There cannot fail to be to-morrow,' said Eugene gravely.

'*I* will see that there is to-morrow,' said Henrietta.

'You will never let me out of your sight?'

Eugene, addressing himself to Henrietta, said: 'Yes, promise her what she asks.'

Henrietta cried: 'She *is* never out of my sight. Who are you to ask me that, you Eugene? Whatever tries to come between me and Sarah becomes nothing. Yes, come to-morrow, come sooner, come – when you like, but no one will ever be quite alone with Sarah. You do not even know what you are trying to do. It is *you* who are making something terrible happen. – Sarah, tell him that this is true! Sarah—'

The others, in the dark on the chairs and sofas, could be felt to turn their judging eyes upon Sarah, who, as once before, could not speak –

– The house rocked: simultaneously the calico window split and more ceiling fell, though not on the bed. The enormous dull sound of the explosion died, leaving a minor trickle of dissolution still to be heard in parts of the house. Until the choking stinging plaster dust had had time to settle, she lay with lips pressed close, nostrils not breathing and eyes shut. Remembering the box, Mary wondered if it had been again buried. No, she found, looking over the edge of the bed: that had been unable to happen because the box was missing. Travis, who must have taken it, would when he came back no doubt explain why. She looked at her watch, which had stopped, which was not surprising; she did not remember winding it for the last two days, but then she could not remember much. Through the torn window appeared the timelessness of an impermeably clouded late summer afternoon.

There being nothing left, she wished he would come to take her to the hotel. The one way back to the fields was barred by Mary's surviving the fall of ceiling. Sarah was right in doubting that there would be to-morrow: Eugene, Henrietta were lost in time to the woman weeping there on the bed, no longer reckoning who she was.

At last she heard the taxi, then Travis hurrying up the littered stairs. 'Mary, you're all right, Mary – *another*?' Such a helpless white face came round the door that she could only hold out her arms and say: 'Yes, but where have *you* been?'

'You said two hours. But I wish—'

'I have missed you.'

'Have you? Do you know you are crying?'

'Yes. How are we to live without natures? We only know inconvenience now, not sorrow. Everything pulverizes so easily because it is rot-dry; one can only wonder that it makes so much noise. The source, the sap must have dried up, or the pulse must have stopped, before you and I were conceived. So much flowed through people; so little flows through us. All we can do is imitate love or sorrow. – Why did you take away my box?'

He only said: 'It is in my office.'

She continued: 'What has happened is cruel: I am left with a fragment torn out of a day, a day I don't even know where or when; and now how am I to help laying that like a pattern against the poor stuff of everything else? – Alternatively, I am a person drained by a dream. I cannot forget the climate of those hours. Or life at that pitch, eventful – not happy, no, but strung like a harp. I have had a sister called Henrietta.'

'And I have been looking inside your box. What else can you expect? – I have had to write off this day, from the work point of view, thanks to you. So could I sit and do nothing for the last two hours? I just glanced through this and that – still, I know the family.'

'You said it was morbid stuff.'

'Did I? I still say it gives off something.'

She said: 'And then there was Eugene.'

'Probably. I don't think I came on much of his except some notes he must have made for Fitzgeorge from some book on scientific farming. Well, there it is: I have sorted everything out and put it back again, all but a lock of hair that tumbled out of a letter I could not trace. So I've got the hair in my pocket.'

'What colour is it?'

'Ash-brown. Of course, it is a bit – desiccated. Do you want it?'

'No,' she said with a shudder. 'Really, Travis, what revenges you take!'

'I didn't look at it that way,' he said puzzled.

Is the taxi waiting?' Mary got off the bed and, picking her way across the room, began to look about for things she ought to take with her, now and then stopping to brush her dress. She took the mirror out of her bag to see how dirty her face was. 'Travis—' she said suddenly.

'Mary?'

'Only, I—'

'That's all right. Don't let us imitate anything just at present.'

In the taxi, looking out of the window, she said: 'I suppose, then, that I am descended from Sarah?'

'No,' he said, 'that would be impossible. There must be some reason why you should have those papers, but that is not the one. From all negative evidence Sarah, like Henrietta, remained unmarried. I found no mention of either, after a certain date, in the letters of Constance, Robert or Emily, which makes it seem likely both died young. Fitzgeorge refers, in a letter to Robert written in his old age, to some friend of their youth who was thrown from his horse and killed, riding back after a visit to their home. The young man, whose name doesn't appear, was alone; and the evening, which was in autumn, was fine though late. Fitzgeorge wonders, and says he will always wonder, what made the horse shy in those empty fields.'

VLADIMIR NABOKOV

THE VISIT TO THE MUSEUM

SEVERAL YEARS AGO a friend of mine in Paris – a person with oddities, to put it mildly – learning that I was going to spend two or three days at Montisert, asked me to drop in at the local museum where there hung, he was told, a portrait of his grandfather by Leroy. Smiling and spreading out his hands, he related a rather vague story to which I confess I paid little attention, partly because I do not like other people's obtrusive affairs, but chiefly because I had always had doubts about my friend's capacity to remain this side of fantasy. It went more or less as follows: after the grandfather died in their St Petersburg house back at the time of the Russo-Japanese War, the contents of his apartment in Paris were sold at auction. The portrait, after some obscure peregrinations, was acquired by the museum of Leroy's native town. My friend wished to know if the portrait was really there; if there, if it could be ransomed; and if it could, for what price. When I asked why he did not get in touch with the museum, he replied that he had written several times, but had never received an answer.

I made an inward resolution not to carry out the request – I could always tell him I had fallen ill or changed my itinerary. The very notion of seeing sights, whether they be museums or ancient buildings, is loathsome to me; besides, the good freak's commission seemed absolute nonsense. It so happened, however, that, while wandering about Montisert's empty streets in search of a stationery store, and cursing the spire of a long-necked cathedral, always the same one, that kept popping up at the end of every street, I was caught in a violent downpour which immediately went about accelerating the fall of the maple leaves, for the fair weather of a southern October was holding on by a mere thread. I dashed for cover and found myself on the steps of the museum.

It was a building of modest proportions, constructed of many-coloured stones, with columns, a gilt inscription over the frescoes of the pediment, and a lion-legged stone bench on either side of the bronze door. One of its leaves stood open, and the interior seemed dark against the shimmer of the shower. I stood for a while on the steps, but, despite the overhanging roof, they were gradually growing speckled. I saw that the rain had set in for good, and so, having nothing better to do, I decided to go inside. No sooner had I trod on the smooth, resonant flagstones of the vestibule than the clatter of a moved stool came from a distant corner, and the custodian – a banal pensioner with an empty sleeve – rose to meet me, laying aside his newspaper and peering at me over his spectacles. I paid my franc and, trying not to look at some statues at the entrance (which were as traditional and as insignificant as the first number in a circus programme), I entered the main hall.

Everything was as it should be: grey tints, the sleep of substance, matter dematerialized. There was the usual case of old, worn coins resting in the inclined velvet of their compartments. There was, on top of the case, a pair of owls, Eagle Owl and Long-eared, with their French names reading 'Grand Duke' and 'Middle Duke' if translated. Venerable minerals lay in their open graves of dusty papier-mâché; a photograph of an astonished gentleman with a pointed beard dominated an assortment of strange black lumps of various sizes. They bore a great resemblance to frozen frass, and I paused involuntarily over them for I was quite at a loss to guess their nature, composition and function. The custodian had been following me with felted steps, always keeping a respectful distance; now, however, he came up, with one hand behind his back and the ghost of the other in his pocket, and gulping, if one judged by his Adam's apple.

'What are they?' I asked.

'Science has not yet determined,' he replied, undoubtedly having learned the phrase by rote. 'They were found,' he continued in the same phony tone, 'in 1895, by Louis Pradier, Municipal Councillor and Knight of the Legion of Honour,' and his trembling finger indicated the photograph.

'Well and good,' I said, 'but who decided, and why, that they merited a place in the museum?'

'And now I call your attention to this skull!' the old man cried energetically, obviously changing the subject.

'Still, I would be interested to know what they are made of,' I interrupted.

'Science . . .' he began anew, but stopped short and looked crossly at his fingers, which were soiled with dust from the glass.

I proceeded to examine a Chinese vase, probably brought back by a naval officer; a group of porous fossils; a pale worm in clouded alcohol; a red-and-green map of Montisert in the seventeenth century; and a trio of rusted tools bound by a funereal ribbon – a spade, a mattock and a pick. 'To dig in the past,' I thought absentmindedly, but this time did not seek clarification from the custodian, who was following me noiselessly and meekly, weaving in and out among the display cases. Beyond the first hall there was another, apparently the last, and in its centre a large sarcophagus stood like a dirty bathtub, while the walls were hung with paintings.

At once my eye was caught by the portrait of a man between two abominable landscapes (with cattle and 'atmosphere'). I moved closer and, to my considerable amazement, found the very object whose existence had hitherto seemed to me but the figment of an unstable mind. The man, depicted in wretched oils, wore a frock coat, whiskers and a large pince-nez on a cord; he bore a likeness to Offenbach, but, in spite of the work's vile conventionality, I had the feeling one could make out in his features the horizon of a resemblance, as it were, to my friend. In one corner, meticulously traced in carmine against a black background, was the signature *Leroy* in a hand as commonplace as the work itself.

I felt a vinegarish breath near my shoulder, and turned to meet the custodian's kindly gaze. 'Tell me,' I asked, 'supposing someone wished to buy one of these paintings, whom should he see?'

'The treasures of the museum are the pride of the city,' replied the old man, 'and pride is not for sale.'

Fearing his eloquence, I hastily concurred, but nevertheless asked for the name of the museum's director. He tried to distract me with the story of the sarcophagus, but I insisted. Finally he gave me the name of one M. Godard and explained where I could find him.

Frankly, I enjoyed the thought that the portrait existed. It is fun to be present at the coming true of a dream, even if it is not one's own. I decided to settle the matter without delay. When I get in the spirit, no one can hold me back. I left the museum with a brisk, resonant step, and found that the rain had stopped, blueness had spread across the sky, a woman in besplattered stockings was spinning along on a silver-shining bicycle, and only over the surrounding hills did clouds still hang. Once again the cathedral began playing hide-and-seek with me, but I outwitted it. Barely escaping the onrushing tyres of a furious red bus packed with singing youths, I crossed the asphalt thoroughfare and a minute later was ringing at the garden gate of M. Godard. He turned out to be a thin, middle-aged gentleman in high collar and dickey, with a pearl in the knot of his tie, and a face very much resembling a Russian wolfhound; as if that were not enough, he was licking his chops in a most doglike manner, while sticking a stamp on an envelope, when I entered his small but lavishly furnished room with its malachite inkstand on the desk and a strangely familiar Chinese vase on the mantel. A pair of fencing foils hung crossed over the mirror, which reflected the narrow grey back of his head. Here and there photographs of a warship pleasantly broke up the blue flora of the wallpaper.

'What can I do for you?' he asked, throwing the letter he had just sealed into the wastebasket. This act seemed unusual to me; however, I did not see fit to interfere. I explained in brief my reason for coming, even naming the substantial sum with which my friend was willing to part, though he had asked me not to mention it, but wait instead for the museum's terms.

'All this is delightful,' said M. Godard. 'The only thing is, you are mistaken – there is no such picture in our museum.'

'What do you mean there is no such picture? I have just seen it! Portrait of a Russian nobleman, by Gustave Leroy.'

'We do have one Leroy,' said M. Godard when he had leafed through an oilcloth notebook and his black fingernail had stopped at the entry in question. 'However, it is not a portrait but a rural landscape: *The Return of the Herd*.'

I repeated that I had seen the picture with my own eyes five minutes before and that no power on earth could make me doubt its existence.

'Agreed,' said M. Godard, 'but I am not crazy either. I have been curator of our museum for almost twenty years now and know this catalogue as well as I know the Lord's Prayer. It says here *Return of the Herd* and that means the herd is returning, and, unless perhaps your friend's grandfather is depicted as a shepherd, I cannot conceive of his portrait's existence in our museum.'

'He is wearing a frock coat,' I cried. 'I swear he is wearing a frock coat!'

'And how did you like our museum in general?' M. Godard asked suspiciously. 'Did you appreciate the sarcophagus?'

'Listen,' I said (and I think there was already a tremor in my voice), 'do me a favour – let's go there this minute, and let's make an agreement that if the portrait is there, you will sell it.'

'And if not?' inquired M. Godard.

'I shall pay you the sum anyway.'

'All right,' he said. 'Here, take this red-and-blue pencil and using the red – the red, please – put it in writing for me.'

In my excitement I carried out his demand. Upon glancing at my signature, he deplored the difficult pronunciation of Russian names. Then he appended his own signature and, quickly folding the sheet, thrust it into his waistcoat pocket.

'Let's go,' he said, freeing a cuff.

On the way he stepped into a shop and bought a bag of sticky looking caramels which he began offering me insistently; when I flatly refused, he tried to shake out a couple of them into my hand. I pulled my hand away. Several caramels fell on the sidewalk; he stopped to pick them up and then overtook me at a trot. When we drew near the museum we saw the red tourist bus (now empty) parked outside.

'Aha,' said M. Godard, pleased. 'I see we have many visitors to-day.'

He doffed his hat and, holding it in front of him, walked decorously up the steps.

All was not well at the museum. From within issued rowdy cries, lewd laughter, and even what seemed like the sound of a scuffle. We entered the first hall; there the elderly custodian was restraining two sacrilegists who wore some kind of festive emblems in their lapels and were altogether very purple-faced and full of pep as they tried to extract the municipal councillor's merds from beneath the glass. The rest of the youths, members of some rural athletic organization, were making noisy fun, some of the worm in alcohol, others of the skull. One joker was in rapture over the pipes of the steam radiator, which he pretended was an exhibit; another was taking aim at an owl with his fist and forefinger. There were about thirty of them in all, and their motion and voices created a condition of crush and thick noise.

M. Godard clapped his hands and pointed at a sign reading 'Visitors to the Museum must be decently attired'. Then he pushed his way, with me following, into the second hall. The whole company immediately swarmed after us. I steered Godard to the portrait; he froze before it, chest inflated, and then stepped back a bit, as if admiring it, and his feminine heel trod on somebody's foot.

'Splendid picture,' he exclaimed with genuine sincerity. 'Well, let's not be petty about this. You were right, and there must be an error in the catalogue.'

As he spoke, his fingers, moving as it were on their own, tore up our agreement into little bits which fell like snowflakes into a massive spittoon.

'Who's the old ape?' asked an individual in a striped jersey, and, as my friend's grandfather was depicted holding a glowing cigar, another funster took out a cigarette and prepared to borrow a light from the portrait.

'All right, let us settle on the price,' I said, 'and, in any case, let's get out of here.'

'Make way, please!' shouted M. Godard, pushing aside the curious.

There was an exit, which I had not noticed previously, at the end of the hall and we thrust our way through to it.

'I can make no decision,' M. Godard was shouting above the din. 'Decisiveness is a good thing only when supported by law. I must first discuss the matter with the mayor, who has just died and has not yet been elected. I doubt that you will be able to purchase the portrait but nonetheless I would like to show you still other treasures of ours.

We found ourselves in a hall of considerable dimensions. Brown books, with a half-baked look and coarse, foxed pages, lay open under glass on a long table. Along the walls stood dummy soldiers in jack-boots with flared tops.

'Come, let's talk it over,' I cried out in desperation, trying to direct M. Godard's evolutions to a plush-covered sofa in a corner. But in this I was prevented by the custodian. Flailing his one arm, he came running after us, pursued by a merry crowd of youths, one of whom had put on his head a copper helmet with a Rembrandtesque gleam.

'Take it off, take it off!' shouted M. Godard, and someone's shove made the helmet fly off the hooligan's head with a clatter.

'Let us move on,' said M. Godard, tugging at my sleeve, and we passed into the section of Ancient Sculpture.

I lost my way for a moment among some enormous marble legs, and twice ran around a giant knee before I again caught sight of M. Godard, who was looking for me behind the white ankle of a neighbouring giantess. Here a person in a bowler, who must have clambered up her, suddenly fell from a great height to the stone floor. One of his companions began helping him up, but they were both drunk, and, dismissing them with a wave of the hand, M. Godard rushed on to the next room, radiant with Oriental fabrics; there hounds raced across azure carpets, and a bow and quiver lay on a tiger skin.

Strangely, though, the expanse and motley only gave me a feeling of oppressiveness and imprecision, and, perhaps because new visitors kept dashing by or perhaps because I was impatient to leave the unnecessarily spreading museum and amid calm and freedom conclude my business negotiations with M. Godard, I began to experience a vague sense of alarm. Meanwhile we had transported ourselves into yet another hall, which must have been really enormous, judging by the fact that it housed the entire skeleton of a whale, resembling a frigate's frame; beyond were visible still other halls, with the oblique sheen of large paintings, full of storm clouds, among which floated the delicate idols of religious art in blue and pink vestments; and all this resolved itself in an abrupt turbulence of misty draperies, and chandeliers came aglitter and fish with translucent frills meandered through illuminated aquariums. Racing up a staircase, we saw, from the gallery above, a crowd of grey-haired people with umbrellas examining a gigantic mock-up of the universe.

At last, in a sombre but magnificent room dedicated to the history of steam machines, I managed to halt my carefree guide for an instant.

'Enough!' I shouted. 'I'm leaving. We'll talk to-morrow.'

He had already vanished. I turned and saw, scarcely an inch from me, the lofty wheels of a sweaty locomotive. For a long time I tried to find the way back among models of railroad stations. How strangely glowed the violet signals in the gloom beyond the fan of wet tracks, and what spasms shook my poor heart! Suddenly everything changed again: in front of me stretched an infinitely long passage, containing numerous office cabinets and elusive, scurrying people. Taking a sharp turn, I found myself amid a thousand musical instruments; the walls, all mirror, reflected an enfilade of grand pianos, while in the centre there was a pool with a bronze Orpheus atop a green rock. The aquatic theme did not end here as, racing back, I ended up in the Section of Fountains and Brooks, and it was difficult to walk along the winding, slimy edges of those waters.

Now and then, on one side or the other, stone stairs, with puddles on the steps, which gave me a strange sensation of fear, would descend into misty abysses, whence issued whistles, the rattle of dishes, the clatter of typewriters, the ring of hammers and many other sounds, as if, down there, were exposition halls of some kind or other, already closing or not yet completed. Then I found myself in darkness and kept bumping into unknown furniture until I finally saw a red light and walked out onto a platform that clanged under me – and suddenly, beyond it, there was a bright parlour, tastefully furnished in Empire style, but not a living soul, not a living soul.... By now I was indescribably terrified, but every time I turned and tried to retrace my steps along the passages, I found myself in hitherto unseen places – a greenhouse with hydrangeas and broken window-panes with the darkness of artificial night showing through beyond; or a deserted laboratory with dusty alembics on its tables. Finally I ran into a room of some sort with coat-racks monstrously loaded down with black coats and astrakhan furs; from beyond a door came a burst of applause, but when I flung the door open, there was no theatre, but only a soft opacity and splendidly counterfeited fog with the perfectly convincing blotches of indistinct street-lights. More than convincing! I advanced, and immediately a joyous and unmistakable sensation of reality at last replaced all the unreal trash amid which I had just been dashing to and fro. The stone beneath my feet was real sidewalk, powdered with wonderfully fragrant, newly fallen snow in which the infrequent pedestrians had already left fresh black tracks. At first the quiet and the snowy coolness of the night, somehow strikingly familiar, gave me a pleasant feeling after my feverish wanderings. Trustfully, I started to conjecture just where I had come out, and why the snow, and what were those lights exaggeratedly but indistinctly beaming here and there in the brown darkness. I examined and, stooping, even touched a round spur stone on the curb, then glanced at the palm of my hand, full of wet granular cold, as if hoping to read an explanation there. I felt how lightly, how naively I was clothed, but the distinct realization that I had escaped from the museum's maze was still so strong that, for the first two or three minutes, I experienced neither surprise nor fear. Continuing my leisurely examination, I looked up at the house beside which I was standing and was immediately struck by the sight of iron steps and railings that descended into the snow on their way to the cellar. There was a twinge in my heart, and it was with a new, alarmed curiosity that I glanced at the pavement, at its white cover along which stretched black lines, at the brown sky across which there kept sweeping a mysterious light, and at the massive parapet some distance away. I sensed that there was a drop beyond it; something was creaking and gurgling down there. Further on, beyond the murky cavity, stretched a chain of fuzzy lights. Scuffling along the snow in my soaked shoes, I walked a few paces, all the time glancing at the dark house on my right; only in a single window did a lamp glow softly under its green-glass shade. Here, a locked wooden gate. . . . There, what must be the shutters of a sleeping shop. . . . And by the light of a streetlamp whose shape had long been shouting to me its impossible message, I made out the ending of a sign – '. . . . *inka Sapog*' ('. . . *oe Repair*') – but no, it was not the snow that had obliterated the 'hard sign' at the end. 'No, no, in a minute I shall wake up,' I said aloud, and, trembling, my heart pounding, I turned, walked on, stopped again. From somewhere came the receding sound of hooves, the snow sat like a skullcap on a slightly leaning spur stone, and indistinctly showed white on the woodpile on the other side of the fence, and already I knew, irrevocably, where I was. Alas, it was not the Russia I remembered, but the factual Russia of to-day, forbidden to me, hopelessly slavish, and hopelessly my own native land. A semi-phantom in a light foreign suit, I stood on the impassive snow of an October night, somewhere on the Moyka or the Fontanka Canal, or perhaps on the Obvodny, and I had to do something, go somewhere, run, desperately protect my fragile, illegal life. Oh, how many times in my sleep I had experienced a similar sensation! Now, though, it was reality. Everything was real – the air that seemed to mingle with scattered snowflakes, the still unfrozen canal, the floating fish house, and that peculiar squareness of the darkened and the yellow windows. A man in a fur cap, with a briefcase under his arm, came toward me out of the fog, gave me a startled glance, and turned to look again when he had passed me. I waited for him to disappear and then, with a tremendous haste, began pulling out everything I had in my pockets, ripping up papers, throwing them into the snow and stamping them down. There were some documents, a letter from my sister in Paris, five-hundred francs, a handkerchief, cigarettes; however, in order to shed all the integument of exile, I would have to tear off and destroy my clothes, my linen, my shoes, everything, and remain ideally naked; and, even though I was already shivering from my anguish and from the cold, I did what I could.

But enough. I shall not recount how I was arrested, nor tell of my subsequent ordeals. Suffice it to say that it cost me incredible patience and effort to get back abroad, and that, ever since, I have foresworn carrying out commissions entrusted one by the insanity of others.

NOTE: The unfortunate narrator notices a shop sign and realizes he is not in the Russia of his past but in the Russia of the Soviets: what gives it away is the absence of one letter which used to decorate the end of words after consonants but is now omitted in the reformed orthography.

Vladimir Nabokov

EUDORA WELTY

CLYTIE

IT WAS LATE afternoon, with heavy silver clouds which looked bigger and wider than cotton-fields, and presently it began to rain. Big round drops fell, still in the sunlight, on the hot tin sheds, and stained the white false fronts of the row of stores in the little town of Farr's Gin. A hen and her string of yellow chickens ran in great alarm across the road, the dust turned river-brown, and the birds flew down into it immediately, seeking out little pockets in which to take baths. The bird dogs got up from the doorways of the stores, shook themselves down to the tail, and went to lie inside. The few people standing with long shadows on the level road moved over into the post office. A little boy kicked his bare heels into the sides of his mule, which proceeded slowly through the town toward the country.

After everyone else had gone under cover, Miss Clytie Farr stood still in the road, peering ahead in her near-sighted way, and as wet as the little birds.

She usually came out of the old big house about this time in the afternoon, and hurried through the town. It used to be that she ran about on some pretext or other, and for a while she made soft-voiced explanations that nobody could hear, and after that she began to charge up bills, which the postmistress declared would never be paid any more than anyone else's, even if the Farrs were too good to associate with other people. But now Clytie came for nothing. She came every day, and no one spoke to her any more: she would be in such a hurry, and couldn't see who it was. And every Saturday they expected her to be run over, the way she darted out into the road with all the horses and trucks.

It might be simply that Miss Clytie's wits were all leaving her, said the ladies standing in the door to feel the cool, the way her sisters had left her; and she would just wait there to be told to go home. She would have to wring out everything she had on – the waist and the jumper skirt, and the long black stockings. On her head was one of the straw hats from the furnishing store, with an old black satin ribbon pinned to it to make it a better hat, and tied under the chin. Now, under the force of the rain, while the ladies watched, the hat slowly began to sag down on each side until it looked even more absurd and done for, like an old bonnet on a horse. And indeed it was with the patience almost of a beast that Miss Clytie stood there in the rain and stuck her long empty arms out a little from her sides, as if she were waiting for something to come along the road and drive her to shelter.

In a little while there was a clap of thunder.

'Miss Clytie! Go in out of the rain, Miss Clytie!' someone called.

The old maid did not look around, but clenched her hands and drew them up under her armpits, and sticking out her elbows like hen wings, she ran out of the street, her poor hat creaking and beating about her ears.

'Well, there goes Miss Clytie,' the ladies said, and one of them had a premonition about her.

Through the rushing water in the sunken path under the four wet black cedars, which smelled bitter as smoke, she ran to the house.

'Where the devil have you been?' called the older sister, Octavia, from an upper window.

Clytie looked up in time to see the curtain fall back.

She went inside, into the hall, and waited, shivering. It was very dark and bare. The only light was falling on the white sheet which covered the solitary piece of furniture, an organ. The red curtains over the parlour door, held back by ivory hands, were still as tree trunks in the airless house. Every window was closed, and every shade was down, though behind them the rain could still be heard.

Clytie took a match and advanced to the stair-post, where the bronze cast of Hermes was holding up a gas fixture; and at once above this, lighted up, but quite still, like one of the unmovable relics of the house, Octavia stood waiting on the stairs.

She stood solidly before the violet-and-lemon-coloured glass of the window on the landing, and her wrinkled, unresting fingers took hold of the diamond cornucopia she always wore in the bosom of her long black dress. It was an unwithered grand gesture of hers, fondling the cornucopia.

'It is not enough that we are waiting here – hungry,' Octavia was saying, while Clytie waited below. 'But you must sneak away and not answer when I call you. Go off and wander about the streets. Common – common –!'

'Never mind, Sister,' Clytie managed to say.

'But you always return.'

'Of course. . . .'

'Gerald is awake now, and so is Papa,' said Octavia, in the same vindictive voice – a loud voice, for she was usually calling.

Clytie went to the kitchen and lighted the kindling in the wood stove. As if she were freezing cold in June, she stood before its open door, and soon a look of interest and pleasure lighted her face, which had in the last years grown weather-beaten in spite of the straw hat. Now some dream was resumed. In the street she had been thinking about the face of a child she had just seen. The child, playing with another of the same age, chasing it with a toy pistol, had looked at her with such an open, serene, trusting expression as she passed by! With this small, peaceful face still in her mind, rosy like these flames, like an inspiration which drives all other thoughts away, Clytie had forgotten herself and had been obliged to stand where she was in the middle of the road. But the rain had come down, and someone had shouted at her, and she had not been able to reach the end of her meditations.

It had been a long time now, since Clytie had first begun to watch faces, and to think about them.

Anyone could have told you that there were not more than 150 people in Farr's Gin, counting Negroes. Yet the number of faces seemed to Clytie almost infinite. She knew now to look slowly and carefully at a face; she was convinced that it was impossible to see it all at once. The first thing she discovered about a face was always that she had never seen it before. When she began to look at people's actual countenances there was no more familiarity in the world for her. The most profound, the most moving sight in the whole world must be a face. Was it possible to comprehend the eyes and the mouths of other people, which concealed she knew not what, and secretly asked for still another unknown thing? The mysterious smile of the old man who sold peanuts by the church gate returned to her; his face seemed for a moment to rest upon the iron door of the stove, set into the lion's mane. Other people said Mr Tom Bate's Boy, as he called himself, stared away with a face as clean-blank as a water-melon seed, but to Clytie, who observed grains of sand in his eyes and in his old yellow lashes, he might have come out of a desert, like an Egyptian.

But while she was thinking of Mr Tom Bate's Boy, there was a terrible gust of wind which struck her back, and she turned around. The long green window-shade billowed and plunged. The kitchen window was wide open – she had done it herself. She closed it gently. Octavia, who never came all the way downstairs for any reason, would never have forgiven her for an open window, if she knew. Rain and sun signified ruin, in Octavia's mind. Going over the whole house, Clytie made sure that everything was safe. It was not that ruin in itself could distress Octavia. Ruin or encroachment, even upon priceless treasures and even in poverty, held no terror for her; it was simply some form of prying from without, and this she would not forgive. All of that was to be seen in her face.

Clytie cooked the three meals on the stove, for they all ate different things, and set the three trays. She had to carry them in proper order up the stairs. She frowned in concentration, for it was hard to keep all the dishes straight, to make them come out right in the end, as Old Lethy could have done. They had had to give up the cook long ago when their father suffered the first stroke. Their father had been fond of Old Lethy, she had been his nurse in childhood, and she had come back out of the country to see him when she heard he was dying. Old Lethy had come and knocked at the back door. And as usual, at the first disturbance, front or back, Octavia had peered down from behind the curtain and cried, 'Go away! Go away! What the devil have you come *here* for?' And although Old Lethy and their father had both pleaded that they might be allowed to see each other, Octavia had shouted as she always did, and sent the intruder away. Clytie had stood as usual, speechless in the kitchen, until finally she had repeated after her sister, 'Lethy, go away.' But their father had not died. He was, instead, paralyzed, blind, and able only to call out in unintelligible sounds and to swallow liquids. Lethy still would come to the back door now and then, but they never let her in, and the old man no longer heard or knew enough to beg to see her. There was only one caller admitted to his room. Once a week the barber came by appointment to shave him. On this occasion not a word was spoken by anyone.

Clytie went up to her father's room first and set the tray down on a little marble table they kept by his bed.

'I want to feed Papa,' said Octavia, taking the bowl from her hands.

'You fed him last time,' said Clytie.

Relinquishing the bowl, she looked down at the pointed face on the pillow. To-morrow was the barber's day, and the sharp black points, at their longest, stuck out like needles all over the wasted cheeks. The old man's eyes were half closed. It was impossible to know what he felt. He looked as though he were really far away, neglected, free. . . . Octavia began to feed him.

Without taking her eyes from her father's face, Clytie suddenly began to speak in rapid, bitter words to her sister, the wildest words that came to her head. But soon she began to cry and gasp, like a small child who has been pushed by the big boys into the water.

'That is enough,' said Octavia.

But Clytie could not take her eyes from her father's unshaven face and his still-open mouth.

'And I'll feed him to-morrow if I want to,' said Octavia. She stood up. The thick hair, growing back after an illness and dyed almost purple, fell over her forehead. Beginning at her throat, the long accordion pleats which fell the length of her gown opened and closed over her breasts as she breathed. 'Have you forgotten Gerald?' she said. 'And I am hungry too.'

Clytie went back to the kitchen and brought her sister's supper.

Then she brought her brother's.

Gerald's room was dark, and she had to push through the usual barricade. The smell of whisky was everywhere; it even flew up in the striking of the match when she lighted the jet.

'It's night,' said Clytie presently.

Gerald lay on his bed looking at her. In the bad light he resembled his father.

'There's some more coffee down in the kitchen,' said Clytie.

'Would you bring it to me?' Gerald asked. He stared at her in an exhausted, serious way.

She stooped and held him up. He drank the coffee while she bent over him with her eyes closed, resting.

Presently he pushed her away and fell back on the bed, and began to describe how nice it was when he had a little house of his own down the street, all new, with all conveniences, gas stove, electric lights, when he was married to Rosemary. Rosemary – she had given up a job in the next town, just to marry him. How had it happened that she had left him so soon? It meant nothing that he had threatened time and again to shoot her, it was nothing at all that he had pointed the gun against her breast. She had not understood. It was only that he had relished his contentment. He had only wanted to play with her. In a way he had wanted to show her that he loved her above life and death.

'Above life and death,' he repeated, closing his eyes.

Clytie did not make an answer, as Octavia always did during these scenes, which were bound to end in Gerald's tears.

Outside the closed window a mocking-bird began to sing.

Clytie held back the curtain and pressed her ear against the glass. The rain had dropped. The bird's song sounded in liquid drops down through the pitch-black trees and the night.

'Go to hell,' Gerald said. His head was under the pillow.

She took up the tray, and left Gerald with his face hidden. It was not necessary for her to look at any of their faces. It was their faces which came between.

Hurrying, she went down to the kitchen and began to eat her own supper.

Their faces came between her face and another. It was their faces which had come pushing in between, long ago, to hide some face that had looked back at her. And now it was hard to remember the way it looked, or the time when she had seen it first. It must have been when she was young. Yes, in a sort of arbour, hadn't she laughed, leaned forward... and that vision of a face – which was a little like all the other faces, the trusting child's, the innocent old traveller's, even the greedy barber's and Lethy's and the wandering peddlers' who one by one knocked and went unanswered at the door – and yet different, yet far more – this face had been very close to hers, almost familiar, almost accessible. And then the face of Octavia was thrust between, and at other times the apoplectic face of her father, the face of her brother Gerald and the face of her brother Henry with the bullet hole through the forehead. ...It was purely for a resemblance to a vision that she examined the secret, mysterious, unrepeated faces she met in the street of Farr's Gin.

But there was always an interruption. If anyone spoke to her, she fled. If she saw she was going to meet someone on the street, she had been known to dart behind a bush and hold a small branch in front of her face until the person had gone by. When anyone called her by name, she turned first red, then white, and looked somehow, as one of the ladies in the store remarked, *disappointed.*

She was becoming more frightened all the time, too. People could tell because she never dressed up any more. For years, every once in a while, she would come out in what was called an 'outfit', all in a hunter's green, a hat that came down around her face like a bucket, a green silk dress, even green shoes with pointed toes. She would wear the outfit all one day, if it was a pretty day, and then next morning she would be back in the faded jumper with her old hat tied under the chin, as if the outfit had been a dream. It had been a long time now since Clytie had dressed up so that you could see her coming.

Once in a while when a neighbour, trying to be kind or only being curious, would ask her opinion about anything – such as a pattern of crochet – she would not run away; but, giving a thin trapped smile, she would say in a childish voice, 'It's nice.' But, the ladies always added, nothing that came anywhere close to the Farrs' house was nice for long.

'It's nice,' said Clytie when the old lady next door showed her the new rosebush she had planted, all in bloom.

But before an hour was gone, she came running out of her house screaming, 'My sister Octavia says you take that rosebush up! My sister Octavia says you take that rosebush up and move it away from our fence! If you don't I'll kill you! You take it away.'

And on the other side of the Farrs lived a family with a little boy who was always playing in his yard. Octavia's cat would go under the fence, and he would take it and hold it in his arms. He had a song he sang to the Farrs' cat. Clytie would come running straight out of the house, flaming with her message from Octavia. 'Don't you do that! Don't you do that!' she would cry in anguish. 'If you do that again, I'll have to kill you!'

And she would run back to the vegetable patch and begin to curse.

The cursing was new, and she cursed softly, like a singer going over a song for the first time. But it was something she could not stop. Words which at first horrified Clytie poured in a full, light stream from her throat, which soon, nevertheless, felt strangely relaxed and rested. She cursed all alone in the peace of the vegetable garden. Everybody said, in something like deprecation, that she was only imitating her older sister, who used to go out to that same garden and curse in that same way, years ago, but in a remarkably loud, commanding voice that could be heard in the post office.

Sometimes in the middle of her words Clytie glanced up to where Octavia, at her window, looked down at her. When she let the curtain drop at last, Clytie would be left there speechless.

Finally, in a gentleness compounded of fright and exhaustion and love, an overwhelming love, she would wander through the gate and out through the town, gradually beginning to move faster, until her long legs gathered a ridiculous, rushing speed. No one in town could have kept up with Miss Clytie, they said, giving them an even start.

She always ate rapidly, too, all alone in the kitchen, as she was eating now. She bit the meat savagely from the heavy silver fork and gnawed the little chicken bone until it was naked and clean.

Half-way upstairs, she remembered Gerald's second pot of coffee, and went back for it. After she had carried the other trays down again and washed the dishes, she did not forget to try all the doors and windows to make sure that everything was locked up absolutely tight.

The next morning, Clytie bit into smiling lips as she cooked breakfast. Far out past the secretly opened window a freight train was crossing the bridge in the sunlight. Some Negroes filed down the road going fishing, and Mr Tom Bate's Boy, who was going along, turned and looked at her through the window.

Gerald had appeared dressed and wearing his spectacles, and announced that he was going to the store to-day. The old Farr furnishing store did little business now, and people hardly missed Gerald when he did not come; in fact, they could hardly tell when he did because of the big boots strung on a wire, which almost hid the cage-like office. A little high-school girl could wait on anybody who came in.

Now Gerald entered the dining-room.

'How are you this morning, Clytie?' he asked.

'Just fine, Gerald; how are you?'

'I'm going to the store,' he said.

He sat down stiffly, and she laid a place on the table before him.

From above, Octavia screamed, 'Where in the devil is my thimble, you stole my thimble, Clytie Farr, you carried it away, my little silver thimble!'

'It's started,' said Gerald intensely. Clytie saw his fine, thin, almost black lips spread in a crooked line. 'How can a man live in the house with women? How can he?'

He jumped up, and tore his napkin exactly in two. He walked out of the dining-room without eating the first bite of his breakfast. She heard him going back upstairs into his room.

'My thimble!' screamed Octavia.

She waited one moment. Crouching eagerly, rather like a little squirrel, Clytie ate part of her breakfast over the stove before going up the stairs.

At nine Mr Bobo, the barber, knocked at the front door.

Without waiting, for they never answered the knock, he let himself in and advanced like a small general down the hall. There was the old organ that was never uncovered or played except for funerals, and then nobody was invited. He went ahead, under the arm of the tiptoed male statue and up the dark stairway. There they were, lined up at the head of the stairs, and they all looked at him with repulsion. Mr Bobo was convinced that they were every one mad. Gerald, even, had already been drinking, at nine o'clock in the morning.

Mr Bobo was short and had never been anything but proud of it, until he had started coming to this house once a week. But he did not enjoy looking up from below at the soft, long throats, the cold, repelled, high-reliefed faces of those Farrs. He could only imagine what one of those sisters would do to him if he made one move. (As if he would!) As soon as he arrived upstairs, they all went off and left him. He pushed out his chin and stood with his round legs wide apart, just looking around. The upstairs hall was absolutely bare. There was not even a chair to sit down in.

'Either they sell away their furniture in the dead of night,' said Mr Bobo to the people of Farr's Gin, 'or else they're just too plumb mean to use it.'

Mr Bobo stood and waited to be summoned, and wished he had never started coming to this house to shave old Mr Farr. But he had been so surprised to get a letter in the mail. The letter was on such old, yellowed paper that at first he thought it must have been written a thousand years ago and never delivered. It was signed 'Octavia Farr', and began without even calling him 'Dear Mr Bobo'. What it said was: 'Come to this residence at nine o'clock each Friday morning until further notice, where you will shave Mr James Farr.'

He thought he would go one time. And each time after that he thought he would never go back – especially when he never knew when they would pay him anything. Of course, it was something to be the only person in Farr's Gin allowed inside the house (except for the undertaker, who had gone there when young Henry shot himself, but had never to that day spoken of it). It was not easy to shave a man as bad off as Mr Farr, either – not anything like as easy as to shave a corpse or even a fighting-drunk field hand. Suppose you were like this, Mr Bobo would say: you couldn't move your face; you couldn't hold up your chin, or tighten your jaw, or even bat your eyes when the razor came close. The trouble with Mr Farr was his face made no resistance to the razor. His face didn't hold.

'I'll never go back,' Mr Bobo always ended to his customers. 'Not even if they paid me. I've seen enough.'

Yet here he was again, waiting before the sick-room door.

'This is the last time,' he said. 'By God!'

And he wondered why the old man did not die.

Just then Miss Clytie came out of the room. There she came in her funny, sideways walk, and the closer she got to him the more slowly she moved.

'Now?' asked Mr Bobo nervously.

Clytie looked at his small, doubtful face. What fear raced through his little green eyes! His pitiful, greedy, small face – how very mournful it was, like a stray kitten's. What was it that this greedy little thing was so desperately needing?

Clytie came up to the barber and stopped. Instead of telling him that he might go in and shave her father, she put out her hand and with breath-taking gentleness touched the side of his face.

For an instant afterward, she stood looking at him inquiringly, and he stood like a statue, like the statue of Hermes.

Then both of them uttered a despairing cry. Mr Bobo turned and fled, waving his razor around in a circle, down the stairs and out the front door; and Clytie, pale as a ghost, stumbled against the railing. The terrible scent of bay rum, of hair tonic, the horrible moist scratch of an invisible beard, the dense, popping green eyes – what had she got hold of with her hand! She could hardly bear it – the thought of that face.

From the closed door to the sick-room came Octavia's shouting voice.

'Clytie! Clytie! You haven't brought Papa the rain-water! Where in the devil is the rain-water to shave Papa?'

Clytie moved obediently down the stairs.

Her brother Gerald threw open the door of his room and called after her, 'What now? This is a madhouse! Somebody was running past my room, I heard it. Where do you keep your men? Do you have to bring them home?' He slammed the door again, and she heard the barricade going up.

Clytie went through the lower hall and out the back door. She stood beside the old rain barrel and suddenly felt that this object, now, was her friend, just in time, and her arms almost circled it with impatient gratitude. The rain barrel was full. It bore a dark, heavy, penetrating fragrance, like ice and flowers and the dew of night.

Clytie swayed a little and looked into the slightly moving water. She thought she saw a face there.

Of course. It was the face she had been looking for, and from which she had been separated. As if to give a sign, the index-finger of a hand lifted to touch the dark cheek.

Clytie leaned closer, as she had leaned down to touch the face of the barber.

It was a wavering, inscrutable face. The brows were drawn together as if in pain. The eyes were large, intent, almost avid, the nose ugly and discoloured as if from weeping, the mouth old and closed from any speech. On either side of the head dark hair hung down in a disreputable and wild fashion. Everything about the face frightened and shocked her with its signs of waiting, of suffering.

For the second time that morning, Clytie recoiled, and as she did so, the other recoiled in the same way.

Too late, she recognized the face. She stood there completely sick at heart, as though the poor, half-remembered vision had finally betrayed her.

'Clytie! Clytie! The water! The water!' came Octavia's monumental voice.

Clytie did the only thing she could think of to do. She bent her angular body further, and thrust her head into the barrel, under the water, through its glittering surface into the kind, featureless depth, and held it there.

When Old Lethy found her, she had fallen forward into the barrel, with her poor lady-like black-stockinged legs up-ended and hung apart like a pair of tongs.

JORGE LUIS BORGES

THE CIRCULAR RUINS

Translated by James E. Irby

And if he left off dreaming about you . . .
Through the Looking Glass, IV

NO ONE SAW him disembark in the unanimous night, no one saw the bamboo canoe sinking into the sacred mud, but within a few days no one was unaware that the silent man came from the South and that his home was one of the infinite villages upstream, on the violent mountainside, where the Zend tongue is not contaminated with Greek and where leprosy is infrequent. The truth is that the obscure man kissed the mud, came up the bank without pushing aside (probably without feeling) the brambles which dilacerated his flesh, and dragged himself, nauseous and bloodstained, to the circular enclosure crowned by a stone tiger or horse, which once was the colour of fire and now was that of ashes. This circle was a temple, long ago devoured by fire, which the malarial jungle had profaned and whose god no longer received the homage of men. The stranger stretched out beneath the pedestal. He was awakened by the sun high above. He evidenced without astonishment that this wounds had closed; he shut his pale eyes and slept, not out of bodily weakness but out of determination of will. He knew that this temple was the place required by his invincible purpose; he knew that, downstream, the incessant trees had not managed to choke the ruins of another propitious temple, whose gods were also burned and dead; he knew that his immediate obligation was to sleep. Towards midnight he was awakened by the disconsolate cry of a bird. Prints of bare feet, some figs and a jug told him that men of the region had respectfully spied upon his sleep and were solicitous of his favour or feared his magic. He felt the chill of fear and sought out a burial niche in the dilapidated wall and covered himself with some unknown leaves.

The purpose which guided him was not impossible, though it was supernatural. He wanted to dream a man: he wanted to dream him with minute integrity and insert him into reality. This magical project had exhausted the entire content of his soul; if someone had asked him his own name or any trait of his previous life, he would not have been able to answer. The uninhabited and broken temple suited him, for it was a minimum of visible world; the nearness of the peasants also suited him, for they would see that his frugal necessities were supplied. The rice and fruit of their tribute were sufficient sustenance for his body, consecrated to the sole task of sleeping and dreaming.

At first, his dreams were chaotic; somewhat later, they were of a dialectical nature. The stranger dreamt that he was in the centre of a circular amphitheatre which in some way was the burned temple: clouds of silent students filled the gradins; the faces of the last ones hung many centuries away and at a cosmic height, but were entirely clear and precise. The man was lecturing to them on anatomy, cosmography, magic; the countenances listened with eagerness and strove to respond with understanding, as if they divined the importance of the examination which would redeem one of them from his state of vain appearance and interpolate him into the world of reality. The man, both in dreams and awake, considered his phantoms' replies, was not deceived by impostors, divined a growing intelligence in certain perplexities. He sought a soul which would merit participation in the universe.

After nine or ten nights, he comprehended with some bitterness that he could expect nothing of those students who passively accepted his doctrines, but that he could of those who, at times, would venture a reasonable contradiction. The former, though worthy of love and affection, could not rise to the state of individuals; the latter pre-existed somewhat more. One afternoon (now his afternoons too were tributaries of sleep, now he remained awake only for a couple of hours at dawn) he dismissed the vast illusory college for ever and kept one single student. He was a silent boy, sallow, sometimes obstinate, with sharp features which reproduced those of the dreamer. He was not long disconcerted by his companions sudden elimination; his progress, after a few special lessons, astounded his teacher. Nevertheless, catastrophe ensued. The man emerged from sleep one day as if from a viscous desert, looked at the vain light of afternoon, which at first he confused with that of dawn, and understood that he had not really dreamt. All that night and all day, the intolerable lucidity of insomnia weighed upon him. He tried to explore the jungle, to exhaust himself; amidst the hemlocks, he was scarcely able to manage a few snatches of feeble sleep, fleetingly mottled with some rudimentary visions which were useless. He tried to convoke the college and had scarcely uttered a few brief words of exhortation, when it became deformed and was extinguished. In his almost perpetual sleeplessness, his old eyes burned with tears of anger.

He comprehended that the effort to mould the incoherent and vertiginous matter dreams are made of was the most arduous task a man could undertake, though he might penetrate all enigmas of the upper and lower orders: much more arduous than weaving a rope of sand or coining the faceless wind. He comprehended that an initial failure was inevitable. He swore he would forget the enormous hallucination which had misled him at first, and he sought another method. Before putting it into effect, he dedicated a month to replenishing the powers his delirium had wasted. He abandoned any premeditation of dreaming and, almost at once, was able to sleep for a considerable part of the day. The few times he dreamt during this period, he did not take notice of the dreams. To take up his task again, he waited until the moon's disc was perfect. Then, in the afternoon, he purified himself in the waters of the river, worshipped the planetary gods, uttered the lawful syllables of a powerful name and slept. Almost immediately, he dreamt of a beating heart.

He dreamt it as active, warm, secret, the size of a closed fist, of garnet colour in the penumbra of a human body as yet without face or sex; with minute love he dreamt it, for fourteen lucid nights. Each night he perceived it with greater clarity. He did not touch it, but limited himself to witnessing it, observing it, perhaps correcting it with his eyes. He perceived it, lived it, from many distances and many angles. On the fourteenth night he touched the pulmonary artery with his finger, and then the whole heart, inside and out. The examination satisfied him. Deliberately, he did not dream for a night; then he took the heart again, invoked the name of a planet and set about to envision another of the principal organs. Within a year he reached the skeleton, the eyelids. The innumerable hair was perhaps the most difficult task. He dreamt a complete man, a youth, but this youth could not rise nor did he speak nor could he open his eyes. Night after night, the man dreamt him as asleep.

In the Gnostic cosmogonies, the demiurgi knead and mould a red Adam who cannot stand alone; as unskilful and crude and elementary as this Adam of dust was the Adam of dreams fabricated by the magician's nights of effort. One afternoon, the man almost destroyed his work, but then repented. (It would have been better for him had he destroyed it.) Once he had completed his supplications to the numina of the earth and the river, he threw himself down at the feet of the effigy which was perhaps a tiger and perhaps a horse, and implored its unknown succour. That twilight, he dreamt of the statue. He dreamt of it as a living, tremulous thing: it was not an atrocious mongrel of tiger and horse, but both these vehement creatures at once and also a bull, a rose, a tempest. This multiple god revealed to him that its earthly name was Fire, that in the circular temple (and in others of its kind) people had rendered it sacrifices and cult and that it would magically give life to the sleeping phantom, in such a way that all creatures except Fire itself and the dreamer would believe him to be a man of flesh and blood. The man was ordered by the divinity to instruct his creature in its rites, and send him to the other broken temple whose pyramids survived downstream, so that in this deserted edifice a voice might give glory to the god. In the dreamer's dream, the dreamed one awoke.

The magician carried out these orders. He devoted a period of time (which finally comprised two years) to revealing the arcana of the universe and of the fire cult to his dream child. Inwardly, it pained him to be separated from the boy. Under the pretext of pedagogical necessity, each day he prolonged the hours he dedicated to his dreams. He also redid the right shoulder, which was perhaps deficient. At times, he was troubled by the impression that all this had happened before.... In general, his days were happy; when he closed his eyes, he would think: *Now I shall be with my son.* Or, less often: *The child I have engendered awaits me and will not exist if I do not go to him.*

Gradually, he accustomed the boy to reality. Once he

ordered him to place a banner on a distant peak. The following day, the banner flickered from the mountain top. He tried other analogous experiments, each more daring than the last. He understood with certain bitterness that his son was ready – and perhaps impatient – to be born. That night he kissed him for the first time and sent him to the other temple whose debris showed white downstream, through many leagues of inextricable jungle and swamp. But first (so that he would never know he was a phantom, so that he would be thought a man like others) he instilled into him a complete oblivion of his years of apprenticeship.

The man's victory and peace were dimmed by weariness. At dawn and at twilight, he would prostrate himself before the stone figure, imagining perhaps that his unreal child was practising the same rites, in other circular ruins, downstream; at night, he would not dream, or would dream only as all men do. He perceived the sounds and forms of the universe with a certain colourlessness: his absent son was being nurtured with these diminutions of his soul. His life's purpose was complete; the man persisted in a kind of ecstasy. After a time, which some narrators of his story prefer to compute in years and others in lustra, he was awakened one midnight by two boatmen; he could not see their faces, but they told him of a magic man in a temple of the North who could walk upon fire and not be burned. The magician suddenly remembered the words of the god. He recalled that, of all the creatures of the world, fire was the only one that knew his son was a phantom. This recollection, at first soothing, finally tormented him. He feared his son might meditate on his abnormal privilege and discover in some way that his condition was that of a mere image. Not to be a man, to be the projection of another man's dream, what a feeling of humiliation, of vertigo! All fathers are interested in the children they have procreated (they have permitted to exist) in mere confusion or pleasure; it was natural that the magician should fear for the future of that son, created in thought; limb by limb and feature by feature, in a thousand and one secret nights.

The end of his meditations was sudden, though it was foretold in certain signs. First (after a long drought) a faraway cloud on a hill, light and rapid as a bird; then, towards the south, the sky which had the rose colour of the leopard's mouth; then the smoke which corroded the metallic nights; finally, the panicky flight of the animals. For what was happening had happened many centuries ago. The ruins of the fire god's sanctuary were destroyed by fire. In a birdless dawn the magician saw the concentric blaze close round the walls. For a moment, he thought of taking refuge in the river, but then he knew that death was coming to crown his old age and absolve him of his labours. He walked into the shreds of flame. But they did not bite into his flesh, they caressed him and engulfed him without heat or combustion. With relief, with humiliation, with terror, he understood that he too was a mere appearance, dreamt by another.

ELIZABETH TAYLOR

POOR GIRL

MISS CHASTY'S FIRST pupil was a flirtatious little boy. At seven years, he was alarmingly precocious and sometimes she thought that he despised his childhood, regarding it as a waiting time which he used only as a rehearsal for adult life. He was already more sophisticated than his young governess and disturbed her with his air of dalliance, the mockery with which he set about his lessons, the preposterous conversations he led her into, guiding her skilfully away from work, confusing her with bizarre conjectures and irreverent ideas, so that she would clasp her hands tightly under the plush tablecloth and pray that his father would not choose such a moment to observe her teaching, coming in abruptly as he sometimes did and signalling to her to continue her lesson.

At those times, his son's eyes were especially lively, fixed cruelly upon his governess as he listened, smiling faintly, to her faltering voice, measuring her timidity. He would answer her questions correctly, but significantly, as if he knew that by his aptitude he rescued her from dismissal. There were many governesses waiting employment, he implied – and this was so at the beginning of the century. He underlined her good fortune at having a pupil who could so easily learn, could display the results of her teaching to such advantage for the benefit of the rather sombre, pompous figure seated at the window. When his father, apparently satisfied, had left them without a word, the boy's manner changed. He seemed fatigued and too absent-minded to reply to any more questions.

'Hilary!' she would say sharply. 'Are you attending to me?' Her sharpness and her foolishness amused him, coming as he knew they did from the tension of the last ten minutes.

'Why, my dear girl, of course.'

'You must address me by my name.'

'Certainly, dear Florence.'

'Miss Chasty.'

His lips might shape the words, which he was too weary to say.

Sometimes, when she was correcting his sums, he would come round the table to stand beside her, leaning against her heavily, looking closely at her face, not at his book, breathing steadily down his nose so that tendrils of hair wavered on her neck and against her cheeks. His stillness, his concentration on her and his too heavy leaning, worried her. She felt something experimental in his attitude, as if he were not leaning against her at all, but against someone in the future. 'He is only a baby,' she reminded herself, but she would try to shift from him, feeling a vague distaste. She would blush, as if he were a grown man, and her heart could be heard beating quickly. He was aware of this and would take up the corrected book and move back to his place.

Once he proposed to her and she had the feeling that it was a proposal-rehearsal and that he was making use of her, as an actor might ask her to hear his lines.

'You must go on with your work,' she said.

'I can shade in a map and talk as well.'

'Then talk sensibly.'

'You think I am too young, I daresay; but you could wait for me to grow up. I can do that quickly enough.'

'You are far from grown-up at the moment.'

'You only say these things because you think that governesses ought to. I suppose you don't known *how* governesses go on, because you have never been one until now, and you were too poor to have one of your own when you were young.'

'That is impertinent, Hilary.'

'You once told me that your father couldn't afford one.'

'Which is a different way of putting it.'

'I shouldn't have thought they cost much.' He had a way of just making a remark, of breathing it so gently that it was scarcely said, and might conveniently be ignored.

He was a dandified little boy. His smooth hair was like a silk cap, combed straight from the crown to a level line above his topaz eyes. His sailor-suits were spotless. The usual boldness changed to an agonized fussiness if his serge sleeve brushed against chalk or if he should slip on the grassy terrace and stain his clothes with green. On their afternoon walks he took no risks and Florence, who had younger brothers, urged him in vain to climb a tree or jump across puddles. At first, she thought him intimidated by his mother or nurse; but soon she realized that his mother entirely indulged him and the nurse had her thoughts all bent upon the new baby: his fussiness was just another part of his grown-upness come too soon.

The house was comfortable, although to Florence rather too sealed-up and overheated after her own damp and draughty home. Her work was not hard and her loneliness only what she had expected. Cut off from the kitchen by her education, she lacked the feuds and camaraderie, gossip and cups of tea, which made life more interesting for the domestic staff. None of the maids – coming to light the lamp at dusk or laying the schoolroom-table for tea – ever presumed beyond a remark or two about the weather.

One late afternoon, she and Hilary returned from their walk and found the lamps already lit. Florence went to her room to tidy herself before tea. When she came down to the schoolroom, Hilary was already there, sitting on the window-seat and staring out over the park as his father did. The room was bright and warm and a maid had put a white cloth over the plush one and was beginning to lay the table.

The air was full of a heavy scent, dry and musky. To Florence, it smelt quite unlike the Eau de Cologne she sometimes sprinkled on her handkerchief, when she had a headache and she disapproved so much that she returned the maid's greeting coldly and bade Hilary open the window.

'Open the window, dear girl?' he said. 'We shall catch our very deaths.'

'You will do as I ask and remember in future how to address me.'

She was angry with the maid – who now seemed to her an immoral creature – and angry to be humiliated before her.

'But why?' asked Hilary.

'I don't approve of my schoolroom being turned into a scented bower.' She kept her back to the room and was trembling, for she had never rebuked a servant before.

'I approve of it,' Hilary said, sniffing loudly.

'I think it's lovely,' the maid said. 'I noticed it as soon as I opened the door.'

'Is this some joke, Hilary?' Florence asked when the maid had gone.

'No. What?'

'This smell in the room?'

'No. You smell of it most, anyhow.' He put his nose to her sleeve and breathed deeply.

It seemed to Florence that this was so, that her clothes had caught the perfume among their folds. She lifted her palms to her face, then went to the window and leant out into the air as far as she could.

'Shall I pour out the tea, dear girl?'

'Yes, please.'

She took her place at the table abstractedly, and as she drank her tea she stared about the room, frowning. When Hilary's mother looked in, as she often did at this time, Florence stood up in a startled way.

'Good-evening, Mrs Wilson. Hilary, put a chair for your mamma.'

'Don't let me disturb you.'

Mrs Wilson sank into the rocking-chair by the fire and gently tipped to and fro.

'Have you finished your tea, darling boy?' she asked. 'Are you going to read me a story from your book? Oh, there is Lady scratching at the door. Let her in for mamma.'

Hilary opened the door and a balding old pug-dog with bloodshot eyes waddled in.

'Come Lady! Beautiful one. Come to mistress! What is wrong with her, poor pet lamb?'

The bitch had stopped just inside the room and lifted her head and howled. 'What has frightened her, then? Come, beauty! Coax her with a sponge-cake, Hilary.'

She reached forward to the table to take the dish and doing so noticed Florence's empty teacup. On the rim was a crimson smear, like the imprint of a lip. She gave a sponge-finger to Hilary, who tried to quieten the pug, then she leaned back in her chair and studied Florence again as she had studied her when she had engaged her a few weeks earlier. The girl's looks were appropriate enough, appropriate to a clergyman's daughter and a governess. Her square chin looked resolute, her green eyes innocent, her dress was modest and unbecoming. Yet Mrs Wilson could detect an excitability, even feverishness, which she had not noticed before and she wondered if she had mistaken guardedness for innocence and deceit for modesty.

She was reaching this conclusion – rocking back and forth when she saw Florence's hand stretch out and turn the cup round in its saucer so that the red stain was out of sight.

'What is wrong with Lady?' Hilary asked, for the dog would not be pacified with sponge-fingers, but kept making barking advances further into the room, then growling in retreat.

'Perhaps she is crying at the new moon,' said Florence and she went to the window and drew back the curtain. As she moved, her skirts rustled. 'If she has silk underwear as well!' Mrs Wilson thought. She had clearly heard the sound of taffetas and she imagined the drab, shiny alpaca dress concealing frivolity and wantonness.

'Open the door Hilary!' she said. 'I will take Lady away. Vernon shall give her a run in the park. I think a quiet read for Hilary and then an early bedtime, Miss Chasty. He looks pale this evening.'

'Yes, Mrs Wilson.' Florence stood respectfully by the table, hiding the cup.

'The hypocrisy!' Mrs Wilson thought and she trembled as she crossed the landing and went downstairs.

She hesitated to tell her husband of her uneasiness, knowing his susceptibilities to women whom his conscience taught him to deplore. Hidden below the apparent urbanity of their married life were old unhappinesses – little acts of treachery and disloyalty which pained her to remember, bruises upon her peace of mind and her pride: letters found, a pretty maid dismissed, an actress who had blackmailed him. As he read the Lesson in Church, looking so perfectly upright and honourable a man, she sometimes thought of his escapades; but not with bitterness or cynicism, only with pain at her memories and a whisper of fear about the future. For some time she had been spared those whispers and had hoped that their marriage had at last achieved its calm. To speak of Florence as she must might both arouse his curiosity and revive the past. Nevertheless, she had her duty to her son to fulfil and her own anger to appease and she opened the Library door very determinedly.

'Oliver, I am sorry to interrupt your work, but I must speak to you.'

He put down the *Strand* magazine quite happily, aware that she was not a sarcastic woman.

Oliver and his son were extraordinarily alike. 'As soon as Hilary has grown a moustache we shall not know them apart,' Mrs Wilson often said, and her husband liked this little joke which made him feel more youthful. He did not know that she added a silent prayer – 'O God, please do nor let him *be* like him, though.'

'You seem troubled, Louise.' His voice was rich and authoritative. He enjoyed setting to rights her little domestic flurries and waited indulgently to hear of some tradesman's misdemeanour or servant's laziness.

'Yes, I am troubled about Miss Chasty.'

'Little Miss Mouse? I was rather troubled myself. I noticed two spelling-faults in Hilary's botany essay, which she claimed to have corrected. I said nothing before the boy; but I shall acquaint her with it when the opportunity arises.'

'Do you often go to the schoolroom, then?'

'From time to time. I like to be sure that our choice was wise.'

'It was not. It was misguided *and* unwise.'

'All young people seem slipshod nowadays.'

'She is more than slipshod. I believe she should go. I think she is quite brazen. Oh, yes, I should have laughed at that myself if it had been said to me an hour ago, but I have just come from the schoolroom and it occurs to me that now she has settled down and feels more secure – since you pass over her mistakes – she is beginning to take advantage of your leniency and to show herself in her true colours. I felt a sinister atmosphere up there and I am quite upset and exhausted by it. I went up to hear Hilary's reading. They were finishing tea and the room was full of the most overpowering scent – *her* scent. It was disgusting.'

'Unpleasant?'

'No, not at all. But upsetting.'

'Disturbing?'

She would not look at him or reply, hearing no more indulgence or condescension in his voice, but the quality of warming interest.

'And then I saw her teacup and there was a mark on it – a red smear where her lips had touched it. She did not know I saw it and as soon as she noticed it herself she turned it round, away from me. She is an immoral woman and she has come into our house to teach our son.'

'I have never noticed a trace of artificiality in her looks. It seemed to me that she was rather colourless.'

'She has been sly. This evening she looked quite different, quite flushed and excitable. I know that she had rouged her lips or painted them, or whatever those women do.' Her eyes filled with tears.

'I shall observe her for a day or two,' Oliver said, trying to keep anticipation from his voice.

'I should like her to go at once.'

'Never act rashly. She is entitled to a quarter's notice unless there is definite blame. We could make ourselves very foolish if you have been mistaken. Oh, I know that you are sure; but it has been known for you to misjudge others. I shall take stock of her and decide if she is suitable. She is still Miss Mouse to me and I cannot think otherwise until I see the evidence with my own eyes.'

'There was something else as well,' Mrs Wilson said wretchedly.

'And what was that?'

'I should rather not say.' She had changed her mind about further accusations. Silk underwear would prove, she guessed, too inflammatory.

'I shall go up ostensibly to mention Hilary's spelling-faults.' He could not go fast enough and stood up at once.

'But Hilary will be in bed.'

'I could not mention the spelling-faults if he were not.'

'Shall I come with you?'

'My dear Louise, why should you? It would look very strange – a deputation about two spelling-faults.'

'Then don't be long, will you? I hope you won't be long.'

He went to the schoolroom, but there was no one there. Hilary's story-book lay closed upon the table and Miss Chasty's sewing was folded neatly. As he was standing there looking about him and sniffing hard, a maid came in with a tray of crockery.

'Has Master Hilary gone to bed?' he asked, feeling rather foolish and confused.

The only scent in the air was a distinct smell – even a haze – of cigarette smoke.

'Yes, sir.'

'And Miss Chasty – where is she?'

'She went to bed, too, sir.'

'Is she unwell?'

'She spoke of a chronic head, sir.'

The maid stacked the cups and saucers in the cupboard and went out. Nothing was wrong with the room apart from the smell of smoke and Mr Wilson went downstairs. His wife was waiting in the hall. She looked up expectantly, in some relief at seeing him so soon.

'Nothing,' he said dramatically. 'She has gone to bed with a headache. No wonder she looked feverish.'

'You noticed the scent.'

'There was none,' he said. 'No trace. Nothing. Just imagination, dear Louise. I thought that it must be so.'

He went to the library and took up his magazine again, but he was too disturbed to read and thought with impatience of the following day.

Florence could not sleep. She had gone to her room, not with a headache but to escape conversations until she had faced her predicament alone. This she was doing, lying on the honeycomb quilt which, since maids do not wait on governesses, had not been turned down.

The schoolroom this evening seemed to have been wreathed about with a strange miasma; the innocent nature of the place polluted in a way which she could not understand or have explained. Something new it seemed, had entered the room which had not belonged to her or became a part of her – the scent had clung about her clothes; the stained cup was her cup and her handkerchief with which she had rubbed it clean was still reddened; and, finally, as she had stared in the mirror, trying to re-establish her personality, the affected little laugh which startled her had come from herself. It had driven her from the room.

'I cannot explain the inexplicable,' she thought wearily and began to prepare herself for bed. Home-sickness hit her like a blow on the head. 'Whatever they do to me, I have always my home,' she promised herself. But she could not think who 'they' might be; for no one in this house had threatened her. Mrs Wilson had done no more than irritate her with her commonplace fussing over Hilary and her dog, and Florence was prepared to overcome much more than irritations. Mr Wilson's pomposity, his constant watch on her work, intimidated her, but she knew that all who must earn their living must have fears lest their work should not seem worth the payment. Hilary was easy to manage; she had quickly seen that she could always deflect him from rebelliousness by opening a new subject for conversation; any idea would be a counter-attraction to naughtiness; he wanted her to sharpen his wits upon. 'And is that all that teaching is, or should be?' she had wondered. The servants had been good to her, realizing that she would demand nothing of them. She had suffered great loneliness, but had foreseen it as part of her position. Now she felt fear nudging it away. 'I am not lonely any more,' she thought. 'I am not alone any more. And I have lost something.' She said her prayers; then sitting up in bed, kept the candle alight while she brushed her hair and read the Bible.

'Perhaps I have lost my reason,' she suddenly thought, resting her finger on her place in the Psalms. She lifted her head and saw her shadow stretch up the powdery, rose-sprinkled wall. 'Now can I keep *that* secret?' she wondered. 'When there is no one to help me to do it? Only those who are watching to see it happen.'

She was not afraid in her bedroom as she had been in the schoolroom, but her perplexed mind found no replies to its questions. She blew out the candle and tried to fall asleep but lay and cried for a long time, and yearned to be at home again and comforted in her mother's arms.

In the morning she met kind enquiries. Nurse was so full of solicitude that Florence felt guilty. 'I came up with a warm drink and put my head round the door but you were in the land of Nod so I drank it myself. I should take a grey powder; or I could mix you a gargle. There are a lot of throats about.'

'I am quite better this morning,' said Florence and she felt calmer as she sat down at the schoolroom-table with Hilary. 'Yet it was all true,' her reason whispered. 'The morning hasn't altered that.'

'You have been crying,' said Hilary. 'Your eyes are red.'

'Sometimes people's eyes are red from other causes – headaches and colds.' She smiled brightly.

'And sometimes from crying, as I said. I should think usually from crying.'

'Page fifty-one,' she said, locking her hands together in her lap.

'Very well.' He opened the book, pressed down the pages and lowered his nose to them, breathing the smell of print. 'He is utterly sensuous,' she thought. 'He extracts every pleasure, every sensation, down to the most trivial.'

They seemed imprisoned in the schoolroom, by the silence of the rest of the house and by the rain outside. Her calm began to break up into frustration and she put her hands behind her chair and pressed them against the hot mesh of the fireguard to steady herself. As she did so, she felt a curious derangement of both mind and body; of desire unsettling her once sluggish, peaceful nature, desire horribly defined, though without direction.

'I have soon finished those,' said Hilary, bringing his sums and placing them before her. She glanced at her palms which were criss-crossed deep with crimson where she had pressed them against the fireguard, then she took up her pen and dipped it into the red ink.

'Don't lean against me, Hilary,' she said.

'I love the scent so much.'

It had returned, musky, enveloping, varying as she moved. She ticked the sums quickly, thinking that she would set Hilary more work and escape for a moment to calm herself

– change her clothes or cleanse herself in the rain. Hearing Mr Wilson's footsteps along the passage, she knew that her escape was cut off and raised wild-looking eyes as he came in. He mistook panic for passion, thought that by opening the door suddenly he had caught her out and laid bare her secret, her pathetic adoration.

'Good-morning,' he said musically and made his way to the window-seat. 'Don't let me disturb you.' He said this without irony, although he thought: 'So it is that way the wind blows! Poor creature!' He had never found it difficult to imagine that women were in love with him.

'I will hear your verbs,' Florence told Hilary, and opened the French Grammar as if she did not know them herself. Her eyes – from so much crying – were a pale and brilliant green and as the scent drifted in Oliver's direction and he turned to her, she looked fully at him.

'Ah, the still waters!' he thought and stood up suddenly. '*Ils vont*,' he corrected Hilary and touched his shoulder as he passed. 'Are you attending to Miss Chasty?'

'Is she attending to me?' Hilary murmured. The risk was worth taking, for neither heard. His father appeared to be sleep-walking and Florence deliberately closed her eyes, as if looking down were not enough to blur the outlines of her desire.

'I find it difficult,' Oliver said to his wife, 'to reconcile your remarks about Miss Chasty with the young woman herself. I have just come from the schoolroom and she was engaged in nothing more immoral than teaching French verbs – that not very well, incidentally.'

'But can you *explain* what I have told you?'

'I can't do that,' he said gaily. For who can explain a jealous woman's fancies? he implied.

He began to spend more time in the schoolroom; for

surveillance, he said. Miss Chasty, though not outwardly of an amorous nature, was still not what he had at first supposed. A suppressed wantonness hovered beneath her primness. She was the ideal governess in his eyes – irreproachable, yet not unapproachable. As she was so conveniently installed, he could take his time in divining the extent of her willingness; especially as he was growing older and the game was beginning to be worth more than the triumph of winning it. To his wife, he upheld Florence, saw nothing wrong save in her scholarship, which needed to be looked into – the explanation for his more frequent visits to the schoolroom. He laughed teasingly at Louise's fancies.

The schoolroom indeed became a focal point of the house – the stronghold of Mr Wilson's desire and his wife's jealousy.

'We are never alone,' said Hilary. 'Either Papa or Mamma is here. Perhaps they wonder if you are good enough for me.'

'Hilary!' His father had heard the last sentence as he opened the door and the first as he hovered outside listening. 'I doubt if my ears deceived me. You will go to your room while you think of a suitable apology and I think of an ample punishment.'

'Shall I take my history book with me or shall I just waste time?'

'I have indicated how to spend your time.'

'That won't take long enough,' said Hilary beneath his breath as he closed the door.

'Meanwhile, I apologize for him,' said his father. He did not go to his customary place by the window, but came to the hearth-rug where Florence stood behind her chair. 'We have indulged him too much and he has been too much with adults. Have there been other occasions?'

'No, indeed, sir.'

'You find him tractable?'

'Oh, yes.'

'And you are happy in your position?'

'Yes.'

As the dreaded, the now so familiar scent began to wreathe about the room, she stepped back from him and began to speak rapidly, as urgently as if she were dying and must make some explanation while she could. 'Perhaps, after all, Hilary is right, and you do wonder about my competence – and if I can give him all he should have. Perhaps a man would teach him more. . . .'

She began to feel a curious infraction of the room and of her personality, seemed to lose the true Florence, and the room lightened as if the season had been changed.

'You are mistaken,' he was saying. 'Have I ever given you any hint that we were not satisfied?'

Her timidity had quite dissolved and he was shocked by the sudden boldness of her glance.

'No, no hint,' she said, smiling. As she moved, he heard the silken swish of her clothes.

'I should rather give you a hint of how well pleased I am.'

'Then why don't you?' she asked.

She leaned back against the chimney-piece and looped about her fingers a long necklace of glittering green beads. 'Where did these come from?' she wondered. She could not remember ever having seen them before, but she could not pursue her bewilderment, for the necklace felt familiar to her hands, much more familiar than the rest of the room.

'*When* shall I?' he was insisting. 'This evening, perhaps? when Hilary is in bed?'

'Then who is *he*, if Hilary is to be in bed?' she wondered. She glanced at him and smiled again. 'You are extraordinarily alike,' she said. 'You and Hilary.' 'But Hilary is a little boy,' she reminded herself 'It is silly to confuse the two.'

'We must discuss Hilary's progress,' he said, his voice so burdened with meaning that she began to laugh at him.

'Indeed we must,' she agreed.

'Your necklace is the colour of your eyes.' He took it from her fingers and leaned forward, as if to kiss her. Hearing footsteps in the passage she moved sharply aside, the necklace broke and the beads were scattered over the floor.

'Why is Hilary in the garden at this hour?' Mrs Wilson asked. Her husband and the governess were on their knees, gathering up the beads.

'Miss Chasty's necklace broke,' her husband said. She had heard that submissive tone before: his voice lacked authority only when he was caught out in some infidelity.

'I was asking about Hilary. I have just seen him running in the shrubbery without a coat.'

'He was sent to his room for being impertinent to Miss Chasty.'

'Please fetch him at once,' Mrs Wilson told Florence. Her voice always gained in authority what her husband's lacked.

Florence hurried from the room, still holding a handful of beads. She felt badly shaken – as if she had been brought to the edge of some experience which had then retreated beyond her grasp.

'He was told to stay in his room,' Mr Wilson said feebly.

'Why did her beads break?'

'She was fidgeting with them. I think she was nervous. I was making it rather apparent to her that I regarded Hilary's insubordination as proof of too much leniency on her part.'

'I didn't know that she had such a necklace. It is the showiest trash that I have ever seen.'

'We cannot blame her for the cheapness of her trinkets. It is rather pathetic.'

'There is nothing pathetic about her. We will continue this in the morning-room and *they* can continue their lessons, which are, after all, her reason for being here.'

'Oh, they are gone,' said Hilary. His cheeks were pink from the cold outside.

'Why did you not stay in your bedroom as you were told?'

'I had nothing to do. I thought of my apology before I got there. It was: "I am sorry, dear girl, that I spoke too near the point".'

'You could have spent longer and thought of a real apology.'

'Look how long papa spent and he did not even think of a punishment, which is a much easier thing.'

Several times during the evening, Mr Wilson said: 'But you cannot dismiss a girl because her beads break.'

'There have been other things and will be more,' his wife replied.

So that there should not be more that evening, he did not move from the drawing-room where he sat watching her doing her wool-work. For the same reason, Florence left the schoolroom empty. She went out and walked rather nervously in the park, feeling remorseful, astonished and upset.

'Did you mend your necklace?' Hilary asked her in the morning.

'I lost the beads.'

'But, my poor girl, they must be somewhere.'

She thought: 'There is no reason to suppose that I shall get back what I never had in the first place.'

'Have you got a headache?'

'Yes. Go on with your work Hilary.'

'Is it from losing the beads?'

'No.'

'Have you a great deal of jewellery I have not seen yet?'

She did nor answer and he went on: 'You still have your brooch with your grandmother's plaited hair in it. Was it cut off her head when she was dead?'

'Your *work*, Hilary.'

'I shudder to think of chopping it off a corpse. You could have some of my hair, now, while I am living.' He fingered it with admiration, regarded a sum aloofly and jotted down its answer. 'Could I cut some of yours?' he asked, bringing his book to be corrected. He whistled softly, close to her, and the tendrils of hair round her ears were gently blown about.

'It is ungentlemanly to whistle,' she said.

'My sums are always right. It shows how I can chatter and subtract at the same time. Any governess would be annoyed by that. I suppose your brothers never whistle.'

'Never.'

'Are they to be clergymen like your father?'

'It is what we hope for one of them.'

'I am to be a famous judge. When you read about me, will you say: "And to think I might have been his wife if I had not been so self-willed"?'

'No, but I hope that I shall feel proud that once I taught you.'

'You sound doubtful.'

He took his book back to the table. 'We are having a quiet morning,' he remarked. 'No one has visited us. Poor Miss Chasty, it is a pity about the necklace,' he murmured, as he took up his pencil again.

Evenings were dangerous to her. 'He said he would come,' she told herself, 'and I allowed him to say so. On what compulsion did I?'

Fearfully, she spent her lonely hours out in the dark garden or in her cold and candlelit bedroom. He was under his wife's vigilance and Florence did not know that he dared not leave the drawing-room. But the vigilance relaxed, as it does: his carelessness returned and steady rain and bitter cold drove Florence to warm her chilblains at the schoolroom fire.

Her relationship with Mrs Wilson had changed. A wary hostility took the place of meekness and when Mrs Wilson came to the schoolroom at tea-times, Florence stood up defiantly and cast a look round the room as if to say: 'Find what you can. There is nothing here.' Mrs Wilson's suspicious ways increased her rebelliousness. 'I have done nothing wrong,' she told herself. But in her bedroom at night: '*I* have done nothing wrong,' she would think.

'They have quite deserted us,' Hilary said from time to time. 'They have realized you are worth your weight in gold, dear girl; or perhaps I made it clear to my father that in this room he is an interloper.'

'Hilary!'

'You want to put yourself in the right in case that door opens suddenly as it has been doing lately. There, you see! Good-evening, mamma. I was just saying that I have scarcely seen you all day.' He drew forward her chair and held the cushion behind her until she leaned back.

'I have been resting.'

'Are you ill, mamma?'

'I have a headache.'

'I will stroke it for you, dear lady.'

He stood behind her chair and began to smooth her forehead. 'Or shall I read to you?' he asked, soon tiring of his task. 'Or play the musical-box?'

'No, nothing more, thank you.'

Mrs Wilson looked about her, at the teacups, then at

Florence. Sometimes it seemed to her that her husband was right and that she was growing fanciful. The innocent appearance of the room lulled her and she closed her eyes for a while, rocking gently in her chair.

'I dozed off,' she said when she awoke. The table was cleared and Florence and Hilary sat playing chess, whispering so that they should not disturb her.

'It made a domestic scene for us,' said Hilary. 'Often Miss Chasty and I feel that we are left too much in solitary bliss.'

The two women smiled and Mrs Wilson shook her head. 'You have too old a head on your shoulders,' she said. 'What will they say of you when you go to school?'

'What shall I say of *them*?' he asked bravely, but he lowered his eyes and kept them lowered. When his mother had gone, he asked Florence:

'Did you go to school?'

'Yes.'

'Were you unhappy there?'

'No. I was homesick at first.'

'If I don't like it, there will be no point in my staying,' he said hurriedly. 'I can learn anywhere and I don't particularly want the corners knocked off, as my father once spoke of it. I shouldn't like to play cricket and all those childish games. Only to do boxing and draw blood,' he added, with sudden bravado. He laughed excitedly and clenched his fists.

'You would never be good at boxing if you lost your temper.'

'I suppose your brothers told you that. They don't sound very manly to me. They would be afraid of a good fight and the sight of blood, I daresay.'

'Yes, I daresay. It is bedtime.'

He was whipped up by the excitement he had created from his fears.

'Chess is a woman's game,' he said and upset the board. He took the cushion from the rocking-chair and kicked it inexpertly across the room. 'I should have thought the door would have opened then,' he said. 'But as my father doesn't appear to send me to my room, I will go there of my own accord. It wouldn't have been a punishment at bedtime in any case. When I am a judge I shall be better at punishments than he is.'

When he had gone, Florence picked up the cushion and the chess-board. 'I am no good at punishments either,' she thought. She tidied the room, made up the fire, then sat down in the rocking-chair, thinking of all the lonely schoolroom evenings of her future. She bent her head over her needlework – the beaded sachet for her mother's birthday present. When she looked up she thought the lamp was smoking and she went to the table and turned down the wick. Then she noticed that the smoke was wreathing upwards from near the fireplace, forming rings which drifted towards the ceiling and were lost in a haze. She could hear a woman's voice humming softly and the floorboards creaked as if someone were treading up and down the room impatiently.

She felt in herself a sense of burning impatience and anticipation and watching the door opening found herself thinking: 'If it is not he, I cannot bear it.'

He closed the door quietly. 'She has gone to bed,' he said in a lowered voice. 'For days I dared not come. She has watched me at every moment. At last, this evening, she gave way to a headache. Were you expecting me?'

'Yes.'

'And once I called you Miss Mouse! And you are still Miss Mouse when I see you about the garden, or at luncheon.'

'In this room I can be myself. It belongs to us.'

'And not to Hilary as well – ever?' he asked her in amusement.

She gave him a quick and puzzled glance.

'Let no one intrude,' he said hastily. 'It is our room, just as you say.'

She had turned the lamp too low and it began to splutter. 'Firelight is good enough for us,' he said, putting the light out altogether.

When he kissed her, she felt an enormous sense of disappointment, almost as if he were the wrong person embracing her in the dark. His arch masterfulness merely bored her. 'A long wait for so little,' she thought.

He, however, found her entirely seductive. She responded with a sensuous languor, unruffled and at ease like the most perfect hostess.

'Where did you practise this, Miss Mouse?' he asked her. But he did not wait for the reply, fancying that he heard a step on the landing. When his wife opened the door, he was trying desperately to light a taper at the fire. His hand was trembling and when at last, in the terribly silent room, the flame crept up the spill it simply served to show up Florence's disarray which, like a sleep-walker, she had not noticed or put right.

She did not see Hilary again, except as a blurred little figure at the schoolroom window – blurred because of her tear-swollen eyes.

She was driven away in the carriage, although Mrs Wilson had suggested the station fly. 'Let us keep her disgrace and her tearfulness to ourselves,' he begged, although he was exhausted by the repetitious burden of his wife's grief.

'*Her* disgrace!'

'My mistake, I have said, was in not taking your accusations about her seriously. I see now that I was in some way bewitched – yes, bewitched is what it was – acting against my judgement; nay, my very nature. I am astonished that anyone so seemingly meek could have cast such a spell upon me.'

Poor Florence turned her head aside as Williams, the coachman, came to fetch her little trunk and the basket-work holdall. Then she put on her cloak and prepared herself to go downstairs, fearful lest she should meet anyone on the way. Yet her thoughts were even more on her journey's end; for what, she wondered, could she tell her father and how expect him to understand what she could not understand herself?

Her head was bent as she crossed the landing and she hurried past the schoolroom door. At the turn of the staircase she pressed back against the wall to allow someone to pass. She heard laughter and then up the stairs came a young woman and a little girl. The child was clinging to the woman's arm and coaxing her, as sometimes Hilary had tried to coax Florence. 'After lessons,' the woman said firmly, but gaily. She looked ahead, smiling to herself. Her clothes were unlike anything that Florence had ever seen. Later, when she tried to describe them to her mother, she could only remember the shortness of a tunic which scarcely covered the knees, a hat like a helmet drawn down over eyes intensely green and matching the long necklace of glass beads which swung on her flat bosom. As she came up the stairs and drew near to Florence, she was humming softly against the child's pleading; silk rustled against her silken legs and all of the staircase, as Florence quickly descended, was full of fragrance.

In the darkness of the hall a man was watching the two go round the bend of the stairs. The woman must have looked back, for Florence saw him lift his hand in a secretive gesture of understanding.

'It is Hilary, not his father!' she thought. But the figure turned before she could be sure and went into the library.

Outside on the drive Williams was waiting with her luggage stowed away in the carriage. When she had settled herself, she looked up at the schoolroom window and saw Hilary standing there rather forlornly and she could almost imagine him saying: 'My poor dear girl; so you were not good enough for me, after all?'

'When does the new governess arrive?' she asked Williams in a casual voice, which hoped to conceal both pride and grief.

'There's nothing fixed as far as I have heard,' he said.

They drove out into the lane.

'When will it be *her* time?' Florence wondered. 'I am glad that I saw her before I left.'

'We are sorry to see you going, Miss.' He had heard that the maids were sorry, for she had given them no trouble.

'Thank you, Williams.'

As they went on towards the station, she leaned back and looked at the familiar places where she had walked with Hilary. 'I know what I shall tell my father now,' she thought, and she felt peaceful and meek as though beginning to be convalescent after a long illness.

WALTER DE LA MARE

THE QUINCUNX

ON OPENING THE door and in no good humour at so late and apparently timid a summons I fancied at first glance that the figure standing at the foot of the four garden steps was my old and precious friend Henry Beverley – unexpectedly back in England again. At the moment there was only obscured moonlight to see him by and he stood rather hummocked up and partly in shadow. If it hadn't been Henry one might have supposed *this* visitor was the least bit apprehensive.

'Bless my heart!' I began – delight mingled with astonishment – then paused. For at that moment a thin straight shaft of moonlight had penetrated between the chimney stacks and shone clear into the face of a far less welcome visitor – Henry's brother, Walter.

I knew he was living rather dangerously near, but had kept this knowledge to myself. And now in his miniature car, which even by moonlight I noticed would have been none the worse off for a dusting, he had not only routed me out, but was also almost supplicating me to spend the night with him – in a house which had, I heard with surprise, been left to him by an eccentric aunt, recently deceased – about two miles away.

Seldom can moonshine have flattered a more haggard face. Had he no sedatives? Sedatives or not, how could I refuse him? Besides, he was Henry's brother. So having slowly climbed the stairs again, with a lingering glance of regret at the book I had been reading, I extinguished my green glass-shaded lamp (the reflex effects of which may have given poor Walter an additional pallor) pushed myself into a greatcoat, and jammed a hat on my head, and in a moment or so we were on our way, with a din resembling that of a van-load of empty biscuit-tins. I am something of a snob about cars, though I prefer them borrowed. It was monstrous to be shattering the silence of night with so fiendish a noise, all the blinds down and every house asleep. 'On such a night . . .' And as for poor Walter's gear-changing – heaven help the hardiest of Army lorries!

'Of course,' he repeated, 'it would be as easy as chalk to dismiss the whole affair as pure fancy. But that being so, how could it possibly have stood up to repeated rational experiment? Don't think I really care a hoot concerning the "ghostly" side of this business. Not in the least. I am out for the definite, I am dog-tired, and I am all but beaten.'

Beaten, I thought to myself not without some little satisfaction. But beaten by what, by whom?

'Beaten?' I shouted through the din. We were turning a corner.

'You see – for very good reasons I don't doubt – my late old aunt could not away with me. She found precious little indeed to please her in my complete side of the family – not even the saintly Henry. My own idea is that all along she had been in love with my father. And I, thank heaven, don't take after *him*. There is a limit to imbecile unpracticality, and—' he dragged at his handbrake, having failed to notice earlier a crossroad immediately in front of us under a lamp-post.

'She never intended me to inherit so much as a copper bed-warmer, or the leg of a chair. Irony was not her strong point – otherwise I think she might have bequeathed me her wheezy old harmonium. I always had Salvation Army leanings. But Fate was too quick for her, and the *house* came to *me* – to me, the least beloved of us all. At first merely our of curiosity, I decided to live in the place, but there's living and living, and there's deucedly little cash.'

'But she must have. . .' I began.

'Of course she must have,' he broke in. 'Even an old misbegotten aunt-by-marriage can't have lived on air. She *had* money; it was meant, I believe – she mistrusted lawyers – for my cousin Arthur and the rest. And' – he accelerated – 'I am as certain as instinct and common sense can make me, that there are stocks, shares, documents, all sorts of riff-raff, and *possibly* private papers, hidden away somewhere in her own old house. Where she lived for donkeys' years. Where I am trying to exist now.' He shot me a rapid glance rather like an animal looking round.

'In short, I am treasure-hunting; and there's interference. That's the situation, naked and a bit ashamed of it. But the really odd thing is – she knows it.'

'Knows what?'

'She knows I am after the loot,' he answered, 'and cannot rest in her grave. Wait till you have seen her face my dear feller, then scoff, if you can. She was a secretive old cat and she hated bipeds. Soured, I suppose. And she never stirred out of her frowsy seclusion for nearly twenty years. And *now* – her poor Arthur left gasping – she is fully aware of what her old enemy is at. Of every move I make. It's a fight to – well, past "the death between us". And *she* is winning.'

'But my dear Beverley . . .' I began.

'My dear Rubbish,' he said, squeezing my arm. 'I am as sane as you are – only a little jarred and piqued. Besides I am not dragging you out at this time of night on evidence as vague as all that. I'll give you positive proof. *Perhaps* you shall have some pickings!'

We came at length to a standstill before his antiquated inheritance. An ugly awkward house, it abutted sheer on to the pavement. A lamp shone palely on its walls, its few beautifully-proportioned windows; and it seemed, if possible, a little quieter behind its two bay-trees – more resigned to night – than even its darkened neighbours were. We went in, and Beverley with a candle led the way down a long corridor.

'The front room', he said, pointing back, 'is the dining-room. There's nothing there – simply the odour of fifty years of lavendered cocoon; fifty years of seed-cake and sherry. But even to sit on, there alone, munching one's plebeian bread-and-cheese, is to become conscious – well, is to become *conscious*. In *here*, though, is the mystery.'

We stood together in the doorway, peering beneath our candle into a low-pitched, silent, strangely-attractive and old-fashioned parlour. Everything within it, from its tarnished cornice to its little old parrot-green beaded footstool, was the accumulated record of one mind, one curious, solitary human individuality. And it was as silent and unresponsive as a clam.

'What a fascinating old lady!' I said.

'Yes,' he answered in a low voice. 'There she is!'

I turned in some confusion, but only to survey the oval painted portrait of Miss Lemieux herself. She was little, narrow, black-mittened, straight-nosed, becurled; and she encountered my eyes so keenly, darkly, tenaciously, that I began to sympathize with both antagonists.

'Now this is the problem,' he said, making a long nose at it, and turning his back on the picture. 'I searched the house last week from garret to cellar and intend to begin again. The doubloons, the diamonds, the documents are here somewhere, and as R.L.S. said in another connection, If she's *Hide*, then I'm Seek. On Sunday I came in here to have a think. I sat there, in that little chair, by the window staring vacantly in front of me, when presently in some indescribable fashion I became aware that I was being stared *at*.' He touched the picture hanging up on its nail behind him with the back of his head. 'So we sat, she and I, for about ten solid minutes, I should think. Then I tired of it. I turned the old Sphinx to the wall again, and went out. A little after nine I came back. There wasn't a whisper in the house. I had my supper, sat thinking again, and fell asleep. When I awoke, I was shivering cold.

I got up immediately, went out, shut the dining-room door with my face towards this one, went up a few stairs, my hand on the banister and then vaguely distinguished by the shadow that the door I had shut was ajar. I was certain I had shut it. I came back to investigate. And saw – *her*.' He nodded towards the picture again. 'I had left her as I supposed in disgrace, face to the wall: she had, it seemed, righted herself. But this may have been a mistake. So I deliberately took the old lady down from her ancestral nail and hid her peculiarly intent physiognomy in that cushion:

> Dare not, wild heart, grow fonder!
> Lie there, my love, lie yonder!

Then I locked windows, shutters and door and went to bed.'

He paused and glanced at me out of the corner of his eye. 'I dare say it sounds absurd,' he said, 'but next morning when I came down I dawdled about for at least half an hour before I felt impelled to open this door. The chair was empty. She was "up"!'

'Any charwoman?' I ventured.

'On Tuesdays, Fridays, and at the weekends,' he said.

'You are *sure* of it?' He looked vaguely at me, tired and protesting. 'Oh, yes,' he said, 'last night's was my fifth experiment.'

'And you want me . . . ?'

'Just to stay here and keep awake. *I can't.* That's all. Theorizing is charming – and easy. But the nights are short. You don't appear to have a vestige of nerves. Tell me who is playing this odd trick on me! Mind you, I *know* already. *Some*how it's this old She's who is responsible, who is manœuvring. But how?'

I exchanged a long look with him – with the cold blue gaze in the tired pallid face; then glanced back at the portrait. Into those small, feminine, dauntless, ink-black eyes.

He turned away with a vague shrug of his shoulders. 'Of course,' he said coldly, 'if you'd rather *not*.'

'Go to bed, Beverley,' I answered, 'I'll watch till morning. . . . We are, you say, absolutely alone in this house?'

'Physically, yes; absolutely alone. Apart from *that* old cat there is not so much as a mouse stirring.'

'No rival heirs? No positive claimants?'

'None,' he said. 'Though, of course. . . . It's only – my aunt.' We stood in silence.

'Well, good night, then; but honestly I am rather sceptical.'

He raised his eyebrows, faintly smiled – something between derision and relief, lifted the portrait from the wall, carried it across the room, leaned it against the armchair in the corner. 'There!' he muttered. 'Check! you old witch! . . . It's very good of you. I'm sick of it. It has relieved me immensely. Good night!' He went out quickly, leaving the door ajar. I heard him go up the stairs, and presently another door, above, slammed.

I thought at first how few candles stood between me and

darkness. It was now too late to look for more. Not, of course, that I felt any real alarm. Only a kind of curiosity – that might perhaps leap into something a little different when off its guard! I sat down and began meditating on Beverley, his nerves, his pretences, his venomous hatred of . . . well, what? Of a dozen things. But beneath all this I was gazing in imagination straight into the pictured eyes of a little old lady, already months in her grave.

The hours passed slowly. I changed from chair to chair – 't.e.g.' gift-books, albums of fading photographs, old picture magazines. I pored over some marvellously fine needlework, and a few enchanting little water-colours. My candle languished; its successor was kindled. I was already become cold, dull, sleepy, and depressed, when in the extreme silence I heard the rustling of silk. Screening my candle with my hand, I sat far back into my old yellow damask sofa. Slow, shuffling footsteps were quietly drawing near. I fixed my eyes on the door. A pale light beyond it began stealing inwards, mingling with mine. Faint shadows zigzagged across the low ceiling. The door opened wider, stealthily, and a most extraordinary figure discovered itself, and paused on the threshold.

For an instant I hesitated, my heart thumping at my ribs; and then I recognized, beneath a fantastic disguise, no less tangible an interloper than Beverley himself. He was in his pyjamas; his feet were bare; but thrown over his shoulders was an immense old cashmere shawl that might have once graced Prince Albert's Exhibition in the Crystal Palace. And his head was swathed in what seemed to be some preposterous eighteenth-century night-gear. The other hand outstretched, he was carrying his candlestick a few inches from his face, so that I could see his every feature with exquisite distinctness beneath his voluminous head-dress.

It was Beverley right enough – I noticed even a very faint likeness to his brother, Henry, unperceived till then. His pale eyes were wide and glassily open. But behind this face, as from out of a mask – keen, wizened, immensely absorbed – peered his little old enemy's unmistakable visage, Miss Lemieux's! He was in a profound sleep, there could be no doubt of that. So closely burned the flame to his entranced face I feared he would presently be setting himself on fire. He moved past me slowly with an odd jerky constricted gait, something like that of a very old lady. He was muttering, too, in an aggrieved queer far-away voice. Stooping with a sigh, he picked up the picture; returned across the room; drew up and mounted the parrot-green footstool, and groped for the nail in the wall not six inches above his head. At length he succeeded in finding it; sighed again and turned meditatively; his voice rising a little shrill, as if in altercation. Once more he passed me by unheeded and came to a standstill; for a moment, peering through curtains a few inches withdrawn, into the starry garden. Whether the odd consciousness within him was aware of *me*, I cannot say. Those unspeculating, window-like eyes turned themselves full on me crouched there in the yellow sofa. The voice fell to a whisper; I think that he hastened a little. He went out and closed the door, and I'd swear my candle solemnly ducked when his was gone!

I huddled myself up again, pulled up a rug and woke to find the candle-stub still alight in the dusk of dawn – battling faintly together to illuminate the little vivid painted face leaning from the wall. And that, on my soul – showing not a symptom of fatigue – in this delicate Spring daybreak, indeed appeared more redoubtable than ever!

I sat for a time undecided what to be doing, what even to be thinking. And then, as if impelled by an inspiration, I got up, took down again the trophy from its nail, and with my penknife gently prised open the back of its gilded frame. Surely, it had occurred to me, it could not be mere vanity, mere caprice or rancour that could take such posthumous pains as this! Perhaps, ever dimly aware of it as he was in his waking moments, merely the pressing subconscious thought of the portrait had lured Beverley out of his sleep. Perhaps . . .

I levered up the thin dusty wood; there was nothing beneath. I drew it out from the frame. And then was revealed, lightly pasted on the back, a scrap of yellowed paper, scrawled with five crosses in the form of a quincunx. In one corner of this was a large, capital Italianate 'P'. And beneath a central cross was drawn a small square. Here was the veritable answer before my eyes. How very like old age to doubt its memory even on such a crucial matter as this. Or was it only doubt?

For whose guidance had this odd quincunx been intended? Not for Walter Beverley's – that was certain. Standing even where I was I could see between the curtains the orchard behind the house pale in the dawn with its fast-fading fruit-blossom. There, then, lay concealed the old lady's secret 'hoard'. We had but to exercise a little thought, a little dexterity and precaution; and Beverley had won.

And then suddenly, impetuously, rose up in my mind an obstinate distaste of meddling in the matter. Surely, if there is any such thing as desecration, *this* would be desecration.

I glanced at the old attentive face looking up at me, the face of one who had, it seemed, so easily betrayed her most intimate secret, and in some unaccountable fashion there now appeared to be something quite other than mere malice in its concentration – a hint even of the apprehension and entreaty of a heart too proud to let them break through the veil of the small black fearless eyes.

I determined to say nothing to Beverley; watch yet again.

And – if I could find a chance – dig by myself, and make sure of the actual contents of Miss Lemieux's treasury before surrendering it to her greedy, insensitive heir. So once more the portrait was re-hung on its rusty nail.

He was prepared for my scepticism; but he did not believe, I think, that I had kept unceasing watch.

'I am sure,' he said repeatedly, 'absolutely sure that what I told you last night has recurred repeatedly. How can you disprove my positive personal evidence by this one failure – by a million negatives? It is you who are to blame – that tough, bigoted *common* sense of yours.'

I willingly accepted his verdict and offered to watch once more. He seemed content. And yet by his incessant restlessness and the curious questioning dismay that haunted his face I felt that his nocturnal guest was troubling and fretting him more than ever.

It was a charming old house, intensely still, intensely self-centred, as it were. One could imagine how unwelcome the summons of death would be in such a familiar home on earth as this. I wandered, and brooded, and searched in the garden: and found at length without much difficulty my 'quincunx'. The orchard was full of fruit trees, cherry, plum, apple: but the five towering pear trees, their rusty crusted bloom not yet all shed, might become at once unmistakably conspicuous to anyone in possession of the clue; though not till then. But how hopeless a contest had my friend set himself with no guidance, and one spade, against such an aunt, against such an orchard!

Evening began to narrow in the skies. My host and I sat together over a bottle of wine. Much as he seemed to cling to my company, I knew he longed for solitude. Twice he rose, as if urged by some sudden caprice to leave me, and twice he sat down again in even deeper constraint.

But soon after midnight I was left once more to my vigil. This time I forestalled his uneasy errand and replaced the portrait myself. I rested awhile; then, when it was still very early morning, I ventured out into the mists of the garden to find a spade. But I had foolishly forgotten on which side of the mid-most tree Miss Lemieux had set her tell-tale square. So back again I was compelled to go, and this time I took the flimsy, precious scrap of paper with me. Somewhere a waning moon was shedding light, for the mists of the garden were white as milk and the trees stood phantom-like above the drenched grasses.

I pinned the paper to the mid-most pear tree, measured out with my eye a rough narrow oblong a foot or two from the trunk and drove the rusty spade into the soil.

At that instant I heard a cautious minute sound behind me. I turned and once more confronted the pathetic bedizened figure of the night before. It was fumbling with the handle of the window, holding aloft a candle. The window opened at length and Beverley stood peering out into the garden. I fancied even a shrill voice called. And then without hesitation, with the same odd, shuffling gait Beverley stepped out on to the dew-damped gravel path and came groping towards me. He stood then, quietly watching me, not two paces distant; and so utterly still was the twilight that his candle-flame burned slim and unwavering in the mist, shedding its small, pale light on leaf-sprouting flowerless bough and dewdrop, and upon that strange set haunted face.

I could not gaze very long into the grey unseeing eyes. His lips moved. His fingers, oddly bent, twitched. And then he turned from me. The large pale eyes wandered to my spade, to the untrampled grasses, and finally, suddenly fixed their gaze on the tiny square of fading paper. He uttered a little cry, shrill and desperate, and stretched out his hand to snatch it. But I was too quick for him. Doubling it up, I thrust it into my pocket and stepped back beneath the trees. Then, intensely anxious not to awaken the sleep-walker, I drew back with extreme caution. None the less, I soon perceived that, however gradual my retreat, he was no less patiently driving me into a little shrubbery where there would be no chance of eluding him, and we should stand confronting one another face to face.

I could not risk a struggle in such circumstances. A wave of heat spread over me; I tripped, and then ran as fast as I could back to the house, hastened into the room and threw myself down in my old yellow sleeping-place – closing my eyes as if I were lost to the world. Presently followed the same faint footfall near at hand. Then, hearing no sound at all, and supposing he had passed, I cautiously opened my eyes – only to gaze once more unfathomably deep into his, stooping in the light of his candle, searching my face insanely, entreatingly – I cannot describe with how profound a disquietude.

I did not stir, until, with a deep sigh, like that of a tired-out child, he turned from me and left the room.

I waited awhile, my thoughts like a disturbed nest of ants. What should I do? To whom was my duty obligatory? – to Beverley, feverishly hunting for wealth not his (even if it existed) by else than earthly right; or to this unquiet spirit – that I could not but believe had taken possession of him – struggling, only *I* knew how bravely, piteously, and desperately, to keep secret – what? Not mere money or valuables or private papers or personal secrets which might lie hidden beneath the shadow of the pear tree. Surely never had eyes pleaded more patiently and intensely and less covetously for a stranger's chivalry, nor from a wilder ambush than these that had but just now gazed into mine. What was the secret;

what lure was detaining on earth a shade so much in need of rest?

I took the paper from my pocket. Light was swiftly flowing into the awakening garden. A distant thrush broke faintly into song. Undecided – battling between curiosity and pity, between loyalty to my friend and loyalty to even *more* than a friend – to this friendless old woman's solitary perturbed spirit, I stood with vacant eyes upon the brightening orchard – my back turned on portrait and room.

A hand (no *man's* asleep, or awake) touched mine. I turned – debated no more. The poor jaded face was grey and drawn. He seemed himself to be inwardly wrestling – possessed against possessor. And still the old bygone eyes within his own, across how deep an abyss, argued, pleaded with mine. They seemed to snare me, to persuade me beyond denial. I held out the flimsy paper between finger and thumb.

Like the limb of an automaton, Beverley's arm slowly raised his guttering candle. The flame flowed soft and blue. I held the paper till its heat scorched my thumb. Something changed; something but just now there was suddenly gone. The old, drawn face melted, as it were, into another. And Beverley's voice broke out inarticulate and feverish. I sat him down and let him slowly awaken. He stared incredulously to and fro, from the window to me, to the portrait, and at last his eye fell on his extraordinary attire.

'I say,' he said, 'what's this?'

'Seemingly,' I said, 'they are the weeds of the malevolent aunt who has been giving you troubled nights.'

'Me?' he said, not yet quite free from sleep.

'Yes,' I said.

He yawned. 'Then – I have been fooled?' he said. I nodded. I think that even tears came into his eyes. The

May-morning choragium of the wild birds had begun, every singer seemingly a soloist in the enraptured medley of voices.

'Well, look here!' he said, nodding a stupid sleep-drowsed head at me, 'look here! What . . . you think of an aunt who hates a fellow as much as that, eh? What you think?'

'I don't know what to think,' I said.

PENELOPE LIVELY

UNINVITED GHOSTS

MARIAN AND SIMON were sent to bed early on the day that the Brown family moved house. By then everyone had lost their temper with everyone else; the cat had been sick on the sitting-room carpet; the dog had run away twice. If you have ever moved you will know what kind of a day it had been. Packing cases and newspaper all over the place... sandwiches instead of proper meals... the kettle lost and a wardrobe stuck on the stairs and Mrs Brown's favourite vase broken. There was bread and baked beans for supper, the television wouldn't work and the water wasn't hot so when all was said and done the children didn't object too violently to being packed off to bed. They'd had enough, too. They had one last argument about who was going to sleep by the window, put on their pyjamas, got into bed, switched the lights out... and it was at that point that the ghost came out of the bottom drawer of the chest of drawers.

It oozed out, a grey cloudy shape about three feet long smelling faintly of woodsmoke, sat down on a chair and began to hum to itself. It looked like a bundle of bedclothes, except that it was not solid: you could see, quite clearly, the cushion on the chair beneath it.

Marian gave a shriek. 'That's a ghost!'

'Oh, be quiet, dear, do,' said the ghost. 'That noise goes right through my head. And it's not nice to call people names.' It took out a ball of wool and some needles and began to knit.

What would you have done? Well, yes – Simon and Marian did just that and I dare say you can imagine what happened. You try telling your mother that you can't get to sleep because there's a ghost sitting in the room clacking its knitting-needles and humming. Mrs Brown said the kind of things she could be expected to say and the ghost continued sitting there knitting and humming and Mrs Brown went out, banging the door and saying threatening things about if there's so much as another word from either of you . . .

'She can't see it,' said Marian to Simon.

''Course not, dear,' said the ghost. 'It's the kiddies I'm here for. Love kiddies, I do. We're going to be ever such friends.'

'Go away!' yelled Simon. 'This is our house now!'

'No it isn't,' said the ghost smugly. 'Always been here, I have. A hundred years and more. Seen plenty of families come and go, I have. Go to bye-byes now, there's good children.'

The children glared at it and buried themselves under the bedclothes. And, eventually, slept.

The next night it was there again. This time it was smoking a long white pipe and reading a newspaper dated 1842. Beside it was a second grey cloudy shape. 'Hello, dearies,' said the ghost. 'Say how do you do to my Auntie Edna.'

'She can't come here too,' wailed Marian.

'Oh yes she can,' said the ghost. 'Always comes here in August, does Auntie. She likes a change.'

Auntie Edna was even worse, if possible. She sucked peppermint drops that smelled so strong that Mrs Brown, when she came to kiss the children good night, looked suspiciously under their pillows. She also sang hymns in a loud squeaky voice. The children lay there groaning and the ghosts sang and rustled the newspapers and ate peppermints.

The next night there were three of them. 'Meet Uncle Charlie!' said the first ghost. The children groaned.

'And Jip,' said the ghost. 'Here, Jip, good dog – come and say hello to the kiddies, then.' A large grey dog that you could see straight through came out from under the bed, wagging its tail. The cat, who had been curled up beside Marian's feet (it was supposed to sleep in the kitchen, but there are always ways for a resourceful cat to get what it wants), gave a howl and shot on top of the wardrobe, where it sat spitting. The dog lay down in the middle of the rug and set about scratching itself vigorously; evidently it had ghost fleas, too.

Uncle Charlie was unbearable. He had a loud cough that kept going off like a machine-gun and he told the longest most pointless stories the children had ever heard. He said he too loved kiddies and he knew kiddies loved stories. In the middle of the seventh story the children went to sleep out of sheer boredom.

The following week the ghosts left the bedroom and were to be found all over the house. The children had no peace at all. They'd be quietly doing their homework and all of a sudden Auntie Edna would be breathing down their necks reciting arithmetic tables. The original ghost took to sitting on top of the television with his legs in front of the picture. Uncle Charlie told his stories all through the best programmes and the dog lay permanently at the top of the stairs. The Browns' cat became quite hysterical, refused to eat and went to live on the top shelf of the kitchen dresser.

Something had to be done. Marian and Simon also were beginning to show the effects; their mother decided they looked peaky and bought an appalling sticky brown vitamin medicine from the chemist to strengthen them. 'It's the ghosts!' wailed the children. 'We don't need vitamins!' Their mother said severely that she didn't want to hear another word of this silly nonsense about ghosts. Auntie Edna, who was sitting smirking on the other side of the kitchen table at that very moment, nodded vigorously and took out a packet of humbugs which she sucked noisily.

'We've got to get them to go and live somewhere else,' said Marian. But where, that was the problem, and how? It was then that they had a bright idea. On Sunday the Browns were all going to see their uncle who was rather rich and lived alone in a big house with thick carpets everywhere and empty rooms and the biggest colour television you ever saw. Plenty of room for ghosts.

They were very cunning. They suggested to the ghosts that they might like a drive in the country. The ghosts said at first that they were quite comfortable where they were, thank you, and they didn't fancy these newfangled motor cars, not at their time of life. But then Auntie Edna remembered that she liked looking at the pretty flowers and the trees and finally they agreed to give it a try. They sat in a row on the back shelf of the car. Mrs Brown kept asking why there was such a strong smell of peppermint and Mr Brown kept roaring at Simon and Marian to keep still while he was driving. The fact was that the ghosts were shoving them; it was like being nudged by three cold damp flannels. And the ghost dog, who had come along too of course, was carsick.

When they got to Uncle Dick's the ghosts came in and had a look round. They liked the expensive carpets and the enormous television. They slid in and out of the wardrobes and walked through the doors and the walls and sent Uncle Dick's budgerigars into a decline from which they have never recovered. 'Nice place,' they said. 'Nice and comfy.'

'Why not stay here?' said Simon, in an offhand tone.

'Couldn't do that,' said the ghosts firmly. 'No kiddies. Dull. We like a place with a bit of life to it.' And they piled back into the car and sang hymns all the way home to the Browns' house. They also ate toast. There were real toast crumbs on the floor and the children got the blame.

Simon and Marian were in despair. The ruder they were to the ghosts the more the ghosts liked it. 'Cheeky!' they said indulgently. 'What a cheeky little pair of kiddies! There now . . . come and give Uncle a kiss.' The children weren't even safe in the bath. One or other of the ghosts would come and sit on the taps and talk to them. Uncle Charlie had produced a mouth organ and played the same tune over and over again; it was quite excruciating. The children went around with their hands over their ears. Mrs Brown took them to the doctor to find out if there was something wrong with their hearing. The children knew better than to say anything to the doctor about the ghosts. It was pointless saying anything to anyone.

I don't know what would have happened if Mrs Brown hadn't happened to make friends with Mrs Walker from down the road. Mrs Walker had twin babies, and one day she brought the babies along for tea.

Now one baby is bad enough. Two babies are trouble in a big way. These babies created pandemonium. When they weren't both howling, they were crawling around the floor pulling the tablecloths off the tables or hitting their heads on the chairs and hauling the books out of the bookcases. They threw their food all over the kitchen and flung cups of milk on the floor. Their mother mopped up after them and every time she tried to have a conversation with Mrs Brown the babies bawled in chorus so that no one could hear a word.

In the middle of this, the ghosts appeared. One baby was

yelling its head off and the other was glueing pieces of chewed-up bread on to the front of the television. The ghosts swooped down on them with happy cries. 'Oh!' they trilled. 'Bless their little hearts then, diddums, give Auntie a smile then.' And the babies stopped in mid-howl and gazed at the ghosts. The ghosts cooed at the babies and the babies cooed at the ghosts. The ghosts chattered to the babies and sang them songs and the babies chattered back and were as good as gold for the next hour and their mother had the first proper conversation she'd had in weeks. When they went the ghosts stood in a row at the window, waving.

Simon and Marian knew when to seize an opportunity. That evening they had a talk with the ghosts. At first the ghosts raised objections. They didn't fancy the idea of moving, they said; you got set in your ways, at their age; Auntie Edna reckoned a strange house would be the death of her.

The children talked about the babies, relentlessly.

And the next day they led the ghosts down the road, followed by the ghost dog, and into the Walkers' house. Mrs Walker doesn't know to this day why the babies, who had been screaming for the last half hour, suddenly stopped and broke into great smiles. And she has never understood why, from that day forth, the babies became the most tranquil, quiet, amiable babies in the area. The ghosts kept the babies amused from morning to night. The babies thrived; the ghosts were happy; the ghost dog, who was actually a bitch, settled down so well that she had puppies – which is one of the most surprising aspects of the whole business. The Brown children heaved a sigh of relief and got back to normal life. The babies, though, I have to tell you, grew up somewhat peculiar.

ALISON LURIE

THE HIGHBOY

EVEN BEFORE I KNEW more about that piece of furniture I wouldn't have wanted it in my house. For a valuable antique, it wasn't particularly attractive. With that tall stack of dark mahogany drawers, and those long spindly bowed legs, it looked not only heavy but top-heavy. But then Clark and I have never cared much for Chippendale; we prefer simple lines and light woods. The carved bonnet-top of the highboy was too elaborate for my taste, and the surface had been polished till it glistened a deep blackish brown, exactly the colour of canned prunes.

Still, I could understand why the piece meant so much to Clark's sister-in-law, Buffy Stockwell. It mattered to her that she had what she called 'really good things': that her antiques were genuine and her china was Spode. She never made a point of how superior her 'things' were to most people's, but one was aware of it. And besides, the highboy was an heirloom; it had been in her family for years. I could see why she was disappointed and cross when her aunt left it to Buffy's brother.

'I don't want to sound ungrateful, Janet, honestly,' Buffy told me over lunch at the country club. 'I realize Jack's carrying on the family name and I'm not. And of course I was glad to have Aunt Betsy's Tiffany coffee service. I suppose it's worth as much as the highboy actually, but it just doesn't have any past. It's got no personality, if you know what I mean.'

Buffy giggled. My sister-in-law was given to anthropomorphizing her possessions, speaking of them as if they had human traits: 'A dear little Paul Revere sugar-spoon.' 'It's lively, even kind of aggressive, for a plant-stand – but I think it'll be really happy on the sunporch.' Whenever their washer or sit-down mower or VCR wasn't working properly she'd say it was 'ill'. I'd found the habit endearing once, but it had begun to bore me.

'I don't understand it really,' Buffy said, digging her dessert fork into the lemon cream tart that she always ordered at the club after declaring that she shouldn't. 'After all, I'm the one who was named for Aunt Betsy, and she knew how interested I was in family history. I always thought I was her favourite. Well, live and learn.' She giggled again and took another bite, leaving a fleck of whipped cream on her short, lifted upper lip.

You mustn't get me wrong. Buffy and her husband Bobby, Clark's brother, were both dears, and as affectionate and reliable and nice as anyone could possibly be. But even Clark had to admit that they'd never quite grown up. Bobby was sixty-one and a vice-president of his company, but his life still centred around golf and tennis.

Buffy, who was nearly his age, didn't play any more because of her heart. But she still favoured yellow and shocking-pink sportswear, and kept her hair in blond all-over curls and maintained her girlish manner. Then of course she had these bouts of childlike whimsicality: she attributed opinions to their pets, and named their automobiles. She insisted that their poodle Suzy disliked the mailman because he was a Democrat, and for years she'd driven a series of Plymouth Valiant wagons called Prince.

* * *

The next time the subject of the highboy came up was at a dinner-party at our house about a month later, after Buffy'd been to see her brother in Connecticut. 'It wasn't all that successful a visit,' she reported. 'You know my Aunt Betsy left Jack her Newport highboy, that I was hoping would come to me. I think I told you.'

I agreed that she had.

'Well, it's in his house in Stonington now. But it's completely out of place among all that pickled-walnut imitation French-provincial furniture that Jack's new wife chose. It looked so uncomfortable.' Buffy sighed and helped herself to roast potatoes as they went round.

'It really makes me sad,' she went on. 'I could tell right away that Jack and his wife don't appreciate Aunt Betsy's highboy, the way they've shoved it slap up into the corner behind the patio door. Jack claims it's because he can't get it to stand steady, and the drawers always stick.'

'Well, perhaps they do,' I said. 'After all, the piece must be over two hundred years old.'

But Buffy wouldn't agree. Aunt Betsy had almost never had that sort of trouble, though she admitted once to Buffy that the highboy was temperamental. Usually the drawers would slide open as smoothly as butter, but now and then they seized up.

It probably had something to do with the humidity, I suggested. But according to Buffy her Aunt Betsy, who seems to have had the same sort of imagination as her niece, used to say that the highboy was sulking; someone had been rough with it, she would suggest, or it hadn't been polished lately.

'I'm sure Jack's wife doesn't know how to take proper care of good furniture either,' Buffy went on during the salad course. 'She's too busy with her high-powered executive job.'

'Honestly, Janet, it's true,' she added. 'When I was there

last week the finish was already beginning to look dull, almost soapy. Aunt Betsy always used to polish it once a week with beeswax, to keep the patina. I mentioned that twice, but I could see Jack's wife wasn't paying any attention. Not that she ever pays any attention to me.' Buffy gave a little short nervous giggle like a hiccup. Her brother's wife wasn't the only one of the family who thought of her as a lightweight, and she wasn't too silly to know it.

'What I suspect is, Janet, I suspect she's letting her cleaning-lady spray it with that awful synthetic no-rub polish they make now,' Buffy went on, frowning across the glazed damask. 'I found a can of the stuff under her sink. Full of nasty chemicals you can't pronounce. Anyhow, I'm sure the climate in Stonington can't be good for old furniture; not with all that salt and damp in the air.'

There was a lull in the conversation then, and at the other end of the table Buffy's husband heard her and gave a kind of guffaw. 'Say, Clark,' he called to my husband. 'I wish you'd tell Buffy to forget about that old highboy.'

Well naturally Clark was not going to do anything of the sort. But he leant towards us and listened to Buffy's story, and then he suggested that she ask her brother if he'd be willing to exchange the highboy for her aunt's coffee service.

I thought this was a good idea, and so did Buffy. She wrote off to her brother, and a few days later Jack phoned to say that was fine by him. He was sick of the highboy; no matter how he tried to prop up the legs it still wobbled.

Besides, the day before he'd gone to get out some maps for a trip they were planning and the whole thing just kind of seized up. He'd stopped trying to free the top drawer with a screwdriver, and was working on one of the lower ones, when he got a hell of a crack on the head. He must have loosened something somehow, he told Buffy, so that when he pulled on the lower drawer the upper one slid out noiselessly above him. And when he stood up, bingo.

It was Saturday, and their doctor was off call, so Jack's wife had to drive him ten miles to the Westerly emergency room; he was too dizzy and confused to drive himself. There wasn't any concussion, according to the X-rays, but he had a lump on his head the size of a plum and a headache the size of a football. He'd be happy to ship that goddamned piece of furniture to her as soon as it was convenient, he told Buffy, and she could take her time about sending along the coffee service.

Two weeks later when I went over to Buffy's for tea her aunt's highboy had arrived. She was so pleased that I bore with her when she started talking about how it appreciated the care she was taking of it. 'When I rub in the beeswax I can almost feel it purring under my hand like a big cat,' she insisted. I glanced at the highboy again. I thought I'd never seen a less agreeable-looking piece of furniture. Its pretentious high-arched bonnet top resembled a clumsy mahogany Napoleon hat, and the ball-and-claw feet made the thing look as if it were up on tiptoe. If it was a big cat, it was a cat with bird's legs – a sort of gryphon.

'I know it's grateful to be here,' Buffy told me. 'The other day I couldn't find my reading-glasses anywhere; but then, when I was standing in the sitting room, at my wits' end, I heard a little creak, or maybe it was more sort of a pop. I looked round and one of the top drawers of the highboy was out about an inch. Well, I went to shut it, and there were my glasses! Now what do you make of that?'

I made nothing of it, but humoured her. 'Quite a coincidence.'

'Oh, more than that.' Buffy gave a rippling giggle. 'And it's completely steady now. Try and see.'

I put one hand on the highboy and gave the thing a little push, and she was perfectly right. It stood solid and heavy against the cream Colonial Williamsburg wallpaper, as if it had been in Buffy's house for centuries. The prune-dark mahogany was waxy to the touch and colder than I would have expected.

'And the drawers don't stick the least little bit.' Buffy slid them open and shut to demonstrate. 'I know it's going to be happy here.'

It was early spring when the highboy arrived and whether or not it was happy, it gave no trouble until that summer. Then in July we had a week of drenching thunderstorms and the drawers began to jam. I saw it happen one Sunday when Clark and I were over and Bobby tried to get out the slides of their recent trip to Quebec. He started shaking the thing and swearing, and Buffy got up and hurried over to him.

'There's nothing at all wrong with the highboy,' she whispered to me afterwards. 'Bobby just doesn't understand how to treat it. You mustn't force the drawers open like that; you have to be gentle.'

After we'd sat through the slides Bobby went to put them away.

'Careful, darling,' Buffy warned him.

'Okay, okay,' Bobby said; but it was clear he wasn't listening seriously. He yanked the drawer open without much trouble; but when he slammed it shut he let out a frightful howl: he'd shut his right thumb inside.

'Christ, will you look at that!' he shouted, holding out his broad red hand to show us a deep dented gash below the knuckle. 'I think the damn thing's broken.'

* * *

Well, Bobby's thumb wasn't broken; but it was bruised rather badly, as it turned our. His hand was swollen for over a week, so that he couldn't play in the golf tournament at the club, which meant a lot to him.

Buffy and I were sitting on the clubhouse terrace that day, and Bobby was moseying about by the first tee in a baby-blue golf shirt, with his hand still wadded up in bandages.

'Poor darling, he's so cross,' Buffy said.

'Cross?' I asked; in fact Bobby didn't look cross, only foolish and disconsolate.

'He's furious at Aunt Betsy's highboy, Janet,' she said. 'And what I've decided is, there's no point any longer in trying to persuade him to treat it tight. After what happened last week, I realized it would be better to keep them apart. So I've simply moved all his things out of the drawers, and now I'm using them for my writing-paper and tapestry wools.'

This time, perhaps because it was such a sticky hot day and there were too many flies on the terrace, I felt more than usually impatient with Buffy's whimsy. 'Really, dear, you mustn't let your imagination run away with you,' I said, squeezing more lemon into my iced tea. 'Your aunt's highboy doesn't have any quarrel with Bobby. It isn't a human being, it's a piece of furniture.'

'But that's just it,' Buffy insisted. 'That's why it matters so much. I mean, you and I, and everybody else.' She waved her plump freckled hand at the other people under their pink and white umbrellas, and the golfers scattered over the rolling green plush of the course. 'We all know we've got to die sooner or later, no matter how careful we are. Isn't that so?'

'Well, yes,' I admitted.

'But furniture and things can be practically immortal, if

they're lucky. An heirloom piece like Aunt Betsy's highboy – I really feel I've got an obligation to preserve it.'

'For the children and grandchildren, you mean.'

'Oh, that too, certainly. But they're just temporary themselves, you know.' Buffy exhaled a sigh of hot summer air. 'You see, from our point of view we own our things. But really, as far as they're concerned we're only looking after them for a while. We're just caretakers, like poor old Billy here at the club.'

'He's retiring this year, I heard,' I said, hoping to change the subject.

'Yes. But they'll hire someone else, you know, and if he's competent it won't make any difference to the place. Well, it's the same with our things, Janet. Naturally they want to do whatever they can to preserve themselves, and to find the best possible caretakers. They don't ask much: just to be polished regularly, and not to have their drawers wrenched open and slammed shut. And of course they don't want to get cold or wet or dirty, or have lighted cigarettes put down on them, or drinks or houseplants.'

'It sounds like quite a lot to ask,' I said.

'But Janet, it's so important for them!' Buffy cried. 'Of course it was naughty of the highboy to give Bobby such a bad pinch, but I think it was understandable. He was being awfully rough and it got frightened.'

'Now, Buffy,' I said, stirring my iced tea so that the cubes clinked impatiently. 'You can't possibly believe that we're all in danger of being injured by our possessions.'

'Oh no.' She gave another little rippling giggle. 'Most of them don't have the strength to do any serious damage. But I'm not worried anyhow. I have a lovely relationship with all my nice things: they know I have their best interests at heart.'

* * *

I didn't scold Buffy any more; it was too hot, and I realized there wasn't any point. My sister-in-law was fifty-six years old, and if she hadn't grown up by then she probably never would. Anyhow, I heard no more about the highboy until about a month later, when Buffy's grandchildren were staying with her. One hazy wet afternoon in August I drove over to the house with a basket of surplus tomatoes and zucchini. The children were building with blocks and Buffy was working on a *gros-point* cushion-cover design from the Metropolitan Museum. After a while she needed more pink wool and she asked her grandson, who was about six, to run over to the highboy and fetch it.

He got up and went at once – he's really a very nice little boy. But when he pulled on the bottom drawer it wouldn't come out and he gave the bird leg a kick. It was nothing serious, but Buffy screamed and leapt up as if she had been stung, spilling her canvas and coloured wools.

'Jamie!' Really, she was almost shrieking. 'You must never, never do that!' And she grabbed the child by the arm and dragged him away roughly.

Well naturally Jamie was shocked and upset; he cast a terrified look at Buffy and burst into tears. That brought her to her senses. She hugged him and explained that Grandma wasn't angry; but he must be very, very careful of the highboy, because it was so old and valuable.

I thought Buffy had over-reacted terribly, and when she went out to the kitchen to fix two gin-and-tonics, and milk and peanut-butter cookies for the children, 'to settle us all down', I followed her in and told her so. Surely, I said, she cared more for her grandchildren than she did for her furniture.

Buffy gave me an odd look; then she pushed the swing door shut.

'You don't understand, Janet,' she said in a low voice, as if someone might overhear. 'Jamie really mustn't annoy the highboy. It's been rather difficult lately, you see.' She tried to open a bottle of tonic, but couldn't – I had to take it from her.

'Oh, thank you,' she said distractedly. 'It's just – Well, for instance. The other day Betsy Lee was playing house under the highboy: she'd made a kind of nest for herself with the sofa pillows, and she had some of her dolls in there. I don't know what happened exactly, but one of the claw feet gave her that nasty-looking scratch you noticed on her leg.' Buffy looked over her shoulder apprehensively and spoke even lower. 'And there've been other incidents – Oh, never mind.' She sighed, then giggled. 'I know you think it's all perfect nonsense, Janet. Would you like lime or lemon?'

I was disturbed by this conversation, and that evening I told Clark so; but he made light of it. 'Darling, I wouldn't worry. It's just the way Buffy always goes on.'

'Well, but this time she was carrying the joke too far,' I said. 'She frightened those children. Even if she was fooling, I think she cares far too much about her old furniture. Really, it made me cross.'

'I think you should feel sorry for Buffy,' Clark remarked. 'You know what we've said so often: now that she's had to give up sports, she doesn't have enough to do. I expect she's just trying to add a little interest to her life.'

I said that perhaps he was right. And then I had an idea: I'd get Buffy elected secretary of the Historical Society, to fill out the term of the woman who'd just resigned. I knew it wouldn't be easy, because she had no experience and a lot of people thought she was flighty. But I was sure she could do it; she'd always run that big house perfectly, and she knew lots about local history and genealogy and antiques.

First I had to convince the Historical Society board that they wanted her, and then I had to convince Buffy of the same thing; but I managed. I was quite proud of myself. And I was even prouder as time went on and she not only did the job beautifully, she also seemed to have forgotten all that nonsense about the highboy. That whole fall and winter she didn't mention it once.

It wasn't until early the following spring that Buffy phoned one morning, in what was obviously rather a state, and asked me to come over. I found her waiting for me in the front hall, wearing her white quilted parka. Her fine blond-tinted curls were all over the place, her eyes unnaturally round and bright, and the tip of her snub nose pink; she looked like a distracted rabbit.

'Don't take off your coat yet, Janet,' she told me breathlessly. 'Come out into the garden, I must show you something.'

I was surprised, because it was a cold blowy day in March. Apart from a few snowdrops and frozen-looking white crocuses scattered over the lawn, there was nothing to see. But it wasn't the garden Buffy had on her mind.

'You know that woman from New York, that Abigail Jones, who spoke on "Decorating with Antiques" yesterday at the Society?' she asked as we stood between two beds of spaded earth and sodden compost.

'Mm.'

'Well, I was talking to her after the lecture, and I invited her to come for brunch this morning and see the house.'

'Mm? And how did that go?'

'It was awful, Janet. I don't mean—' Buffy hunched her shoulders and swallowed as if she were about to sob. 'I mean, Mrs Jones was very pleasant. She admired my Hepplewhite table and chairs; and she was very nice about the canopy bed in the blue room too, though I felt I had to tell her that one of the posts wasn't original. But what she liked best was Aunt Betsy's highboy.'

'Oh yes?'

'She thought it was a really fine piece. I told her we'd always believed it was made in Newport, but Mrs Jones thought Salem was more likely. Well that naturally made me uneasy.'

'What? I mean, why?'

'Because of the witches, you know.' Buffy gave her nervous giggle. 'Then Mrs Jones said she hoped I was taking good care of the highboy. So of course I told her I was. Mrs Jones said she could see that, but what I should realize was that my piece was unique, with the carved feathering of the legs, and what looked like all the original hardware. It really ought to be in a museum, she said. I tried to stop her, because I could tell the highboy was getting upset.'

'Upset?' I laughed, because I still assumed that it was a joke. 'Why should it be upset? I should think it would be pleased to be admired by an expert.'

'But don't you see, Janet?' Buffy almost wailed. 'It didn't know about museums before. It didn't realize that there were places where it could be well taken care of and perfectly safe for, well, almost forever. It wouldn't know about them, you see, because when pieces of furniture go to a museum they don't come back to tell the others. It's like our going to heaven, I suppose. Only now the highboy knows, that's what it will want.'

'But a piece of furniture can't force you to send it to a museum,' I protested, thinking how crazy this conversation would sound to anyone who didn't know Buffy.

'Oh, can't it.' She brushed some wispy curls out of her

face. 'You don't know what it can do, Janet. None of us does. There've been things I didn't tell you about – But never mind that. Only in fairness I must say I'm beginning to have a different idea of why Aunt Betsy didn't leave the highboy to me in the first place. I don't think it was because of the family name at all. I think she was trying to protect me.' She giggled with a sound like ice cracking.

'Really, Buffy—' Wearily, warily, I played along. 'If it's as clever as you say, the highboy must know Mrs Jones was just being polite. She didn't really mean—'

'But she did, you see. She said that if I ever thought of donating the piece to a museum, where it could be really well cared for, she hoped I would let her know. I tried to change the subject, but I couldn't. She went on telling me how there was always the danger of fire or theft in a private home. She said home instead of house, that's the kind of woman she is.' Buffy giggled miserably. 'Then she started to talk about tax deductions, and said she knew of several places that would be interested. I didn't know what to do. I told her that if I did ever decide to part with the highboy I'd probably give it to our Historical Society.'

'Well, of course you could,' I suggested. 'If you felt—'

'But it doesn't matter now,' Buffy interrupted, putting a small cold hand on my wrist. 'I was weak for a moment, but I'm not going to let it push me around. I've worked out what to do to protect myself: I'm changing my will. I called Toni Stevenson already, and I'm going straight over to her office after you leave.'

'You're willing the highboy to the Historical Society?' I asked.

'Well, maybe eventually, if I have to. Not outright; heavens, no. That would be fatal. For the moment I'm going to leave it to Bobby's nephew Fred. But only in case of my accidental death.' Behind her distracted wisps of hair, Buffy gave a peculiar little smile.

'Death!' I swallowed. 'You don't really think—'

'I think that highboy is capable of absolutely anything. It has no feelings, no gratitude at all. I suppose that's because from its point of view I'm going to die so soon anyway.'

'But, Buffy—' The hard wind whisked away the rest of my words, but I doubt if she would have heard them.

'Anyhow, what I'd like you to do now, Janet, is come in with me and be a witness when I tell it what I've planned.'

I was almost sure then that Buffy had gone a bit mad; but of course I went back indoors with her.

'Oh, I wanted to tell you, Janet,' she said in an unnaturally loud, clear voice when we reached the sitting-room. 'Now that I know how valuable Aunt Betsy's highboy is, I've decided to leave it to the Historical Society. I put it in my will to-day. That's if I die of natural causes, of course. But if it's an accidental death, then I'm giving it to my husband's nephew, Fred Turner.' She paused and took a loud breath.

'Really,' I said, feeling as if I were in some sort of absurdist play.

'I realize the highboy may feel a little out of place in Fred's house,' Buffy went on relentlessly, 'because he and his wife have all that weird modern canvas and chrome furniture. But I don't really mind about that. And of course Fred's a little careless sometimes. Once when he was here he left a cigarette burning on the cherry pie table in the study; that's how it got that ugly scorch mark, you know. And he's rather thoughtless about wet glasses and coffee cups too.' Though Buffy was still facing me, she kept glancing over my shoulder towards the highboy.

I turned to follow her gaze, and suddenly for a moment I shared her delusion. The highboy had not moved; but now it looked heavy and sullen, and seemed to have developed a kind of vestigial face. The brass pulls of the two top drawers formed the half-shut eyes of this face, and the fluted column between them was its long thin nose; the ornamental brass keyhole of the full-length drawer below supplied a pursed, tight mouth. Under its curved mahogany tricorne hat, it had a mean, calculating expression, like some hypocritical New England Colonial merchant.

'I know exactly what you're thinking,' Buffy said, abandoning the pretence of speaking to me. 'And if you don't behave yourself, I might give you to Fred and Roo right now. They have children too. Very active children, not nice quiet ones like Jamie and Mary Lee.' Her giggle had a chilling fragmented sound now; ice shivering into shreds.

'None of that was true about Bobby's nephew, you know,' Buffy confided as she walked me to my car. 'They're not really careless, and neither of them smokes. I just wanted to frighten it.'

'You rather frightened me,' I told her.

Which was no lie, as I said to Clark that evening. It wasn't just the strength of Buffy's delusion, but the way I'd been infected by it. He laughed and said he'd never known she could be so convincing. Also he asked if I was sure she hadn't been teasing me.

Well, I had to admit I wasn't. But I was still worried. Didn't he think we should do something?

'Do what?' Clark said. And he pointed out that even if Buffy hadn't been teasing, he didn't imagine I'd have much luck trying to get her to a therapist; she thought psychologists were completely bogus. He said we should just wait and see what happened.

All the same, the next time I saw Buffy I couldn't help

enquiring about the highboy. 'Oh, everything's fine now,' she said. 'Right after I saw you I signed the codicil. I put a copy in one of the drawers to remind it, and it's been as good as gold ever since.'

Several months passed, and Buffy never mentioned the subject again. When I finally asked how the highboy was, she said, 'What? Oh, fine, thanks,' in an uninterested way that suggested she'd forgotten her obsession – or tired of her joke.

The irritating thing was that now that I'd seen the unpleasant face of the highboy, it was there every time I went to the house. I would look from it to Buffy's round pink face, and wonder if she had been laughing at me all along.

Finally, though, I began to forget the whole thing. Then one day late that summer Clark and Bobby's nephew's wife, Roo, was at our house. She's a professional photographer, quite a successful one, and she'd come to take a picture of me.

Like many photographers, Roo always kept up a more or less mindless conversation with her subjects as she worked; trying to prevent them from getting stiff and self-conscious, I suppose.

'I like your house, you know, Janet,' she said. 'You have such simple, great-looking things. Could you turn slowly to the right a little? . . . Good. Hold it . . . Now over at Uncle Bobby's – Hold it . . . Their garden's great of course, but I don't care much for their furniture. Lower your chin a little, please . . . You know that big dark old chest of drawers that Buffy's left to Fred.'

'The highboy,' I said.

'Right. Let's move those roses a bit. That's better . . . It's supposed to be so valuable, but I think it's hideous. I told Fred I didn't want it around. Hold it . . . Okay.'

'And what did he say?' I asked.

'Huh? Oh, Fred feels the same as I do. He said that if he did inherit the thing he was going to give it to a museum.'

'A museum?' I have to admit that my voice rose. 'Where was Fred when he told you this?'

'Don't move, please. Okay . . . What? . . . I think we were in Buffy's sitting room – but she wasn't there, of course. You don't have to worry, Janet. Fred wouldn't say anything like that in front of his aunt; he knows it would sound awfully ungrateful.'

Well, my first impulse was to pick up the phone and warn my sister-in-law as soon as Roo left. But then I thought that would sound ridiculous. It was crazy to imagine that Buffy was in danger from a chest of drawers. Especially so long after she'd gotten over the idea herself, if she'd ever really had it in the first place.

Buffy might even laugh at me, I thought; she wasn't anywhere near as whimsical as she had been. She'd become more and more involved in the Historical Sociery, and it looked as if she'd be re-elected automatically next year. Besides, if by chance she hadn't been kidding and I reminded her of her old delusion and seemed to share it, the delusion might come back and it would be my fault.

So I didn't do anything. I didn't even mention the incident to Clark.

Two days later, while I was writing letters in the study, Clark burst in. I knew something awful had happened as soon as I saw his face.

Bobby had just called from the hospital, he told me. Buffy was in intensive care and the prognosis was bad. She had a broken hip and a concussion, but the real problem was the shock to her weak heart. Apparently, he said, some big piece of furniture had fallen on her.

I didn't ask what piece of furniture that was. I drove straight to the hospital with him; but by the time we got there Buffy was in a coma.

Though she was nearer plump than slim, Buffy seemed horribly small in that room, on that high flat bed – like a kind of faded child. Her head was in bandages, and there were tubes and wires all over her like mechanical snakes; her little freckled hands lay in weak fists on the white hospital sheet. You could see right away that it was all over with her, though in fact they managed to keep her alive, if you can use that word, for nearly three days more.

Fred Turner, just as he had promised, gave the highboy to a New York museum. I went to see it there recently. Behind its maroon velvet rope it looked exactly the same: tall, glossy, top-heavy, bird-legged and claw-footed.

'You wicked, selfish, ungrateful thing,' I told it. 'I hope you get termites. I hope some madman comes in here and attacks you with an axe.'

The highboy did not answer me, of course. But under its mahogany Napoleon hat it seemed to wear a little self-satisfied smile.

RAY BRADBURY

ANOTHER FINE MESS

THE SOUNDS BEGAN in the middle of summer in the middle of the night.

Bella Winters sat up in bed about three a.m. and listened and then lay back down. Ten minutes later she heard the sounds again, out in the night, down the hill.

Bella Winters lived in a first-floor apartment on top of Vendome Heights, near Effie Street in Los Angeles, and had lived there now for only a few days, so it was all new to her, this old house on an old street with an old staircase, made of concrete, climbing steeply straight up from the low-lands below, one hundred and twenty steps, count them. And right now . . .

'Someone's on the steps,' said Bella to herself.

'What?' said her husband, Sam, in his sleep.

'There are some men out on the steps,' said Bella. 'Talking, yelling, not fighting, but almost. I heard them last night, too, and the night before, but . . .'

'What?' Sam muttered.

'Shh, go to sleep. I'll look.'

She got out of bed in the dark and went to the window, and yes, two men were indeed talking out there, grunting, groaning, now loud, now soft. And there was another noise, a kind of bumping, sliding, thumping, like a huge object being carted up the hill.

'No one could be moving in at this hour of the night, could they?' asked Bella of the darkness, the window, and herself.

'No,' murmured Sam.

'It sounds like . . .'

'Like what?' asked Sam, fully awake now.

'Like two men moving—'

'Moving what, for God's sake?'

'Moving a piano. Up those steps.'

'At three in the *morning*!?'

'A piano and two men. Just listen.'

The husband sat up, blinking, alert.

Far off, in the middle of the hill, there was a kind of harping strum, the noise a piano makes when suddenly thumped and its harp strings hum.

'There, did you *hear*?'

'Jesus, you're right. But why would anyone steal – '

'They're not stealing, they're delivering.'

'A *piano*?'

'I didn't make the rules, Sam. Go out and ask. No, don't; I will.'

And she wrapped herself in her robe and was out the door and on the sidewalk.

'Bella,' Sam whispered fiercely behind the porch screen. 'Crazy.'

'So what can happen at night to a woman fifty-five, fat, and ugly?' she wondered.

Sam did not answer.

She moved quietly to the rim of the hill. Somewhere down there she could hear the two men wrestling with a huge object. The piano on occasion gave a strumming hum and fell silent. Occasionally one of the men yelled or gave orders.

'The voices,' said Bella. 'I know them from somewhere,' she whispered and moved in utter dark on stairs that were only a long pale ribbon going down, as a voice echoed:

'Here's *another* fine mess you've got us in.'

Bella froze. Where have I heard that voice, she wondered, a million *times*!

'Hello,' she called.

She moved, counting the steps, and stopped.

And there was no one there.

Suddenly she was very cold. There was nowhere for the strangers to have gone to. The hill was steep and a long way down and a long way up, and they had been burdened with an upright piano, *hadn't* they?

How come I know *upright*? she thought. I only *heard*. But – yes, *upright*! Not only that, but inside a box!

She turned slowly and as she went back up the steps, one by one, slowly, slowly, the voices began to sound again, below, as if, disturbed, they had waited for her to go away.

'What *are* you doing?' demanded one voice.

'I was just—' said the other.

'*Give* me that!' cried the first voice.

That *other* voice, thought Bella, I know that, *too*. And I know what's going to be said next!

'Now,' said the echo far down the hill in the night, 'just don't stand there, *help* me!'

'Yes!' Bella closed her eyes and swallowed hard and half fell to sit on the steps, getting her breath back as black-and-white pictures flashed in her head. Suddenly it was 1929 and she was very small, in a theatre with dark and light pictures looming above the first row where she sat, transfixed, and then laughing, and then transfixed and laughing again.

She opened her eyes. The two voices were still down there, a faint wrestle and echo in the night, despairing and thumping each other with their hard derby hats.

Zelda, thought Bella Winters. I'll call Zelda. She knows everything. She'll tell me what this is. Zelda, yes!

Inside, she dialed Z and E and L and D and A before she

saw what she had done and started over. The phone rang a long while until Zelda's voice, angry with sleep, spoke halfway across L.A.

'Zelda, this is Bella!'

'Sam just *died*?'

'No, no, I'm sorry—'

'*You're* sorry?'

'Zelda, I know you're going to think I'm crazy, but . . .'

'Go ahead, be crazy.'

'Zelda, in the old days when they made films around L.A., they used lots of places, right? Like Venice, Ocean Park . . .'

'Chaplin did, Langdon did, Harold Lloyd, sure.'

'Laurel and Hardy?'

'What?'

'Laurel and Hardy, did *they* use lots of locations?'

'Palms, they used Palms lots, Culver City Main Street, Effie Street.'

'*Effie* Street!'

'Don't yell, Bella.'

'Did you say *Effie* Street?'

'Sure, and God, it's three in the morning!'

'Right at the top of Effie Street!?'

'Hey, yeah, the stairs. Everyone knows them. That's where the music box chased Hardy downhill and ran over him.'

'Sure, Zelda, *sure*! Oh, God, Zelda, if you could *see*, hear, what *I* hear!'

Zelda was suddenly wide awake on the line. 'What's going *on*? You *serious*?'

'Oh, God, yes. On the steps just now, and last night and the night before maybe, I heard, I hear – two men hauling a – a piano up the hill.'

'Someone's pulling your leg!'

'No, no, they're there. I go out and there's nothing. But

the steps are haunted, Zelda! One voice says: "Here's another fine mess you've got us in." You got to *hear* that man's voice!'

'You're drunk and doing this because you know I'm a nut for them.'

'No, no. Come, Zelda. Listen. Tell!'

Maybe half an hour later, Bella heard the old tin lizzie rattle up the alley behind the apartments. It was a car Zelda, in her joy at visiting silent-movie theatres, had bought to lug herself around in while she wrote about the past, always the past, and steaming into Cecil B. DeMille's old place or circling Harold Lloyd's nation-state, or cranking and banging around the Universal backlot, paying her respects to the Phantom's opera stage, or sitting on Ma and Pa Kettle's porch chewing a sandwich lunch. That was Zelda, who once wrote in a silent country in a silent time for *Silver Screen*.

Zelda lumbered across the front porch, a huge body with legs as big as the Bernini columns in front of St Peter's in Rome, and a face like a harvest moon.

On that round face now was suspicion, cynicism, scepticism, in equal pie-parts. But when she saw Bella's pale stare she cried:

'Bella!'

'You *see* I'm *not* lying!' said Bella.

'I *see*!'

'Keep your voice down, Zelda. Oh, it's scary and strange, terrible and nice. So come on.'

And the two women edged along the walk to the rim of the old hill near the old steps in old Hollywood, and suddenly as they moved they felt time take a half turn around them and it was another year, because nothing had changed, all the buildings were the way they were in 1928 and the hills beyond like they were in 1926 and the steps, just the way they were when the cement was poured in 1921.

'Listen, Zelda. *There!*'

And Zelda listened and at first there was only a creaking of wheels down in the dark, like crickets, and then a moan of wood and a hum of piano strings, and then one voice lamenting about this job, and the other voice claiming he had nothing to do with it, and then the thumps as two derby hats fell, and an exasperated voice announced:

'Here's *another* fine mess you've got us in.'

Zelda, stunned, almost toppled off the hill. She held tight to Bella's arm as tears brimmed in her eyes.

'It's a trick. Someone's got a tape recorder or – '

'No, I checked. Nothing but the steps, Zelda, the steps!'

Tears rolled down Zelda's plump cheeks.

'Oh, God, that *is* his voice! I'm the expert, I'm the mad fanatic, Bella. That's Ollie. And that other voice, Stan! And you're *not* nuts after all!'

The voices below rose and fell and one cried: 'Why don't you do something to *help* me?'

Zelda moaned. 'Oh, God, it's so *beautiful*.'

'What does it mean?' asked Bella. 'Why are they here? Are they really ghosts, and why would ghosts climb this hill every night, pushing that music box, night after night, tell me, Zelda, why?'

Zelda peered down the hill and shut her eyes for a moment to think. 'Why do *any* ghosts go anywhere? Retribution? Revenge? No, not *those* two. Love maybe's the reason, lost loves or something. *Yes?*'

Bella let her heart pound once or twice and then said, 'Maybe nobody *told* them.'

'Told them *what*?'

'Or maybe they were told a lot but still didn't believe, because maybe in their old years things got bad, I mean they were sick, and sometimes when you're sick you forget.'

'Forget *what*!?'

'How much we loved them.'

'They *knew*!'

'*Did* they? Sure, we told each other, but maybe not enough of us ever wrote or waved when they passed and just yelled "*Love!*" you think?'

'Hell, Bella, they're on TV every *night*!'

'Yeah, but that don't count. Has anyone, since they left us, come here to these steps and *said*? Maybe those voices down there, ghosts or whatever, have been here every night for years, pushing that music box, and nobody thought, or tried, to just whisper or yell all the love we had all the years. Why not?'

'Why not?' Zelda stared down into the long darkness where perhaps shadows moved and maybe a piano lurched clumsily among the shadows. 'You're right.'

'If I'm right,' said Bella, 'and you say so, there's only one thing to do—'

'You mean you and *me*?'

'Who else? Quiet. Come on.'

They moved down a step. In the same instant lights came on around them, in a window here, another there. A screen door opened somewhere and angry words shot out into the night:

'Hey, what's going *on*?'

'Pipe down!'

'You know what *time* it is?'

'My God,' Bella whispered, 'everyone *else* hears now!'

'No, no.' Zelda looked around wildly. 'They'll spoil everything!'

'I'm calling the cops!' A window slammed.

'God,' said Bella, 'if the cops come—'

'What?'

'It'll be all wrong. If anyone's going to tell them to take it easy, pipe down, it's gotta be us. We *care*, *don't* we?'

'God, yes, but—'

'No buts. Grab on. Here we go.'

The two voices murmured below and the piano tuned itself with hiccups of sound as they edged down another step and another, their mouths dry, hearts hammering, and the night so dark they could see only the faint streetlight at the stair bottom, the single street illumination so far away it was sad being there all by itself, waiting for shadows to move.

More windows slammed up, more screen doors opened. At any moment there would be an avalanche of protest, incredible outcries, perhaps shots fired, and all this gone forever.

Thinking this, the women trembled and held tight, as if to pummel each other to speak against the rage.

'Say something, Zelda, quick.'

'*What?*'

'Anything! They'll get hurt if we don't—'

'*They?*'

'You know what I mean. Save them.'

'Okay. Jesus!' Zelda froze, clamped her eyes shut to find the words, then opened her eyes and said, 'Hello.'

'Louder.'

'Hello,' Zelda called softly, then loudly.

Shapes rustled in the dark below. One of the voices rose while the other fell and the piano strummed its hidden harp strings.

'Don't be afraid,' Zelda called.

'That's good. Go on.'

'Don't be afraid,' Zelda called, braver now. 'Don't listen to those others yelling. We won't hurt you. It's just us. I'm Zelda, you wouldn't remember, and this here is Bella, and we've known you forever, or since we were kids, and we love you. It's late, but we thought you should know. We've loved you ever since you were in the desert or on that boat with ghosts or trying to sell Christmas trees door-to-door or in that traffic where you tore the headlights off cars, and we still love you, right, Bella?'

The night below was darkness, waiting.

Zelda punched Bella's arm.

'Yes!' Bella cried, 'what she *said*. We love you.'

'We can't think of anything else to say.'

'But it's enough, yes?' Bella leaned forward anxiously. 'It's *enough*?'

A night wind stirred the leaves and grass around the stairs and the shadows below that had stopped moving with the music box suspended between them as they looked up and up at the two women, who suddenly began to cry. First tears fell from Bella's cheeks, and when Zelda sensed them, she let fall her own.

'So now,' said Zelda, amazed that she could form words but managed to speak anyway, 'we want you to know, you don't have to come back anymore. You don't have to climb the hill every night, waiting. For what we said just now is it, isn't it? I mean you wanted to hear it here on this hill, with those steps, and that piano, yes, that's the whole thing, it had to be that, didn't it? So now here we are and there you are and it's said. So rest, dear friends.'

'Oh, there, Ollie,' added Bella in a sad, sad whisper. 'Oh, Stan, Stanley.'

The piano, hidden in the dark, softly hummed its wires and creaked its ancient wood.

And then the most incredible thing happened. There was a series of shouts and then a huge banging crash as the music box, in the dark, rocketed down the hill, skittering on the steps, playing chords where it hit, swerving, rushing, and ahead of it, running, the two shapes pursued by the musical beast, yelling, tripping, shouting, warning the Fates, crying out to the gods, down and down, forty, sixty, eighty, one hundred steps.

And half down the steps, hearing, feeling, shouting, crying themselves, and now laughing and holding to each other, the two women alone in the night wildly clutching, grasping, trying to see, almost sure that they *did* see, the three things ricocheting off and away, the two shadows rushing, one fat, one thin, and the piano blundering after, discordant and mindless, until they reached the street, where, instantly, the one overhead streetlamp died as if struck, and the shadows floundered on, pursued by the musical beast.

And the two women, abandoned, looked down, exhausted with laughing until they wept and weeping until they laughed, until suddenly Zelda got a terrible look on her face as if shot.

'My God!' she shouted in panic, reaching out. 'Wait. We didn't mean, we don't want – don't go *forever*! Sure, go, so the neighbours here sleep. But once a year, you *hear*? Once a year, one night a year from to-night, and every year after that, come back. It shouldn't bother anyone so much. But we got to tell you all over again, huh? Come back and bring the box with you, and we'll be here waiting, won't we, Bella?'

'Waiting, yes.'

There was a long silence from the steps leading down into an old black-and-white, silent Los Angeles.

'You think they heard?'

They listened.

And from somewhere far off and down, there was the faintest explosion like the engine of an old jalopy knocking itself to life, and then the merest whisper of a lunatic music from a dark theatre when they were very young. It faded.

After a long while they climbed back up the steps, dabbing at their eyes with wet Kleenex. Then they turned for a final time to stare down into the night.

'You know something?' said Zelda. 'I think they *heard*.'

ACKNOWLEDGMENTS

JORGE LUIS BORGES: 'The Circular Ruins' by Jorges Luis Borges, translated by James E. Irby, from *Labyrinths*, copyright © 1962, 1964 by New Directions Publishing Corp. Reprinted by permission of New Directions Publishing Corporation and Pollinger Limited.
ELIZABETH BOWEN: 'The Happy Autumn Fields' by Elizabeth Bowen. Reproduced with permission of Curtis Brown Group Limited, London, on behalf of the Estate of Elizabeth Bowen. Copyright © Elizabeth Bowen 1944.
'The Happy Autumn Fields', from *The Collected Stories of Elizabeth Bowen* by Elizabeth Bowen, copyright © 1981 by Curtis Brown Limited, Literary Executors of the Estate of Elizabeth Bowen. Used by permission of Alfred A. Knopf, a division of Random House, Inc.
RAY BRADBURY: 'Another Fine Mess' by Ray Bradbury. Reprinted by permission of Don Congdon Associates, Inc. Copyright © 1995 by Ray Bradbury. First published in the *Magazine of Fantasy and Science Fiction* and collected in *Quicker Than the Eye* (HarperCollins, 1996).
WALTER DE LA MARE: 'The Quincunx' by Walter de la Mare, from *A Beginning and Other Stories* (Faber & Faber). Reprinted by permission of The Literary Trustees of Walter de la Mare and the Society of Authors as their representative.
L. P. HARTLEY: 'W.S.' by L. P. Hartley, from *Complete Short Stories* (Hamish Hamilton). Reprinted by permission of the Society of Authors as the Literary Representative of the Estate of L. P. Hartley.

PENELOPE LIVELY: 'Uninvited Ghosts' from *Uninvited Ghosts* by Penelope Lively. Text Copyright © Penelope Lively 1974. Published by Egmont UK Limited, London. Used with permission.
'Uninvited Ghosts' from *Uninvited Ghosts & Other Stories* by Penelope Lively (Heinemann). Reprinted with permission from David Higham Associates.
ALISON LURIE: 'The Highboy'. Copyright © Alison Lurie 1990. From *Women and Ghosts.* Originally published in *Redbook*. Reprinted with permission by Melanie Jackson Agency, LLC.
'The Highboy' from *Women and Ghosts* by Alison Lurie. Reprinted with permission from A. P. Watt on behalf of Alison Lurie.
VLADIMIR NABOKOV: 'The Visit to the Museum' by Vladimir Nabokov; copyright © 1963 by Vladimir Nabokov; reprinted here by arrangement with the Estate of Vladimir Nabokov and Weidenfeld & Nicolson, a division of The Orion Publishing Group Ltd. All rights reserved.
ELIZABETH TAYLOR: 'Poor Girl' by Elizabeth Taylor (Copyright © Elizabeth Taylor, 1957). Reprinted by permission of A. M. Heath & Co. Ltd.
EUDORA WELTY: 'Clytie' by Eudora Welty, from *Collected Stories.* Reprinted by permission of Marion Boyars Publishers Limited.
'Clytie' by Eudora Welty, from *A Curtain of Green and Other Stories.* Reprinted by permission of Russell & Volkening, Inc., as agents for the author. Copyright © 1941 by Eudora Welty, renewed in 1969 by Eudora Welty.
'Clytie' from *A Curtain of Green and Other Stories*, copyright © 1941 and renewed 1969 by Eudora Welty, reprinted by permission of Houghton Mifflin Harcourt Publishing Company.

Everyman's Pocket Classics are
typeset in the classic typeface Garamond and
printed on acid-free, cream-wove paper
with a sewn, full-cloth binding.